The Country Village Winter Wedding

Cathy Lake is a women's fiction writer who lives with her family and three dogs in beautiful South Wales. She writes uplifting stories about strong women, family, friendship, love, community and overcoming obstacles.

Also by Cathy Lake
The Country Village Christmas Show
The Country Village Summer Fête

The Country Village Winter Wedding

CATHY LAKE

ZAFFRE

First published in the UK in 2021 by
ZAFFRE
An imprint of Bonnier Books UK
4th Floor, Victoria House, Bloomsbury Square, London, England, WC1B 4DA
Owned by Bonnier Books
Sveavägen 56, Stockholm, Sweden

A CIP catalogue record for this book is
available from the British Library.

ISBN: 978–1–83877–604–6

Also available in ebook and audio

3 5 7 9 10 8 6 4

Typeset by IDSUK (Data Connection) Ltd
Printed and bound in Great Britain by Clays Ltd, Elcograf S.p.A.

Zaffre is an imprint of Bonnier Books UK
www.bonnierbooks.co.uk

For my husband and children, with love always

Chapter 1

'Yes, that's right. The power went off last night before I went to bed, but I thought it was a local power cut . . . Yes, that's what I said . . . I live in the flat above my office and I'm meant to be opening today. Yes, all right then . . . I'll hold.'

Hazel Campbell pressed the speaker option on her new smartphone, resisting the urge to roll her eyes because that was something a teenager, not the sophisticated business-woman she was supposed to be, would do, then placed it on her brand-new and very tidy desk.

She crossed the office and stood in front of the bay window. Rain lashed at the glass and the wind howled outside. The weather and lack of power were hardly good omens for her fresh start, she thought, as she gazed past the silver-grey writing painted on the window glass to the street outside. From inside, the name of her business, *Country Charm Weddings*, was backwards, which was appropriate because her whole life felt as though it was in reverse. She'd had it all, been heading in the right direction for a charmed life and then – BOOM! Everything had been blown apart. She'd lost her direction and her whole world with it.

'Yes, indeed,' she said to the room, 'the love of your life was an utter bastard and you had no idea. Funny, right? Well, ironic, really, that a wedding planner such as yourself should end up being jilted on the eve of your wedding. Or, not really jilted, I suppose, because Lennox said he'd still go through with it – but at that point he was still physically joined to your maid of honour, and, well, who'd want to marry a cheat?'

'I'm sorry?' The tinny voice came from her phone. 'Did you say something about being cheated?'

'Hello?' Hazel hurried over to the desk and snatched her phone up.

'Sorry for having to put you on hold, Ms Campbell. It looks like there was an error on the system and your power should be turned back on today.'

'Why was it turned off in the first place?'

'A mix-up with the billing as the previous tenant left owing money.'

The previous tenant had, to Hazel's knowledge, passed away some years ago (although not in the flat, thank goodness) and the office and flat had been left vacant until a local business-woman had bought and renovated them. Surely someone had paid off the debts since? The renovation itself would have required power. She shrugged. Confusions like this happened, data wasn't always input properly into computer systems, and if she had power soon, what did it matter?

'What time will it be back on?'

'I'm sorry?'

Goodness, this energy company employee liked the word *sorry*.

'What time today?'

The line went dead. Hazel looked at her phone screen and suppressed a scream, feeling as though steam might start pouring out of her ears. Bloody energy company! Or was it the phone company? Her signal appeared to have died, and while she knew it could be the weather, it didn't make it any less frustrating. She'd had fabulous signal just about everywhere with her former mobile phone provider but after she'd decided to leave Scotland, that had changed. She'd deleted her contacts and most photos and videos from her phone and cloud storage, destroyed the SIM card and sent the shell of the phone back to the company. Severing all ties with her old life had seemed imperative. But this new phone company did not have the great signal or service it had promised when she'd signed the eighteen-month contract.

She closed her eyes and inhaled slowly, trying to fill herself with positive energy and expel the negativity that loomed over her like the dark clouds currently drifting over the village. Little Bramble was a beautiful location; she had happy memories of a childhood holiday here with her parents and that was why she'd chosen the village to run away to. When she'd been at her most desperate, wondering what to do and where to go, she'd Googled the village and devoured the photos she'd found online, had lapped up the Tripadvisor reviews claiming a delightful community spirit there with things like Christmas shows and summer fetes. Hazel liked the idea of being part of a close-knit community, of having people she could rely on, because being totally alone was quite scary at times. But had she made the right choice moving here?

She opened her eyes and blinked; she had to make the best of the situation and, as soon as she had power, she would do exactly that.

Suddenly, the office was illuminated from above as the lights came on, making her blink hard, and she smiled as one of her mum's sayings sprang to mind: *You have to come through the darkness before you can appreciate the light.*

❄

The morning had passed with Hazel tidying her already tidy desk, making cups of coffee and browsing the internet. But not one person had come to the door, peered through the window or telephoned with an enquiry. It was, of course, only day one for Country Charm Weddings, but even so, Hazel had hoped that things might have got off to a better start than this.

She was used to being busy. Extremely busy. In Edinburgh, where she'd lived since she was twelve, life had been hectic. The business she'd co-owned there for the past eight years with her best friend, Valentina Partridge, had been a well-established success. They'd arranged weddings across Scotland throughout the year and barely had a weekend wedding-free, even in the winter. It was why, even though she'd set up in Little Bramble in the middle of October, outside peak wedding season, she'd hoped to have some business come her way. Before moving to the area, she'd checked it out, of course – she wasn't stupid – and found that there wasn't a similar business for miles so there should be no competition. There were, however, a variety of venues suitable for weddings and lots of businesses such as florists, wedding dress boutiques and wedding cake bakers she could work with. It was also a short train ride to London, so she hoped to develop contacts in the city to grow her business over time.

Hazel knew that she could do this.

She really could.

So why were her palms clammy, why was her heart racing and why was she overwhelmed with a longing to call her mum?

✻

Jack Hurst wiped a raindrop from his cheek and stopped walking, turning instead to gaze out to sea. He'd come down to Oxwich Bay, a gorgeous location on the Gower Peninsula, to walk, something he often did when the walls of his house closed in around him and he needed to feel the wind on his face, the crunch of the wet sand beneath his feet and to hear the waves crashing against the shore. The beach symbolised freedom for him because of the seemingly endless horizon and it offered him an escape from his reality, however temporary that might be.

It was a dreary afternoon, the sky gunmetal grey, the khaki-green sea choppy. The sand looked dark too, sodden from recent heavy rainfall and the slowly retreating tide, with clumps of seaweed scattered across its surface like mini mountains. The wind buffeted him as he stood there, forcing him to lock his knees to steady himself. The last thing he wanted right now was to fall over and get his jeans wet, although the thought of feeling something physical, rather than the ache inside, wasn't completely unappealing. It was one of the reasons why he'd started running again. Growing up, he'd been a keen competitor in school track events, had medals and trophies displayed in his parents' Woking home, but once he'd gone to university in Swansea his running had lapsed as he'd enjoyed the student life of late nights and plenty of beer.

How carefree he'd been back then, the younger child of loving parents, adored and spoilt by his older sister and excited about life. He'd decided to study history at Swansea University because, while he loved his family, he'd wanted to go some distance from home. The idea of spreading his wings as he flew the nest appealed and Swansea provided that, as well as a sprawling campus, pleasing accommodation, a bustling city centre with plenty of bars and nightclubs and beautiful sandy beaches nearby.

He'd thrown himself into student life with enthusiasm and had a great three years, the best part of which was meeting and falling in love with Danni Williams in the second year. Danni had been studying nursing and was passionate about her career choice; Jack, consumed by his love and desire for her, pushed aside his initial thoughts of studying for another year to become a teacher. Instead, he'd decided to start earning immediately after graduating in order to support her as she went on to study a postgraduate course in long-term and chronic-condition management.

Jack had taken a job working in telesales for an insurance company and had enjoyed earning a regular wage and being able to set up home with Danni. She'd continued her studies and, for a while, the job had been enough for Jack. It hadn't been the most exciting role, but it had paid the bills. Also, with his and Danni's university debts to pay off, going back to university to train as a teacher in the years that followed had seemed frivolous and irresponsible, especially when they had started thinking about starting a family in the near future.

A seagull cried as it soared overhead, dragging him from his thoughts. He sighed and turned away from the sea, deciding to walk towards the cliffs that separated Oxwich from Three Cliffs Bay. Life didn't always work out as planned and it could be such a smack in the face, especially when he'd seemed to have everything. But losing Danni had been more complicated than he could ever have imagined. His grief was twofold and he wondered if he'd ever be the same person he was before his life had shattered into tiny pieces.

He sincerely doubted it.

Chapter 2

Two weeks had passed since Hazel had opened her business in Little Bramble and, so far, she hadn't had a flicker of interest. She was wondering if the decision to sell her half of the business in Edinburgh to Valentina and let Lennox buy her out of the house so she could move to this small Surrey village had been a big mistake. After all, how responsible was it really to upend her whole life and move somewhere based on memories of a magical family holiday? Surely nostalgia and a longing for happier times with her beloved parents meant she was wearing rose-tinted glasses. Maybe she should have held her nerve and stayed in Scotland. Someone tougher might have done that instead of running away. If her parents had still been alive to support her, maybe she would have done. But she'd felt so alone, so isolated and so bereft because the two people she'd loved most in the world – her best friend and her boyfriend – the only two people she had left, had betrayed her and she couldn't bear to spend any more time around them.

She had left just about everything behind, not wanting the furniture she'd chosen with Lennox or the curtains, cushions – anything that would be a constant reminder of the life she'd had, or thought she'd had. But everything had been one big fat lie and so the things they'd bought as they'd planned their future together were tainted. All she had brought from Scotland were her clothes, her laptop, some bits and bobs from her childhood and, of course, Fleas Witherspoon, her Ragdoll cat.

Sitting in the village café, her laptop open in front of her, a latte on one side and a toasted teacake slathered in golden butter on the other, she found her gaze drawn to the customers who came in. The café was busy, the sounds of the coffee grinder, the clinking of cutlery, the murmur of conversation and the hum of the fridge all blending into a comforting melody. She could sit there all day, watching and listening, pretending to work while she ate her bodyweight in cakes and toasted sandwiches, and no one would care. The air was delicious, fragranced with freshly ground coffee beans and aromatic spices, baking cakes and savoury pastries. She could have been anywhere in the world right now and that thought was at once reassuring and disconcerting.

A couple came into the café then and Hazel watched them from behind her laptop. The woman had long brown hair and striking green eyes that Hazel avoided as they scanned the café. She was dressed casually in boots, jeans and a black jumper beneath an open wax jacket, and she looked effort-lessly stylish in the way Hazel imagined someone living in the English countryside would. The man with her was handsome, tall and broad-shouldered with brown eyes and short Afro hair. Even at the counter, they held hands, as if they couldn't bear to not touch.

When they'd ordered, they came over to the table next to Hazel's, bringing with them the scent of outdoors and a hint of the woodsmoke that seemed to permeate the air in the village, especially during the evenings. From the corner of her eye, she saw them remove their coats and place them on the backs of chairs, then sit down and start chatting with the ease of a couple in love.

Of course, couples in love were Hazel's favourite type of couples because they often meant weddings. This couple seemed a bit older, possibly in their forties, and when Hazel glanced at the woman, she spotted a sparkling diamond on her ring finger but no wedding band. She had a trained eye for these things, not because she thought everyone should get married or be in a relationship, but because weddings were her business. Weddings were – or had been – her passion. And she wanted that passion back because, without it, she didn't know who she was. Lennox and Valentina had taken so much from her and she hated them for it, so much so that she was glad she'd taken revenge, however petty it might have seemed.

'What do you think?' the woman asked her companion.

Hazel knew she shouldn't be listening but she couldn't help wanting to know more about this couple.

'I'm not sure.' He blew out his cheeks and rubbed his hands over his head. 'We've only got – what? – eight and a half weeks until Christmas.'

'It's come around so quickly.'

'I know. And to think that this time last year we were just getting to know each other!' He smiled. 'Oh, I love you, Clare.'

'And I love you, Sam.'

Hazel turned her laptop slightly so she could see the couple better – or was it spy on them better? – her heart pounding at the way they gazed at each other. They were obviously deeply in love, believed in each other and what they had between them. A flicker of unexpected jealousy pierced her heart.

'So,' Clare said, 'eight and a half weeks. But if we went for the eighteenth, as we discussed, that's seven and a half weeks.'

'Less than two months to plan a wedding?' Sam sighed. 'Is that even possible?'

Hazel had to sit on her hands. Was this really happening? Had her mum been listening to her and stepped in to help like some heavenly fairy godmother?

'Well, we don't want a big wedding, do we? Just family and friends – and Goliath, of course.'

'And Scout.'

'Definitely.'

Were Goliath and Scout their children?

'So, shall we start looking at venues seriously?' Sam reached across the table and took Clare's hand.

'I did ring around a few last week, just in case, but there wasn't much availability anywhere. It *is* late notice.'

'It is.' He nodded. 'We could always go abroad, run away, just the two of us.'

Clare shook her head. 'No, we should do it here, with family and friends. I left Little Bramble once and I don't want to do it again, not for our wedding.'

They gazed at each other, both lost in their thoughts of what could be but what might not be possible. Hazel felt that the air in the café was filled with a sense of anticipation – and if she didn't take a chance, she could miss an opportunity . . .

'Excuse me,' Hazel turned her chair to face the couple and summoned up her best professional smile, 'I couldn't help overhearing that you're getting married.'

Sam laughed and his face lit up. He certainly was handsome. She could already picture him in a dark-grey morning suit with a gold cravat and shiny black shoes.

'Hello there. That was the plan, yes, but we've left it quite late. I proposed in the summer and we were going to wait until next year, but then we started talking about how nice a winter wedding would be and we really don't want to wait until next year but it's not looking great at the moment.'

Hazel's body tingled and goosebumps rose on her arms. She was a problem solver; they had a problem to solve.

'I understand that. You're in love, you want to marry now – and why wait?' She shrugged. 'I'm Hazel Campbell; I recently moved to the village.'

'I'm Clare and this is Sam,' the woman said, smiling warmly.

'Pleased to meet you both.' Hazel shuffled her chair a bit closer to their table. 'I'm actually a wedding planner.'

Clare's eyebrows rose. 'A wedding planner?'

'That's right. I've set up my business, Country Charm Weddings, here. I have an office just off the main street behind the grocer and the butcher on Acorn Street.'

'Oh, right,' Clare replied. 'It'll be one of the renovated buildings then, Sam.'

'I know it,' he said.

'I've rented the flat above the shop too. A bit of a work-from-home set-up.' Hazel laughed, aware that even though she'd spoken to hundreds of couples in the past, she was suddenly very nervous. It seemed that Lennox and Valentina had taken some of her professional confidence too.

'So . . . is something like that, having your wedding planned, quite costly?' Clare asked, her eyes flickering to her fiancé.

'Actually,' Hazel leant forwards, 'I'm offering a special winter discount. Plus, you'd be my first customers from the village, so if you'd like my help we could certainly come to a reasonable arrangement.' She held her breath, silently praying for them to agree. If she could just get one wedding on the books, it would be a positive step *and* they seemed like such a nice couple. Clare would make a beautiful bride and Sam an attractive groom. 'And I'm sure your children, Goliath and Scout, would be delighted with a Christmas wedding.'

Clare and Sam snorted with laughter. 'Our children?'

'Yes . . . uh . . . are they not?'

Sam shook his head. 'They're our *dogs*.'

'But they are kind of like our children,' Clare added.

'And you'd like the dogs at your wedding?'

'Of course.' They both smiled.

'How lovely.' Hazel was completely unfazed. People wanted all sorts of things at their weddings; she'd had one couple have their enormous snake present and another their Shetland pony, so dogs were nothing in comparison. 'Look, no pressure at all. I know you need to think about this so how about I give you my card and you take a look at my website and some of my testimonials and then you can get in touch if you want to talk more?'

Clare and Sam looked at each other, communicating silently. Hazel felt suddenly very lonely. At one time, she could communicate with Lennox like that, could trust him to know what she was thinking, and there had been so much comfort in it. Being part of a couple had mattered to Hazel and she'd treasured it. Lennox, it seemed, had not.

'That would be great.' Clare held out a hand and Hazel gave her a business card.

'Just so you know, the testimonials are from weddings I planned in Scotland. I've not long moved from Edinburgh and so, as I said, I have yet to plan a wedding locally, but I do know my business – and I'm very good at it.' She bit the inside of her cheek. She didn't want to come across as desperate, but she didn't want them to be put off by the fact she was new to the area.

'I love your accent,' Clare said, 'but it doesn't sound strictly Scottish. There's something else there too.'

'My mum is Welsh.' Hazel winced inwardly at the use of the present tense. When would she get used to the fact that her mum was gone? 'My dad was Scottish.'

Clare smiled warmly. 'That would explain the beautiful musical lilt to your words.'

'Kind of like I can't make up my mind where I come from?' Hazel laughed; it wasn't the first time someone had commented on her accent.

'It's charming.' Clare pulled a purse from her coat pocket and placed Hazel's card inside. 'There we go. All safe.'

'Right.' Hazel closed her laptop and stood up. 'I'd better get back to the office.' She didn't want to put any pressure on them by hanging around. They needed to talk and so she would give them space. It was all part of being good at sales, letting the customer have the information they needed then backing away to let them think about things. Besides which, if she was going to stay in the village, she didn't want the locals ducking their heads and avoiding her for fear that she'd be on the hard sell all the time. 'Take care both and hopefully I'll speak to you soon.'

She pulled on her coat, packed up her things and left the café, wondering if they would contact her and hoping with all her heart that they would. She needed this – and she really would ensure that they had the most wonderful winter wedding ever.

Chapter 3

Jack sat back and stared at the screen of his laptop as he waited. Over the past year, time had lost all meaning and he often had no idea what day it was. The past two weeks had passed in a blur with him trying to make an effort to get on with his life but still not quite getting there. However, his sister wanted to speak to him today on Zoom. He'd been able to avoid a virtual face to face for a while but he couldn't avoid her forever, and so today he had showered and shaved and put on a clean T-shirt. If he didn't look presentable then Bella would worry and he didn't want to stress her out.

As if by magic, his sister's face appeared.

'Hello, baby brother.'

'Hi, Bella.'

She hadn't changed since she was a teenager. She still had the same dark brown hair with a full fringe, though it was cut in a choppy bob now and didn't brush her shoulders as it used to, the same warm hazel eyes and same perfect smile that she'd acquired after wearing braces for several years growing up. Bella was one of life's happy people – she had a permanently sunny disposition and it seemed to emanate from her like a warm glow.

'So, what's new with you?' she asked, leaning closer to the screen.

'Oh, you know . . .' Jack shrugged. What *was* new with him?

'Have you given any more thought to looking for a job?'

He avoided her gaze.

'Jack?'

'No . . . I-I'm just not in the right place at the moment. I've been looking, though,' he fibbed, thinking it best to let Bella think he was at least trying to decide what to do with his life, 'at some courses at the university. If I decide to go for it, it should be straightforward enough to do a postgrad course . . . if I want to.' He'd brought the website up on his laptop and looked at it then shut it down, but Bella didn't need to know that.

'That's positive news, Jack, and you can certainly afford it, especially if you sell the house.'

'Yeah.' He nodded. 'It's on the market and when it sells, I'll have some funds in the bank.'

'And with the life insurance as well . . .'

He sighed and rubbed his eyes.

'Sorry, Jack, I don't mean to sound callous, but the money's there and you do need to start thinking about your life and your future.' She gave him a small smile. 'It's been almost a year.'

'A year next month.'

'Yes.'

He met Bella's eyes. 'That's not long, you know.'

She pursed her lips. 'It's not. I know how much you've struggled, Jack, believe me I do, and I love you so much and wish desperately that I could take your pain away. But sadly, no one can. What I do know, though, is that Danni would absolutely not want you to drift along like this for the rest of your life. You need to put your big boy pants on and get back in the game.'

'Pardon?' He gave a wry laugh. 'My big boy pants? The *game*?'

Bella rolled her eyes. 'I know, Jack, I'm mixing my metaphors, but I do spend eight hours a day with children and sometimes I need to get them to understand what I mean by providing images that they can visualise. They always laugh at *big boy pants* and who doesn't like the idea of life being like a game?'

'It's OK, I know what you mean. It just made me think of superheroes wearing their pants over their trousers.'

'You can do that if you like, as long as you start moving again.'

'I will, I promise. Try to figure my life out, I mean, not wear my pants over my jeans. Anyway, how are my nieces?'

As Bella launched into a monologue about her daughters, Jack occasionally raised his eyebrows and made noises to show he was paying attention. He hadn't seen enough of his nieces over the years and the guilt of that added to his low mood, but they had lived in Woking and he had lived in Swansea and so get-togethers had been limited to a few times a year. Children grew so quickly and changed daily, it seemed, and when he did see Penny and Bobby, they tended to be a bit shy and awkward around him, as they would be with anyone they didn't know well.

'What do you think?' Bella was chewing at her bottom lip, a sign that she was anxious about her question.

What had she asked? He'd been thinking about his nieces and his attention had drifted.

'Uhhh . . .'

'Oh, come on, Jack. If you don't have a job and don't have any intention of getting one this side of Christmas, you might just as well come and stay with us.'

'When?'

'As soon as possible. We have that apartment over the garage and you'd be quite comfortable in there. You could have your privacy and space but also join us for meals and have company when you want it.'

'Oh, right. Uh . . .'

'It would give you a chance to spend some time with the girls and me, and you and Lee have always got on well, so that wouldn't be an issue.'

'Isn't Lee using that space above the garage as an office?'

Bella laughed. 'As a games room, more like. He's set up his Xbox in there and was hoping to sneak off for some quiet time, but he rarely has the chance.'

'Really? I'd hate for him to feel I'd kicked him out of his man cave.'

'Man cave is exactly what he'd like it to be. Honestly, it's fine. He has a million jobs to do around the house anyway and the girls are always asking for lifts or attention, so the apartment is basically unused. When we moved in we decorated and furnished it and it's such a waste, so you'd be doing us a favour, really.'

Jack liked how Bella was calling it an apartment. He'd seen photos and it looked like a bedsit above the garage at the side of the house. It had a bedroom, bathroom, kitchen-lounge

19

area and windows that overlooked the large back garden that Bella had told him bordered the village park and playing fields.

'When were you thinking?' She'd mentioned Christmas so Jack thought she might mean middle to late December.

'Seeing as how the anniversary's looming, why don't you come before then?'

'Well, the house needs to be tidied and readied for viewings so I'll need to get things organised first.'

'OK, then do that and give the estate agent the key and they can take care of the viewings.'

Jack took a slow, deep breath. Selling the house he'd bought with Danni had been a hard decision to make, but it was a family home with four bedrooms and a large back garden and he rattled around in it on his own. There were also reasons why he didn't want to stay there that were all muddled up in his grief and so he'd reasoned that selling the house would be better than trying to live in it. Of course, he'd need to find somewhere to live once it sold, but he was trying to take things one step at a time. The house had risen significantly in value since they'd bought it ten years ago and with disposable income from the house sale, along with Danni's life insurance, he could, basically, move anywhere as long as he didn't splurge the money and lived sensibly. And he did want to get a job but not in insurance sales this time; he knew he couldn't do that for the rest of his life. It just wasn't for him, long-term. That was why he'd started to wonder – on his better days – if he could return to uni and study to be a teacher as he'd once dreamt of doing. It would be a challenge, though, and one that he wasn't sure he had the strength for just yet. However, a change of scenery could help.

'Can I think about it?'

'Yes, think about spending some time here with us in a beautiful English village with gorgeous woodland walks, cosy country pubs, your big sister's excellent culinary skills and people around who love you. It'll be good for you, I'm sure it will.'

He looked at Bella, at her pleading hazel eyes and her warm smile, and knew he couldn't refuse.

'OK. Give me a few days to get everything sorted and I'll be there.'

'Yay!' Bella clapped her hands. 'I'm so glad you've said yes. We'll have the loveliest time. You can come and get settled in, then in December we'll go and watch the girls' school play and you can help with the Christmas tree and come to carols at the village green and – and just all those gorgeous, festive things.'

'It's not even November yet!' Jack laughed.

'I know, but time will fly and I'll just feel better if you're here safe with us. It broke my heart last year when you insisted on being alone for Christmas.'

He cleared his throat. 'I had to do it.'

'I know, even though it must have been awful with you being so newly bereaved and with Mum and Dad being so far away.'

'It was probably a good thing that they were in Florida, to be honest.'

'They did want to come back for the funeral.'

'I know. But with Dad having that operation, it wasn't a good idea for him to fly and I definitely didn't want Mum coming all that way alone, or leaving him.'

Bella sighed. 'You always think about everyone else and never about yourself, Jack.'

'That's not strictly true, but I was suffering anyway and there was no point in them going through it too.'

'I guess not, but family should support you through good times *and* bad.'

'I know you're always there for me, Bella,' he said. 'Anyway, haven't you got children to feed?'

'Nope. Lee's making spag bol for dinner.'

'Nice.'

'He's a good cook too, so you'll be well fed.'

'I'll look forward to it.'

'Good, because you're looking a bit too thin right now.'

'I've started running again, so I've lost a few pounds.'

'I'm glad to hear that. About the running, I mean. It's good for you, physically and mentally.'

'I know. Getting out does help a lot. By the way, do I need to bring anything when I come?'

'Just yourself. And some clothes, obviously. We don't want you walking around starkers, do we?'

'Perish the thought.'

'Let me know when you've spoken to the estate agent. Love you, Jack.'

'Will do. Love you too.'

He ended the Zoom call and closed his laptop. When Bella wanted something, she usually got it. But her heart was in the right place. Last year he'd been in no fit state of mind to be with anyone over the holidays. This year, he'd thought to have a quiet one again, but he could tell that Bella would be worried about him and if going to stay with her for a while would stop her worrying, then he could do that. Also, having some time away from Swansea might be good for him. As long as he lived here there were too many reminders of Danni and he'd find it difficult to move on. While in some ways the memories were comforting, in others they were a reminder of what he'd lost and, possibly, of what he'd never really had. His life had been more complicated than even he'd known.

He shook his head and pressed the heels of his hands into his eyes. No point thinking about that right now. Better to get up and get moving. He could go for a run, come home and shower, then start thinking about tidying and packing. Not that he was going just yet, but if he was going to be away for about two months, he'd need to take most of his clothes with him. He'd also need to give the house a good clean for the estate agent to show people around. Being busy would kill some time and then he could head off and spend a while with his sister's family.

It would be a positive thing to do.

Suddenly, he realised he was actually kind of looking forward to the idea of a family Christmas. He just hoped he'd be able to smile and be positive.

Chapter 4

Hazel ended the call and put her phone down, then she stood up and walked around the desk to stand in the middle of the small office.

She took a deep breath.

Then she shouted, 'YES! YES! YES! Get in there, Hazel!'

This was followed by her punching the air several times, a bit of a dance, then more air punches before returning to her desk and sitting down, straightening her blouse as she did so.

'Here it begins, Hazel. You've got the job and you *can* do this.'

She turned her computer on and sat back in her chair. She'd just spoken to Clare Greene, who had asked her to plan a Christmas wedding for herself and her fiancé Sam Wilson. They ideally wanted to marry on 18th December, which would be the Saturday before Christmas, and they would prefer a late afternoon or evening ceremony. They didn't want anything religious, and the village church was about to undergo some structural repairs, so would have to be ruled out even if they had wanted the ceremony there. Clare had told her that slipped roof tiles had been missed and there had been consequential damage as rainwater had leaked through and caused issues with the walls and floor. As the church was a listed building, the repairs had to be done by specialists and with the right materials, and that could take weeks, possibly months. They had asked Hazel to search for locations including hotels, barn conversions and historical sites.

Hazel rubbed her hands then clicked the internet explorer icon. There was nothing she loved more than planning a wedding and although the timing was tight with this one, she was sure she could pull it off.

It had been four days since she'd handed Clare and Sam her business card in the café and in that time, hoping that they'd call, she'd started looking at local venues just in case and there were some lovely hotels and other sites nearby, but she knew that with it being so close to Christmas, she might struggle to secure somewhere as they'd be booked up with other weddings and Christmas parties. However, it wasn't impossible, and Hazel would now search in earnest. December was a wonderful time of year to get married and she could have a lot of fun with planning the finer details of a winter wedding once the venue had been secured. First, though, she needed to email a questionnaire to Clare and Sam to find out their likes and dislikes.

She opened her emails and took a deep breath.

'Here we go . . .'

❄

Jack taped the side of the box down then stood up. He'd phoned the estate agent the day after his conversation with Bella and she'd said that she already had people who she thought would be interested in the house. A comfortably-off middle-aged couple were moving to Swansea because the woman had got a job in the city and they were looking for a property. They'd sold their home in Coventry and needed to buy quickly. As Jack didn't have a chain, his house was really appealing.

And so the past three days had involved Jack packing his things, taking some stuff to the charity shop and putting some of it into storage. The time constraints had, in a way, made it easier and his actions had been mechanical, unaffected by sentiment or emotion. If he'd had more time then things like deciding what to do with his wedding album would have been more difficult, but as it was, he'd packed it carefully in a box to go into storage along with the rest of their photographs, except for the ones he'd thought Danni's parents might want. He planned on dropping a box of Danni's things at her parents' house over the weekend.

The estate agent had told him that the potential buyers wanted to view the property in person and would be in Swansea at the start of next week, so he'd decided to stay until after their viewing in case they made an offer and he could get the ball rolling straight away. At least then he'd know where he stood in terms of what to do with furniture and larger items, but he'd put as much as he could into the storage facility now so there was less to do if the house did sell straight away.

He'd got rid of Danni's clothes and some of her other things earlier in the year. After a bleak Christmas, January had rolled in as it always did with dark days and plenty of rain. The cold had seemed to seep into his bones and he'd wondered how he'd ever feel hope again. But one morning he'd woken up to find a bright spring day and he'd felt the urge to go for a run. It had hurt, but that had been good; just to feel something other than agonising grief or the numbness that came over him sometimes. The throbbing in his calves, the burning in his lungs and the sweat that dripped off him were good things because they reminded him that he was still alive; he was still breathing, still moving, still human. His fitness had soon increased and running had become part of his routine – even on the days when he wanted to stay in bed – and it had been an integral one after he'd quit his job in the summer, having used up a lot of sick days and with the company offering him counselling and a support plan that he didn't want. It had seemed easier to quit than to keep plugging away at a job he had no passion for. When he went out, he ran for miles and miles, along woodland paths and beaches, through housing estates and open fields. It gave him a purpose and it made him feel better, stronger, more able to cope with everything. That feeling didn't always last, but when he was running, he could forget about everything else and that was addictive for him.

He hoped there would be some good places to run in Surrey because he couldn't cope without his daily fix. There was nothing quite like it and he couldn't imagine there being anything better, not any more anyway.

❉

Hazel slumped over her desk. She'd been on the phone and email all day trying to find a venue that wasn't booked up on 18th December, but she'd had no luck at all. Not one place near the village had the date free and even when she'd tried for the day before and the day after, it had been the same. She'd asked them to let her know if there were any cancellations but no one she spoke to seemed very optimistic.

What on earth was she going to do? This was her chance to prove herself in the community as a capable business-woman. Reputation was everything in her business and word of mouth and online reviews were incredibly important to her success. If she failed at the first hurdle, her name would be mud, surely? Clare and Sam seemed lovely, but she'd promised she'd plan them a wonderful wedding and even though they had yet to sign on the dotted line, as it were, they wouldn't be happy if she couldn't sort something out for them. Besides which, apart from the reputation aspect, they really did seem nice and she wanted them to have the perfect wedding. They deserved it.

She just needed to think outside the box, to use one of the phrases her university tutor had repeated over the years of her degree. A successful businessperson had to look at a situation and see opportunities, not obstacles. That was, of course, easier said than done, but Hazel Campbell was no quitter and she *would* find a solution.

A cup of coffee and a blank notepad would be a good place to start. They always helped to get her brain whirring and she was determined to do just that.

Chapter 5

Jack parked his black Ford Kuga outside the large house in a Mumbles side street and sat for a moment, thinking about how many times he'd parked outside Danni's parents' home over the years. Like those in the early days of their relationship when he'd been anxious about making a good impression, when their love had been new and they'd been unable to keep their hands off each other. Everything had seemed so exciting back then and nostalgia swept through him, making his chest ache with longing for how things used to be.

But that was a long time ago, sixteen years to be precise, and while his and Danni's relationship had still been good in some ways (or so Jack had thought) the initial passion and intensity had waned, morphing into something else, a more comfortable existence. And that had been fine; Jack was a realist and knew that relationships didn't stay the same way for ever, that desire wasn't always going to burn as brightly when work and life and tiredness crept in. What he hadn't expected was to have his wife torn away from him so young, to never have the chance to do all the things they had planned when they first got together, when they'd whispered about their hopes and dreams as they lay entwined, their hearts seeming to beat as one.

He shook himself. He wasn't here to reminisce or to bathe in regret, he was here to drop off some things for his in-laws and then to get home and finish the packing and cleaning. Time was of the essence and there was none spare for moping.

He got out of the car, retrieved the box from the boot then let himself into the garden and walked to the front door. He rang the bell, shivering as the freezing morning breeze swirled around his legs and crept under his collar like icy fingers.

'Oh, hello, Jack.' Fenella Williams eyed him with surprise as if she hadn't been expecting him, even though he'd called the day before to check it would be OK.

'Fenella.' He gave a nod.

'I suppose you'd better come in.' She stepped back and he entered the large hallway with its wide central staircase and mezzanine landing. The house smelt of spices, as it always had done, and Fenella gave off a floral powdery scent that made Jack think of crushed lilies.

'I've got the things we spoke about in here.' He directed a nod at the box in his arms.

Fenella's left eye twitched and she touched it briefly then glanced at the box. 'Leave it on the hall table, I'll look at it later.'

'Of course.' Jack set the box down, taking care not to knock the vase of fresh flowers there over, then turned back to Fenella.

'Stuart's not here. He had a meeting with an old colleague about something or other. Would you like coffee?'

'Uh . . .' Jack wasn't sure that she wanted him there. She had always been quite aloof and he'd often wondered if she'd been disappointed that her youngest child chose to marry him, but as he was going away, he felt that he should make the effort to spend at least ten minutes with her, so he agreed. 'Sure. Thanks.'

Fenella made a face that suggested she'd have preferred to have coffee with a serial killer, then headed for the kitchen, her movements tight and strained. For a seventy-five-year-old woman she had excellent posture and Jack knew that her years as a ballet dancer then actress had probably instilled that in her.

Coffee made, they sat at the round table that overlooked the back garden. Fenella placed a plate of lemon shortbread in front of Jack along with the cafetière and a small crystal jug of cream.

'Well, Jack, how have you been?'

Jack met her pale-blue eyes. It was as if a shutter had come down since she'd made tea. She could have been doing long multiplication in her head or cursing him with every swear word she knew and he'd have been none the wiser. 'I'm OK, thanks. Plodding along. You?'

She inclined her head. 'We're fine. Busy as always.'

'Of course,' he said.

Fenella and Stuart had been involved with a variety of clubs and groups for as long as he'd known them. They had three other children and several grandchildren, although none of them lived locally, so they didn't see them that often. Only Danni had stayed close to home, attending Swansea University and then getting a nursing job at the hospital after her

31

postgraduate course. She'd told Jack that, as the youngest of four children, she'd felt it was up to her to stay local. Danni had adored her parents and refused to hear a bad word about them from anyone – not that Jack would have spoken badly of them, but at times he'd been frustrated at how Fenella and Stuart behaved, biting his tongue on many occasions. Danni had been there for them and yet it had always been their eldest daughter, Prudence, who'd been their favourite and it was she they'd always raved about, with her wealthy husband and estate in Oxford, her two perfect sons and their perfect life. Danni had barely got a look in when Fenella had started on about Pru's latest achievements, and yet Danni had always listened patiently and shown genuine pride in her older sister, even though that sister had seemed barely aware of Danni's existence. Danni had come along unexpectedly when Fenella was in her forties and Jack thought that might have explained Fenella's air of resentment towards her youngest child and, in turn, towards Jack.

After Danni's death, it had been harder for Jack to keep quiet his belief that Fenella and Stuart had been neglectful of Danni and hadn't recognised how much she had achieved as a nurse, but he'd known that there was no point trying to get through to them. Prudence, Alain (now in Dubai) and Geraint (in New York) had all come before Danni and even after her death, nothing had changed.

'I wasn't sure how much of Danni's stuff you'd want so I've put some photos of hers in the box and a few other bits, like one of her journals that she wrote a few years ago. It's really nice . . . filled with cuttings from magazines and some little poems and memories about her childhood. It's—'

Fenella was shaking her head. 'I'm sure you mean well, Jack, but there was no need. It will just add to the things we have to sort out here – and lord knows there's a lot of that. Stuart ordered a skip just last week to clear out some of the old toys and whatnot from the attic. We're not getting any younger and the last thing we want is to leave a load of old junk behind when we go. Poor Pru does *not* need that on her to-do list.'

Silenced, Jack stared at her, taking in the light film of powder that sat on her skin and the mascara that had seeped into the fine lines around her eyes. Her hair was immaculate as always, a white helmet that barely moved, even in strong winds, and she wore a string of pearls and matching earrings along with her uniform of pale-pink blouse and cream cashmere cardigan. She looked smart and demure, could have been a loving mum, and yet her eyes were cold. They had always been cold.

He sighed inwardly, part of him wondering why he had bothered and yet knowing that he had to come. It was who he was, even although he'd known that this reaction would be the most likely one. It was why he'd seen very little of Fenella and Stuart since they'd lost Danni, why he knew that he couldn't seek comfort from them nor try to offer them any.

He drank the coffee, declined a lemon shortbread then stood up.

'I'm leaving the house keys with the estate agent,' he said as Fenella walked him to the door. 'I'm going to stay with Bella for a while.'

'Bella?'

He fought the urge to roll his eyes. 'My sister. She lives in Surrey.'

'Oh, of course.'

'I'll let you know when the house sells and what I intend to do then.'

'Intend to do?' A small frown marred her brow.

'Yes. Where I'm going to live afterwards . . .' He let his sentence trail off. There was no need to say more. Fenella obviously didn't care and he knew that if he did leave Swansea and move away, he would probably never see her again.

He opened the door then turned and looked at his mother-in-law, perhaps for the final time. He searched her face for similarities to Danni's but there weren't many. The slight Cupid's bow of her mouth and the high cheekbones were all that he could find. Danni's eyes had been a brighter blue, her hair chestnut brown, whereas Fenella, even in her youth, had been ash blonde, pin thin and heavily made-up. He wondered for a moment what had happened to make her the way she was, knew that everyone had a story to tell, a reason why they held themselves a certain way and why they treated others as they did, but he also knew that Fenella would never reveal anything of herself to him and that, apart from Danni, they had nothing in common at all.

'Goodbye, Fenella,' he said.

'Take care,' she replied, closing the door before he'd even reached the gate.

Getting into his car, Jack was surprised to find a lump in his throat. It was a physical embodiment of sadness for all that had passed, for all that had never been, and also one of relief because he'd done his part now and he could leave without feeling guilty. He had tried over the years to develop a relationship with his in-laws, but they had barely wanted to know when Danni had been around and, after her passing, it was crystal clear that they had no interest in him whatsoever.

But that was OK. Jack could go and stay with his kind and caring sister now and know that she had always accepted him for who he was, had always loved him, quirks and all – and never, ever judged him.

He started the engine, something fluttering inside him, and he wondered for a moment what the unfamiliar feeling was. But as it grew and a warmth spread through his chest, he sat up straighter. He didn't know if it would last but as he drove away, he realised what the feeling was.

It was hope.

Chapter 6

Hazel yawned and stared at her reflection in the bathroom mirror. She had purple shadows under her eyes and her skin was grey. She hadn't slept well and had been worrying all weekend. She'd thought that moving would mean leaving her worries behind, but had she been ridiculously naïve? She'd believed that as she'd set up one successful wedding planning business, setting up another should be easy. However, so far, she'd gained one couple for her books and had been unable to find them a venue.

'I'm a failure,' she said to her reflection. 'A failure in love and a failure at my job. I'm rubbish. I'm . . .' She tried to think of another insult to throw at herself. Why not? If she was going to give herself a hard time then she might as well do it in style. But her mind had gone blank and, as she held her own gaze, the ridiculousness of her situation bubbled inside her and suddenly a snort burst from her. And another. She watched as her lips curled upwards and she pressed a hand to her belly.

'Sort yourself out, Hazel Campbell, you bloody idiot! You can do this, but you have to get your brain into gear.'

She pulled her hair into a high ponytail, slicked on some lip gloss, then headed for the bedroom.

Fleas Witherspoon, named after Hazel's favourite actress, was stretched out on the bed, fast asleep. Hazel gazed at her for a moment, wishing she could have just an ounce of the cat's peace of mind, wondering how it would be to lie in bed all day and have someone prepare all her meals. But then, Fleas hadn't had a good start in life, had been mistreated, in fact, and it had left her with some emotional scars. Her previous owners had abandoned her when they'd left the area and she'd been rescued by a neighbour who had cats of her own and couldn't home another and taken to a local animal charity. She was severely underweight, her fur was knotted and she had bald patches from scratching at fleas. Urgent care was administered and then, when she was stronger, she'd been put up for adoption. Hazel had seen Fleas on a Facebook post for the charity and felt compelled to contact them about her. As soon as she'd met the cat, she'd known that Fleas belonged in her life and, despite Lennox's disapproval, she'd adopted her. Caring for Fleas gave Hazel a sense of purpose, because she loved the cat and knew that the feeling was mutual.

Once she'd dressed in skinny black jeans and a fine-knitted black jumper, she pulled on socks and knee-high boots. There was something about dressing all in black that she liked. It was smart but also like a uniform and yet it gave nothing away about her to anyone.

The bijou flat she was renting above her office was clean and cosy, the perfect space for a single woman. In the bedroom, she had a comfortable double bed, wardrobe, chest of drawers and dressing table. There was a bathroom with a bath and power shower over it, a sink and a toilet. The lounge had two fat purple sofas with scatter cushions, an oak coffee table and a large bookcase, both of which looked as if they'd been made of reclaimed wood and she wondered if there was somewhere nearby that did that type of work. And finally, there was the kitchen-diner, complete with a two-seater table, freestanding fridge-freezer and plenty of cupboard space for her meagre collection of kitchenware. She knew she'd been lucky finding a flat with an office below it and for the price she was paying. There was a sense of security in having her own little space where she could be herself. Choosing Little Bramble as her new home had been a good decision, even if there were no wedding venues nearby with the date she needed free.

At the sash window she gazed out at the leafy, treelined side street, appreciating how quiet it was, although knowing that this also meant that it lacked the footfall of her office in the centre of Edinburgh. She'd have to use other techniques to bring in custom and the first part of that was planning the best wedding Little Bramble had ever seen. In order to do that, she needed to know a bit more about the village, so it was time to get out there and have a good look around. She had walked around the village in the three weeks since she'd opened her business, but only to pick up some shopping and to grab a coffee at the green, so today's walk would be different. The weather had not been great recently but today looked like a good day for a walk.

She gave Fleas a stroke, grabbed her red wool coat, black beret and gloves, then headed downstairs, enjoying the sense of determination that was building inside her. Hazel had always liked a challenge and this was a good one.

The morning was cold but bright and, as Hazel walked briskly along the street, she breathed in the fresh, clean air.

At the end of the street was an opening that took her towards the cluster of village shops, including a grocer, a butcher, a bakery, a sweetshop and a charity shop. There was also a hair salon; as she passed it, she caught a waft of styling products on the air along with the hum of a hairdryer as the door opened and a woman went inside. Ahead of Hazel was the very old church, surrounded by a low stone wall and grounds that included a graveyard. A shingle-clad spire on the church roof pointed towards the sky and there was a Victorian lychgate covered with holly and ivy halfway along the stone wall. It was easy to see how repairs to a listed building like that would need extra care and attention.

She walked alongside the wall, gazing over it at the well-tended headstones, many of which had flowers in pots, and admiring the large yew tree in the far corner of the church yard. That tree probably had a few stories to tell, she thought, smiling to herself.

A memory stopped her in her tracks and she wobbled slightly as she tried to pin it down. Yes! She'd looked at that tree with her parents during that wonderful holiday when she was ten. Her maternal grandmother had a friend who lived in the village and she'd rented them a holiday cottage. The friend was long since gone and Hazel wondered if the cottage was too. She thought she knew where it might be, but her memory of its exact location was hazy, although something told her it was near allotments and lots of trees, possibly even a stream. She'd take a look soon, but for now she was content to remember walking around the yew tree with her mum and dad, admiring the tree that her mum had told her was a symbol of rebirth and regeneration, representing the cycle of life.

How innocent she had been back then as she'd gazed lovingly up at her parents, held both their hands tightly and thought the three of them would be together forever. Their love had made her feel safe and secure so as a child she'd felt invincible. It was a good thing that she'd had no idea what lay ahead, that she'd lose them both by the time she was thirty-one and within a three-year window. Bowel cancer had taken her dad and her mum had suffered a fatal heart attack, but Hazel was convinced that it had been grief that led to the heart attack. Her parents had loved each other deeply and that love had spread to their only child and wrapped around her like a security blanket, one she sorely missed every day.

Focusing on the church building again, Hazel thought that some clients would want a church wedding in future, and it would be a beautiful place to get married. The history of a church like that would be rich and varied and she'd take a good look inside when she had the chance, probably after the repairs had been done. But for now, she needed to walk and think, to find inspiration, and she felt sure that this pretty little village had that in abundance.

Past the church was the village primary school, along with playing fields and a children's park. She could hear the shouts and laughter of children in the schoolyard and she guessed it must be morning break for them. One of the many things she'd felt excited about with her job was the idea that when she and Lennox had children, she'd have the flexibility to do the school run some days, and she'd said it to him on more than one occasion. She'd imagined being part of a group of mums and dads who shared the school run and had pictured collecting a brood of excited little people and taking them for pizza or ice cream before heading home to her handsome husband. There would also be a cat and, hopefully, a dog or two in their large, detached home. But the years had passed and she'd not been able to get Lennox to commit to when they were going to start trying for a family. There had always been a reason to wait a while, whether it was her job or his, a holiday they wanted to have or something else that – now she looked back – seemed to be simply another excuse. Things hadn't been right and that was why. Thank goodness, in light of what had happened, that they hadn't started a family.

She pressed her hands to her chest as the familiar pain welled, hating Lennox for hurting her but hating herself even more for allowing him to hurt her. How blind had she been and for how long? She had to shake this off and get on with her life, but everything seemed to be a reminder of what she'd lost, even when she'd moved so far away.

Sucking in deep breaths, Hazel continued with her stroll, passing a row of small but pretty cottages and a pub called The King's Arms on her left. There was a bistro, a veterinary surgery, a café and more cottages, all surrounding a large village green. Finally, she reached the village hall and re-alised she'd done a circle of the core of Little Bramble with just The Red Squirrel ahead of her and the lane that led to the train station entrance.

The front doors to the village hall were closed but she could see lights on inside and decided to have a peek. Having spent most of her life in Edinburgh, she'd never been inside an English country village hall but seeing as how she was a part of this community now she should know what the hall was like and what it offered to the community.

She climbed the steps, pushed the door open then stepped inside.

The village hall was warm, a stark contrast to the bitterly cold air outside, and aromas of coffee and pastries greeted Hazel, along with some other smells like paint and a faint waft of chips that made her think of school. It was, she realised, how she'd expect a village hall to smell. A notice-board on the wall was covered in colourful flyers advertising a range of classes including baby band, bread making, yoga, tai chi, Zumba and crochet. Well, at least she knew there was plenty to do here.

The sound of instruments being played very badly, reminiscent of the screeching and yowling of fighting cats, led her towards double doors, one of which was propped open, and she peered into what must be the main room of the hall. To one side was a stage and a large, covered piano and ahead was a group of people sitting in a circle with babies and small children at their sides, on their laps and in front of them. Prams and pushchairs were lined up in front of the windows that overlooked the green. The noise was coming from the circle and Hazel realised it must be some sort of baby music club.

Baby Band! Of course. She'd seen the flier.

Some of the children were shaking tambourines and maracas, others were blowing into recorders and some had bongos. Looking at the parents sitting in the circle, she wondered how they could bear the noise. Her eyes landed on one woman with a sleek blue-black bob who was wearing smart trousers and a white silk blouse and looked more as though she should be at a business meeting than a baby group. She didn't have a baby with her but was holding the hand of a woman at her side who had fair hair pulled into a messy bun. The fair-haired woman was cupping her softly rounded belly in the way Hazel had noticed some pregnant women did. Were they both oblivious to the noise even though it didn't look like they had any children with them? Did parenthood and even pregnancy numb your senses or deafen you to such an awful racket?

A woman with grey, bobbed hair and glasses with thick black frames was walking around the circle, occasionally moving her hands and nodding as if she was conducting the London Symphony Orchestra. She also seemed oblivious to the noise. She looked up as Hazel faltered in the doorway and gestured at her to come in.

Hazel considered backing away, but as the music faltered then stopped and heads turned towards her, she felt it would be rude not to say hello, so she approached the circle cautiously.

'Hello there! Have you come to join us?' the grey-haired woman asked.

'Oh . . . uh . . . no. I don't have a child,' Hazel said apologetically, holding up her hands as if to prove it. 'I recently moved to the village and I was taking a look around.'

The woman gave a small nod, her blue eyes appraising Hazel and Hazel felt like she'd just walked into the head teacher's office at school.

'I'm Elaine Hughes.' She held out a hand and Hazel shook it.

'Hazel Campbell.'

'Is that a Scottish accent?' Elaine asked, her brows meeting.

'Partly, but there's also a hint of Welsh in there.'

'Thought so.' Elaine tilted her head. 'Are you the wedding planner?'

'That's right. How did you know?'

'Clare Greene is my daughter.'

'Oh, right.' Hazel swallowed a comment about it being a small world because it was, obviously, a small village.

'Clare is incredibly relieved to have some help with the wedding planning, I can tell you. I offered to help, and their wedding is one of the main reasons why I've come back to Little Bramble after some time away travelling, but I'm also planning the Christmas Show this year as it was a bit much for Clare to do along with getting married.' Elaine waved her hands around her head. 'It's all been rather chaotic, to be honest, so we're very glad you're on board to help. I'm sure you'll like living here and that you'll have lots of business coming your way.'

'I hope so,' Hazel said, aware of the many pairs of eyes watching them from the circle.

'And this, as you can see, is Baby Band. I only set it up a few weeks ago but it's very popular already, even with those of our village who have yet to birth their babies, like Phoebe Baxter-Cheng over there with her wife, Lucie.' The women waved as they were mentioned. 'Although,' Elaine leant closer to Hazel, 'I think I'll need two ibuprofen and a lie-down in a dark room afterwards. Perhaps even a large G & T.'

'I'd better let you get back to it.' Hazel gestured at the circle, where a toddler had started to grizzle and where a blonde woman wearing designer yoga gear and with immaculate makeup lifted a baby and sniffed at its behind. She grimaced, then got up and picked up another baby from a blanket that was spread out in front of her. She carried both babies over to them.

'Elaine?' the blonde woman said.

'Yes, Jenny?'

'I have to change this or she'll stink the hall out.' She smiled at Hazel. 'My daughter might be cute but she can fill a nappy with poo so toxic it could clear a stadium in seconds.'

'Let me have him and you go and sort her out.' Elaine took the one baby. 'Before you go, though – this is Hazel, our newly arrived wedding planner.'

'You're planning Clare and Sam's wedding?'

'That's right.' Hazel inclined her head. No pressure at all, then; it seemed that everyone knew!

'Great to meet you. I'm Jenny Rolands and I'm the maid of honour. Or is it matron of honour? So we'll be seeing more of each other.'

'Lovely.' Hazel smiled.

'I would shake your hand but I'm worried this one has leaked so I'd better get her changed asap.' Jenny hurried away, her black yoga wear making Hazel think of the so-called yummy mummies she'd met in Scotland, including one whose wedding to a giant rugby player, the star of the international team, she'd planned. Pleasing them had been a challenge but Hazel had risen to it and then some. Hazel had, however, drawn the line when the bride had requested flamingos at the reception. She'd said that they would complement her enormous dress perfectly and wanted them to take part in a choreographed ballet routine that involved lifting the edges of her train and carrying it around as she pirouetted. Hazel had calmly explained that such things took place only in cartoons and that, until she could harness the powers of Disney, she'd be unable to provide dancing flamingos, or any other wild birds for that matter. Luckily, the bride had been satisfied with a video of flamingos on a projector screen that Hazel had set up as a background to the dance floor and the wedding reception had been a great success.

'Anyway,' Elaine patted Hazel's arm, bringing her back to the room, 'I'll see you very soon, no doubt. I can't wait to see what venues you've come up with.'

'Great.' Hazel grinned so hard her teeth felt like they'd snap, then she walked away. When the cooler air of the hallway met her cheeks, she sighed with relief. She really did love her job but being unable to find a venue was a worry, especially with her reputation on the line. She'd known that Clare and Sam had family and friends, of course she had, because they'd mentioned them all, but in a village like this, if Hazel didn't come up trumps on all counts, then her reputation could be in tatters before she'd even begun.

She closed her eyes for a moment, trying to keep calm, then opened them and peered along the hallway. There was what must be a kitchen at the end of it and the walls either side of her were, she now realised, lined with photographs.

She turned and looked at the wall behind her, taking in the details. Some of the photographs appeared to have been taken inside a different hall that looked older and more dated, possibly one that had been in the village before, and showed photographs of people on a stage wearing costumes that made her think of the Broadway shows she'd seen advertised. There were others of performers in Christmas outfits, including Santa hats and tinsel, and some that looked as though they were from pantomimes.

The other side of the hallway had photographs that had been taken outside, including some that seemed to be of summer fetes and what looked like a dog show with lots of greyhounds. One photograph higher up caught her eye and she stood on tiptoes to see it better. It was of a snow-covered landscape with a large Christmas tree draped with colourful lights. People stood around it holding mugs of what she suspected were mulled wine or hot chocolate. Everyone was smiling, the lights on the tree appeared to be twinkling and the snow was pure and white.

Pure. White. Smiling.

Something stirred in her brain like a butterfly and she tried to pin it down. She knew this process; her mind was working things out and problem-solving, as it always did.

She hurried to the doors and back out into the morning sun, then jogged across the road. There was the tree, a large, splendid thing at the centre of the green. She could picture it draped with twinkling lights, snow frosting its branches and covering the grass. There could be some sort of archway . . . an aisle created from chairs or benches . . . fairy lights on surrounding trees, a band or choir . . .

And there it was! The solution.

If she couldn't find an indoor venue, then why not hold the wedding outside? As long as she could get local council approval, it could be magical.

The tree would be the perfect backdrop for a wedding, especially if it snowed. And if not, they could always hire a snow machine.

47

Goosebumps rose on her skin and a tingle traced down her spine. She'd need to look into it and check that it was allowed, to ensure there was no annoying red tape to prevent a wedding being held there, but experience told her that most things could be overcome by speaking nicely to the right people.

She needed to get back to the office so she could look into this further and, if all was well, then she could pitch the idea to the bride and groom and hope that they liked it as much as she did.

Her mum had always told her to see opportunities not obstacles, and Hazel was convinced that, over the years, it had helped her to do just that. There were few problems in life that couldn't be solved, except perhaps for those that came with a broken heart. Although she felt sure that her mum would have had a way of reframing even that into something positive.

Chapter 7

'Jack!' Bella screamed as she opened the door and flung herself into his arms. 'You're here.'

He laughed as she clung to him, his lovely older sister with her shiny brown hair, bright-patterned wool jumper (that she had probably knitted herself), jeans and UGG boots. She had always managed to pull off slouchy style effortlessly and he was glad to know that hadn't changed. He found her consistency comforting. She smelt the same as she always did, too, like orange blossom, as if she'd spent the day making marmalade and cutting flowers.

'You knew I was coming, Bella.'

'I know, but I've missed you so much.'

She released her brother and stood back to look at him, her eyes shining.

'If I'd known you were missing me that much I'd have come sooner.'

She squeezed his shoulders, then planted a kiss on his cheek.

'You're here now and I'm going to take *such* good care of you.'

'Thanks.' He pushed away the urge to tell his older sister that he didn't need looking after. Bella was caring, had always looked out for him when they were children, and just because they were adults it didn't mean they couldn't support each other. Plus, he had a feeling that it would be nice to have someone looking after him for a change. He'd had enough of being alone. 'I'll just grab my bags.'

He went back out to the car then lifted his rucksack and his holdall out of the boot. He'd brought plenty to last him for the duration of his planned stay, during which time he hoped to sort himself and his life out. Having a clearer head and a sense of what he was going to do next would be, he imagined, an incredible feeling. He just hoped it worked.

Inside, he set his bags down in the hallway and looked around. He was ashamed to admit that he hadn't once visited Bella in her new home. She'd moved to the village in the late summer, after Lee got a job as a carpenter at a place called The Lumber Shed, and Jack hadn't made it down to visit. It was a bit of a trek, though, the journey taking over three hours by car and almost four by train with changes, so there was that. Anyway, he was here now, and he intended to pull himself together and be a better brother from here on. He had no doubt that it wouldn't be easy to climb out of the slump he'd sunk into, but with Bella's help, he had a better chance than if he was alone, surrounded by ghosts of the past.

The hallway had a carpeted staircase to the left, an open door to the right and a corridor that led towards another door. Jack glanced through the door to the right and saw a light and airy lounge with two large grey sofas at right angles to each other, a huge flat-screen TV and an open fireplace. Three fat white candles sat on a rectangular coffee table between the sofas and there was a hint of vanilla and woodsmoke in the air. The room was very light with two large windows, one overlooking the front garden and driveway and the other the side of the house where Jack knew – because Bella had told him – there was more garden, the garage and the apartment she'd told him he could use.

He ducked out of the room and walked along the hallway, the wooden boards clean and polished. Under the staircase was a space with a desk and a cupboard where he suspected they kept coats, shoes and other things they wanted out of sight.

Bella was in the kitchen at the back of the house.

'Wow, Bella! This is amazing.'

The kitchen-diner was big enough to have a kitchen area to the left with a giant free-standing fridge, range cooker and apron-fronted sink, all set in and around oak cabinets with shiny chrome handles. To the right was a dining area with a six-foot table and six green leather chairs. More candles like the ones in the lounge sat in the middle of the table. To the right of the doorway was a Welsh dresser and over to the left in front of the bifold doors was a two-seater sofa and another TV.

Bella saw him looking at it. 'With two children we need to have more than one TV downstairs, or they fight over who's watching what.'

'I bet.' He nodded.

'Plus, I always wanted a kitchen with room for a sofa and a TV area where we could all gather.'

'It's perfect.'

He went over to the bifold doors and looked out into the garden.

'Large garden too.'

'A lot of these old houses have fabulous gardens. It was perfect for the girls because they have a trampoline out there and a swing and I have a vegetable and herb patch and a greenhouse.'

'Oh yes, I can see it,' Jack said. 'Beyond the fruit trees?'

'Yes. It's a dream come true having fruit trees. It's very different to what we had in Woking.'

'It is.' Jack thought of the townhouse Bella and Lee had had in Woking with its concrete driveway out front and tiny box of a garden out back. Their view had been more houses, identical to theirs, and while there was nothing wrong with that, he knew that Bella had always wanted a house with a big garden so she could grow fruit and veg and have somewhere for the girls to play. He was sure she'd mentioned something about chickens too. 'So, do you have every Thursday and Friday off?'

'I do,' she replied as she filled the kettle. 'I work three days at the village school as a teaching assistant. I only started in September but I love it. I was doing the same job in Woking so had the experience the local school was looking for. I job-share now with another mum and it's perfect. Finally, I have the work-life balance I needed.'

'I'm very happy to hear that. I wish I could find what it is that I'm meant to do.'

Bella made tea then carried two mugs and a plate of biscuits to the table and they sat down.

'You're still not sure?'

He shook his head. 'I'm hoping that it'll come to me, although I'm thinking that perhaps a return to university could be in order, as we discussed on Zoom.'

Since they'd spoken, he had made the effort to look at some postgraduate training courses and it seemed that he met the entry requirements. He hadn't got as far as applying, but one step at a time was the best he could do right now.

'To train as a teacher?' She raised her eyebrows.

'Yes.'

'At last!' She clapped her hands. 'You'll be so good with the children.'

'Well, that remains to be seen. And it's something I'm thinking about doing, not *actually* doing – not yet, anyway.'

He reached for his tea and a custard cream, already feeling relaxed in his sister's home and aware that it was very nice indeed to have a cuppa, a biscuit, and a chat with his oldest friend.

※

Hazel had arranged to meet Clare and Sam at the The King's Arms pub to broach the subject of holding their wedding on the village green. She had checked with the local council and there was no issue with a civil ceremony being held there, as long as a registrar carried out the service or was present at the ceremony.

She'd put together a portfolio of ideas and images for the couple to give them some ideas of what their wedding could be like. She hadn't yet told them that she'd been unable to find an alternative venue because she wanted to do it in person in order to gauge their reaction. It was the only way she'd know if this was right for them. Otherwise, they'd need to reconsider when they got married and possibly postpone until next year and she knew they'd be disappointed with that.

She arrived at The King's Arms at quarter to seven and went inside, shivering a bit from the cold and partly from nerves. If this was wrong for Clare and Sam then she had no idea what to suggest next.

She ordered a glass of house red at the bar then sat at a corner table so she could set up her laptop and keep an eye on the door. The fire in the large hearth was lit and it sent a welcoming warmth into the room. There were other people at tables, some eating bar meals, and some just chatting over drinks. It seemed like a typical English pub, she thought, as she sipped her wine, feeling the alcohol seeping into her bloodstream and relaxing her.

The doors opened and she looked up expectantly, but it wasn't Clare and Sam, it was a tall man with dark hair and a woman with a very shiny brown bob that made her think of Claudia Winkleman. She returned her gaze to the screen of her laptop and tried to focus but her stomach was fluttering and she knew it wouldn't stop until she had spoken to Clare and Sam. She sipped more wine, hoping it would take the edge off her nerves.

When she raised her gaze again, the man and woman who'd come in were standing at the bar. The woman was speaking to a male bartender but the man was looking around the pub. His eyes landed on Hazel and her breath caught in her throat. He was gorgeous, with eyes the colour of dark chocolate and thick black eyebrows. His chin was shaded with stubble and he'd removed his coat, revealing his broad shoulders which were encased in a navy shirt, the sleeves rolled up to the elbows showing off muscular forearms dusted with dark hairs.

And he was staring at her!

Searing heat flooded her cheeks and she broke off eye contact, furious with herself for blushing and for gawking at him in the first place. He'd come in with a woman, and while she might not be his wife or girlfriend, Hazel should not be looking at him. She was here in a business capacity, not to ogle the attractive locals. Besides which, while she could appreciate a handsome man, Lennox had put her off dating for the rest of her life. Hazel's business would be everything to her now because at least that wouldn't betray her and break her heart.

'Get a grip,' she muttered to herself, fighting the urge to check if Handsome Man was still looking her way. She'd been with Lennox since she was fifteen and he was sixteen; they'd got together one evening at a mutual friend's party and she hadn't even looked at another man properly since then. Why would she when she'd loved Lennox so much? She shook her head as if to dislodge the thought because Lennox was a shit and he didn't deserve any space in her heart or her head.

A gust of cold air rushed around Hazel's ankles and she spotted Clare and Sam coming through the door to the pub. Breathing a sigh of relief, she waved at them and they came over to her table.

'Hello, Hazel, lovely to see you.' Clare greeted her with a friendly smile. 'Can we get you a drink?'

Hazel was about to decline but she looked at her glass and saw that it was almost empty.

'Oh, go on then.'

'House red?' Clare asked.

'Yes, please.'

Clare went to the bar while Sam sat down.

'Cold out.' He grimaced.

'It is. And it's dark so early now.' Hazel slipped into the easy exchange of weather and winter evenings, aware that it was a good way to relax her client and to move on to more important topics.

'I always feel like I should be home by four in the winter and in bed by seven.' Sam laughed.

'I know what you mean. So, Sam, what's it like being the village vet?'

'One of the vets,' he said. 'I have a business partner, Miranda Fitzalan. We share the workload.'

'I'm sure it's a tiring job.'

'It is, but very rewarding too.' Sam ran a hand over his springy curls. 'Although I don't always get time to do normal things like get a haircut.'

Hazel smiled. 'And with a salon in the village too.'

'I know. You'd think it would be manageable.'

'Definitely.' *Like falling in love and being true to that person when they weren't true to you.*

'Here you go.' Clare placed a bottle of red on the table along with two more glasses. 'I thought it would be easier to share a bottle.'

'Great idea, thank you,' Hazel said.

When Sam had filled their glasses, Hazel turned her laptop around on the table so they could all see the screen.

'Right, I've made a bit of a presentation because I wanted to see what you thought about an idea I've had.'

'OK,' Clare and Sam said together.

'I'd better be honest with you from the offset . . . I was unable to get you booked into any venues on the eighteenth.'

Clare's face fell and Hazel saw Sam take his fiancée's hand. Hazel pressed her lips together and inhaled slowly through her nostrils.

'But please don't despair, because I have an idea.'

'It's not the church, is it?' Sam asked, a small frown darkening his brow. 'Because it's in a terrible state at the moment inside.'

'It's not the church.' Hazel shook her head. 'It's something a bit different, actually.'

'Right.' His expression changed.

'I'll talk you through this and then we can see what you think.'

She ran through the PowerPoint, showing them the images she'd collected of outdoor weddings, along with some suggestions about where they could hold the ceremony, where they could have the aisle if they wanted one and what music they could consider. She had also put together some ideas for outdoor heating because they did want to marry in December and it was likely to be cold, possibly even snowing.

Clare and Sam listened and nodded at intervals, their eyes lighting up at some of the PowerPoint slides, and a few times they glanced at each other, communicating in the way that couples who know each other intimately are wont to do.

'What do you think?' Hazel asked when she'd closed the presentation and her laptop. 'No need to tell me now, actually, I can just leave you to have a chat and then let me know your thoughts once you've had time to digest it.'

Clare and Sam were gazing at each other as if the whole world had faded away.

'Tell you what . . .' Hazel got up. 'I'll just pop to the toilet. No pressure on you to decide now, though. Just let me know if you need more time. Oh, and before I forget, there's a wedding fayre being held in a hotel on the outskirts of Guildford a week on Saturday. If you fancy it, we could go and take a look. Have a think about it, anyway.'

She stood up, grabbed her bag and headed past the bar and towards the toilets. She'd thought she'd seen some positive signs as she'd talked them through the presentation but perhaps she'd been wrong. After what had happened with Lennox, she didn't trust her instincts the way she used to; if she could be wrong about the man she loved and about her best friend, then she could be wrong about anyone.

In the toilets she splashed some cold water over her face and patted it dry with a paper towel then fluffed her hair. She'd left it down this evening and it felt strange because she tied it back most of the time these days. Lennox had liked her to wear it down and so she'd pulled it back off her face recently in a kind of futile rebellion, she guessed. It's not as if Lennox would notice, though. He wasn't there and, anyway, he was far too busy running his hands through Valentina's ginger pixie cut and gazing into her glassy grey eyes, that he'd once commented had reminded him of a stormy sky. Had he been trying to throw Hazel off the scent even then by making out that he thought Valentina wasn't attractive when in fact he couldn't wait to get her knickers off?

Hazel leant over the sink and groaned. When would this anger leave her? When would she stop caring?

'Hello?'

She turned abruptly and looked around. There was no one there.

'Are you OK?'

The voice came from one of the cubicles. She hadn't realised anyone was in there.

'Yes, thanks. I'm fine,' Hazel said with what she hoped was a breezy air.

'That's all right then. I heard groaning and wondered if you were in pain or something.' A toilet flushed then the door to the cubicle opened and a woman emerged. Hazel recognised her as the one she'd seen in the bar with the shiny brown bob.

'No.' Hazel shook her head vigorously. 'I'm not in pain.'

'Glad to hear it.' The woman frowned. 'Are you new to the village? It's just that I don't think I've seen you around.'

Hazel supposed she'd have to get used to this; it was a small village and most people would know each other.

'I moved here a few weeks ago.'

'From Scotland?'

She'd also have to get used to that, as her accent wasn't going anywhere anytime soon.

'That's right.'

'That's a long way. I'm Bella Thornton and I moved here recently too, in the summer, actually, with my husband Lee and two children. I work at the primary school as a teaching assistant and my husband works at The Lumber Shed.'

'Nice to meet you, Bella, I'm Hazel Campbell.'

'I love the way your name sounds. Camp-bell is just musical when you say it.'

'Thanks.' Hazel laughed. 'I think.'

'Did you come here tonight for work or pleasure?'

'Work.' Hazel was surprised by how easily the word slipped out and felt the need to qualify it. 'Although I get a lot of pleasure from my job.'

'Good to hear that. What do you do?'

'I'm a wedding planner.'

'How exciting!' Bella's eyes lit up. 'Gosh, you must have some amazing stories.'

'I have some good ones, yes.' Hazel nodded, enjoying the interest Bella was showing in her.

'I bet you've had bridezillas and fainting grooms and all sorts, haven't you? Best men giving it to bridesmaids behind the altar.' Bella laughed but Hazel swallowed hard; Bella was a bit closer to the mark than was comfortable.

'Something like that.' She turned to the mirror and fluffed her hair again for something to do. She tried to think of something funny to tell Bella, but her mind had gone blank after the bridesmaids' comment.

'Oh, look at me chatting away when you've got things to do. Actually, I think I saw you in the bar with Clare and Sam, didn't I?'

'You did.'

'Are you planning their wedding? Oh wow, how wonderful! I don't know them very well but they seem like lovely people.'

'They are wonderful.'

'Well, it was very nice meeting you.' Bella placed a hand on Hazel's arm. 'We'll probably see more of each other and should have a coffee sometime or a few drinks.'

'I'd like that.'

They left the toilets together and Bella gestured at the bar, where the man she'd come in with was standing. 'Better get back to Jack. He'll be thinking I fell down the toilet.'

Hazel had thought Bella said her husband was called Lee.

'See you around,' Hazel said, glancing at the man Bella had called Jack as she passed, and realising that she had, in fact, been right when she'd seen him earlier.

He was drop-dead gorgeous, a dead ringer for Aidan Turner.

The thought annoyed the hell out of her because it was as though she was betraying herself just by noticing him.

❉

'Who was that?' Jack asked as Bella rejoined him at the bar.

'Who?'

'That woman.' He looked in the direction of the pretty blonde woman Bella had been chatting to as she emerged from the toilets.

'That's Hazel Campbell. She only moved here recently too. I haven't met her before but she seems really nice.'

'You think everyone's nice.'

Bella wrinkled her nose. 'And? What's wrong with seeing the best in people?'

'Nothing, I guess.'

'She's a wedding planner and has set up her business here in the village.'

'A wedding planner?' Jack rolled his eyes. 'Flogging costly wedding packages to bridezillas and grooms who just want the excuse of heading off on a stag weekend. Taking advantage of people when their common sense has been replaced by desire and romance and who think having some money in the bank isn't important because, of course, you can live on love and fresh air and no one's feelings will ever change.'

'Jack, what's made you so cynical? You never used to be like this. You were the man who surrendered your own career dreams to support your wife through her studies. You were very romantic with Danni and completely devoted to her.'

Jack picked up his beer and drained the bottle, feeling abashed and a bit shocked at his own outburst. 'I'm not cynical. At least, I don't mean to sound like I am. I'm sure lots of people need wedding planners.'

'It sounds like a fascinating job. She's planning a wedding for a gorgeous couple from the village. See over there . . . the people she's with?' Bella gestured at a table where Hazel was sitting with a man and woman.

'I can see them.' He returned his gaze to the bar, not wanting to be caught staring again. He'd noticed Hazel when he'd come in and caught her staring at him.

'That's Clare Greene and Sam Wilson. They're both delightful.'

Jack nodded. What could he say? He didn't know them but they looked nice enough. Mind you, Bella would see the good in anyone and always had done.

'Also . . .' Bella nudged his arm. 'Hazel's very pretty, isn't she?'

'What?'

'I didn't see a ring on her finger and she didn't mention a partner.'

Jack sighed and met his sister's teasing gaze. 'Bella, I am here to spend some time with you and to try to sort my life out. As much as I appreciate that you're being kind, I'm not interested in women right now. After what I've been through, I don't think I'll ever be interested again.'

Bella squeezed his arm. 'I know, Jack, and I wasn't trying to set you up or anything. I was just saying that Hazel is very pretty and I did see you looking at her. You *are* allowed to find women attractive, you know, without feeling guilty.'

He shook his head. 'I'm simply not interested.'

He hadn't told Bella the full story about Danni and what he'd found out because he hadn't wanted to admit to what had gone on. Danni had been perfect in his eyes and he didn't want to ruin that by chewing over what he'd discovered because, out in the open, it would feel real.

'Give yourself time, Jack. One day, you might – hopefully – be able to consider another relationship or at least a bit of dating. Life is short so you have to make the most of it.'

'I'm very aware that life is short,' he snapped, then he rubbed a hand over his face. 'I'm so sorry, Bella, I didn't mean for it to come out like that. It's just that Danni was only just thirty-four and that was a very short life indeed.'

'I know.'

He looked up into Bella's shining eyes and guilt coursed through him. The last thing he wanted was to make his sister feel bad.

'It's fine, honestly. I just need some time.'

He wrapped an arm around her shoulders and leant his head against hers.

'How do you feel now that you've looked through the presentation for a second time?' Hazel asked. She was so tense that her shoulders were aching and her neck was stiff, making her movements feel jerky. When she'd got back from the toilet, Clare and Sam had asked to see the presentation again.

Clare looked at Sam and he nodded.

'We love it.' Clare smiled. 'We'd thought about what it would be like to hold the wedding in the village but the idea of having the ceremony on the green itself hadn't occurred to us.'

'We think it would be perfect.' Sam raised his glass. 'We could have mulled wine for the adults, hot chocolate for the children . . .'

'That's a great idea.' Hazel made a note on her phone. 'We can also make sure the guests are warm enough with outdoor heaters and blankets.'

'We both love walking and spending time in the fresh air, so this wedding idea suits us perfectly,' Clare said. 'And it'll be perfect for the dogs as well. Let's go for it.'

'You're sure?' Hazel asked.

'Oh yes, 100 per cent.'

'OK,' Hazel said. 'I'll start pricing things up and get back to you after the weekend.'

'Brilliant!' Clare poured more wine in their glasses. 'And we'd love to attend the wedding fayre too.'

'Great news.' Hazel almost bounced in her seat. 'Let's celebrate.'

As Hazel shut down her laptop, she glanced over at the bar. Bella was leaning against the tall man and he had his arm around her shoulders. Hazel was sure Bella had said her husband was called Lee and the man she was with was called Jack, so was he a close friend? Hazel had never had a close friendship with a man, except Lennox, and that didn't count, and she had no brothers or cousins either, so had no knowledge of how such relationships worked. Of course, Bella could be having an affair with Jack, but she'd be flaunting it a bit by being so tactile at the local pub. Plus, Bella had seemed nice, very down to earth, the type of woman Hazel would like to be friends with if she was ever able to trust another woman again.

She picked up her wine and drained the glass then set it on the table.

'Right, I'd better be off. I have to get back to feed Fleas.'

'You feed fleas?' Sam grimaced.

'No!' Hazel laughed. 'My cat is called Fleas Witherspoon.'

Sam raised his eyebrows. 'Ahhhh. As a vet you had me worried there for a minute. Fleas are pesky things that you need to get rid of or they'll infest your whole house.'

'Tell me about it. Fleas had them a few times and Lennox went mad!' She jolted as she realised what she'd just said. When would that stop? Why did so much of her life have to be connected to him? It felt like he'd always be there, weighing her down.

'Who's Lennox?' Clare asked, smiling.

'Oh, no one.' Hazel shook her head then realised that sounded ridiculous. She wasn't fourteen, after all. 'Actually, he was my partner but we, uh, split up a while back and he's still in Scotland.'

'I'm sorry.' Clare frowned.

'Don't be.' Hazel laughed but it sounded fake, even to her own ears. 'I had a lucky escape.' She swallowed hard to stop herself saying anything else because a full rant about how Lennox had shagged her bestie the day before their wedding was not the way to win clients. A wedding planner whose wedding had been called off was not a good advertisement at all.

'Sometimes that's the way.' Clare gave a wry smile.

'Indeed.' Hazel stood up and put her coat on, then stuffed her laptop into her bag. 'Well, thank you so much for trusting me with this. I promise you I'll ensure that you have an amazing wedding. And don't forget that you need to give notice that you intend to marry at the local registry office at least twenty-nine days before the ceremony.'

'We'll sort that out this week,' Sam said. 'Pop by the veterinary surgery soon and we can get Fleas on the system. I'll do a complimentary health check for you as a way of thanking you for the wedding planning.'

'Great, thanks.' Hazel nodded. 'That's very kind of you.'

She left Clare and Sam smiling at each other and headed for the door. She pushed it but the door stayed fast and she bounced off it then staggered back slightly, gripping onto her laptop bag for dear life. A pair of strong hands caught her shoulders and stopped her falling over.

'Steady there.'

She turned her head and looked up into chocolate brown eyes.

'I bet that door fools everyone. Might be an idea to slow down though, just in case.' He smiled but Hazel's cheeks burned instantly and she stepped away from him.

'Thank you.' She stared down at the floor, her ears now so hot she was worried they'd spontaneously combust.

'It's no problem.'

She glanced at him and found those gorgeous eyes watching her, filled with something that she couldn't quite work out. Was he laughing at her or feeling sorry for her?

'I'd better g-go,' she stuttered.

'Take care now.'

This time, she made sure to pull, not push, the door, then she hurried out into the night, hoping she hadn't just created a bad first impression on Jack or shown herself up in front of the locals.

Exhaustion hit her suddenly with the fresh air and all she wanted was to get back to her flat, snuggle up with Fleas and forget that there was a whole world outside.

Back in the apartment over Bella's garage, Jack closed the curtains and switched off the lamp in the lounge. He was tired after the excitement of the day and looking forward to getting into bed. Even if it was a strange bed. He'd driven a long way, been reunited with his sister and her family, and it had been quite an emotional day. His nieces were adorable, but understandably shy meeting him after so long, but he hoped that they'd come around and get used to him over the coming days. Seeing how different they were from the last time he'd spent time with them, he realised he wanted to have a relationship with them, not be the distant uncle they didn't know. They were growing so quickly and he didn't want to miss another minute of that and risk living with regrets.

He brushed his teeth, changed into pyjama shorts then turned off the light and slid between the soft cotton sheets. It was quiet above the garage and the double glazing kept the sounds of the countryside at night out of his room, so he should be able to drop off to sleep easily . . .

But as he lay there, the pretty face of the woman from the pub kept popping into his head. He hadn't had that kind of feeling on meeting someone new in years. She was a wedding planner, had moved to the village recently to start her business. She was clearly a strong, independent woman and yet . . . As he'd caught her and stopped her falling onto the pub floor then met her gaze he'd seen something in her eyes. It was vulnerability, he felt sure; he'd seen it in his own eyes when looking in the mirror. He'd been trying to hide his pain for almost a year and he wondered if it was the same for Hazel and if she'd ever be able to unburden herself to another human being, someone who could help her to deal with whatever it was that had hurt her.

Jack hoped so, even if he'd been unable to do that very same thing himself.

Chapter 8

Jack sat bolt upright in bed, the screech of tyres and the crunch of metal in the room with him. He gasped and pushed back the quilt then got out of bed, his heart racing, his forehead damp with sweat. The room was grey with early morning light, the chest of drawers and chair in the corner dark shadows. Even though he'd been there for just over a week, the bedroom still seemed unfamiliar and every morning when he woke he had to overcome his surprise at his surroundings.

That damned nightmare! It seemed he couldn't escape it, even though he'd come so far from Swansea. He went to the bathroom and swilled his face, then he drank some cold water straight from the tap. In the mirror above the sink, he gazed at his reflection. In the dim light, his eyes were dark hollows and his face was a ghostly oval, which was ironic because that was how he felt. Dark. Hollowed out.

A run would help to shake the dream off, to expunge the image of a car skidding on ice and ploughing into Danni's from his mind. If he tried to go back to sleep, it would remain in his head all day, like a migraine hangover. He dressed quickly in his running gear, let himself out of the apartment and trotted down the steps to the driveway. The house was still dark and silent, but all around him the dawn chorus began, seeming to echo in the rural morning air like the song of a choir in a cathedral.

After a quick warm-up, he set off, breathing deeply as he tried to clear his mind and find a sense of peace.

❋

Hazel climbed back into bed, her early morning cup of tea on the bedside table, Fleas curled up next to her. She was still getting used to waking up alone, to having breakfast alone and to knowing that when she came home at the end of the day, she would be alone. There would be no one to text to ask what he wanted for dinner, no one to snuggle in bed at night when she felt sad that her parents were gone. Lennox might not have been the most sympathetic of partners but sometimes, just having another human being close was comforting. But now it was just Hazel and Fleas and it was likely to be that way for quite some time. Hazel's heart was broken and the idea of being with anyone else was something that seemed impossible and improbable.

❋

'What are you doing today, Uncle Jack?'

He looked up from his poached egg on toast into his six-year-old niece's inquisitive green eyes.

'Uhh . . . I'm not sure, Bobby.' He shrugged. 'Just spending some time with your mum, I guess.'

'I want to stay and spend time with you both!' Bobby folded her arms over her chest and scowled at him.

'Now, now, Bobby, you have to go to school,' Bella said, winking at Jack over Bobby's head. 'I'm taking Uncle Jack shopping because we have a very important task to complete.'

'Do you?' Ten-year-old Penny's eyes widened.

While Bobby was sports mad, boisterous and brimming with self-confidence, her older sister Penny was quiet, studious and reserved. Bobby had a head of ginger curls the same colour as her dad and Penny had silky brown hair like her mum, but they both had bright green eyes like Lee.

'We do.' Bella carried her cereal bowl to the sink and swilled it out.

'What is it?' Bobby unfolded her arms and leant forwards.

'Uncle Jack and I are going to go and look for some inspiration for your costume for the Christmas play.'

'Wow!' Bobby's eyes widened. 'I wish I was coming.'

'Well, you can't, but I will pick up a treat for you for after school. How does that sound?'

'It sounds good.' Bobby nodded. 'Thank you.'

'You're welcome.' Bella came back to the kitchen table and sat down. 'Right, girls, go and brush your teeth and get your school bags ready. We'll leave in ten minutes.'

Jack sat back, enjoying the good-quality coffee that Bella had made. Lee had left an hour ago, bidding Jack a brief goodbye as he'd headed off for work. Jack was enjoying the mornings now, having breakfast with his sister and nieces and anticipating what the day would bring. Even on the days when Bella was working, he knew he'd have an evening meal with company and it was making a difference to how he felt after just a week.

71

Following his run that morning, he'd showered and dressed then waited until he saw signs of life in the house before knocking on the back door and going inside. Bella had given him a key, but he hadn't wanted to barge in. Goodness only knew what he might find and as much as Bella wanted to have him there, her family still needed some privacy.

'You OK with a shopping trip?' Bella asked him.

'Sure. It sounds intriguing. What's her part in the play?'

'Penny's the narrator and Bobby's a Christmas fairy.'

'What type of play is it?'

'Oh, you know how it is these days. It's an amalgamation of different things – more commercial Christmas than nativity play.'

'Is Bobby happy being a fairy?'

'Kind of. She loves being centre stage but wants to be more of a superhero fairy than a girly princess one.'

'And you want me to help with this?'

'Why not? You were good at making costumes when we were young.'

'That was a long time ago and I don't think anything I made was that good.'

Bella grinned. 'It'll be fine. Bobby will soon tell you if she doesn't like what you've done.'

'OK, then.'

'I thought we could have lunch out too then get back for the girls at home time. You can accompany me on the school run. You'll be a hit with the mums and dads and I can't wait to show you off.'

'Uhhh . . .' Jack grimaced. 'Really? That sounds a bit like my idea of hell.'

'Oh, come on, Jack. If you're going to become a teacher, you need to get used to being surrounded by other adults and their offspring.'

'That's different; and anyway, I didn't say I am going to become a teacher . . . I'm just considering it.'

'We'll see.' She stood up. 'Right, I'm going to check that Bobby has actually brushed her teeth and not just rubbed toothpaste over her lips like she sometimes does when she can't be bothered to brush, and then we can go.'

'I'll grab my coat.'

'See you in ten.'

Jack let himself out of the house and jogged up the steps to the apartment over the garage. Being shown off at the school gate was not something he was looking forward to, but a day out with his sister certainly was. It had been a long time since he'd been out for the day and he couldn't imagine better company than Bella.

But first he'd better make himself look presentable because he didn't want anyone thinking that Bella's brother was a scruff bag.

❄

Hazel decided to take another walk to the village green to take some photos for the wedding planning. She had created the PowerPoint of ideas and images for Clare and Sam but she had also created a private Pinterest board for herself because she found it helped her to get organised and boosted her creative thinking. She dressed warmly in boots and a down-filled jacket, then pulled a woolly hat on and set off.

Smiling as she walked, she thought of Fleas and how the cat had eaten breakfast then gone back to the bedroom, happy to stay in bed for the morning. While she was out, Hazel realised she could pop into the vet's and make an appointment for Fleas to see Sam, as he'd suggested. It was important to get Fleas registered with a local vet, just as Hazel also needed to register with a GP and a dentist. That was the thing with moving – there was quite a lot to take care of on top of running a business.

Hazel walked the long way around, not wanting to wait outside the veterinary surgery until it opened, passing the church and the school. She paused for a moment to check that she had her phone on her, to take some photos of the green, and looked up when someone called her name.

'Hazel! It is you, isn't it?'

Hazel pushed her hat back a bit to see better.

'Oh . . . hello, Bella.'

The other woman headed straight for Hazel, two young girls and a tall man in tow.

'How are you this morning?' Bella asked.

'Good, thanks.'

'Going anywhere nice?'

Hazel was aware that the two girls were staring at her, as was the man, and when she glanced at him, she realised it was Jack.

'No. Not really. I'm going to book my cat, Fleas, in at the vet and take some photos of the green.'

'I hope there's nothing wrong.' Bella tilted her head, inviting confidence.

'No, I'm fine.'

'With your cat!' Bella raised her eyebrows. 'You said you're making her a vet appointment.'

'She's fine.' Hazel nodded. 'She just needs to be registered with a local vet and Sam Wilson said to take her there.'

'I've heard that Sam's a great vet so your cat will be in good hands,' Bella said. 'Oh, before I forget . . . This is my brother, Jack, and my daughters, Penny and Bobby.'

Brother?

'Yes, we met last week.' Jack cocked an eyebrow at Hazel and she looked away.

'Hello, girls. Lovely to meet you.' Hazel smiled at the children and they smiled shyly back. 'And yes, Jack kind of saved me last week when I was leaving the pub and I . . . tripped.'

'When you bounced off the door, you mean,' he said, a teasing smile on his lips.

'Yes. That.' Hazel sighed. She wasn't about to engage in verbal sparring with this man, who seemed to have the confidence of the very attractive (teasing her when he barely knew her), in front of his family, who all seemed very nice. 'Anyway, I'd better let you get going. You don't want to be late for school.'

'Don't forget that we need to arrange that coffee,' Bella said. 'I work Monday to Wednesday but have Thursdays and Fridays free, so we could easily arrange something.'

'That would be lovely.'

'Can I have your number then?'

Hazel pulled out her phone and exchanged numbers with Bella, all the while aware of Jack's eyes on her, of his towering presence nearby. Perhaps it was just because she was newly single that she was so conscious of him. She didn't normally give men a second thought, other than as customers or friends of Lennox. She certainly couldn't usually care less if they were attractive or if they had a deep sexy voice or any of that nonsense. Why would she? She'd been engaged, believed she was going to spend the rest of her life with one man. But now it was as if her hormones had kicked in and some primal part of her was on high alert, looking for a new man, preferably one with shoulders as broad as Jack's and lips as kissable. Perhaps it was because of the way he looked at her, as if he was trying to work her out and wanted to know more. Lennox hadn't seemed to care how she was feeling for such a long time that having a man look at her as if he was interested in her as a person, rather than as someone to cook his meals and pick his dirty pants up off the floor, was novel indeed.

She froze. Where on earth had those thoughts come from? This was ridiculous and she needed to stop it right now.

'Call me soon,' Bella said, then she walked away with Jack and her two beautiful daughters.

Hazel hurried along the road to the green, keen to start taking photographs and get into work mode. Her career was her safe place, the one thing she could rely on in life, and she had to forget about everything else.

It was the only way to survive . . .

At the school gates, Jack plastered on his best smile as Bella introduced him to everyone she knew. Some of them were colleagues, because it was where she worked, but some were parents and grandparents of children from the school. He could feel people evaluating him, weighing him up and assessing his eligibility, like a scene from a Regency romance. He just hoped that he'd made a good impression because he could see how important it was to Bella that her family settled in Little Bramble. Overall, though, everyone he met was friendly and, as the girls headed into school surrounded by groups of friends, he could see the attraction of village life and of having a family.

Although having a family had been something he'd already wanted over recent years and had tried to persuade Danni to consider. They were still young, but he had friends who'd experienced fertility problems and he knew that it was better to find out if they had any issues while time was on their side. When he'd broached the subject with Danni, she'd laughed and shaken her head. It hadn't been the end of the conversation though; he'd raised it several times over the next year, but each time had left him wondering exactly where he stood. He'd known that Danni loved her job, but she took on more and more overtime and they saw less and less of each other and eventually Jack had started to feel like he was alone in the marriage. Danni had dismissed his concerns, citing exhaustion and work demands, but he'd had a feeling during the last few months of their time together that something wasn't quite right.

'You OK?' Bella asked now as the school doors closed and they stood gazing at the empty yard.

'Yeah, yeah, I'm fine.' He coughed to clear his throat.

'You drifted away for a moment there.'

'Just thinking about how life can be so full for some people,' he explained. 'It's wonderful to see you so happy.'

Bella slid her arm through his. 'I want the same for you, Jack.'

'I had all I needed.'

'*Had.* Not have. You are still entitled to a full life, you know. I don't want to sound insensitive, but you're young and good-looking. I'm sure we can find you a bride.'

They started walking in the direction of the train station. 'Find me a *bride*. This isn't Regency England, you know,' he said, his thought from just moments ago returning.

'I sometimes think it would be so much easier if it was. We could marry you off to some stunning debutante and that would be that.'

'Bella!' Jack shook his head. 'Nothing is ever that straightforward. I loved Danni – I still love her – and the idea of being in a place mentally and emotionally where I could even consider being with another woman is still beyond me.'

'Well, don't give up on the idea yet, because there are plenty of amazing women out there and you're a lovely man.'

He leant over and kissed the top of her head, hoping she'd leave the matter there. All he wanted now was to be with his sister and her family and to forget about dating, romance, sex and all that malarky. There was, as he knew from experience, far too much to lose.

'Try this on,' Bella said as she held up a shirt.

Jack frowned, wondering if this was why they'd detoured via a department store at the retail park. 'I thought we were shopping for craft supplies.'

Bella shrugged. 'We are, but it won't hurt to pick up a few things for you too.'

'I don't need anything.'

Bella placed her hands on her hips. 'Jack, haven't you ever heard of retail therapy?'

'Yes, of course. But I don't need clothes.'

'You're staying for a while, and over Christmas, so I think it would be nice if you updated your wardrobe.'

'What exactly are you trying to say about my wardrobe?' He laughed.

'Nothing at all. But I doubt you've bought anything new in a while and so this is part of my pl—' Her eyes widened.

'Your what? Your *plan*?'

She bit her lip and held up her hands. 'I just want to help get you back on your feet.'

Jack sighed inwardly. So Bella had a plan to fix him, did she? He'd had a feeling she might have some ideas along those lines and could understand her motivation. She wanted to help, and he didn't want to throw her efforts back in her face.

'All right, I'll try it on.' He looked around the men's clothing section of the store. 'Anything else while we're here?'

'Now you're talking.' Bella giggled and skipped off among the rails, selecting a variety of shirts and jackets before heading towards the denim section.

Jack followed her, smiling at her enthusiasm. How could he possibly say no when she wanted to help him so badly and when she was clearly enjoying herself?

An hour later he'd tried on so many shirts, jackets and pairs of jeans that he was exhausted and ravenous, but Bella's joy made it worthwhile. She'd stood outside the changing rooms and told him to show her each shirt and jacket along with each pair of jeans, and then she'd led him to the tills to pay for the things they'd selected. He now had two bags of new clothes and although he hadn't known he was coming clothes shopping, he had found the experience uplifting. Shopping for clothes alone had never been something he'd enjoyed, and although Danni had gone with him in the early days of their relationship, in more recent times she'd been busy and he hadn't liked to ask her to accompany him. However, with someone to help, it was certainly different. After Danni had seemed to lose interest in clothes shopping with him, he'd had to go alone. On those rare occasions, he'd looked at the store mannequins and located the outfits they had on, then bought them. Of course, this didn't always work because he didn't have the exact proportions of a store mannequin – he had a wider waist, broader shoulders and a thicker neck. He'd complained to Danni after those disastrous solo shopping trips that he wasn't a normal size and she'd laughed and told him that there was no such thing as a normal size. As a nurse, she'd seen plenty of bodies over the years and everyone was different. Apparently, though, it was the same for women when they were shopping. A size twelve in one store could be completely different from a size twelve in another. Clothes were a bit like people, it seemed. There was no one-size-fits-all and no two garments were ever the same.

'Can we get a drink and a snack now, *please*?' Jack asked as they left the store and walked back out into the central area of the shopping centre.

'You sound like a little boy.' Bella grinned at him. 'Of course, we can. Come on, I know just the place.'

They passed shops selling clothes, electrical goods, children's toys and perfumes. It was fairly quiet because, according to Bella, it was a school day, and that was one of the advantages of working part-time as she did: she could go shopping while other people were still at work.

'How does this look?' She stopped in front of a café with a bright red sign and several tables out front.

'It looks good.' Jack's stomach was grumbling now so he'd have said yes to anywhere.

'Shall we sit inside?'

'It'll be cosier.' The glass-ceilinged shopping centre was cool and airy and Jack knew that if they sat outside the café, although they'd still be effectively indoors, it was November and he fancied a quiet corner table where he could fill his belly and recharge before Bella resumed shopping. Jack was fit but not shopping fit; that was, it seemed, a different thing altogether.

He followed Bella inside and they headed towards the back of the café, where they placed their bags under a table – Bella had picked up a few things for Lee too – and hung their coats on the backs of chairs. They went up to the counter and ordered, then waited at the end while the barista made their coffees and told them she'd bring the paninis to the table.

Jack groaned when he sat down and Bella giggled.

'Shopped till you dropped, baby brother.'

'Don't laugh. You've worn me out.'

'Jack, we've only done one shop.'

He shrugged. 'You made me try on so many things that I'm exhausted – and look at my hair.'

'What's wrong with it?'

'It's full of static.'

He ran a hand over his head and there was a crackle as it rose up to meet his fingers.

'Oops.'

'Oops indeed.' He winked at her. 'I don't mind, though. I have some stylish new clothes to wear now, so I can impress your friends.'

'It wasn't about that.'

She placed a hand over his where it rested on the table.

'I know.'

He sipped his latte, glad he'd asked for the extra shot of espresso, and settled back in his seat.

'This is nice.'

'It's brilliant,' Bella replied, her hands wrapped around her coffee. 'I didn't think I'd ever get you here.'

'Really?'

She inclined her head. 'You seemed so lost after Danni died and I was incredibly worried. I said to Lee so many times that I wanted to come to Swansea and get you.'

'What, pack me into the car and kidnap me?'

'It seemed like an idea at one point, yes. With Mum and Dad being so far away and you being so bloody independent, I knew you wouldn't have anyone to rely on.'

'I have friends.'

'But I bet they all think you're fine now, don't they? You men don't always talk about your feelings and I know what you're like. You'd have told them all that you were managing and a lot of men would just accept that. Not because they don't care but because they're busy and it's easier to believe that their mates are fine. I think Lee would be the same.'

'They're all busy with their own lives, Bella.'

'Exactly. Too busy to allow themselves to wonder if you are all right, if you are actually coping. I mean, I felt so bad myself for being busy, what with the girls and moving and my job. It's no excuse, but I just felt that I didn't know when I'd find time to come to you.'

'I wouldn't have wanted you to anyway, Bella. Your children and husband come first. I'm a grown man and I can take care of myself. I *do* take care of myself.'

'I know you can do the basics, that you'd eat and drink and wash, but what about everything else? After losing a partner, anyone would be lost. My heart broke for you.'

'It's been awful but I'm managing.'

'Managing . . .' Bella shook her head. 'But are you *happy*, Jack?'

He swallowed and looked across the café at the windows, watching a woman struggling to get a toddler into a push-chair. 'What's happy? Where's the benchmark for happiness?' He cleared his throat. 'I like running, watching Netflix, eating pasta. I occasionally go for a pint with some of my friends. I have – *had* – a nice home.'

'But are you happy?' Bella repeated, leaning forwards, her eyes glued to his face.

'I . . .' Could he say this to her? It seemed wrong to admit to being unhappy when he had so much more than many others did. 'I'm happy sometimes.'

Bella nodded as if his response was exactly what she'd expected.

'Sometimes.'

'Yes.' He drank some more coffee, breathing in the aroma of freshly ground beans. It was comforting, familiar, real. 'No one's happy all the time.' He looked at her. 'Except for maybe you.'

Bella met his gaze and smiled. 'Do I seem that way?'

'You're the happiest person I know and I love that about you.'

'I'm not happy every minute of every day, but I do appreciate what I have and strive to be positive.'

'You're one of life's eternal optimists.'

'But when it comes to you I feel sad that I can't help you more.'

'You *are* helping me, Bella. Just knowing you're there, that you care, that I have a sister as amazing as you . . . that helps me.'

'It does?'

'Absolutely.'

Their food arrived then and they waited quietly until the waitress had gone.

'I think what I'm trying to say is that I do have happy moments,' Jack said. 'Like now. Being here with you, having good coffee and a very tasty-looking lunch in front of me is something that does make me feel happy.'

'Well, it's a start.' Bella said. 'And we need to start somewhere.'

The basket over Jack's arm was full and so was the one that Bella was carrying. After their coffee break they'd hit the shops again and now they were in the craft supplies and Bella, it seemed, was buying every single thing that Bobby could possibly need to make her costume.

'I don't think you have enough glitter,' Jack said, cocking an eyebrow.

Bella turned to him. 'No?'

'You've only got five colours and that won't be enough, surely?'

'You don't think so?' She furrowed her brows. 'Shall I get some of the pink as well?'

Jack snorted. 'I was teasing you.'

'Oh.' She poked her tongue into her cheek. 'It's just that I want to make sure we don't run out.'

'Bella, your floors will be sparkling until 2050 with all of this.'

'It's a good job we have mainly tile and wood floors, then.'

'Ha! Indeed it is.'

'The thing is, Jack, we need glitter for the costumes but also for the Christmas cards.'

'I'm sorry?'

'We're going to make Christmas cards too.'

'*We?*'

'Yes. Remember we used to do it when we were children?'

He blinked. 'We did?'

'Yes! Mum would get us some card and glitter and we'd draw snowmen and holly and Christmas trees and then cover them in glue and sprinkle them with glitter.'

'I don't remember that.'

'It was fun.'

'I'm sure it was.'

'Dad used to go mad about the mess, but he always put the cards on the mantelpiece.'

'You think he was proud?'

'Always. And that angel you once made went on the top of the tree every year after, even when it was flat and yellowing.'

'I made an angel?'

'Don't you remember *anything* from when we were kids?'

'Of course, I do. It's just that we probably remember different things.'

'Mum and Dad always made Christmas really special, and I've tried to do the same for the girls.'

'I would have too.' He froze.

'If you'd had children?'

'I was . . . uh, looking forward to all that.'

'Oh, Jack . . .' Bella placed a cool hand over his where it held the basket handle. 'You'd make a great dad.'

'Well, I guess I'll never know now, will I?'

'You might meet someone else and have a family one day. You're young. There's loads of time.'

He shrugged. 'Who knows, right?'

There was more to it than Bella knew and he couldn't bring himself to tell her right now. They were having such a nice day and he hadn't told anyone else about Danni's feelings, feelings he'd only found out about after she'd gone.

'Anyway, we're going to make cards with the girls, are we?'

'Yes. They love it and over the next few weeks we'll also make a Christmas cake, mince pies and more.'

'We're going to be busy.'

'We are.' She coughed then swiped the back of her free hand over her cheek.

'Are you getting emotional?'

'Maybe. I'm just excited that you'll be with us. Christmas will be even more special this year because you'll be there to enjoy it too.'

'Bella Thornton, you are such a softy.'

'I know.' She leant against him for a moment, her head against his shoulder, and he felt a rush of love for her, his amazing sister with a heart of gold. Over the years they hadn't seen as much of each other as he would have liked but now they were together again it was as if their old closeness had been reawakened.

God, he had missed her!

Chapter 9

Hazel got out of her car and looked around. The Lumber Shed was a converted barn set in a gorgeous location just outside the village. It was surrounded by established trees and fields and what seemed to be endless sky stretched out around her. She'd driven because she wasn't sure how far away it was, plus it was freezing out, and so it hadn't taken her five minutes to get there.

Trees swayed in the wind, some still holding their leaves, others with bare branches reaching into the sky like gnarled fingers. The sky looked ominous: slate-grey clouds were being swept along by the wind and she felt sure that there was rain in the air.

The name she'd found on the website the previous day, after seeing Bella and Jack taking Bella's children to school, was Connor Jones. It was his business and he also worked there, had moved the business to this location after his father had started it many years before. Hazel liked the idea of family-run businesses, especially in a village like Little Bramble. It meant that the owners had their roots here, that they belonged. It had been a while since Hazel had felt she belonged somewhere. As a child, Wales had been her home but then they'd moved to Scotland and, as the years passed, she'd felt at home there. However, after Lennox had betrayed her, nothing looked the same or felt the same there, and she'd been overwhelmed by an urge to leave so she didn't have to keep seeing the same things, people and places that she'd seen when she'd been in love with Lennox.

The door to The Lumber Shed opened and a man stepped outside, looking as if he'd just come out for a breath of fresh air. He scanned the car park then his gaze fell on Hazel and he raised a hand in greeting.

Hazel pushed her lips into a smile, locked the car then strode forwards over the gravel, determined to make a good impression. If this was Connor Jones – and it looked like the man whose photo was on the website, someone she could easily have mistaken for George Clooney – then she had a very special request to make.

After they'd introduced themselves, Connor invited Hazel inside. She looked around the workshop of The Lumber Shed, breathing in the scent of wood, varnish and machinery, unfamiliar and yet pleasant, reminding her of the Design and Technology classrooms at school where she'd spent a lot of time years ago. As a teenager she'd become interested in creating things, especially in sewing, and had progressed from small purses to scarves and then dresses. Her mum had an old Singer sewing machine and together they'd made a wide variety of clothes over the years. Delyth Campbell was so talented that she'd even made her own wedding dress and, as a child, Hazel had loved it when her mum got the dress out of the box she'd kept it in and let Hazel try it on. Of course, back then it had been too big for her, but Hazel had hoped to wear it for her wedding to

Lennox, though he'd not been keen on the idea at all. He'd said it was old-fashioned and that she should have something new and not a fusty dress that was older than she was, especially as their friends and family would all be there to see her in it. She was overwhelmed by an urge to look at the dress and decided to do so later as it always made her feel closer to her mum. Hazel's interest in sewing had waned when she'd got together with Lennox, as he'd always kept her busy, but it still meant that she appreciated how much work went into creating the beautiful wedding dresses available and how talented anyone who could create something from scratch really was. Just like Connor Jones, it seemed.

'This is impressive,' she said, smiling up at him.

It was a large open space with workbenches, complicated-looking machinery, plenty of tools and people working. Music filled the space from speakers above the doorway and behind the music came the hum of machinery as Connor's employees used saws and sanders.

'Thanks, I think so. I love this place and what we do here.' His green eyes sparkled with enthusiasm.

'So, you use reclaimed wood?'

'We do. Sometimes there's a need to use a new piece but mostly we use reclaimed and we upcycle furniture, floorboards and more. I wanted the business to be environmentally friendly and it is, as far as possible, and we're committed to improving this all the time.'

'That's brilliant. I wonder if you made some of the furniture in my flat?'

'It's highly likely.' He laughed. 'We've furnished a lot of properties around here. What is it that you're looking for?'

Hazel filled Connor in with what she was thinking about for the wedding and he listened carefully.

'We can do whatever you like with reclaimed wood, even driftwood, and after the wedding, we can move it to Clare and Sam's garden.'

'Kind of like a wedding gift?'

'Exactly,' he said. 'Sam is a good mate of mine and I'd like to do this free of charge.'

'Oh, I couldn't ask that of you.'

'It would be my pleasure. I've lived here all my life and I'm always happy to give back what I can. The community of Little Bramble is wonderful so I really want to do this.'

'Well, that's incredibly generous of you. Thank you so much.'

'Come on up to my office and we can have a look at some designs, then I'll get started right away.'

'Right away?'

'I'll fit it around everything else, don't worry.'

'Fabulous.' Hazel followed Connor up a staircase to a small office, delighted that she'd come here to ask for his help and even more so because this wouldn't cost the bride and groom a penny.

'Take a seat,' Connor said as he gestured at a chair in front of a desk that was covered in paperwork. 'Excuse all the paper but I wasn't expecting anyone today. And this will all be recycled.' He grinned.

'I'm sorry, Connor. I should have made an appointment, but I just had an idea in my head and needed to see what you thought. If you'd been unable to do it, I'd have had to go elsewhere.'

'It's fine.' He waved a hand. 'Would you like tea or coffee?'

'No, thanks. I'm good.'

'OK, then.' He sat behind the desk then opened a drawer and pulled out an A4 pad and a pencil. 'If you describe what you're thinking of, I'll draw it and we can adjust as necessary then. Depending on size, etc., you might need to obtain permission.'

'I've spoken to the council and they have no concerns because it's not a permanent structure.'

'Of course.' He nodded his grey head. 'It's kind of like setting up the fete stalls there, so as long as everything's tidied up afterwards, they'll be fine about it all.'

Hazel described her vision and, after donning a pair of black-framed glasses, Connor sketched away, pausing occasionally to look up then returning his gaze to the paper.

'So you said you've always lived locally?'

'I have. Born and bred in Little Bramble.'

'That must be nice.'

'In many ways it is. Over the years there were times when I wished I'd left, but they didn't last long.'

'Do you have family here?'

'My mother and my partner. My daughter's in Paris at the moment, studying fashion design, and my mother's retired, but she's very involved with the local greyhound rescue charity. As for my partner, Emma, she's a fiction editor.'

'That's exciting! About all of them.'

Connor laughed. 'My daughter's talented and will do very well, I'm sure. My mother's dog mad and my partner's very intelligent.' He looked up. 'Emma's not my daughter's mum. We were together when we were younger but then we split up and Emma went off to London. It was a difficult time . . . I'm only telling you because, no doubt, you'll soon know everyone's business – this village is like that – but I'd rather tell you myself.' He shrugged. 'Everyone knows just about everything about everyone else.'

'I can imagine.' Hazel shuddered at the thought of people knowing all about her past. Would they see her as a failure because her partner had cheated on her, or would they feel sorry for her? She didn't want either reaction. She wanted to be known as a woman in her own right, not someone's reject or someone to pity.

'It's OK, though, no one's malicious.'

'Good to know.'

'Do you have family with you?' he asked.

'No.' Hazel shook her head. 'It's just me and my cat.'

'Cats are good. Not great with greyhounds, though. Emma has a greyhound called Harmony. Well, Emma and her dad, Greg, do. Beautiful girl, she is.'

'Emma?'

'Emma *and* the greyhound. Although Emma would laugh at me now for calling her a girl. We're in our fifties and only recently got back together, even though we first fell in love when we were at school. Can you believe it? We wasted years not being together but then, if we had been, I wouldn't have had my daughter, and so I can't have any regrets. I'm just glad we're together now.'

No regrets? That would be nice and must come with a sense of freedom. Hazel watched him as he gazed at the pad, his hand sweeping across the paper expertly. So he'd rekindled his love for his childhood sweetheart. How romantic! Would they be getting married too? She dared not ask. It was far too forward, but her professional side wanted to know. Not now though, another time.

'That must be amazing,' Hazel said.

'What? That we got back together?'

'Yes. And after so long apart.'

'I always loved her and I always missed her. But things happened as they did and all that matters is that we've found each other again.'

Hazel swallowed back a surge of emotion. Love could work out, even if people fell out, lost their way, went in different directions. It was possible to fall in love and be happy, but it just hadn't happened for her.

Connor held up the pad so Hazel could see what he'd been drawing.

'What do you think?'

'That's perfect.'

'Is it what you imagined? Because I can always tweak it.'

'No, please don't – it's absolutely spot on.'

'I'm delighted to hear that.'

Hazel breathed a sigh of relief, hoping that Connor was right. He was clearly a kind and gentle man. He'd let her into his confidence by telling her about his past and she was surprised by that in some ways, but not overly so. In her experience, men sometimes spoke about their emotions, especially when they were very much in love. She'd organised weddings for couples who'd reunited after time apart and their bonds always seemed so deep and solid. She could see that reflected in Connor as he spoke about Emma and rediscovering their love for each other.

'I'll let you know when I've chosen the wood and if you give me your number and email address, I'll send regular updates.'

'Thank you so much, Connor.'

'No problem at all. The wedding will be wonderful for Clare and Sam but also for the village.'

'Yes, a Christmas wedding is always magical.'

Hazel swiped her phone and went to her to-do list, then placed a tick next to the top item. There was a lot to do in not much time, but every single thing ticked off the list was an achievement to be proud of.

When she went back out to her car, she looked around. The rain had held off so far and the temperature had risen slightly, although it was quite clearly winter. Connor was standing in the doorway so she called to him, 'I meant to ask – are there allotments around here somewhere? I visited them as a child on a family holiday and I haven't seen them yet.'

He pointed to his left. 'If you walk that way, you'll come to an overpass that will take you over the road and the train tracks. You'll come to some fields, then a dirt track; the allotments are there next to the stream and a big old house.'

Hazel frowned. A big old house sounded familiar, as did the stream.

'Is it OK to leave my car here for a bit if I walk there?'

'Of course.'

'Brilliant, thank you.'

Connor waved then disappeared inside and Hazel opened her boot and got out her wellies, woolly hat, gloves and duck-down jacket that she'd packed in case of a break-down. She'd always had a similar kit in her car living in

Scotland, because the winters were so cold. It seemed even more imperative that she took precautions now that she was single and an orphan with no one to call for help other than a faceless breakdown company.

Once she'd donned her warm clothing, she set off in the direction Connor had pointed, keen to see if the allotments had changed much over the past twenty-three years.

When she came to the overpass, she ascended at a brisk pace, and found herself at the highest point. She paused and looked around. In one direction there was a clear view back to The Lumber Shed and the village and in the other lay more road and adjacent train tracks. The sky was pewter, the air chilly and she knew she had to keep moving or she'd start to feel the cold in spite of her warm clothes.

At the end of the overpass, she found herself on a footpath that led in three directions, two following the paths of the train tracks and road in either direction, the other leading to a gate. She approached the gate and peered at a weather-worn sign attached to a post. She could just about make out the words *Little Bramble Allotments*. Her heart squeezed; she was heading in the right direction.

She let herself through the gate, making sure to close it after her, then trudged across the field. The smell of damp earth and decay rose up to meet her and a few times she almost slipped on leaves that had fallen from surrounding trees and rotted on the ground. There was something else too, but she wasn't sure what, although it made her think of farms and animals. Off to her left, large old trees dotted the field and to her right was a footpath and a building. She froze and stared at it. Why was it familiar?

Then it hit her. That was the cottage she'd stayed in as a child! She hurried towards it, her breath steaming in front of her, and only slowed down when she reached the fence. The outside of the stone cottage was exactly how she remembered it, with a slate roof and a low wall surrounding it. There were four windows at the front and a door in the middle of the lower two. The small front garden was coated with leaves and natural debris and tatty net curtains hung in the windows. Up close, it looked neglected. She leant against the fence and swallowed the lump that had risen in her throat. She'd had such a happy holiday there with her parents, had memories of the sun shining and of the windows being open to let in the fresh country air. Out the back there was a cottage garden with a swing and her mum and dad had taken turns to push her on it every afternoon then they'd sat outside and had a barbecue and Hazel had drunk fizzy orange while her mum and dad had drunk red wine. Afterwards, they'd had blackberry and apple pie or cherry pie from the local farm shop, with thick golden cream, and watched as the sky had turned pinky-orange then purple before the stars had come out. She'd sat on her mum's lap, snuggled in a blanket, and dozed as her parents had spoken about their hopes and dreams, for them and for her, and she'd felt so content and so safe.

She wiped at her cheek and stared at the tear on her glove. The memories were good ones and they'd stirred her emotions, made her miss what had once been and also grieve for what could have been. She'd thought she'd have that with Lennox, had even, on occasion, thought that they might return to the cottage with their own children and relive the holiday she'd once had. But now she knew that was just silly and sentimental, that she'd been dreaming about a life that had never been hers. Her parents' love for each other and for her had been special, and what she'd had with Lennox hadn't come close. All the trying in the world couldn't create love and loyalty when one partner didn't feel the same. Hazel had been all in; Lennox had not.

Before the pain in her chest could completely overwhelm her, she pushed her shoulders back and turned around. Across the field to her right, she could make out a building beyond the trees. Frowning, she cast her mind back, and then it came to her. The big old house had belonged to a woman, as had the land the allotments were built on. She'd seemed old, small and wiry and Hazel had been a bit afraid of her when they'd come across her at the allotments, but her parents had seemed to like the woman and she'd even given them some fresh vegetables from her plot for their dinner. She'd had an unusual name. What was it?

'Zelda!' Hazel grinned, happy that she'd remembered it. Would Zelda still own the big old house? It was possible, although a long time had passed.

Hazel continued past the cottage and through some trees and found herself in another field, which overlooked the allotments. She looked across the patchwork of square plots and sighed. There were some new additions such as small sheds and some of the surrounding trees had grown significantly, altering the landscape, but the basic layout was the same. Her dad had liked the allotments and said that if he'd lived in the village he'd have wanted one. Her mum had said she'd prefer a garden of her own, but her dad had said that an allotment was something special, a place reserved for self-sufficiency, a place where people could go to escape everything and work on the land. Hazel could recall her mum laughing and calling her dad an old romantic. It dawned on Hazel that she was a lot like her dad; she had inherited his tendency to romanticise things and had done so in her own life, and also as a wedding planner. She had what she liked to think of as vision, and she could picture what a wedding would be like and how to create it to suit a couple perfectly. It lay within her romanticism and also within her creative flair that she'd got from her mum.

Resting her arms on the fence, she gazed at the land ahead of her, enjoying the idea of herself as a visionary. It was a positive way to see herself and far nicer than some of the things Lennox had called her.

Something at the corner of her left eye made her turn. She was sure she'd seen movement in the bushes. She watched for a moment then shrugged. It was probably just the wind.

Then there was a terrible noise and she shuddered. What the hell was that?

It sounded like someone shouting, 'Maaa!' but it was eerie and unsettling. It came again, 'Maaaaaa!'

Hazel scanned the field, but she couldn't see anything. Then again, though, there were trees growing everywhere and over in the far corner there was some sort of a wooden construction a bit like a small shed.

The sky darkened and the wind rolled around the field, shaking the trees and causing their remaining leaves to fall to the ground. Somewhere a crow squawked and a dog barked. There didn't seem to be a human being around for miles and Hazel realised that she wanted to go back to her cosy little flat, snuggle up with Fleas and watch an old movie on TV.

She started to march across the field, heading back the way she'd come, trying to conjure the happy memories she'd had earlier when gazing at the cottage and the allotments. *Yes, such lovely memories . . .*

Then she saw it.

Staring at her as it emerged from behind a tree.

It had black eyes. Horns. Hoofs.

'Shit!' She started to run, suddenly terrified. And as if spurred on by her running, the creature started to run too.

Her feet slid on the damp grass in her wellies and she almost fell a few times, catching her balance just in time. She waved her arms and kept her eyes pinned on the gate where she could escape the field and what seemed to be a very angry-looking goat.

Once, she glanced back, and it was fatal. The goat was gaining on her. She tried to push forwards, but her ankle twisted and she fell face down in a pile of something brown and very smelly.

She turned her head cautiously, wondering if she should play dead. Wasn't that what the wildlife experts advised when a wild animal chased you?

She held her breath, fought the urge to wipe her face and closed her eyes.

Please leave me alone. Don't bite me or butt me or anything else horrible!

She lay there for what felt like hours, but was really only a minute or two, and silence fell over the field. When she slowly opened her eyes, she hoped she'd find herself alone again, but instead there were now three goats staring down at her.

'Maaaaa!' they bleated.

Hazel groaned. 'Maaaaa to you too,' she said as she cautiously stood up and started to back away. When she felt it was safe to do so, she started to run again and didn't stop until she reached the gate and threw herself at it, then climbed over and fell to the ground on the other side.

The goats were still staring at her, their eyes blank, and she wondered if they were curious or utterly convinced that human beings were very silly creatures indeed. What Hazel couldn't fathom as she trudged back to her car was why anyone would ever choose to keep goats. But then again, she'd always been a city girl. Living in the countryside was completely new to her, so she was the one who needed to adjust and learn about her new surroundings. She just hoped that none of her clients would want goats at their weddings – because after that experience, she suspected she'd probably developed a phobia.

Chapter 10

'Capraphobia,' Kyle said, looking up from his phone.

'Sorry?' Hazel frowned.

'Darling, you said you thought you might have a phobia of goats after your little incident yesterday and goat phobia is called capraphobia.'

'Oh . . . right.' Hazel nodded. She was watching Clare and Sam as they looked around the wedding fayre. She'd driven them all to the hotel on the outskirts of Guildford and Kyle had not come up for air throughout the whole journey. Clare's son, Kyle, was certainly a character and Hazel had found herself warming to him immediately with his easy smile and effervescent personality.

'So were you really covered in goat poo?'

'It stank and it was so . . . sticky.'

Kyle shuddered. 'It sounds disgusting, although you never know, it could become one of those faddy skincare products at some point.'

Clare had picked up a sparkling tiara and Sam was smiling as she placed it on her head.

'Oh God, look at Mum doing her best Princess Di.'

'It suits her.'

'It does and I can just imagine her marrying a prince. Although I wouldn't say no to a prince either.'

'Do you want to get married then?'

Kyle smiled and fluttered his eyelashes. 'Are you asking?'

'Ha! No.' Hazel giggled. 'But I'm sure someone will one day.'

'I'm not sure if it will be Magnus. He's my partner. He's gorgeous, such a hunk of a man, but I have sampled female delights too.'

'Good to know.'

'To me, people are people, and I couldn't care less what appendages they do or don't have. Love is love, right!'

'I agree!'

Hazel had planned weddings for lots of different couples and one of the most moving had been for a gay couple who'd been together for three decades. The men were both in their fifties and had hidden their relationship from one man's parents because they were very old-fashioned and he'd been afraid of being disowned. When his father had become old and frail, he'd finally told him, not wanting to miss his chance to let his dad know who he really was. Instead of scorn and rejection, his father had hugged him and told him he'd always suspected and that he didn't mind. He said that, years before, he'd have struggled to witness his son marrying another man, but now he wanted to be able to give him away to the person he loved. The wedding had been beautiful and emotional – even thinking about it now gave Hazel goosebumps.

'Perhaps you can plan my wedding too one day.' Kyle nudged Hazel, a dreamy look in his eyes.

'I'd like that.'

'What do you think, Kyle?' Clare was holding up a dress. It was lavender with large puffy sleeves and a frilly hem.

'Mother!' Kyle threw up his hands. 'You simply cannot wear that.'

'I wasn't thinking of it for me.' Clare winked at Hazel. 'I thought it might do for you.'

Kyle rolled his eyes. 'Pull the other one, Clare, it plays jingle bells.'

'Fancy looking at the suits, Kyle?' Sam gestured at a display across the room.

'Absolutely.' Kyle squeezed Hazel's arm. 'Do *not* let her order anything until she's shown it to me. We have to make sure that she looks gorgeously demure for this wedding and not at all like mutton dressed as ham or whatever it is they say.'

'I'll do my best,' Hazel replied, making her way over to Clare.

They walked around looking at stalls of dresses, shoes, tiaras and fascinators. Clare picked things up, peered at them, then put them back down again.

'See anything you like?'

Clare gave a tight smile that didn't reach her eyes. 'It's all so lovely but . . .' She glanced around as if to check that they were out of earshot of Sam and Kyle. 'Although I'm delighted to be marrying Sam and it's like a dream come true, I'm just feeling a bit overwhelmed.'

'That's understandable,' Hazel said softly.

'I love him so much and I want to be his wife, but this is all so elaborate and expensive and I'm . . .'

'You're what?' Hazel reached out and squeezed Clare's arm.

'I'm a bit old for it all, aren't I?'

'Oh, Clare, bless you.' Hazel shook her head. 'You're not old at all. You and Sam are such a beautiful couple and clearly very much in love. Just because you're not twenty-somethings, why shouldn't you have a lovely wedding?'

Clare looked across the room at Sam, who was standing patiently while Kyle fastened a bow tie around his neck.

'My marriage to Kyle's dad was good at first, but we were very young, and we didn't have much money. It's different, now, because while we're not rich, Sam and I are comfortable and yet . . . I think being older and wiser means that I'm reluctant to spend money that doesn't need to be spent.'

'And that's fine. There are ways to save money, but it doesn't mean you can't have an amazing wedding. The most important thing is that you and Sam are able to make your vows to each other in the way you want.'

Clare's eyes were glistening. 'Thank you.' She sniffed and Hazel handed her a tissue. 'I know you're right. It's just that I get a bit anxious about it all sometimes. I mean, I can't believe how lucky I am to have found Sam. He's such an amazing person.'

'As are you.' Hazel smiled. 'Oh my goodness, look at Kyle!'

There was a catwalk at the far end of the room, set up for later when there would be a wedding attire show, and Kyle was standing on it.

Clare gasped. 'I can't take him anywhere. He's been like this since he was about five years old and then I could excuse it, but now?'

They hurried over to the catwalk where Kyle was standing, hands on hips, wearing a leopard print suit with a white shirt, bright-pink bow tie and pink brogues. He had a matching pink fedora on his head and, as they watched him, he tilted it slightly so it shadowed his face, then twirled around.

'Kyle Greene!' Clare raised her voice. 'What *are* you doing?'

Kyle pushed the hat back and grinned at her. 'I'm trying out the catwalk, Mother dear, can't you see?'

'Yes, I can, but why?'

He shrugged. 'Why not? I always fancied myself as a bit of a model and in this suit and with this hat on – well, it seemed too good an opportunity to waste.'

Clare covered her face with her hands and Hazel noticed that she was shaking. She put a hand on Clare's shoulder, worried that she was crying, but when Clare looked up, although there were tears running down her cheeks, she was grinning from ear to ear.

'Are you OK?' Hazel asked.

'I'm fine.' Clare wiped at her face with a tissue. 'It's just my son. He's one in a million.'

'He certainly is,' Hazel agreed.

Sam appeared at Clare's side. 'What *is* he doing?'

Kyle sashayed off along the catwalk then did another graceful turn before walking towards them again. People had gathered round and a hush fell over the room. Phones were raised and Hazel heard some people murmuring to each other about whether or not Kyle was a celebrity hired to publicise the event.

'He's being Kyle,' Clare replied, leaning against Sam.

As Kyle posed for photographs, Hazel took some too, keen to capture the moment for her website and Clare's wedding album, as part of the lead-up to the big day section.

'Did you find a suit?' Clare asked.

'I did, but there are two I'm keen on, so I need you to help me decide.'

'I can do that.'

'Are you coming, Hazel?' Clare pointed at the stall of suits.

'I'll be along in a bit.' Hazel waved her phone. 'I'll just capture a few more shots.'

'You'll be there all day at this rate. My son is a proper show-off.' Clare laughed then walked away with Sam.

Kyle was a show-off, but he was also funny and lovely and Hazel wanted to get to know him better. He might be loud and flamboyant and more confident than she could ever dream of being, but he was also honest, caring and unafraid of being himself. As Hazel watched him she realised that she could probably learn a lot from him in terms of building her self-esteem, and she hoped she'd have the opportunity to try.

❄

Later on that day, Hazel dropped Clare, Sam and Kyle off in the village, then drove to her flat. It had been a busy, successful day and she was exhausted. Kyle had ended up taking part in the catwalk show because the suit company had liked how he wore their leopard print and he had seemed tireless as he strutted his stuff surrounded by gorgeous male and female models. He didn't seem at all daunted by how beautiful they were and thoroughly enjoyed himself. Watching him, Hazel had realised exactly how eroded her own confidence was. Growing up with loving parents, she'd believed in herself and what she could achieve, but years spent with Lennox had chipped away at who she had been and left her a shell of her former self. She'd even found herself wanting to hop up on stage next to Kyle to soak up some of his sparkle, as if she could glean it from him just by being near.

Back in her flat, Hazel fed Fleas then went to her bedroom and pulled the old box that had belonged to her mum from under the bed. She opened it and gently moved the tissue paper, then gazed at her mum's wedding dress, the dress she had made with her own hands. It was ivory silk, pure and perfect, and Hazel lifted it out and held it to her face. It smelt of roses and paper, of the lavender that her mum had packed in with it.

Overwhelmed by a need to feel close to her mum, Hazel stripped off and put the dress on. It was an almost perfect fit because her figure was so much like her mum's had been. She reached around to button the dress up, then went to the mirror. She scooped up her hair and gazed at her reflection, trying to see herself as others would. How did she come across? Did she seem confident and self-assured or vulnerable and fragile? She could be all those things and how she felt varied by the hour, but today had been a good day and she was keen to cling to that. She'd been Hazel the wedding planner, assisting a couple, but she'd also felt like a friend, that she was slotting into a relationship with Clare and Sam – and Kyle too. Planning weddings was bound to be a reminder of what she had lost, and yet the experience today had been bittersweet because while she had been forced to face up to the fact that she'd never had her wedding, she'd also been able to take joy from sharing in how happy Clare and Sam were.

She went to her dressing table and picked up the wedding photo of her mum and dad. It was in colour but not as sharp as the resolution of contemporary ones. In the simple silk sheath dress, with her wavy blonde hair loose and a white rose tucked behind her ear, her mum looked elegant and beautiful. Next to her, Hazel's dad was handsome in a white shirt, black tie and trousers. They had dressed simply for their wedding, but they looked so happy that they both shone. Hazel touched the glass of the frame, catching herself before she could try to spread her thumb and forefinger to zoom in as she would do with a digital photo. Things had changed so much since the eighties and although her mum had only passed away two years ago, a lot more had changed in that time. There were things she wished she could share with her mum and dad but would never have the chance to.

She kissed the photograph, as she often did, then set it back on the dressing table and went to the lounge. There was only one thing for it when she was feeling this way: a lounge disco complete with fizz and chocolates. She grabbed both from the kitchen then popped the cork on the mini bottle of Prosecco and poured it into a glass before turning on the TV. She found a music channel then turned the volume up, took a swig of fizz and started to dance.

Gloria Gaynor was belting out her hit about surviving when Hazel's mobile started to ring. She picked it up and saw that it was Kyle. They'd exchanged numbers earlier and though she was surprised that he was ringing her already, she was also happy to see his name.

'Hello?'

'Hazel?'

'Yes, it's me.' She sipped her wine then burped as a bubble rose in her throat.

'What's all that noise?'

'Oh . . . nothing. Just the TV.'

'Are you having a party?' he asked.

'No. Not really . . .'

'You are! Let me in quick.'

'What?'

'I'm outside. I've been pressing the buzzer but you can't have heard me because your music is so bloody loud.'

'Hold on and I'll come down.'

Hazel ended the call then looked around. The room was fairly tidy and Fleas had retreated to the bedroom, so there was nothing to worry about. She opened the door and trotted down the stairs then unlocked the front door.

Kyle stood there smiling, a bottle of wine in each hand.

'I didn't know if you liked red or white, so I went for one of each.'

'Uhhh . . .'

'Darling, I thought you seemed a little sad today and the thought of you coming back here and being alone all evening was too much for me to bear so here I am with wine and a listening ear. Alternatively, if talking isn't your thing, we can binge-watch Netflix, but only once you've shown me how you boogie.'

'Boogie?'

He cocked an eyebrow. 'You were having a lounge disco when I arrived, weren't you?'

Hazel chewed at her bottom lip.

'Admit it, honey, there's no shame in it.'

'I was,' she said grudgingly.

'Excellent. Well, we have booze, and by the look of it you have chocolate . . .'

'What?'

He tucked one of the bottles under his arm then reached out and wiped the side of Hazel's mouth with his thumb. 'Chocolate all over your face, you mucky pup.'

'Oops.' Hazel wrinkled her nose.

'And what are you wearing?'

Hazel glanced down at herself, cheeks burning.

'Is that a *wedding* dress?'

'It's my mum's. I tried it on earlier and . . . uh . . . forgot to take it off.'

'It suits you. Don't change on my account. If I'd known I'd have borrowed Nanna's.'

'What?'

'Nanna has a cracking old frock in her attic and it almost fits me. I could at least have brought her veil.'

'I have a fascinator you can borrow.'

'Excellent! Well, come on then, are you going to invite me in or do I have to stand on your doorstep all evening so the neighbours can gossip?'

'Come in.' Hazel stepped back and Kyle entered the shop, then she led the way up to the flat.

'I'll grab you a glass.'

Kyle had opened the white wine when Hazel returned to the lounge, so she swallowed down the rest of her Prosecco and let him fill her glass. When she'd grabbed the fascinator from the bedroom – a large purple silk rose with two blue feathers – and Kyle had pinned it in his hair, he clinked his glass against hers.

'To new friends and to happy times.'

'Cheers.' She swallowed the lump in her throat. Kyle saw her as a friend already and that made her feel special in a way she hadn't in a long time.

'Now, turn up the music and let's have a dance.'

Hazel turned up the TV and they bounced around the lounge. At first, she felt a bit shy, but as the wine flowed and she laughed with Kyle, she began to relax and let go. Right now, she didn't feel the need to talk or to bring Lennox and her past into the room, but having some company was, she realised, an excellent balm to soothe her wounds. And all she cared about was having some fun.

Chapter 11

It was always going to be a difficult day. Jack had known it would be, but as the anniversary of Danni's death dawned, the emotions that swept through him were almost suffocating.

He'd been in Little Bramble for three weeks and each day that passed had brought him hope because the more time he spent with Bella and her family, the better he felt in himself. He was running daily, walking with Bella and the girls, had been out with Lee for a few pints and he was eating better than he had done when he lived alone. He knew the importance of good nutrition and how it affected physical and mental health, but cooking for one hadn't exactly inspired him. However, eating with others had led him to make an effort to cook again, and he was enjoying his time in the kitchen. Though no miracle had happened to heal him, he felt stronger – and even somewhat happy, which surprised him. Bella and her family had shown him that he could find happiness in simple things.

But today was different because exactly a year ago his life had been upended and the events of that night had changed him forever. That morning, he'd stayed in the apartment over the garage while Lee left for work and Bella took the children to school, needing to stay quiet and calm. Putting on a brave face would have been too much of a struggle and so he'd hidden away, hoping that Bella would understand.

He didn't even have the energy to go for a run. Instead, he lay in bed with the curtains drawn, trying to remember the good times he'd had with Danni. That first time he'd seen her, he'd been bowled over by how gorgeous she was, how intelligent she seemed, how she sparkled with energy and enthusiasm. She was driven, focused and knew what she wanted from life. At the time, they'd both been university students and Jack had believed that everything was ahead of them, that nothing was impossible. He hadn't suffered loss, had no idea that someone could be cut down in their prime, even though he saw stories on the news and in the papers. It just wasn't something that happened to people he knew.

They had dated, gone to the cinema and bars, dancing until dawn then headed down to the beach for a dip in the sea. Danni's energy had been infectious, and she'd attracted people to her; everyone wanted to be her friend, to bask in her glow.

After university, when Jack had decided to get a job to support Danni through her postgraduate studies, initially she'd tried to persuade him to do his PGCE, but her resistance hadn't lasted long when she'd realised that he was serious about supporting her. She did have money from her parents, but the emotional support wasn't there and so Jack did everything he could to always have her back. He knew she'd appreciated it, she had told him and shown him all the time, and yet, without being aware of it, his sacrifice had created its own problem – one he wouldn't know about for years.

He hadn't supported Danni to be thanked or rewarded, though. He'd done it because he loved her and wanted her to be happy. Wasn't that what loving someone was all about?

A gentle knock at the door to the apartment brought him back to the present and he sat up and rubbed his hands over his face. He threw back the duvet, grabbed his jogging bottoms and pulled them on, then padded to the door and unlocked it.

'Hey.' It was Bella, holding an umbrella over her head and wearing yellow wellies along with a yellow raincoat. She looked like a children's TV presenter. 'How're you doing?'

'Morning.' He pushed his lips up into a smile. 'Sorry . . . I must've overslept.'

'I thought you'd need some time alone this morning.' She reached out a hand to him and rubbed his shoulder. 'But I'm also worried. Everyone else has gone now so would you like to come and have some breakfast with me?'

'Oh . . . uh . . .' He looked down at himself.

'It's OK. I'll go and put the kettle on and you can come and join me once you're dressed.'

'OK.' He nodded. He could hardly decline when Bella was clearly worried.

'Also, I have someone I'd like you to meet.'

'You do?' He peered out at the goose-grey sky and shivered. 'It's not a – a woman is it?'

'Goodness no! What do you take me for, Jack? And on the anniversary too.' Bella was shaking her head vigorously.

'Right, that's OK then. Sorry. I just . . . I'm not in the right frame of mind for any introductions of the romantic kind.'

'Of course you're not, and I'm not an insensitive idiot – even though Bobby might claim otherwise when I'm trying to detangle her hair.' She stepped backwards. 'Come on over when you're ready. I have croissants and fresh coffee.'

'Thanks. I won't be long.'

Jack closed the door and returned to his bedroom. Looking at the bed, he fought the urge to dive back in and pull the duvet over his head. As much as he might feel like hiding away, he couldn't do that to Bella. He couldn't give in to the grief; he had to eat, drink and join the human race again.

He raised his arm and sniffed then grimaced. Before he went anywhere, he badly needed a shower.

❄

'Chicken or fish?' Hazel asked herself quietly as she held up two boxes of cat food. Fleas liked both, so Hazel put them in the trolley.

She'd driven to the supermarket just outside Little Bramble to stock up. The village shop had plenty of choice, but Hazel had wanted to get in the car and drive somewhere today. She wasn't sure why she'd woken up feeling restless as there was nothing significant about the date and it was Friday, surely the best day of the week? But after sitting in front of her laptop for an hour, she'd known that she needed a change of scenery before she'd get much done and so, with it raining heavily, Tesco had seemed like a good place to go. She'd considered sending Kyle a text, but she didn't want to take up too much of his time. Kyle was in a relationship with Magnus and he had family around, so he didn't have as much disposable time as Hazel and she didn't want to seem needy. Despite the fact that Kyle was eleven years younger than her, they liked a lot of the same things and while he was a lot of fun, he often seemed more mature than his years, so they'd been getting on really well. In the two weeks since their lounge disco, they'd met for coffee twice and he'd messaged her a few times too, usually with some random fact that had made her laugh. She liked him a lot, enjoying his company and sense of humour.

Looking down into her trolley, she sighed. It was a challenge, shopping for one. Even after almost six months, she was still getting used to trying to buy less because large bags of salad and potatoes just ended up being wasted, as would a whole chicken, a pack of minced beef or two portions of cod. Although, having said that, she could cook both pieces of cod and give some to Fleas.

Not for the first time she wondered what Lennox was doing. Was he shopping alone or with Valentina in some form of domestic bliss, fingers entwined as they strolled the aisles adding family-sized bags of crisps and boxes of chocolates (not that Valentina ate much), oysters to slide down their throats and champagne for when they rolled into bed together to—

Ew! She shuddered. She would NOT go there. What was the point? Seeing what she had when she'd caught them had been traumatic enough without a live-action replay. *Cheating gits!* Lennox had cheated on her and so had Valentina, destroying years of trust and friendship.

Hazel pushed the trolley to the bread aisle and threw a loaf of freshly baked tiger bread into the trolley along with a pack of scones, some wholemeal wraps, seeded bagels and a tub of millionaire shortbread bites. Be dammed with it, she was going to stuff her face with carbs until she couldn't feel anything anymore! An afternoon of comfort eating was exactly what she needed.

Wasn't it?

She pushed the trolley away from the aromas of baking and towards the freezers. At least there she could blame the chill in her heart on the cold.

Half an hour later, Jack knocked on Bella's back door then went inside. The kitchen smelt incredible and his mouth watered as the smell of freshly baked croissants and coffee greeted him.

'Hello!' he called, removing his boots by the door and setting them on the mat to dry. He'd only come from the garage but it was raining heavily. He shrugged out of his jacket and hung it on a radiator then grabbed a piece of kitchen roll and dried his hands.

'Jack?' Bella's voice came from the hallway.

'Yes, it's me.'

'I'll be there in a moment.'

He sat on the sofa in the kitchen and leant on his knees. He had no idea what she was up to but really hoped she wasn't about to introduce him to someone like the village vicar or a friend who was also a counsellor. He'd had some counselling sessions after Danni's accident but hadn't gone for long, finding it all far too painful to dig through everything each week, preferring to run to let off steam. He knew there had been some benefits to the counselling, but he hadn't been able to tell her what he'd found out after Danni had died.

'Are you ready?' Bella called.

'I guess so.' He took a deep breath, trying to steady himself for whatever was coming.

The kitchen door opened and Bella stood there smiling.

'I'd like you to meet the newest addition to our family.'

'What?' He half stood as Bella entered the kitchen and stepped aside. There was a skittering then a grey-blue shape with four long spindly legs ran at him and jumped onto the sofa, making him yelp and raise his hands to protect himself.

'This is Aster.' Bella joined them on the sofa, where Jack was now laughing as the dog sniffed at his face and tried to lick his ears. 'She's a rescue greyhound.'

'Stop! Ha! Ha! Cut it out.'

Jack managed to get the dog to stop licking him then he sat back and she stood on the sofa, turned in a circle then landed with her head on his lap, her long body curled up next to him.

'I knew she'd like you.'

Jack looked down at the dog. 'She's lovely, but I had no idea you were getting a dog.'

'Little Bramble has a big greyhound community,' Bella explained. 'There's a kennels just outside the village and they have a lot of dogs needing homes. We'd seen people around the village with greyhounds and asked about them because – as you can imagine – the girls are desperate for a dog. After enquiring about what they're like as pets, Lee and I looked into it a bit more then we went to the kennels a few weeks ago to meet some of the dogs. We did all this without letting the girls know because if it didn't work out then we didn't want them to be disappointed. However, following a successful home check and a meet-and-greet, as well as walking Aster several times, we were told that she could come home with us.'

'She's beautiful.' Jack ran his hand from the greyhound's head, along her body and back again, rubbing her silky ears and making her grunt. 'Is that OK? I didn't hurt her?'

'Not at all. Greyhounds let out a funny grunt or groan when you do something they like.'

'So the girls have no idea?'

'None at all. The thing is, when we lived in Woking, I was working full-time and having a dog wasn't an option, but now I'm down to three days, we thought it would be possible. I can come home at lunchtime and let her out – and now that you're here for a while . . .'

'Oh, I see.' He tilted his head. 'Uncle Jack's going to help out, is he?'

'Do you mind? I don't want to take advantage, Jack.'

'Not at all. I love dogs. And I'm really happy to help.'

'Thank you so much.'

'It's nothing, Bella. Look at what you've done for me.'

'I've barely done a thing, Jack.'

'You invited me for Christmas – well, for most of the winter, actually. You stopped me wallowing in sadness this morning by getting me over here for breakfast. And now you've given me a companion for the days when you're at work.'

Bella smoothed a hand over Aster's fur. 'She's not like some of the others who are terrified of their own shadows. She was born to a greyhound who came to the kennels heavily pregnant. Her mother was having some health issues and the owners couldn't pay for her medical costs, then decided they didn't want her or her pups. Aster is only eight months old and grew up at the kennels and in foster homes.'

'Is that why she's OK with me?' he asked.

'I think so. I know from speaking to other greyhound owners that some of the hounds are terrified of men because of how some of the trainers on the race circuit treat them. But Aster was lucky to only know good treatment and so, according to Zoe Jones, who works at the kennels, Aster actually loves men.'

'I don't know how anyone could mistreat a sweet creature like this.'

'Nor me.' Bella's voice wavered. The idea of the dog suffering was horrific. 'Do you think the girls will like her?'

'They'll be over the moon when they get home.'

'That's why I wanted her here in the day first, so she'll have a chance to settle a bit before they get back.'

'Good plan.' He placed a hand over his belly as it rumbled.

'I almost forgot our breakfast!' Bella laughed. 'I'll get it sorted now.'

'Need a hand?'

'No, thanks. You stay there and keep Aster company while I get it ready.'

Bella stood up and Aster briefly raised her head then settled it again on Jack's leg.

'Good girl,' he said, appreciating the warmth of her long body and the softness of her fur under his hand. It was, he thought, impossible to feel entirely sad when a dog was cuddling up to you. Her very presence was incredibly comforting and he had a feeling that his sister had known exactly what she was doing by bringing the greyhound home today of all days.

Chapter 12

'I'm so excited it's Friday!' Bobby jumped up and down on the sofa in the kitchen, her ginger curls bouncing around her head like springs. 'We get a whole weekend to spend with Aster!'

Jack looked around for Bella, wondering if she'd mind her youngest daughter using the sofa as a trampoline. He was holding Aster's lead and the dog was pulling to get to Bobby, but he didn't think it would be a good idea for both of them to jump around so he held it tight. When Penny and Bobby had got home, he'd been waiting with Aster in the kitchen so Bella could surprise them. The girls had entered the kitchen in what he now knew to be their usual happy, chaotic return with clothes, bags and shoes flying everywhere, to find him sitting on the sofa holding Aster's collar. Penny and Bobby had spotted Aster and squealed then hurried over to meet her. The dog had wagged her long arc of a tail, whimpering with excitement, and Bella had wiped at her eyes with a tissue, overcome by the joy of the moment. It had taken Bobby fifty questions to ensure that Aster was, truthfully, honestly and definitely staying with them, then she'd burst into tears and sobbed into Aster's fur. The dog had stood

122

there and let Bobby hug her, apparently already aware of her role in the family as chief giver of hugs, tear-drier, comforter, playmate and centre of the world.

'I'm excited too,' Penny said, standing next to Jack, already in her coat and warm boots, hat on her head and gloves in one hand. 'But I'm older than Bobby so I don't act like a baby.'

Bobby stopped jumping and glared at Penny. 'I'm not a baby! Don't call me a baby!' Her little face went puce and she balled up her hands into fists.

'I didn't say you were a baby,' Penny said, rolling her eyes. 'I said I don't *act* like one. There's a difference.'

Jack gritted his teeth, worried about where this was going, but Bella strode into the kitchen at that moment and Bobby sprang off the sofa faster than if it had caught on fire.

'Bobby?' Bella put her hands on her hips. 'Were you bouncing on the sofa?'

'No . . .' Bobby looked down at her socks.

'I saw you standing on it.' Bella scowled.

'Was not.'

'Bobby!' Bella shook her head. 'Are you fibbing?'

Bobby chewed at her bottom lip and Jack thought she was about to lie again but instead she pouted then said, 'I'm sorry, Mummy. I was just so excited. It's having Aster and it being Friday and because we are going to the turning on of the bloody Christmas lights!' Bobby grinned, showing off her small white teeth and her cheeky dimples.

'Don't say bloody, Bobby. It's rude.' Penny looked up at Jack and wrinkled her nose. 'She doesn't realise.'

He raised his eyebrows and Penny gave him a faint smile.

'Bobby, go and get your shoes. Penny, help her, will you?' Bella was rooting around in drawers, looking increasingly flustered.

'What've you lost?' Jack asked.

'My phone. Can you believe it? Always have the bloody thing on me and now I've put it somewhere and I can't bloody well find it.'

'Have you checked your pockets?' Jack asked, trying not to grin because it was obvious where Bobby had got *bloody* from. Bella had always resorted to minor swear words whenever she was stressed.

Bella patted her jeans then sighed as she pulled her phone from her back pocket. 'How did it get in there?'

'Beats me.' Jack shrugged. 'What time is Lee back?'

'He said he'll meet us there. He got stuck in traffic following a business meeting outside the village that he went to with Connor. I just hope he makes it in time as we've been looking forward to this for weeks.'

'Will Aster be warm enough?' Jack looked down at the greyhound in her fleecy coat.

'I think so. We can take a blanket in case. And, thankfully, the rain has stopped.'

'Ready!' Bobby bounded into the room wearing a padded jacket, bright red bobble hat and matching mittens.

'OK then, let's go.' Bella ushered them all out of the house.

Jack followed, still holding Aster's lead tightly, grateful to have something to hold on to because as much as he knew this was meant to be a community event, he was a bit nervous about attending. Last year he had ignored Christmas, let the gifts that he and Danni had already placed under the

124

tree remain unopened and the lights stayed turned off. There seemed no point in pretending that his life was anything other than broken, his world destroyed.

Today, though, in spite of the anxiety that was making his palms clammy and his heart race, he was glad to be with family. At least he could enjoy the Christmas celebrations for them, even if his own festive spirit still lay dormant.

✾

Hazel had wondered whether to go to the turning on of the lights. She was tired and it was cold out, but it was either that or a microwave meal for one along with an evening in front of the TV. As tempting as that sounded, it would be the same as the majority of her evenings, so she decided to make the effort to dress warmly and walk to the village green. She was curious to see what it would be like. She'd been to see other Christmas lights turned on in Scotland, but they had been much bigger affairs and this was a small community event so it would surely be more intimate.

Once she'd put on long boots, a black down-filled coat with a faux-fur trimmed hood, a hat and gloves, she checked on Fleas. The cat had eaten and was now stretched out on the sofa, her fluffy belly ready for tickles. Hazel gave her a stroke and told her she'd be back in an hour, then left the flat.

As soon as she got outside, the chill enveloped her, making her shiver. She was glad she'd put layers on under her jacket and tugged her hat lower over her ears. It wasn't the most glamorous outfit, but it would be warm. It wasn't as if she was heading out to try and pull, so what did it matter what she looked like?

When she reached the village green, she was surprised to find quite a crowd had gathered. It was already dark at just after six, but the streetlights cast a welcoming orange glow over the green and surrounding streets.

She found a quiet spot on the grass and stood there trying not to look at anyone directly in case they saw the loneliness in her eyes. The last thing she wanted was to have people pitying her.

'Hazel? Is that you?' A familiar voice made her look up.

'Oh, hello, Connor.'

'It is you. I wasn't sure because it's hard to tell with the hat and coat. Anyway, how are you?'

'I'm good, thanks. How are you?'

'Great, thanks. I've already made a start on *you know what*.'

'Really? That's brilliant.' It had been two weeks since she'd gone to The Lumber Shed but she knew that Connor had a lot on – the workshop had been very busy – but knowing that he was working on the project for Sam and Clare made Hazel happy.

He shrugged. 'I love a secret project.'

'Thank you so much.'

'Before I forget . . .' He turned around. 'Emma! Come here a minute.'

A woman approached them, an affable smile on her face, two mugs in her hands. She gave one to Connor.

'Emma, this is Hazel Campbell. She's new to the village and is our very own wedding planner.'

'Hello, Hazel. I'm Emma.'

'Emma's my significant other.' Connor wrapped an arm around the woman's shoulders and they gazed at each other as if everything else had disappeared.

'Nice to meet you.' Hazel smiled, recalling what Connor had said about the years he and Emma had been apart and how glad he was to be reunited with her. Some people did have happy times after heartbreak.

'Are you here with anyone?' Connor asked, looking around.

'No. Just me.' Hazel grinned, hoping she didn't seem pitiful. She didn't mind being alone, but people often found it hard to see, as if everyone had to have someone. Not that Hazel wouldn't like to have friends and family, but it just wasn't that way and so she wasn't about to mourn what she didn't have. Not tonight, anyway.

'Have you tried the mulled wine?' Emma asked, her big brown eyes fixed on Hazel's face.

'I haven't. Is it good?' Hazel looked over to where Emma was pointing towards a stall.

'Wonderful. Let me go and get you a mug.'

'No! It's fine, honestly. I can get one.'

'It's no problem.' Emma shook her head.

'No, it's really fine. Thanks so much.' Hazel held up a hand. 'I'll go and grab one. Standing still is making me cold.'

'OK, if you're sure,' Emma said. 'It's freezing out here.'

'I'll see you in a bit.' Hazel flashed a smile then marched over to the mulled wine stall. People in the village were so friendly and generous. She'd forgotten how kind human beings could be.

At the stall she ordered a mulled wine then picked up a napkin and wandered closer to the giant Norwegian Spruce.

There was a small platform near the tree and a few people were standing on it, holding up wires and scratching their heads. It seemed that there was a power issue. Was the village renowned for that then? she wondered, recalling her own electricity issues when she'd been due to open her office.

'Hello!' A voice echoed around the green and Hazel looked over at the platform. 'It's me, Marcellus David, your friendly neighbourhood postie.'

The man's voice was laced with a Caribbean accent and his smile brightened his whole face under his baggy beanie hat.

'Welcome to the annual Little Bramble turning on of the lights. I hope you've all purchased a hot chocolate or a mulled wine to enjoy as we feast our eyes on this year's magnificent illuminations. We have to give special thanks this year to our local sponsors The Lumber Shed, The Bistro and Betty's Bakery. Your sponsorship is greatly appreciated and without your help, we would be unable to continue improving our festive lighting.'

A round of applause spread through the crowd and Hazel joined in, clapping one hand against her other wrist while being careful not to spill her wine. Perhaps next year she'd be in a position to sponsor the lights. It would be an incredible feeling to be able to do that and it would really cement her business in the community.

'And so, without further ado, I give you – the Little Bramble Christmas Lights!'

A hush fell over the crowd then as lights flickered on around the green, oohs and ahhs filling the air. There were coloured lanterns, gold and silver baubles and flashing reindeer that had been hung from streetlights and around the many trees. Then the Christmas tree at the centre of the green lit up from the top and the light spread downwards like a helter-skelter slide, thousands of tiny twinkling amber stars coming to life.

Hazel stood watching, shivers of delight running up and down her spine and goosebumps rising on her arms. Set against the backdrop of the wintery darkness, the lights were truly beautiful. Her breath emerged in clouds in front of her and the scents of oranges and cloves coming from the mulled wine made her mouth water.

Then a memory assaulted her: last year, waiting for Lennox to get home. They were meant to be going out to see the Edinburgh Christmas lights being turned on and then meet friends for dinner. Hazel was ready and waiting, excited to go out, but Lennox came home late. He had phoned to say he'd been held up at work and couldn't make it. Hazel had been disappointed but understanding; these things happened, didn't they? She could have gone without him but it hadn't seemed right as the people they were meeting were his friends really, not hers. So instead she'd changed into her pyjamas and settled down in front of the TV. Lennox hadn't got home until gone midnight, the scent of beer on his breath and what she'd thought was perfume on his clothes. He'd told her not to be silly, that it was air freshener from the car. Hazel had chosen to believe him; he was her fiancé after all, the man she'd been with for her whole adult life. He wouldn't cheat . . . Oh, how naïve she had been!

What if he had been cheating with Valentina back then? It was possible. The beer he'd explained as a quick pint after he'd finally finished his meeting, but Hazel knew now that he had probably been lying and she had let him get away with it because the alternative would have meant blowing her life apart – right before Christmas too.

And now look at her. A year on and she was out alone, independent, doing what she should always have done. She was her own person and not relying on anyone else. She could do this; she definitely could.

'Hazel?'

'Hey, Bella.'

In spite of her pride at being a strong and independent woman it was nice to see a friendly face.

'It's so good to see you again.'

'You too.'

'What do you think?' Bella gestured towards the green.

'It's a beautiful display.'

'I know. I'm so impressed.'

'You haven't been here for the lights before?' Hazel asked.

'No, we only moved here in the summer so this is a first for us too. Imagine if we're both still here for this in years to come?' Bella hugged herself. 'Wouldn't that be wonderful?'

'It would.' Security. Constancy. A place to call home.

'Is that mulled wine?' Bella looked at the mug Hazel was holding.

'Yes, and it's delicious.'

'Come on, let's go and get another.'

'Oh . . . OK.'

Bella tucked her arm through Hazel's and led her over to the drink stall, chatting all the way about her daughters and their new dog and how happy she was to have her brother with her for Christmas. Before she knew it, Hazel had another mug of wine and had agreed to go to Hazel's for Sunday lunch.

As they made their way back to the tree, a sound caught on the gentle breeze then it gained momentum and soon, everyone around them was singing 'White Christmas'. Bella squeezed Hazel's arm, smiling warmly, then she started to sing.

What else could Hazel do other than join in?

Chapter 13

Hazel stared at the pile of clothes on her bed and tried to ignore the rising panic. It was only a lunch invitation and yet she'd been up since six trying to decide what to wear. She wasn't even sure why she was in such a state over it. At the turning on of the lights the night before last, Bella had invited Hazel for Sunday lunch and Hazel had not been able to think of a reason why she couldn't go. In fact, she hadn't wanted to think up an excuse, because the idea of a home-cooked Sunday roast was incredibly appealing.

Why she'd become so worried about what to wear she wasn't sure. Bella had told her it would be a casual lunch with her family and therefore, Hazel reasoned, she should wear something comfortable. Hazel was just keen to make a good impression on people and didn't want to do anything to mess that up. Damn Lennox for shredding her confidence so badly.

She picked up the black cotton A-line dress with the long sleeves and rounded neckline. It was smart but not overly dressy and would go well with thick tights and knee-high boots. She would wear a colourful scarf and silver jewellery and she'd feel good about herself and, since it was loose, she could eat without worrying about a waistband digging into her belly.

She put the dress on, tidied her other clothes away then curled her hair and did her makeup, keeping it minimal so she wouldn't look overdone. Glancing at her parents' photo, she sent out a silent wish to them to help her to be strong and stay calm.

❄

Jack looked at the pile of potatoes Bella had put in front of him on the kitchen table.

'Problem?' Bella asked, raising her eyebrows.

'How many people are coming for dinner?'

'Clare, Sam and Hazel.'

'So that makes eight of us.'

'That's right.'

'So why this many spuds?'

'Have you seen how many roast potatoes Lee can put away? That man likes a roastie more than anyone I've ever met.'

'I like roasties too.' Jack licked his lips. 'But will we really eat this many?'

'I'm making mash as well.'

'Right. That makes sense.' Jack started peeling. Radio 2 was on in the kitchen and the sun shone through the bifold doors, warming the room. There was a joint of beef in the oven and it smelt delicious. Lee had prepared the beef and the vegetables while Bella helped the girls with some homework at the kitchen table. When they'd finished, Lee went off to shower and the girls had gone to watch some TV (that they both liked) in the lounge.

'Fancy some wine?' Bella asked.

Jack glanced at the clock on the wall.

'It's only just gone twelve.'

'And?' She held up her hands. 'Everything's ready except for the spuds and the gravy and we can sit and have a chat while you peel.'

'Go on, then.'

'I have some delicious reds here from that online wine company. Would you prefer Chianti or Shiraz?'

'I really don't mind.'

Bella opened a bottle while he continued peeling, placing the potatoes in a colander once they were done. He found that he was looking forward to the idea of socialising, as well as eating the dinner itself, and so was Aster by the looks of things! She'd taken a seat on the kitchen sofa and though she appeared to be snoozing, her ears kept flicking and one eye crept open every so often. She clearly liked what she could smell.

'Aster's settling in well.'

'She is.' Bella handed him a glass of wine and he took a sip, nodding.

'That's delicious.'

'I know, right? It always feels quite decadent having wine in the afternoon but when you work hard through the week and make a special Sunday lunch, I figure it's well-deserved.'

'I agree.' Jack put his glass down, smiling. He was having a great time staying with Bella, felt so welcome and at home there. His brother-in-law was a friendly, easy-going chap and he'd made Jack feel very comfortable. His nieces were funny, sweet and adorable. Aster was proving to be a little character, as well as incredibly affectionate. And then there was Bella. No man could wish for a better big sister, he was sure of it.

'Did you enjoy the turning on of the lights?' Bella asked, sitting back in her chair, one hand resting on the stem of her wine glass.

'Very much. There was definitely a community feel to it all.'

'That's what I thought. Seeing how everyone gathered together and knowing that they've done this for decades made it all the more special. If we stay here, which we're hoping to do as I really do not fancy moving again, then the girls will be able to enjoy the turning on of the lights every year and one day, who knows . . . Lee and I might have our grandchildren here to see it too.'

'You think that far ahead?' he asked.

'Of course. Don't you?' She winced. 'God, I'm so sorry. I—'

'It's fine, honestly. I used to think ahead – perhaps not as far as grandchildren! – but I did want to be a dad. I thought Danni and I would have children at some point. We'd even started talking about it but I think it was more my dream than hers.'

He sipped his wine. He *knew* it was more his dream than hers.

'She was very career-oriented, wasn't she? And I don't say that to be negative. She had an amazing job and did so much for so many people.'

'She was an incredible nurse and she believed fiercely in what she did and in the NHS.'

'But you don't think she was as keen on starting a family?'

He shook his head. 'For me, it was more a case of I had a job but it wasn't a career. I could have gone back to uni, but you know how it is . . .'

'Life flies past while we're living.'

'Exactly that. And I was content, you know?'

'You loved her.'

'Very much.'

'I'm sure she felt the same.'

'I don't. I . . .' How could he form the words he hadn't even been able to say out loud to himself? He'd read them, thought them, turned them over in his mind, but to say them out loud and share them would make them real. It would end all former perceptions of his marriage and there would be no going back. Part of him still wanted to hold on to the image of the fairy-tale marriage. Just for a while longer.

'It's OK, Jack. I know that some things are harder to share than others. I'm here if you want to tell me and if you don't – or can't – then that's absolutely fine too.'

'Thank you.'

'There's no need to thank me. I've tried to put myself in your position and to think how I'd cope . . . how I'd feel if I lost Lee. I love that man with all of my heart and he's my best friend. We share so much and have done throughout our marriage. If I lost him, I-I would crumble.'

'No, Bella, you're strong and you'd manage. It wouldn't be easy, of course not, but you'd keep going for the girls and for yourself and for him. Lee would never want you to give up if something happened to him.'

'I know that and you must think the same about Danni as well?'

'She'd want me to go on.'

'Exactly. Thinking about losing Lee even just for a few seconds is horrid. The pain would be . . . overwhelming. So, although I haven't been through what you have, I can try to empathise. It doesn't mean I understand, because only those who've experienced something can do that fully, but I can try to. I wish I could ease your pain and make it all better.'

'Bella, you *are* helping me. You have no idea how much, clearly. Inviting me here, as much as I might have seemed a bit reluctant to come, has been amazing. I've not even been here for a month yet but I feel a lot better for being here.'

'Do you?'

'I do.'

Bella's eyes were shining.

'I thought that shutting people out was the best way to deal with everything,' he went on, 'and perhaps for a while it was. I needed to process my loss and to come to terms with it but there comes a point when it's time to get back out there and live, and I think my time is now. I'm never going to stop grieving for Danni and I can't imagine the pain completely receding, but I can – at last – start to think that there might be a way forward.'

'I'm so happy to hear that.'

'It's been a year now and everyone says that time's a great healer. Some days it feels like a long time since I last saw Danni and others it's like it was yesterday and yet — and yet I find that I can't always remember the sound of her voice or the feel of her in my arms. There are things that I can't share just yet because I don't know how to say them. I want to, but . . .'

'Don't worry. As I said, I'm here for you.'

He raised his wine glass. 'And I am incredibly grateful. I love you, big sis.'

'I love you too.'

They clinked glasses and drank, then Jack carried on peeling potatoes and Bella wiped discreetly at her eyes. She really did have a heart of gold and Jack knew that she was there for him and always would be. He wanted her to feel that same sense of security from him. Whatever happened to her, he'd be her rock as she was being his.

※

'Come on in!' Bella stepped back and gestured at the hallway. 'I'm so glad you could make it.'

'Thank you.' Hazel smiled as she stepped inside. 'Oh my goodness, dinner smells delicious.'

'I'm glad you think so. You should see the size of Jack's Yorkshire puddings.'

'I love Yorkshire puds.'

'Well then, you're in for a treat. They're bigger than your head.'

Hazel giggled at the image. 'I'm glad I wore a loose dress then because I'm clearly going to have a very full belly after this feast.'

'It's our mission to fill people up whenever they come here for dinner, so yes, elastic waistbands or loose clothing are a must!' Bella patted her own stomach. 'I bought these harem pants and they have a drawstring waist so I can loosen them as needed and the blouse covers the rest.'

'You look amazing.'

'You're too kind. Come on through.'

Hazel followed Bella, admiring the purple silk tunic top and colourful harem pants Bella was wearing with a pair of black UGG boots. She was one of those people who could throw anything on and just look stylish.

In the kitchen, Lee and Jack were standing at the counter chatting and Clare and Sam were sitting at the table with glasses of wine.

'Hello!' Clare got up and kissed Hazel's cheeks. 'Good to see you.'

'Lovely to see you both too.' Hazel held up her hands. 'Bella, these are for you. The sweets are for your daughters. I hope that's OK.'

'That's very kind of you,' Bella said as she accepted the gift bags. 'Ooh . . . that's one of my favourite wines. Look, Lee.'

'Yum! That'll go excellently with the beef.'

'Hazel, take a seat with Clare and Sam and we'll get everything ready.'

'Thank you.'

Do you want a glass of wine?' Lee asked.

'Yes, please.'

Hazel sat on a chair next to Clare and the other woman filled her in on some of the wedding dresses she'd been looking at since the wedding fayre. It had given Clare some ideas and inspiration, but she hadn't found *the* dress at the fayre and had decided to keep looking. It was too late to have anything bespoke made but she had looked in a few charity shops and high street boutiques as well as online and found a few designs she really liked.

'Of course,' Clare said, 'at my age I don't want to seem like I'm trying to look younger. That would be quite sad. Kyle keeps telling me that I must ensure I don't look like mutton dressed as ham. Of course, he means lamb, but he's teasing me.'

'You have a gorgeous figure and you're very pretty,' Hazel said. 'And Kyle is quite the tease.'

'I keep telling her how perfect she is.' Sam took Clare's hand. 'But will she listen?'

Clare's cheeks flushed. 'I'm forty-six so not exactly a young bride.'

'What does that matter?' Hazel asked. 'I've planned weddings for couples in their sixties and seventies. I've yet to plan one for a couple in their eighties or nineties but it's on my bucket list.'

'Well, hold that thought because you never know, Mum and Iolo might get married at some point.'

'If they do, please send them in my direction, because I'd love to help.'

'Will do.'

'Right, you lot, everything's just about ready so I'll call the girls and we can get stuck in.'

As Bella, Lee and Jack brought a variety of steaming dishes to the table, Hazel's mouth watered. Everything looked and smelt incredible and she couldn't wait to load up her plate and get eating. The wine was good, the food appealing and the company delightful.

❄

'That was the best meal I've eaten in a long time,' Hazel said as she put her knife and fork down.

'Glad you enjoyed,' Bella said. 'We have Lee and Jack to thank for it.'

Jack stood up and Hazel peered up at him from under her lashes. 'I only peeled potatoes,' Jack said.

'And made the Yorkshires.' Bella stood up too. 'No one can deny that they were the biggest ones we've ever seen.'

'Now, now, Bella!' Lee shook his head. 'It's not all about size.'

The adults sniggered while Penny and Bobby frowned at each other. Hazel stood up and pushed her chair under the table then picked up her plate and reached for Jack's. He'd been in the chair next to her while Clare had been the other side. She'd been conscious of his long legs and the faint scent of his cologne as he'd accepted the various bowls of vegetables from her. Under the cologne was something else, fresh and sharp, like citrus, and she wondered if it was his shower gel. She had glanced at him a few times, feeling as shy as a teenager, and she couldn't help admiring him. He was so tall, his shoulders broad and his jaw strong. He could have been a model or an actor with his looks and she wondered what he did. The fact that he could cook also impressed her. Lennox hadn't been able to make beans on toast – or at least he'd made out that he couldn't – and the cooking had been left to Hazel. He really had taken her for a long ride.

The conversation around the table had flowed with a focus on weddings and dogs, with frequent references to Aster and how she was settling in, so Hazel had been unable to ask Jack any direct questions. It was probably a good thing, though, because what she had found out was that he was here for Christmas but intended to return to Swansea, so he wasn't going to be around for long in the New Year. He probably had a wife or partner back there and a successful career as a sports coach or businessman, she had thought. But then, if that was the case, how would he have some of November and the whole of December off to stay with his sister? Perhaps he was a freelance magazine features writer or an author. That would certainly be exciting. In any case, Clare and Sam had invited him to the wedding and he'd accepted, so Hazel knew he'd at least be there.

'Hazel, sit down. We can sort this then we'll have dessert.' Bella smiled at her over the table.

'No, let me help, please. I need to move a bit anyway if I'm to manage dessert. I'm currently stuffed.'

'Me too, Mummy,' Bobby said. 'Can I please leave the table?'

'You may,' Bella said. 'But make sure you go and wash your hands and clean that gravy off your chin. You too, Penny.'

Penny rolled her eyes. 'I'm not a baby.'

'I know that, darling, but sometimes I forget. Blame my age if you like.'

Bella poked her tongue out at Penny and Hazel saw the girl smile. Bella had a lovely relationship with her daughters, the type that Hazel would have loved to have with her children – if she ever had any. But that felt as though it was becoming increasingly unlikely. She had often thought that when she did have children she'd want to be like her mum had been: loving, caring, funny, a good listener. She missed her mum so much it was as though someone had dragged a rake through her insides and she'd never be able to put them right again. In some ways she thought she probably missed her mum more than she missed Lennox. Her mum had never been that keen on Lennox, and yet she'd told Hazel that she had to make her own choices and that she would never stick her nose in. She'd be there for Hazel when she needed her, but it was up to her to choose the person she wanted to spend her life with.

Lennox had not exactly been her mum's number one fan either, but they'd tolerated each other for Hazel's sake. As for her dad, he'd raised his eyebrows a few times but tended to leave the romance talk to his wife while making it clear that he was there for Hazel whenever she needed him. And that was how it should be, she guessed; when parents met their son or daughter's partner they should do their best to accept that person for the sake of their child.

Lennox had been respectful of Hazel's dad and slightly intimidated by him, she'd thought on more than one occasion, as if he felt he needed to be on his best behaviour around him. Perhaps Lennox hadn't liked her mum much because he'd known even then that she saw through him, that she could tell that he'd probably hurt Hazel at some point down the line. She'd never know now. And after her parents were gone, Lennox had done the worst thing he could have done, as if their presence had prevented him from showing his true colours in all their cheating glory.

Hazel carried some plates to the kitchen counter then went back for more. As she reached for the bowl of peas in front of Jack, he did the same and their hands brushed. Something tightened inside her as the heat of his skin seemed to sear into hers and she gasped then met his eyes. They were such a rich chocolate brown with thick dark lashes and she couldn't look away. As she gazed into them, his pupils dilated and his eyebrows raised slightly, as if in challenge or question. Not knowing him, she wasn't sure which and so she sucked in a deep breath and returned her focus to clearing the table, but as she carried the bowls to the kitchen counter, she could still feel the brush of his hand and only wonder at the effect it had

had upon her. When she set the bowls down, her hands were trembling and her heart was doing a jig behind her ribs.

She excused herself and went through the door to a small utility room that led to the downstairs toilet. Locking the toilet door behind her, she leant against it and tried to slow her breathing, to work out what had just happened to her. Was she that sex and affection starved that the first touch of a man, however innocuous, had just set her hormones racing? Granted, it had been months since she'd been held by Lennox and, now she thought about it, a fair while longer since they'd been intimate. Jack was gorgeous, yes, but she didn't know him or anything about him and therefore she had no right to have any feelings towards him at all. The magazines she'd read over the years encouraged women to see themselves as sensual human beings with every right to sexual feelings and that was a message she knew she should reinforce in herself. Just because she had feelings and urges it didn't mean she was going to jump into bed with just about anyone. Sitting next to Jack, drinking good wine and laughing with his family had shown her a life that she could have had if things were different. That was all.

She flushed the chain so no one would wonder what she'd been up to, washed her hands then fluffed her curls and left the toilet. There was every possibility that Jack hadn't felt any attraction to her at all so she should just let it go.

❄

Jack finished loading the dishwasher then added a tablet and closed the door. He switched it on then washed his hands over the sink. He'd eaten so much he felt like his belly was bulging over the waistband of his jeans, but he didn't mind because dinner had been amazing. He'd made roast dinners before, usually with Danni's help, but his Yorkshires had always gone wrong. This time, wanting to impress everyone, he'd read some tips online and they had worked. The Yorkshires had been truly enormous and Bella had been over the moon, telling him that he must teach her how to make them. He had tried not to enjoy the praise too much, but who didn't like it when their older sibling told everyone how wonderful they were?

He gazed through the kitchen window at Bella. She was outside, trying to get Aster to go for a wee. The dog was circling repeatedly and he wasn't sure if it was stage fright at being watched so closely or fear that if she stayed out there too long then all the Yorkshire puddings and beef would be gone and she wouldn't get any more. Aster had eaten her fair share of the food as Bella, Lee and the girls had been unable to resist her cold, wet little nose when it nudged at them or her big blue eyes as she blinked at them. She was just the right height to see over the table and she took advantage of that fact. Aster was going to have a fantastic life with his sister and would likely be the most spoilt dog in the whole of England.

He was about to turn away when he saw Hazel join Bella in the garden. She approached her slowly then Bella turned and smiled at her.

Hazel had been sitting next to him at the table and he'd been very aware of her, sneaking glances at her, the curves he couldn't help noticing, her wavy blonde hair that caught the light and her button nose that he had the strangest urge to touch with the tip of his finger. He hadn't been aware of a woman in as long as he could remember, other than Danni, but there was something about Hazel that he couldn't ignore. And she smelt so good! Like vanilla and berries and something else that he couldn't pinpoint. His eyes had been drawn to the curve of her neck more than once and he'd found himself wondering if she would smell like vanilla there and how her skin would feel beneath his lips.

He had to blame the strong wine and good company for these thoughts, surely. If it was more than that, then Hazel must be special. She was stirring him in ways he'd forgotten existed. He'd been so young when he'd fallen in love with Danni, and now he was a grown man. He knew how good things could be between consenting adults and how it felt to hold a woman he adored in his arms. But Danni was gone and, though he hated to admit it, that side of their marriage hadn't been right for a long time before he lost her. She was always too tired or too busy to make love. He had been patient, respectful and tried to do what he could to make life easier for her, but it hadn't meant he didn't want her, that he didn't yearn to be with her as they used to be. And now . . . now it seemed that his body was going through some form of reawakening and he was feeling things he hadn't felt for ages, thinking thoughts that made him blush. But surely it was just a passing attraction. He barely knew this woman.

He grabbed the dish sponge and started to run it around the edge of the sink slowly, making out that he was cleaning so he could stay there and watch Hazel for a bit longer and try to figure out what it was that he was actually feeling. It wasn't horrible, that was for sure, and if he was being honest with himself, it was a bit of a relief because he'd felt shut down for such a long time that he'd wondered if he'd ever be attracted to anyone ever again.

Chapter 14

'Not like that!' Bobby tutted and shook her head.

'Oh, sorry.' Hazel bit her lower lip and put her hands in her lap. Somehow, after lunch, she had been roped into helping Bobby and Penny make Christmas cards. Penny was quiet and sweet, nodding her approval at Hazel's work, but Bobby had turned out to be a tiny tyrant. So far, Hazel had not used the glue stick correctly, had drawn a hideously wonky snowman and selected the wrong colour of glitter. Hazel was not doing well at all and she wondered how this would look on a parenting CV. She doubted she'd be approved at this stage.

'What's the problem?' Jack asked. He was sitting opposite Hazel and, apparently, was the greatest card-maker since Hallmark. Hazel and Jack had been left alone with the girls and it was proving to be quite a challenge, especially as Hazel was sleepy after all the good food and wine.

'I've done it wrong again.' Hazel met his gaze.

'I thought there was no way to get this wrong. Isn't it all about free expression?' He shrugged and Bobby groaned.

'Uncle Jack, it has to be arse-teticly pleasing.'

'Arse-teticly?' His eyes widened and he flashed Hazel a teasing look.

'Yes. My teacher says that cards need to be arse-teticly pleasing or they won't make the rect-ip-ient smile.'

'Such big words from one so young.'

'You mean aesthetically, Bobby.' Penny raised a hand to her forehead and closed her eyes. 'Will you never learn?'

'I'm only six, Penny, you bloody know-it-all.'

'I actually prefer the sound of arse-teticly pleasing, don't you, Hazel?' Jack's lips quivered and Hazel bit the insides of her cheeks to stop herself laughing. 'And less of the *bloody*, please, Bobby. I'm not used to such language.'

'If you do become a teacher like Mummy says you will, then you'd better get used to bad words, Uncle Jack,' Penny said. 'People at school are the worst for using bad words and we hear them all the time.'

'Is that right?' Jack nodded. 'Thanks for the warning.'

'Are you thinking of going into teaching?' Hazel asked, accepting a tube of silver glitter from Bobby and sprinkling it carefully over the sky that Bobby had coloured in with a black pen.

'Well . . .' Jack looked down at the reindeer he was sketching. 'I'm not sure yet. It's something I'm considering. It's a big deal, retraining at my age though.'

'Uncle Jack is OLD,' Bobby said.

'Hey, that's not true. I'm only seventy-four.'

Bobby squealed with laughter and her ginger curls bounced as she tapped Jack's arm. 'You are not!'

'I am indeed.' Jack folded his arms over his broad chest and looked indignant.

'He's not.' Bobby shook her head. 'He's thirty-five.'

'Oh, that's right. I forgot.' Jack grinned at his niece. 'Silly me.'

'You *are* silly.' Bobby looked at Hazel. 'He's such a joker.'

Hazel was enjoying this time with Jack and his nieces. Penny was definitely more serious than Bobby, but she also seemed to be a talented young artist. She'd drawn a beautiful wintery scene complete with snow-covered fields and trees along with a lone deer.

'That's amazing, Penny.'

The girl flushed scarlet.

'Hazel's right, Pen. That's fantastic.'

Penny kept her gaze on the card. 'It's OK.'

'Penny's a good drawer-er . . . no, a good . . . artist!' Bobby jabbed the air with her finger. 'She's going to be a braphic designer when she grows up.'

'Maybe.' Penny poked her tongue out from the side of her mouth as she shaded the landscape then smudged it with the pad of her thumb. 'It's a long time away though. And it's graphic, not braphic.' She whispered the last sentence as if to avoid another outburst from Bobby.

Aster trotted into the kitchen and sniffed at the table.

'You looking for seconds?' Jack asked her, rubbing her head with a large hand. 'I think you'll probably need a walk soon to burn off some of what you've already consumed today. We can't have a fat greyhound now, can we?'

Hazel sat back and let Bobby critique her latest effort at card making and watched as Jack spoke to the dog and his nieces. He seemed like a nice person; gentle, funny and kind. He'd helped with dinner and cleaned up, as Hazel had always thought men should do but hadn't seen from Lennox. As her mum had always said, men shouldn't 'help', but should do their fair share. He'd then sat with Penny and Bobby for the past forty-five minutes and helped them with their crafting, showing enormous patience and a wicked sense of humour. She could see how he'd make a good teacher; he had all the qualities required and similarly he'd be a good dad one day too. If he wanted children, that was.

'How's the card factory coming along?' Bella asked as she entered the kitchen.

'It's going well,' Jack said. 'Although Hazel's not cut out for the work, according to Bobby.'

'She's not great.' Bobby shook her head. 'But it's OK, Hazel, you're never too old to learn.'

'Uh, thanks.' Hazel looked at Bella, who was shaking her head.

'Apologies for my youngest daughter. She doesn't spare anyone's blushes.'

'So I'm finding out.' Hazel gestured at the card in front of her. 'I did my best though and that's all anyone can ask for.'

'Very true.' Jack was smiling at her and she felt an unwelcome heat bloom in her cheeks. 'And I think your best is pretty good indeed.'

'Thanks.' She dropped her gaze to the table, feeling a little embarrassed.

'Why have you gone so red?' Bobby asked, not missing a thing.

'It's because she likes Uncle Jack,' Penny said, and Hazel looked up in horror.

'I . . . I . . . It's not that,' Hazel spluttered. 'I'm just . . . I'm . . .' *Oh God!* Where had all the words gone? Why couldn't she think of a thing to say? And now everyone was staring at her, waiting. This was the longest time that no one had said anything ever. She was on the spot, her cheeks flaming, her armpits tingling with embarrassment and her mind was blank.

'Hazel, would you like to help me make a cup of tea?' Bella asked.

'I'd like that very much,' Hazel said as she stood up and tucked her chair under the table, avoiding eye contact with Jack, Penny and Bobby. Head down, she followed Bella across the kitchen and stood in front of the sink, staring at the window but not seeing anything.

'Are you OK?' Bella whispered as she filled the kettle.

'I think so.'

'I'm sorry about my daughters. They can be so frank. They embarrass me all the time.'

'Really?' Hazel asked.

'Oh yes.' Bella knitted her brows. 'When we lived in Woking and I started work as a teaching assistant, I was at a school where one of the teachers didn't seem to like me. He wasn't a bad person as such but he was a perfectionist and he had a way of making me feel that I got a lot of things wrong. I tried not to let it get to me but it was hard. No one wants to feel like a failure, do they?'

'Of course not.' Hazel watched Bella's face, her heart going out to this kind and caring woman who couldn't possibly have deserved such treatment.

'Anyway, I spoke to the head teacher about it in the end because I thought I needed more training or some help to do a better job and it turned out that he was the same with all female colleagues. He had a chip on his shoulder and so the head teacher spoke to him and things improved. However, I digress . . . My point was that the girls have always managed

152

to show me up in some way or another. During that difficult period, I had quite an upset tummy. The GP said it wasn't IBS but rather an anxiety thing. I used to need the toilet a lot more than usual. Excuse me if this is TMI, but some mornings I'd need to go two or three times before I left the house.'

'How awful.'

Bella gazed past Hazel's shoulder, remembering. 'Tell me about it. Lee was very concerned and so was I. It did pass eventually, but one day, as I was about to get the girls into the car, I needed to go to the toilet again so I ran inside and did what I had to do while Lee waited with the girls. When I came back out, Bobby, who was only three at the time, shouted at the top of her voice, "Mummy three poos!".'

Hazel's mouth fell open. 'She didn't.'

'She did and I was mortified. She was right, but I didn't exactly want the neighbours knowing.'

'But it got better?'

'Yes. After the anxiety died down. It was stress at the thought of going into work and being told I was getting everything wrong again.'

'That was bullying, you know?'

'I know. Lee said as much but I didn't want to rock the boat and so I kind of let it go after the head teacher dealt with it. But it's something I never want to go through again and something I never want anyone else to experience.'

'Bella, that's awful.'

Bella's eyes brightened. 'It's in the past now, and the school here is fabulous. All the staff are friendly and I'm thoroughly enjoying myself. Not that my daughters don't drop me in it from time to time, but I'm more able to laugh it off now.

Bobby has a big mouth and tells everyone my secrets, so I have to laugh or I'd never go anywhere.'

'Kids, eh?'

'Wouldn't be without them, but they don't spare my blushes. Anyway, I *am* sorry that they made you squirm too, but I'm hoping there was no harm done.'

'None at all.' Hazel looked over at the table where Jack was sitting very still as Bobby dabbed at his cheek.

'Looks like Bobby's found a way to make Jack sparkle,' Bella said.

'He seems like a good man,' Hazel said before she could stop herself. 'Especially with glittery cheeks.'

Bella nodded. 'He is. He's been through some tough times but he's coming out the other side now. I'm so glad he's come to stay for Christmas and, if I get my way, he'll move here too.'

'With his partner?' Hazel asked, feigning interest in a fingernail that somehow had glitter under it.

'No.' Bella handed Hazel a mug and gazed over at her brother and sighed. 'He'd be alone if he wasn't here.'

'Oh.' Hazel wondered what had happened to Jack and if he'd been through something similar to her.

'It's one of the reasons I want him here. I want to involve him in our family more and keep an eye on him. He's my baby brother and with our parents living in Florida, I worry about him. I know he's a grown man and all that, but everyone needs family around, don't they?'

Hazel sipped her tea, avoiding replying. She wished she had family around, a big sister like Bella to be there for her and nieces she could spend Sunday afternoons with.

'Thanks so much for inviting me over, Bella. I've had a lovely time.'

'Even with bossy Bobby?'

'Especially with her. Your girls are adorable and I've laughed more this afternoon than I've done in ages.'

'That's good to hear.' Bella placed a hand on her arm. 'You're always welcome at our table.'

Hazel nodded, not trusting herself to speak. Jack was a lucky man and he should definitely stay in the village where he'd have everything he needed to help him to heal from whatever it was he'd been through. As for Hazel herself, she was glad she'd moved here and she hoped that Bella would be her friend because she was one of the kindest people Hazel had ever met. Hazel knew she wasn't at her most trusting right now after what had happened in Scotland, but a friend like Bella could help with that; she was the type of person who invited confidence and inspired faith in humanity.

'Once you've finished your tea, do you fancy taking Aster for a walk?' Bella asked.

'I'd love that.' Hazel said.

'Jack!'

'Yes, sister dear.'

'Have a cuppa then take Aster out, will you? Hazel said she could do with a walk to burn off your Yorkshire puddings.'

'No problem,' Jack said then returned his attention to Bobby.

Hazel looked at Bella. She'd been expecting to go with Bella and possibly the girls. Was her new friend trying her hand at matchmaking? But Bella's expression was one of innocence.

'You don't mind, do you?' Bella asked as she loaded mugs and biscuits onto a tray. 'I just thought it might be nice for you to have a chat without the girls around and to enjoy a walk in the fresh air.'

'N-no, I don't mind at all.'

'Wonderful.' Bella flashed her a smile. 'I'll take these through to the others. Are you coming or are you staying here with Jack and the girls?'

Bella had placed an emphasis on *Jack*, Hazel felt sure, and she willed herself not to blush again.

'I'll come through with you for a moment. I need to check something with Clare and Sam about their wedding attire.'

'Fabulous.'

Bella carried the tray through to the lounge and Hazel followed her, trying not to notice Jack's eyes on her as she left the kitchen, trying not to notice the way her heart had fluttered at the thought of spending some time with him.

Alone.

Very soon.

❄

Jack clipped Aster's lead to her harness then stepped out of the front door. The chill hit him immediately, swirling around his legs and making him grateful for his jeans and thick socks.

'It's chilly out here,' he said to Hazel. 'Do you have a hat and gloves?'

'I have gloves and my coat.'

'I can lend you a hat. Hold on.' Bella went to the under-stairs cupboard and returned with a red bobble hat. 'It's clean.'

'Thanks. I wouldn't have thought otherwise.' Hazel smiled and pulled the bobble hat on.

'Suits you,' Jack said.

'That's good to know. I'd hate to look like a fashion disaster on a dog walk through the woods.'

He laughed. Hazel was funny and sweet. He'd enjoyed their afternoon card making session with his nieces and could tell that Hazel was kind and patient; she'd certainly been patient with Bobby who was, though he hated to admit it, a bit of a mini diva.

'Have fun, you two.' Bella closed the door and they set off.

'Do you have poo bags?' Hazel asked.

'Yes.' He patted his coat pocket. 'Bella made sure I had a roll of them. Aster likes to go a lot.'

Hazel giggled. 'My cat's like that.'

'You have a cat?'

'I do,' she replied. 'She uses a litter tray at the moment, though. I haven't let her outside yet because I wanted her to settle in properly first. I'm just worried that she'll go out and run off but I guess I'll have to let her out sooner or later.'

'What breed is she?'

'A Ragdoll.'

'I don't think I've heard of that one.'

'She's fluffy and cream with a brown tail and paws. She's adorable.'

'Was she expensive?' he asked.

'No, she's a rescue. I paid a fee to the RSPCA for her but that was all. She's really sweet and affectionate.'

'I like cats.'

'You do?'

'Well, I like all animals, really,' he said.
'Me too.'

❄

Jack just kept getting better and better. Lennox had hated Fleas and resisted Hazel's attempts to adopt another cat. But Jack liked animals and Hazel believed that showed a person's true character. Another advantage of being single – she tried to list these advantages daily – was that she could have Fleas in bed with her. Lennox had always complained if Fleas went upstairs, hating that her fur got on his clothes and complaining that her morning breath was repellent. Hazel had bitten her tongue to stop herself retorting that his morning breath was far worse than any cat's, but now she wished she'd told him and not saved his feelings. That was something she'd make sure she did if ever she got into another relationship – which she wouldn't do, of course, but she would allow herself the thought – she'd be completely honest and not spare her partner's feelings as much as she had with Lennox. He'd been pretty emotionally brutal with her at times, even though back then she'd tried to ignore how some of his comments could sting because she loved him and didn't want to rock the boat. Relationships were about compromise and back then she'd believed that she had to accept that Lennox did not see her in the way she often wished he had, and she'd told herself that it was OK because they were only human and no relationship was without flaws.

Having lost her mum and her dad within a year of each other, Lennox had been Hazel's only family and so she had clung to him and to what they had. The funny thing was, though, now she actually was alone it wasn't that bad at all. She was able to look at herself and her abilities and to start trusting herself again. During her relationship with Lennox she had lost sight of herself and who she was, had compromised so far that she was bending over backwards while he got his own way. It was only now, being apart from him, that she had the space to realise these things. There was no man highlighting her weaknesses, insinuating that she was 'highly strung' for asking him to put his dishes in the dishwasher or for crying when she felt sad. How did those things make someone highly strung? It was downright insulting and yet Lennox had said it to her and she'd let him. Love was complicated and led to people accepting things they never thought they would and Hazel wanted nothing more to do with it.

Never again!

'Are you OK?' Jack asked as they walked past the children's park and the pub The King then past the bistro.

'I'm fine, thanks. Sorry . . . I got a bit lost in my thoughts there.'

'Happens to us all.' He flashed her a smile.

'I haven't been this way before,' Hazel said. 'Is it nice?'

'Yes. It's very quiet and pretty, even in winter.'

Soon, they were on the path that led through the woodland. Trees towered over them, mature English oaks, purple-brown alders and silvery-grey sycamores. Many were completely bare of leaves, their branches reaching towards the sky like gnarled fingers. The vivid red of holly berries and prickly green leaves added colour to the palette of browns and greys. Ahead of them, a tiny robin, its red breast a beautiful burst of colour, hopped from a tree to the ground then back again as if leading the way.

'They say that robins are the spirits of loved ones come to see us,' Hazel said. 'I like to think that that could be my mum.'

Jack glanced at her. 'You think that robin could be your mum?'

'Well . . . It would be nice if she did come back to see me.'

'When did you lose her?'

'Two years ago. She had a heart attack.'

'I'm sorry. What about your dad?'

'We lost him the year before. He had cancer. He was a smoker in his youth but had quit a few years before. Too late to make a difference, it seemed. I think my mum was literally broken-hearted and after she lost him she faded away, then her heart gave up.'

'That's sad. They must have loved each other very much, but it must have been difficult losing them both within such a short space of time.'

'I miss them terribly.'

'Did they live in Scotland?'

'Yes, but Mum was Welsh.'

'Where in Wales was she from?' he asked.

'She was from Cardiff and Dad was from Edinburgh. They met when Mum was in her early twenties. She was on holiday in Scotland with some friends and when she and Dad met, they fell hard for each other. Dad came to Cardiff to be with her and they married soon after. They simply couldn't bear to be apart. They were lucky to find love like that.'

'Very lucky. It sounds like a fairy tale. So how did you end up in Edinburgh?'

'My dad worked for my maternal grandfather's building firm and when my grandad died, they moved to Scotland to be near his mother, who wasn't well by that point.'

'So that explains your accent then.'

'My mixed-up accent.'

'I like it. I'm used to the Welsh accent because I live in Swansea but I like how your accent has some Scottish in it too. It's really musical.'

Hazel laughed. 'Thanks.'

'So why did you move here?'

Hazel pulled her collar up and hugged herself.

'I . . . I had a wedding planning business in Edinburgh. It was very successful.'

'Inspired by your parents' love?'

'I think so. They were meant to be and who wouldn't find that inspirational? I wanted to see other couples be as happy as they were.'

'You love your job?'

'Very much.'

'So you've come here to spread that enthusiasm for love.'

He'd picked up on her hesitation when he'd asked why she'd moved to England and didn't want her to feel uncomfortable by pressing for more information.

'Exactly.' She flashed him a smile. 'And I found my fiancé and maid of honour together . . . the day before my wedding.'

'Shit!' He frowned. 'That's awful.'

'It was.'

They slowed their pace as Aster sniffed at a bush and Jack met Hazel's gaze.

'Are you all right now?'

She shrugged. 'Some days. It was only back in June.'

'Not long at all.'

She shook her head. 'After that happened I tried to stay in Scotland but it was too difficult. My maid of honour was also my business partner and I couldn't bear seeing her every day so I sold my half of the business to her and fled.'

'How did you end up in Little Bramble?'

Hazel blushed. 'I stuck a pin in a map.'

'Wow!'

'I'm joking! I came here when I was ten on a family holiday. When I needed somewhere to go, I thought of this beautiful village.'

He smiled, liking that she'd teased him. 'I think that you were incredibly brave doing that.'

'You do?' Her brows furrowed.

'Yes. You left everything you knew behind and moved to make a fresh start. You've not only moved a long way to a place I'm taking it you didn't know very well, but you've also set up a new business. In fact, you're probably the bravest person I've ever met.'

Hazel looked away, gazing through a gap in the trees across the fields. He watched her, admiring how her turquoise-blue eyes seemed luminous in her pretty face and wondered how anyone could have hurt her. She seemed so gentle and sweet, determined and yet vulnerable. She'd lost both of her parents in a short space of time and that would have damaged anyone, but to then have her fiancé break her heart on top of it all would have been dreadful. And yet here she was, still standing, rebuilding her business in a different location. She was strong and brave, braver than he could ever imagine being. At least he had Bella, but it sounded like Hazel had no one. Her fiancé must be a horrible person and if Jack ever met him he'd like to give him a piece of his mind!

'You know what?' he said. 'When you first mentioned the robin thing, I was a bit taken aback. I'm not religious or superstitious and it sounded a bit . . . daft. But now that I know more about you, it makes sense. Whether that robin is just a pretty little bird or some sort of spiritual sign doesn't matter. What does matter is that seeing it gives you some comfort.'

Hazel watched his face carefully, wondering if he was being genuine. 'Do you mean that?'

'Why?' His eyes widened slightly.

'Well . . .' She looked down at her boots and scuffed the toe of one over a clump of grass. 'Because some people think it's silly to believe things like that.'

'Well, we all lose people in one way or another and any loss is awful. Whether we've lost a partner to . . . death or an affair, it's going to hurt and we're going to grieve.' He leant over and rubbed Aster's soft head and the dog wagged her long tail.

'I don't want to pry into *your* past,' she said. 'But if you ever want to talk, I'm a good listener.'

'Thanks, I appreciate that. And the same here – if you ever want someone to talk to about things.'

She sighed. 'We're like some sort of lonely-hearts club.'

Jack looked up and felt himself smile in spite of the nature of their conversation. 'I guess we are. A card making, dog walking club for two.'

'I guess that means we can be friends then? If we have something so important in common.'

'I guess so.' He felt a tug on the lead and looked at Aster. 'Great timing, girl!'

Hazel giggled as he pulled the roll of poo bags from his pocket.

'Never work with animals or children.'

'There's sense in that.' He tidied up after Aster. 'Right then, let's find a poo bin then head back to Bella's, shall we? I don't know about you but I can feel an urge for a hot chocolate coming on.'

'Sounds like a great idea.'

'Come on, Aster.'

The greyhound trotted along next to him on one side and Hazel walked on the other. She was close enough that he could have wrapped an arm around her shoulders if he'd felt it was appropriate. He would have liked to hug her just to reassure her that everything was going to be all right, but he wasn't sure how welcome his touch would be. However, he was happy to have Hazel as a new friend, because he liked her company and suspected that she felt the same way about him. He wished he was ready to open up fully about his past but he wasn't quite there, not yet.

Chapter 15

'Where shall we start?' Kyle asked, hands clasped over his chest, a big grin on his face.

Hazel had caught the train into London with Clare, Kyle and Jenny, the maid of honour. It had been three days since she'd had lunch at Bella's and since then she'd thought a lot about what Jack had said about her being brave. She hadn't thought of herself as brave before; she'd seen what she did as running away. But she liked how Jack had framed it and perhaps he was right; there was something brave about starting again on your own.

'I'm still not sure this is a good idea.' Clare gnawed at a cuticle. 'I'm forty-six. Do they make wedding dresses for women of my age? I mean, none of the dresses at the wedding fayre seemed right for me.'

'Mum!' Kyle rolled his green eyes then fluffed his thick brown hair. 'Will you stop saying that? I'm sick of hearing it and I'm sure Hazel is too. You are *not* old and you are going to find a gorgeous dress. Sam will be expecting a beautiful bride and that's what we're going to give him.'

'Give?' Clare grimaced.

'You know what I mean. Now, ladies, let's shop till we drop. We're hitting Oxford Street first.'

Kyle grabbed Clare's hand and dragged her along while Hazel and Jenny followed. Hazel had agreed to join them to provide an extra opinion as Clare had confided on Sunday afternoon that she was worried about what Kyle would try to get her to buy. Hazel was actually quite excited at the thought of a shopping trip with company and wondered what Kyle would get up to today because so far he'd proved to be fabulous company.

They walked past shops selling well-known brands of clothing, mobile phones and jewellery then past some boutiques and shoe shops, but Kyle kept driving them forwards.

'Where are we going, Kyle?' Clare asked, slightly breathless. 'We've passed some shops we could have looked in.'

'You are not getting your wedding dress from just any shop, Mum.'

'But I don't want to fuss too much, Kyle.'

'No more protests. I know the perfect place.' Kyle flashed a smile at Hazel and Jenny. 'You've been unable to make up your own mind, even after that fabulous wedding fayre Hazel took us to, so now you're going to get a little help.'

With less than a month until Christmas, the city was busy. People hurried along laden with shopping bags, heads down, staring at smartphones and eating on the go, as if they didn't even have time to stop for lunch. When Kyle suddenly stopped walking, Hazel almost crashed into the back of him.

He pulled his phone out of his pocket and looked at the screen. Over his shoulder Hazel saw that he was using Google Maps.

'It seems to be along this side street. Come on.'

He turned and Clare glanced backwards at Hazel and Jenny and grimaced. She was worried about where her son was taking them.

'OK.' Kyle held up his hands and they all stopped. 'There's a new boutique here that I read about. It's small and not cheap, but I think it will be perfect for Mum because it's classy, just like her.'

'You think I'm classy?' Clare asked.

'You are the classiest woman I know, Mum.' Kyle smiled at Clare, his eyes shining.

Clare placed a hand over her chest and gazed at Kyle. 'I'm so lucky to be your mum.'

'Yes, well . . .' Kyle sniffed then fluttered his eyelashes. 'We know that, don't we?' He laughed and they all joined in.

'Are we going in?' Hazel asked, keen to see what type of dress Kyle thought would suit Clare.

'Indeed we are.' Kyle gave a small bow. 'After you, ladies.'

As the door opened, an old-fashioned bell tinkled, making Hazel wonder if they'd been catapulted back in time. The boutique smelt of lilies and jasmine, a strong but not unpleasant scent. There wasn't much room inside because of the rails groaning with garments that stood in the middle of the floor and those fixed around the walls, but it was like walking into an Aladdin's cave of silk, satin and rhinestones. Every surface had shoes, tiaras, handbags and other wedding paraphernalia on it and there were mirrors everywhere – behind the rails, on every spare inch of wall and behind the counter – and light bounced off them, making the shop seem very bright. A tall, thin woman with a snow-white bouffant hairstyle was standing behind the counter, weighing them up. Hazel could imagine her wondering if they were serious shoppers or just there for a nose and if they could afford what she was selling.

'Hello.' Kyle approached the counter.

'Hello.' The woman raised her purple-tinged, pencilled-in eyebrows a fraction. 'Is there anything I can help you with today?'

'There is indeed.' Kyle leant an arm on the counter. 'We are looking for a beautiful dress for my beautiful mother.'

A smile graced the woman's lips and she softened in front of their eyes. 'Well, my name's Agnes and I'm here to help. Which one of you is the bride?'

'That's me.' Clare raised a hand like a pupil in class, looking as uncomfortable as if she was being singled out by a particularly strict teacher.

Agnes came around the counter and slid a tape measure from around her neck. 'Summer wedding, is it?'

Panic crossed Clare's face. 'Winter, actually.'

'Next year?' Agnes fired the question.

'This month, actually.' Clare had gone ashen, as if she feared that she was about to have a telling-off from Agnes. 'And it's outdoors too.'

'Well . . .' Agnes held up the tape measure. 'We'd better get a move on.'

'It's too late, isn't it? I told Kyle that we should just get something from Marks & Spencer or John Lewis. They'll have something perfectly nice, I'm sure.'

'That might well be true, Mum, but you never spoil yourself and I want you to try this place first.'

'We have some very reasonably priced dresses or wedding outfits if you want something less traditional,' Agnes said as she wrapped the tape measure around Clare, moving her this way and that as if Clare was a mannequin. 'OK, I have your measurements so I'll go and get some garments in your size then you can try them on.'

'Thanks.' Clare tried to smile but her face contorted strangely and Hazel worried that she was about to cry.

'Push that curtain there aside and go on through to the changing rooms.' Agnes gestured at a yellow velvet curtain at the rear of the boutique. 'You can all go with her.'

Agnes disappeared behind a different curtain and they heard footsteps ascending a staircase.

'She's gone upstairs to find the best dresses.' Kyle grinned. 'This is so exciting! I can't wait to see what she brings down for you.'

'I'm not so sure about this, Kyle.' Clare grabbed his arm. 'Perhaps we should make a run for it now.'

'Have you seen the prices of some of this stuff?' Jenny's eyes widened as she held up the label on a cream bolero jacket hanging on the rail next to her.

'How much?' Clare's voice was barely a whisper.

'Three thousand and fifty.'

'Pounds?' Clare gasped.

'Yes.'

'We need to leave!'

Kyle was shaking his head. 'Absolutely not.' He pushed his mother towards the changing room and Hazel and Jenny followed them in.

'I can't afford this.' Clare was shaking her head.

'It's fine. Nanna gave me some money that she said was for your wedding and Sam did too and—'

'Nanna? My mother gave you money?' Clare frowned. 'She had money for my wedding? But I've been married before and she helped out with that wedding. I don't understand.'

'She said that she had money put aside for you anyway for when she dies and that she wanted you to have some of it towards a wedding outfit. Plus, Sam knew you'd be worried and so he's contributed to the fund too.'

'What? Kyle, how long have you been organising this?'

Kyle tapped the side of his nose. 'That's for me to know and for you to stop worrying about. You have a very generous budget so just find something you like and I'll let you know if you can afford it.'

Clare looked at Jenny then at Hazel. 'My mother said she couldn't make it today and that's fine, I didn't expect her to come shopping because it's not really her thing. Obviously, I've done this before, and I'm hardly a sweet young blushing bride, but . . . Oh, I don't know what I'm trying to say really. I'm just surprised that she's done this. Not that she's not got a generous side but putting money away for me? I am surprised at that. I'm not wasting lots of money on a dress I'll never wear again, though. I'll choose something sensible that I can wear again for another special occasion. I'm not about to buy some flouncy, frilly, lacey—'

'Mum.' Kyle pointed at where Agnes was standing in the doorway, holding a variety of dresses over her arms.

'I guess it would be rude not to try them on.' Clare shrugged and Kyle nodded vigorously.

Jack carried one end of the wooden bench while Lee carried the other. He'd come to The Lumber Shed to help out and was enjoying spending time with other people as well as the physical labour. He liked his brother-in-law and the boss, Connor Jones. The rest of the staff at the workshop had made him feel very welcome and he'd also enjoyed the banter among them.

'Anything else to put in the van?' he asked Lee.

'I think that's it but I'll just double-check with Connor,' Lee said. 'We'll probably have to do a few more deliveries later anyway. With Christmas just around the corner there's plenty to do. People like to get their homes just right for the big day.'

'Strange how we do that, isn't it?' Jack shook his head. 'So much fuss just for Christmas.'

'Madness, right? But, having said that, it gives people an excuse to get things in order, I suppose.'

'True.'

'Back in five.' Lee jogged back inside and Jack leant against the van and gazed at The Lumber Shed. It was a large converted barn and the simple exterior concealed the hive of activity inside. A bit like people, he thought. A bit like Hazel.

Since his walk with Hazel on Sunday, he'd thought about her quite a bit. Aside from the fact that she was very attractive, there was so much more to her and he wanted to get to know her better. The thought was uplifting and yet scary at the same time, because he worried that he didn't know his own mind after what he'd been through and the last thing he wanted was to hurt Hazel.

He decided to try to go with the flow and not to rush into anything. He didn't even know if she liked him anyway, so there was, he guessed, no point in counting his chickens. After all, no one knew what would happen tomorrow and it was best just to take life one day at a time.

✻

'Here you go.' Agnes carried a tray of champagne into the changing rooms. When everyone had a glass, she smiled. 'If you need any help, just call me.'

'Thanks, Agnes.' Kyle bobbed his head.

'I thought they only did this in movies.' Jenny grinned. 'It's a bit special, isn't it?'

'And one of the reasons why I chose this boutique.' Kyle sniffed, then pulled out his smartphone.

Hazel cringed inwardly. He wasn't going to start taking photos in here, was he? Clare had gone into a cubicle with one of the dresses and pulled the heavy gold curtain across, leaving Hazel, Kyle and Jenny sitting on the gold velvet sofa outside while she changed.

'Where's that music coming from?' Clare's voice came from behind the curtain.

Hazel looked around. She hadn't realised that music was playing, but now she was aware that she'd been tapping her foot to the beat.

'It's on my phone, Mum,' Kyle said. 'It's the *Pretty Woman* soundtrack. I thought it would be perfect to listen to while you shopped.'

'Kind of like a soundtrack to my life,' Clare said.

'Exactly.' Kyle raised his glass, pinky finger sticking out as he drank.

'OK, I'm ready.'

'Well, come on out then,' Kyle said, crossing his legs and leaning back against the plush fringed cushions.

The curtain swished across and Clare stood there.

Kyle snorted.

Hazel bit her tongue.

Jenny gasped.

'It's awful, isn't it?' Clare shuffled out to them, her top half seeming to move a lot faster than her legs.

'You look like a penguin.' Kyle handed Hazel his glass then stood up and went over to Clare. He placed his hands on her shoulders and turned her around so Hazel and Jenny could see the back of the dress. 'I mean, for a start it's black and white. And what's with the tight hem and the . . . God, this side zip won't even do up, Mum!'

Clare's cheeks were glowing as she clung to the bodice of the dress. 'I think this was made for people with very strange proportions.'

'Jessica Rabbit, perhaps?' Kyle raised his eyebrows and shook his head. 'Get it off and try another.'

Clare shuffled back behind the curtain.

Kyle sat down again, making Hazel bob on the sofa. He placed a hand on his forehead and muttered, 'I bloody well hope the next one is better than that otherwise we'll have to consider an alternative shop.'

'It wasn't the best, was it?' Jenny said. Her eyes were shining and Hazel noticed that she'd already downed most of her drink. Jenny saw Hazel looking at her glass and grinned. 'I don't drink much these days because of the babies so this has gone straight to my head.'

'It's nice to have a treat though,' Hazel said, wondering how Jenny managed with two young babies. It must be exhausting. 'And I'm sure you deserve a day off.'

'It's very nice to have a break, although I'll be glad to get back to them later. That's motherhood for you. You love them so much you can't bear to be parted from them but you long for some time alone just to breathe. I mean, I don't even get time to go to the toilet alone most days because one of them always needs me.'

'That must be challenging.'

'It can be. Although I have mastered the art of peeing superfast while almost standing up, sometimes with one of the twins under my arm like a rugby ball.'

Hazel's mind boggled. She couldn't even imagine how that would work.

'Jenny, darling . . .' Kyle widened his eyes. 'Please, please tell me we're not about to enjoy a rendition of how low are my baby boobs and how bad is my post-natal incontinence?'

'Kyle, you cheeky bugger! I'm not that bad.' Jenny chuckled.

'She is, Hazel! I've heard it all when her and Mum get going. Leaky boobs, stretch marks from one hip to the other and as for the lady garden stories!' He shuddered. 'It's enough to put you off for life.'

'Don't listen to him. Kyle likes women too.'

'Of course I do. Women and men are equally beautiful in my eyes. I just don't want to think about stitched perineums or varicose veins popping out where the sun doesn't shine.'

Hazel sniggered. Kyle did not hold back.

'Ta da!' Clare stood before them once more and it was like a scene in a movie. Everything seemed to stop as she floated towards them.

'That's a lot of feathers, Dame Edna.' Kyle stood up and went over to his mother. 'Good job you're not allergic.'

'I quite like this even if it is a bit over the top.' Clare twirled for them and the white feathers made her look as though she was about to take off.

'It's a bit much, Mum.' Kyle wrinkled his nose. 'Imagine how Goliath would react if he saw you in this.'

Clare chewed at her bottom lip. 'He'd probably try to eat it and I'm sure Scout would have a go too.'

'And then you'd be walking down the aisle in just a sheath.'

'You're right.' Clare floated back to the changing cubicle.

'Let's hope the next one's better,' Hazel said.

'How are we getting on?' Agnes popped her head around the curtain that led to the shop floor.

'Two down, two to go.' Kyle sighed as if Agnes had really let him down.

'Which ones has she tried?' Agnes asked.

'Penguin and ostrich,' Kyle said.

'Oh . . . shame. I thought they'd suit her. Shout if you need me. I have plenty more if the other two aren't right.'

'We will.'

Agnes disappeared and there was a swoosh as Clare pulled back the curtain and emerged in a waterfall of champagne silk. The dress was like something out of a regency drama, gathered in just under the bust with a long floaty skirt that almost reached the floor. It had lace sleeves and, as Clare turned, Hazel saw that the back was made of lace too. Kyle buttoned it up, from Clare's waist to her nape, then she turned again, and tears sprang into Hazel's eyes.

'Oh my goodness, Clare, that's the one!'

Clare gazed down at herself. 'I think it is. It fits so well, it could have been made for me.'

'Do the catwalk, Mum.'

'Really?' Clare grimaced.

'Yes!' Kyle clapped his hands and Clare walked towards one wall then turned and walked towards the other.

'Only me!' Agnes announced as she hurried in. 'Brought these to go with the champagne dress . . . Wow!' She froze as she admired Clare. 'I *knew* that one would be perfect.'

'I love it.' Clare looked down at herself.

'Try these.' Agnes set a pair of champagne-coloured lace boots on the floor in front of Clare. She slid them onto Clare's feet then tied the ribbon laces. 'They're Victorian style so look very elegant, but you can wear thick socks under them to keep your feet warm.'

'Good thinking,' Clare replied.

'And this.' Agnes held out a faux fur wrap that she placed over Clare's shoulders then fastened in place. 'I have gloves that match it so you can fully coordinate if you like.'

'It will be perfect for an outdoor wedding.' Hazel stood up and admired the outfit.

'It will – but I do hope you're having heaters.'

'It's all taken care of,' Hazel said. 'I'm a wedding planner.'

Agnes' eyes lit up. 'Why didn't you say anything before? That's incredibly exciting. We must exchange details and we can cross-promote.'

'That would be wonderful.' Hazel gave herself a mental high five. This was what she needed. Women in business supporting one another, recommending each other to clients. It was how a successful business grew.

'Jenny? What do you think?' Clare stepped forwards and Jenny stood up, swaying slightly. 'Are you crying?'

'A bit.' Jenny accepted a tissue from Agnes, who seemed to have all bases covered. 'It's the champagne making me emotional. I won't hold it together as maid of honour.'

'You're the maid of honour?' Agnes asked.

'I am,' Jenny replied.

'I have just the thing!'

Agnes disappeared and they heard her climbing the stairs then moving around above their heads.

'I didn't mean for that to happen,' Jenny said.

'It's fine.' Kyle drained his glass. 'We've budgeted for you too.'

Jenny looked bewildered as Clare slid an arm around her shoulders and they waited for Agnes to return.

An hour and a half and another two glasses of champagne later, they emerged onto the street in a bubble of laughter and excitement. The dress Agnes had brought down for Jenny was perfect, everything had been paid for and they'd arranged to collect the dresses the Monday before the wedding.

They walked down to Oxford Street and Hazel sighed as she looked around her. It was the perfect December scene. Shop fronts were decorated with fake snow, lights and Christmas scenes. Fairy lights hung from lampposts and crisscrossed over the road, twinkling like suspended stars. There was a sense of festive magic in the air and her skin tingled while something stirred in her belly. It was a pleasant feeling, one she hadn't felt in some time and she embraced it, recognising it as hope and even excitement. Life had been hard recently and she'd kept going even when she'd wanted to hide under the duvet and ignore the world. But now, with the worst year of her life behind her and a new one on the horizon, she could start again. She had a new home, a new business and, best of all in her opinion, new friends.

When her phone started ringing in her bag, she accepted the call without hesitation, even though the screen showed a number she didn't recognise.

'Hello! This is Hazel Campbell from Country Charm Weddings. How can I help you today?'

But as a familiar voice said her name, the sky crashed down around her ears and her knees almost buckled.

Kyle took her arm and mouthed, *What's wrong?* She shook her head but held on to him, fearing that if she let go she'd end up on the pavement.

'How did you get this number, Lennox?'

Chapter 16

Jack had been for a run, showered and dressed then gone over to Bella's house to make breakfast for everyone. He'd picked up supplies from the village shop on his way back from the run because he thought it would be nice to surprise them with a cooked breakfast.

He'd been right. Sitting at the table in Bella's kitchen with Aster's head resting on his thigh, he looked around at his family. *His family . . .* That sounded so good. How could he have thought he was alone for so long when Bella and her family had been right there? Of course, he was conscious of not wanting to crowd them and that they needed their space, but Bella and Lee always made him feel so welcome and the girls had accepted him into their home with the same love and enthusiasm they'd had for Aster.

He sneaked Aster another piece of toast dipped in egg and she swallowed it down as if she hadn't eaten in weeks.

'She'll get fat, you know.' Bella shook her head. 'You're spoiling her.'

'She has such beautiful eyes and whenever she looks at me I just want to make her happy.'

'If you react like that towards every pretty female with beautiful eyes you'll find yourself very popular in this village.' Lee laughed then forked a piece of sausage into his mouth. 'Great breakfast, by the way,' he said when he'd swallowed.

'I've only got eyes for Aster,' Jack said, gazing down at the dog, who was gazing right back up at him.

'You'll have to stay forever now, Uncle Jack, because Aster loves you.'

Jack laughed. 'I'm here for Christmas because your mum and dad have been very generous in inviting me to stay but after that I'll have to get back to Swansea.'

'What?' Bobby slammed her knife and fork down. 'You are never bloody leaving this house!'

Jack looked from Bobby to Bella and tried to swallow his laughter.

'Bobby! What've I told you?' Bella frowned at her daughter.

'I know, stop saying *bloody*, but I don't want Uncle Jack to go. He has to stay.'

Bella looked over at Jack and she didn't need to say a word; he could see in her eyes how she was feeling. She didn't want him to go back to Wales either.

'Let's have a smashing Christmas then we can see if we can persuade Uncle Jack to stay in the village.' Lee gave Jack a brief nod, rescuing him from his family and letting him know that he wanted him to stay too. Lee and Jack got on well, but Jack knew it was more than that: Lee loved his wife and wanted her to be happy and he knew that she loved having her brother around.

'What are your plans today then, Uncle Jack?' Penny asked.

'Oh, well, I've been for a run and cooked breakfast so I'll probably take Aster for a W-A-L-K.' They'd taken to spelling the word because Aster became incredibly excited if she heard the word itself. Her ears pricked up at her name though and she tilted her head as if trying to work out what Jack had said.

'It's my day off too, so I'll do the food shop at some point, Jack, if you want to come.'

'Sure.' He nodded at Bella.

'Excuse me.' Lee held up his phone. 'It's Connor from work.'

He left the table and went through to the hallway.

'It's naughty to answer your phone at the table.' Bobby pouted.

'That's true, sweetheart, but if it's Daddy's work it could be important.'

'My teacher says there's nothing as important as spending time with family.' Bobby reached for her orange juice. 'She said you should always make the most of your family because you don't know how long they'll be around.'

Bobby's wisdom never ceased to amaze Jack, although, having said that, she could switch from being some sort of oracle to being a complete diva in seconds.

'That was rather insensitive, Bobby,' Penny said as she set her knife and fork down on her plate.

'What? What does that mean?' Bobby scowled at her sister.

'It means that you said something that could hurt someone's feelings.' Penny gestured at Jack.

'Why?' Bobby sipped her juice.

'Are you really *that* stupid?' Penny stood up and picked up her plate.

'Penny, please don't speak to your sister like that.' Bella yawned. 'Let's all try and be respectful.'

'Why am I stupid?' Bobby whined.

'Uncle Jack lost his wife,' Penny muttered, as if Jack wasn't sitting in the room with them.

'Oh!' Bobby slammed her hand over her mouth. 'I'm sorry.'

'It's fine.' Jack reached for her hand. 'I'm OK, I promise.'

'I didn't mean that about you. I was just saying what my teacher said.'

'And it's very good advice.' Jack smiled at her. 'Come here.'

Bobby got up and went to his side and he wrapped an arm around her.

'I love you being here, Uncle Jack. Please don't go back to Wansea.'

He hugged her tightly, smiling into her curls that smelt like the vanilla custard baby shampoo that Bella told him she used on Bobby. Apparently if she got shampoo in her eyes, she'd scream the house down. It had happened once when they'd moved to the village and the bathroom window had been open. A passer-by had thought something terrible was happening and knocked on the door to check no one was being murdered.

'I'll have a good think about staying here and not going back to Wansea after Christmas, OK?'

Bobby looked up at him. 'I'm going to ask Santa to buy you a house so you can live here near us.'

'That's very kind of you.' A lump rose in Jack's throat and he had to swallow hard. Being around his sister and nieces was making him more emotional than he knew how to handle. He looked down at Aster, who still had her head on his knee in spite of the fact that Bobby was leaning against her.

'How about if you sneak Aster one more small piece of toast then I'll sort the dishes?'

Bobby grinned and did as Jack suggested and the dog wagged her long tail.

'Sorry about that.' Lee came back into the kitchen. 'Connor asked if I could go in a bit early. We've got a lot on with Christmas coming and he's had two staff call in sick. Some winter bug that's going around.'

'I hope you don't catch it.' Bella went to her husband's side.

'Me too.' Lee rubbed a hand through his hair. 'Uh . . . Jack. I don't suppose you fancy another day at The Lumber Shed, do you? I know Bella loves having you here but there's some more furniture to shift and deliver and some of it's pretty heavy. Connor said he'd pay you for your time.'

Jack stood up. 'I'd love to help out.' It was the least he could do when his brother-in-law was asking him a favour. Besides which, he had enjoyed helping out there the previous day.

'Dress warmly then because we'll be outside again, loading and unloading. And wear something sturdy on your feet. Those trainers you had on yesterday wouldn't protect your toes if you dropped something on them.'

'I'll pop next door and get changed but I'll just do the dishes.'

'There's no need,' Lee said. 'I'll do them, you get ready.'

'Are you sure about this, Jack?' Bella asked as Jack went to the door.

'Absolutely.' Jack replied. 'I'm happy to help out if I can.'

As he let himself out, he thought that it would be nice to do something different today and to feel useful. He was conscious of not wanting to be a burden and moving furniture was certainly something he could do.

❄

The day had flown past and Jack had thoroughly enjoyed himself. As he stood in the workshop waiting for Lee to get his things, Connor clapped him on the back.

'Thanks for your help again today, Jack. We really appreciated you coming in.'

'It's no problem at all. I'm happy to help, although I can't do much.'

'Helping with the heavy lifting makes a big difference.' Connor smiled. 'Loading furniture on and off the vans is not easy.'

Jack shook his head. 'It's good exercise.'

'I don't suppose you fancy helping out again tomorrow, do you? I'll pay the going rate. It looks like that bug has wiped out some of my employees until next week and we could really use you again.'

'Sure. I'd like that.' Jack's back and shoulders were aching and he was tired but it had been a good experience. Jack had been impressed when Lee had shown him some of his carpentry work as well as Connor's. It seemed that Connor was putting something together for Sam and Clare's wedding and it was, Jack thought, pretty special.

'Are you staying in Little Bramble for Christmas?' Connor asked.

'Yes. I'll head back to Swansea in the New Year.'

'Do you have a job there?'

Jack shook his head. 'I'm between jobs, as they say.'

'He thinks he's going back but Bobby has other ideas,' Lee said as he arrived with his coat and bag.

'Oh yeah?' Connor laughed. 'Little girls and their strong wills. My Grace was the same at that age. She knew what she wanted and she wouldn't let it go. The times she drove Sadie up the wall by asserting her independence.' He gazed into the distance as if lost in his memories. 'You have any children, Jack?'

'Uh . . . no.' Jack shook his head. He shouldn't be surprised by the question but sometimes it did catch him off guard. People always wanted to know if he was married and if he had a family. It was, he guessed, natural to ask.

'It's not compulsory.' Connor shrugged. 'I was happily single for a long time.'

'Connor's back with his first love now,' Lee explained.

'Emma.' Connor's eyes lit up. 'Never thought it would ever happen but I'm over the moon that it did. We were apart for a very long time then she came back to the village to spend some time with her dad, Greg, and—'

'They couldn't stay away from each other,' Lee said.

'How'd you know all that?' Connor laughed.

'Legend has it.' Lee chuckled.

'Legend?'

'Yes. People talk in a small village.' He laughed. 'Besides which, every village should have a legend or two and Connor here is an absolute legend as a boss and as a friend.'

'Aww, thanks, mate.' Connor grinned at Lee. 'You after more time off over Christmas, are you?'

'Are you mad?' Lee shook his head. 'Bobby and Penny will be like bottles of pop and the more time I have away from that, the better.' He looked at Jack. 'Joking! As if I'd leave my beautiful Bella to deal with those two alone. We have a tricky situation this year too because Bobby is all excited about Santa coming and Penny . . . well, she's ten, so it's kind of different.'

'I remember those days.' Connor sighed. 'But my Grace is still in Paris and she will be until the spring. Emma and I went out to see her but she's so busy now and so . . . sophisticated. She hasn't really been my *baby* girl for a while so enjoy it while you can, Lee.'

'I try.'

'And you enjoy being an uncle, Jack.' Connor patted his pocket. 'Someone's ringing me so I'd better go. See you tomorrow.' He pulled his phone from his pocket then jogged up the stairs to his office.

'You ready then?' Lee asked.

'Ready.' Jack pulled on his coat.

'Fancy grabbing a beer on the way home?'

'Sounds like a great idea.' Jack smiled. 'This day just gets better and better.'

Chapter 17

Hazel strolled around the festive fayre at Hampton Court. Set in front of the magnificent palace, the fayre was the perfect Christmas attraction with fairy lights twinkling on the small white stalls. It was the first Saturday of December and winter was settling in like an unwelcome visitor, taking hold of England in its icy grip and making the wind freezing, the ground frosty and the clouds shimmer with the possibility of snow.

Hazel, though, liked winter. Living in Scotland, she was used to cold winters and she didn't mind them. Winter had always been a time to snuggle up in front of a roaring fire and drink hot chocolate while reading a good book. She'd done this over the years with her mum and dad and then with Lennox, although he'd tended to watch sport on TV while she read. But it had worked for them. She missed that part of their relationship more than anything, the security of being able to sit comfortably with someone without talking, her feet on his lap, a throw over her legs. She'd thought they'd been in the same place, even if it wasn't the romantic place she'd hoped for after witnessing how much in love her parents had been. Lennox had been a bit tight with money, a bit grumpy now and then and he'd been addicted to watching sport, whereas Hazel liked reading romantic comedies. They'd had things in common but separate interests too and she'd thought that was how it should be. Getting together so young, they hadn't had the earth-trembling desire and the fireworks for a long time, but she'd been all right with that because their relationship seemed solid. Or so she'd thought. Then Lennox had apparently decided that he'd wanted the fireworks that were hiding underneath Valentina's tiny lacy thong.

She shuddered. She'd been so close to Valentina; the woman had been her supposed best friend for most of her adult life. They had been very different but that had never mattered before. Valentina believed in going after the men she wanted and Hazel had admired her for that. There was no sitting at home pining after men who didn't call. She was strong and independent, a good businesswoman, and together with Hazel they'd been a dream team. But outside of their wedding planning business, Hazel had wondered how Valentina could flit between sexual partners so quickly, as if they were pairs of shoes. Hazel never could imagine herself doing the same. She'd have got names confused for a start and was also quite shy, so the idea of being naked with a veritable stranger was more than she could stomach. Valentina, though, with her statuesque physique, cropped ginger hair and slate-grey eyes had no qualms about getting her kit off. Not even, as it turned out, with Hazel's fiancé.

Hazel stopped at a stall selling Christmas ornaments and picked up a small robin made of resin which she sat on the palm of her hand. It was so realistic she had to raise it to her face to have a closer look. Christmas songs travelled through the chilly air and part of her mind sang along, conditioned to do so since she was a child.

Lennox had told Hazel during their phone call three days ago, when she was in London with Clare, Jenny and Kyle, that it was all over between him and Valentina. Kyle had been holding Hazel up for support when Lennox had told her that he'd got her number from her new website after tracking her down on Google. He'd needed to tell her what a huge mistake he'd made. It had only taken him more than half a year but he said he'd needed that time to clear his head after Valentina had bewitched him. Hazel had almost laughed at that, then squeezed Kyle's hand so tightly he'd let out a screech that had almost brought Oxford Street to a standstill. She'd had to apologise profusely to him after she'd ended the call.

She'd been polite, she thought, as she stroked the robin's little brown head, had refrained from telling Lennox what a pig he was and had listened as he'd babbled on. But she'd felt nothing. Well, not nothing; she was only human and she had felt a spark of anger, but she'd managed to control it. She'd surprised herself with how different she felt now when not long ago she'd been furious with him and wondered if she'd ever stop feeling angry. She'd let Lennox get out everything he had to say, then told him that she had to go because she was with friends. He'd tried asking her more about her thoughts and feelings but she'd cut him off, only hearing the last thing he said: *I'll be in touch soon.* She bloody well hoped not, because Lennox Macanroy was the last person she wanted to see right now, just when she was getting her life back together again.

She put the robin back down on the table. She decided she'd come back later and, if he was still there, she might buy him. He was a little symbol of hope and enduring love and she needed more of that in her world.

❄

'Uncle Jack, I want a hot chocolate with cream and marshmallows and I want some roasted chestnuts and I want sweeties and—'

'Stop wanting things.' Penny interrupted, scowling at her younger sister. 'You can't have everything, you know.'

Bobby pouted and Jack had to swallow his laughter. He'd come to the festive fayre with Bella, Lee and the girls, and even though they'd only been there for five minutes, Bobby wanted a lot of things already. It was OK, though, because he was finding her enthusiasm infectious. With young children around there was no time for maudlin thoughts and self-pity.

'Uncle Jack!' Bobby gestured at him to come closer so he crouched down and she whispered in his ear, 'I also really, *really* want to see Santa.'

'I'm sure we can arrange that for you.' He winked at her and she gave him a cute smile that brightened everything around them. Christmas with his family was going to be very special indeed.

'Uncle Jack?' Penny tapped his arm, so he turned to her.

'Yes, Penny?'

'Are you any good at ice skating?'

Jack followed her finger, which was pointing to a sign for the open-air ice rink.

'I've been known to manage to stay upright on the ice.' He waggled his eyebrows.

'I've never tried and I'd like to have a go.'

'Penny Thornton, you have never been ice skating?'

She shook her head, a shy smile on her lips.

'Well, that is something we must remedy today.'

'It says you have to book a time slot.'

'Let's go and do that right now then.'

'Are we all going on the ice?' Bella asked.

'I will if you will.'

'Yes, please.' Bella nodded.

'I'll book for five then.' He pulled out his wallet.

'What about Aster?' Lee asked as they all looked down at the dog. She'd come with them because they hadn't wanted to leave her home alone all day. In her cosy, colourful fleece with her bright red collar and matching harness and lead, she looked very smart.

'We can take it in turns,' Jack said.

'Good plan,' Lee replied. 'I don't think Aster will want to get out on the ice.'

'She could use one of the penguins I've seen on the news when they show the ice skating at Hampton Court,' Penny said.

'Aster?' Jack frowned, wondering how that would work. Would they attach her lead to the penguin or place her front paws on the penguin's handles?

Penny laughed. 'Maybe not. It would be far too cold for her paws anyway.'

'Yes, it would.' Bella crouched down and gave Aster a hug. 'And we don't want our precious girl getting cold.'

'Back in a minute,' Jack said, then he jogged off with Penny to book a slot for later that day.

On the way back, he spotted a familiar figure weaving her way through the crowds. He watched as Hazel stopped at a stall and picked up a small robin, gazing at it as if it held the answers to every question she'd ever wanted to ask. Then she set it back down on the stall and moved on.

Jack knew what he had to do.

❄

'Hazel!'

She turned to see Jack waving at her.

'Oh, hello. Nice to see you here.'

He reached her and she found herself admiring the flush on his cheeks, his clear skin and brown eyes. He had the loveliest eyes and she felt sure that they emanated integrity and warmth.

'I'm here with Bella, Lee and the girls. And Aster, of course.'

'How lovely.'

'If you . . . uh . . .' He coughed. 'You're very welcome to join us.'

'Oh.' She raised her eyebrows.

'No pressure, though. I'm sure you have plenty to . . . look for . . . or to buy . . . or perhaps you're just here to visit Santa?' he said, hoping to lighten the mood.

'Santa's here?'

'Bobby's desperate to see him,' Jack said.

'I remember that feeling. My parents used to take me to see Santa when I was a little girl. Before we moved to Edinburgh, there was an old department store in Cardiff and we'd go to see him and his elves and I'd always come away filled with festive magic. It was such a special time and the excitement I felt was through the roof.'

Hazel closed her eyes for a moment as emotion surged, the grief for her parents hitting her like a fresh wave. Perhaps if she'd had a sibling she would have dealt with the pain better as there would have been someone there who understood, who had been a part of her wonderful family, but she hadn't been that lucky. She had always felt that she'd missed out by not having a brother or sister to reminisce with about her mum and dad and her happy childhood.

❄

'I can remember going with Bella and my parents in Woking,' Jack said, watching as Hazel closed her eyes for a moment then opened them, a faraway look passing across them for a few seconds, as if she'd been swept up in a memory.

He fell silent for a moment as he thought about his own happy times. He'd been so lucky to grow up in a loving home with a big sister he adored.

'There's nothing like the magic of Christmas when you're a child, is there?' Her tone was wistful, her eyes glistening.

Jack was hit by an urge to hug Hazel. He wanted to hold her to his chest, to feel her curves pressed against him and to stroke her soft hair. She deserved to feel excited about Christmas and to enjoy herself, not to feel sad or alone.

'Bobby has it in bucketloads.' He laughed. 'Look, I know you're probably busy but you could always join us for an hour or so – or perhaps later? It'll be worth it just to see Bobby meet Santa and Penny hit the ice for the first time.'

'Sorry?' Hazel's eyes widened.

'That came out wrong. God, I hope she doesn't hit the ice literally. Penny wants to go ice skating as she's never been before and I said I'd take her. I've booked us all in for a session after lunch. You could join us if you like.'

He watched her face carefully, trying to read her expression.

'That's very kind of you.'

He thought she was about to decline.

'And I'd love to.'

'You would?'

'Yes, please. I do need to have a mosey around first because I'm looking for some inspiration for Clare and Sam's wedding, but I could meet up with you in a bit?'

'Great!' He nodded perhaps a bit too enthusiastically. But he found himself really wanting her to join them. 'Here, have my number just in case anything pops up.'

Hazel typed it into her phone and sent him a text message with a smiley face that made his heart flutter. There was something about knowing that he had Hazel's number that made him feel excited.

'Shall we meet by the Christmas tree in an hour?' he asked.

'Brilliant.'

Hazel smiled at him then touched his arm. With her gloves and his thick jacket between them, there was no skin-to-skin contact, but something about it sent a thrill through him all the same.

As he headed back to his family, he found himself grinning as if he'd just received the best Christmas gift ever.

✳

Hazel checked her mobile for the time and saw that she had just five minutes left until she was due to meet Jack. She wished her stomach wouldn't keep somersaulting and that she could stop worrying about not having washed her hair – she had a hat on, after all. She didn't know why she was so anxious. Jack was a friend and so was Bella. She'd bumped into him and he'd invited her to spend some time with them today. There was nothing more to it than that. And yet . . . she liked Jack. In spite of all her reservations about ever being with another man, she couldn't help it. Not only was he hot, but he was kind and funny, a good brother and uncle, generous with his time and company. He did, however, have some baggage; anyone who'd been hurt would. Hazel, of course, had her own and she wondered if two people who had been hurt could have a successful relationship with each other. While she didn't know exactly what had happened to Jack, she knew he'd been married and that he wasn't any longer. They'd both probably needed time to heal before they could ever consider being with someone else. Hazel knew that Lennox had left her with some issues and that she would struggle to trust anyone else. She'd just have to accept that she did find Jack attractive and that was OK, but she couldn't take things further.

She hooked her shopping bag over her arm and made her way to the Christmas tree. Everywhere she looked, people were smiling, talking, eating and drinking. The air was laced with the smell of frying onions, hot dogs, glühwein, crêpes and other delights, and her mouth watered. Christmas music was being pumped out from speakers around the market and there was a chill in the air that made her wonder if there might be a possibility of snow. She pulled her coat collar tighter around her neck and her hat lower over her ears. Her life had changed immeasurably in the past year but Christmas would always be a magical time. She might not have a partner or her own wedding to look forward to, but she had things to be happy about. She had a roof over her head, her own baby business, her beloved cat and now she had friends who were waving to her from near the enormous tree that was draped with lights and tinsel.

Hazel knew she had a lot to be grateful for and she intended to focus on trying to forget about her past, not worrying about the future and enjoying today.

❄

Jack carried a tray of crêpes and frites over to the table where Bella was sitting with Hazel, Penny and Bobby. Lee had another tray laden with drinks. They set them down on the table then Jack sat down between Bella and Hazel.

'This looks delicious,' Bella said as she rubbed her hands.

'The hot chocolates are for Penny and Bobby and Lee wanted a Coke because he's driving.' Jack flashed Lee a smile. 'Sorry, Lee. Then the mugs of glühwein are for Bella, Hazel and me.'

'I'm glad I caught the train,' Hazel said.

'You could have had a lift back with us if we had room,' Bella said. 'But with Aster in there too, we're chock-a-block.'

'It's fine.' Hazel shook her head. 'But thank you.'

'Here you are, girls.' Bella handed them small cardboard trays of frites while Jack gave Hazel hers and then he sat back and sipped his drink. Warm and spiced with cinnamon and cloves, it warmed him right through and added to how festive he was feeling. He was surprised that he felt that way because the previous December had been dreadful and in the years before that Christmas had often been hectic, what with Danni working, visits to her parents and friends. He'd often been glad when it was all over so they could get back to normal, especially when Danni had to work Christmas Eve and Christmas Day, because he would often spend those days alone. He'd enjoyed Christmas when he was growing up and hoped to enjoy sharing in his nieces' excitement this year because when it came down to it, the holiday would be better for him with other people to focus on. He'd picked up some gifts this morning and hoped to get some more later because there was no way he was going to leave his Christmas shopping to the last minute like some sort of bad Santa.

After frites, everyone tucked into the crèpes with their various fillings and Bobby made them all laugh with her excitement over what she would ask Santa for and how she thought he would respond. Penny nudged her sister a few times and Bobby poked out her tongue, but now and then they smiled at each other as if they were conspirators involved in some great festive plot. Jack did wonder what they were planning but then, as sisters, they likely had plenty of secrets.

'That was delicious, thank you.' Hazel dabbed at the corners of her mouth with a napkin. 'There's something special about eating outdoors.'

'Definitely. Alfresco dining is always enjoyable,' Jack said.

'What does alfresco mean?' Bobby asked, rubbing a hand over her mouth and smearing melted chocolate up her cheek.

'Outdoors,' Penny replied.

'Oh.' Bobby frowned. 'Jade Jones in my class said her parents like to do it alfresco.'

Bella spurted glühwein over the table and Lee gasped in horror. Next to Jack, Hazel folded over with laughter.

'Does that mean they like eating outdoors too?' Bobby asked.

'Something like that.' Bella used a wet wipe that she'd got from a packet in her bag to clean the table. 'We should probably go and see Santa now, shouldn't we?'

'We should.' Lee stood up and loaded one tray on top of the other. 'Penny, hold Aster's lead while I take these back.'

'Yes, Daddy.'

'Never a dull moment,' Hazel whispered to Jack as she pulled on her gloves.

'Not with this lot.' He held her gaze for a moment before Bobby tugged at his hand. 'Come on, Uncle Jack, we've an old man in a red suit to speak to.'

'*You* do, you mean.'

'Well, yes, but it wouldn't hurt to ask if he can give you what you want for Christmas too.'

Jack glanced at Hazel and she shrugged.

'I guess there's no harm in asking,' he said. 'Come on, then. Let's go see what he can do.'

Bobby gripped his hand tightly and, even though the day had got colder, he felt very warm inside.

❄

Santa's Grotto turned out to be a wooden chalet decorated with fake snow and lots of glitter. It was set back from the other stalls in a corner of the gardens. Christmas trees in pots had been arranged around the cabin so that there was only one way in and one way out and each tree was decorated with a different colour, including matching lights.

'Look at that,' Bobby said in awe as they approached. 'It's amazing.'

'It is,' Hazel agreed, goosebumps rising on her skin. The organisers had clearly made a lot of effort and, even better, was the fact that all donations to Santa went to a children's charity. She was aware that the man playing Santa was a celebrity who regularly appeared in a popular TV soap and that he'd given up his time to support the charity. She just hoped that none of the children recognised him.

'Take your place in the queue, then,' Bella said to Bobby.

'Will you come with me, Uncle Jack?' Bobby asked. She was still holding his hand and Hazel suspected that she didn't intend on letting go anytime soon.

'Of course I will,' he said.

'And Hazel.' Bobby turned the full force of her gaze on Hazel, who felt her mouth fall open.

'Me?'

Bobby held out her free hand.

'Do you mind?' Bella asked quietly. 'She's taken a liking to you.'

'No, I don't mind at all. In fact, I'm honoured.' Hazel took Bobby's hand and they lined up behind other parents and their children.

'I think you should ask Santa to improve your art skills,' Bobby said, looking up at Hazel.

'Oh.' Hazel blinked. 'OK.'

'He might be able to help, but if not, don't plan on becoming an artist. That's what my teacher says to the class.'

'Your teacher tells a class of six-year-olds not to plan on becoming artists if she doesn't think their artwork is good enough?' Jack asked, incredulity in his tone.

Bobby shrugged. 'Something like that. She's very strict.'

'She sounds it.' Jack pulled a face over Bobby's head and Hazel had to stifle a giggle. It did sound rather harsh but she felt sure that the teacher hadn't meant it quite like that.

Soon it was Bobby's turn and they climbed the wooden steps to the grotto, where a very pretty female elf smiled at them.

'Hello there. Are you ready to see Santa? He's looking forward to seeing you.'

'Yes, we are!' Bobby jumped up and down as Jack handed the elf their donation.

'Well, go on in and say hello.'

The doorway was decorated with flashing fairy lights and their warm glow reflected on the floorboards. Inside the cabin it was cosy with heaters blowing warm air. Santa sat on what looked like a throne in the corner, a large red sack on the floor next to his chair.

'Ho! Ho! Ho!' Santa laughed, his red-gloved hands on his ample padded belly. 'And who do we have here?'

'You should know that,' Bobby replied.

'I should, shouldn't I?' Santa's eyes moved to Jack who mouthed Bobby to him. 'Hello there, young Poppy.'

'What?' Bobby dropped Hazel and Jack's hands and folded her arms. 'Poppy! Who the bloody hell is Poppy?'

Santa looked aghast so Hazel mouthed *Bobby* to him.

'I was just teasing you,' Santa said. 'Hello . . . Bobby.' He glanced at Hazel and she gave a crisp nod.

'That's better.' Bobby's shoulders visibly relaxed and she went closer to him.

'So, Bobby, what would you like for Christmas?'

Bobby pulled a piece of paper from her pocket and Hazel could see from where she was standing that there was a long list written on it. Bobby frowned, shook her head and folded the paper back up then pulled a different piece from her pocket. She handed it to Santa.

'Let me get this right . . .' He frowned. 'You don't want any toys or games?'

'I have plenty of those things. I did want some but then I thought this would be better and my big sister agreed with me.'

Santa pushed his hat back and scratched at his bald head. 'I can't promise to make this happen, but I'll certainly do my best.'

'Thank you, Santa.'

'It's my pleasure, Bobby. Let me give you a small gift from my sack.' He reached inside and brought out a small package that he handed to Bobby.

'Thanks. I'm going to show this to my mummy and daddy.'

Bobby turned and skipped out of the cabin while Jack thanked Santa.

'Are you, by any chance, Uncle Jack?' Santa asked him.

'I am.'

'You might want to see this. Your niece clearly loves you very much indeed.'

'Thanks.' Jack took the paper and unfolded it.

'Can I see?' Hazel asked, worried at how his face had changed. He almost looked as if he was going to cry.

'Sure.' He handed it to her.

On the paper, in Bobby's large childish writing were the words:

Dear Santa,

I have everything I need so for Christmas, I would like you to make my Uncle Jack happy again. He misses his wife very much and he's been very sad and lonely. Please help him.

Love Bobby x

Hazel's vision blurred. It was the most adorable Christmas letter she had ever read. As she handed it back to Jack, their fingers touched and for a moment, he held on to her, gazing out at the Christmas trees. A solitary tear trickled down his cheek and Hazel couldn't help herself: she reached up and brushed it gently away.

Jack slid his hand into his pocket to check that the note Bobby had written for Santa was still there. It was something he knew he'd always treasure. His young niece thought so much of him that she would prefer to see him happy than to have any toys or games for Christmas. Bobby was a sweet and clearly sensitive child and she'd picked up on the fact that Jack was carrying a deep sadness. He felt bad knowing that, because the last thing he wanted was to sadden his family, but at the same time, he was grateful for their love and empathy.

At the ice rink, he looked at Bella. 'Who's staying with Aster? I'm happy to if you like.'

'No, no, it's fine,' Lee said. 'I'll stay with her and watch you all. I don't want to risk falling over. I can't afford the time off work.'

'You'll be fine if you skate with me.' Bella laughed. 'I'm quite good at this.'

'She is, you know,' Jack said to Hazel. 'Bella used to be a whiz on the ice. I'm not bad but she literally spins circles around me.'

Hazel's eyes widened. 'I'm not good at all. I've only been once before and I ended up on my backside. I was soaked through and had a massive bruise on my bu— on my behind.'

Jack laughed. 'We'll have to make sure that you don't fall over this time.'

He handed their tickets to the young man at the counter then went through the gate to get their skates. When they were all kitted out, Jack stood up and helped Hazel up too. It was strange wearing skates after so long but his feet soon remembered how to move with them on and he helped Hazel and Penny to the rink while Bella helped Bobby.

On the ice, he held Hazel's hand as she wobbled precariously, then he reached for Penny, but she shook her head.

'I can't. I'm afraid.'

'Use one of the penguins,' Bella said as she stepped onto the ice. 'I'll get you one.' She whizzed off then returned with two penguins that she set in front of Bobby and Penny. The girls took hold of the handles either side of the penguins' heads and relief crept over Penny's features.

Jack skated slowly at Penny's side while Hazel clung to his right arm. Bella stayed with Bobby, occasionally circling her expertly and making Bobby chuckle with delight.

'Do you want to go a bit faster?' Jack asked Hazel.

She glanced at him, her face white with terror. 'I can't. I'll fall.'

'I know you feel tense right now but if you can manage to loosen up a bit, you'll find it easier. Otherwise your legs are going to ache tonight.'

'They're already aching,' she said. 'I'm so sorry. Look, if you can get me back to the side I'll stay there and you can go and have a proper skate.'

'No, it's fine. I'm happy staying with you.'

Hazel's right foot turned and she pirouetted on her left one, screaming as she turned around but Jack caught her and she landed up against him, clinging to his waist. She was breathing heavily and her cheek was pressed flat against his chest.

'It's OK,' he said, holding on to her. 'I've got you.'

'Don't let me fall.'

'I won't. I promise.'

He moved his feet slowly, still holding Hazel, and he felt her surrender to him, letting him push her backwards while she held on tight. He'd thought about how it might feel to hold her this close but hadn't imagined it would be in front of lots of other people, his sister and nieces included, though when he glanced at them they seemed lost in what they were doing and oblivious to him and Hazel.

When they reached the side, he was struck by a sense of disappointment at the thought that he'd soon have to let her go, because it was nice holding Hazel and being held. He had missed being that close to someone and liked feeling needed, liked even more that Hazel was relying on him to keep her safe, even if it was only to stop her slipping on the ice.

He took her hand and placed it on the barrier at the side of the rink and she looked up at him, colour slowly seeping back into her cheeks.

'Thank you so much. I didn't mean to freeze like that but there were so many people whizzing around us and I just stiffened up completely and couldn't move. You . . . you saved me.'

'I only stopped you from losing your balance.'

She looked at him from beneath her eyelashes.

'Thank you.'

His heart squeezed and heat rushed through his veins. He could still feel her warmth against him, still smell her scent on his coat.

'Happy to come to your rescue any time, Hazel.' His voice was gruff, his senses overwhelmed.

'Just kiss her, Uncle Jack!' Bobby sailed past, her penguin leading the way.

'You know you want to.' It was Penny, a grin on her face as she pushed her penguin along.

Jack looked back at Hazel and she held his gaze.

Was she thinking the same as he was? Had his nieces been able to tell that kissing Hazel right now was what he wanted more than anything? Part of him was embarrassed but the rest of him didn't care.

He moved a fraction closer to Hazel and saw her release her hold on the barrier. He gazed at her pink lips, her porcelain skin and her pretty eyes.

Then her face changed and suddenly she lost her balance and spun, and before he knew it, she was on the ice at his feet and Jack was glaring at the teenaged boy who'd been showing off to his friends and so crashed into Hazel.

Chapter 18

Hazel ran a cool iron over the jumper then held it up to check it. It was clean, dry and pressed. She wanted to return it to Jack as soon as possible in case he needed it, but she also wanted to see him again – and soon.

Yesterday, Jack had just kept on surprising her. When they'd gone onto the ice, she'd expected him to skate away. Lennox would have been long gone, keen to test his own skills, but Jack was happy to stay and help her. He was so different from Lennox and she felt as if her eyes had been opened, especially after her fall. Jack had helped her to the side and then away from the ice to sit down. He'd checked her over and ensured that she was OK before gently removing her skates and then taking off his own jumper and offering it to her, as her coat and top were wet. She'd only had a vest top on under the tunic top, so she'd changed then and there and, as she'd pulled the jumper over her head, she'd been conscious that it was still warm from his body and smelt of him. It had been way too big but he'd smiled and told her that oversized clothes were in fashion and that she looked good. Then he'd put her tunic top and coat in a bag and tried to give her his coat as well, but she'd drawn the line at that, knowing that he couldn't walk around the market in just a T-shirt.

Hazel believed in women being strong and independent and going after what they wanted in life, and she knew that in some ways she had compromised that during her relationship with Lennox, but Jack's tenderness and the way he'd taken care of her made something inside her start to unfold. She could imagine being with Jack and not having to sacrifice any part of who she was, being strong and yet vulnerable, able to trust in him and to relax with him, knowing that he wouldn't hurt her.

After everyone had come off the ice, Penny and Bobby speaking excitedly about how much they'd enjoyed skating and watching their mum behaving like a professional skater, they'd gone to get hot chocolates and to listen to a university group singing carols live at the park bandstand. As the music had floated around them, filling the air with festive cheer, the temperature had dropped dramatically and Hazel had started to shiver. Jack had noticed and again tried to give her his coat. When she declined, he held out an arm and she tucked herself under it, nestling close to keep warm. Perhaps it should have felt awkward or uncomfortable because she'd only known him four and a half weeks, but it hadn't. For some reason she felt as if she had known Jack far longer, as if they shared a bond that had formed quickly and was based on mutual trust and respect. It was different to anything she'd ever experienced before and yet her mum had often told her about how quickly she'd fallen for her dad, that as soon as she'd met him she'd known he was the one for her. Hazel didn't think she was in love with Jack and nor did she think he was some kind of soulmate, but she did feel something for him and she was curious to see if it could become anything, despite their past experiences. She even felt differently about herself when she was with him, more positive than she had done with Lennox, and that was because Jack built her up, whereas Lennox had repeatedly torn her down.

The afternoon had been magical, with lights twinkling around them, people singing along to the carols and a few stray snowflakes drifting through the air, so that it had seemed OK to stand so close to Jack, and Hazel had sensed that he found it comforting too. The best part about the day had been when Jack told Bella he would catch the train home with Hazel – to ensure that she'd fully recovered after being shaken by her fall – and they'd sat side by side on the train and chatted all the way back to Little Bramble. They hadn't talked about anything heavy, just about films, music, Netflix, people they'd met in the village and about Aster and how adopting animals was such a wonderful thing. Jack was certainly becoming a friend and Hazel knew how important it was to have friends she could trust.

It was dusk by the time the train stopped at Little Bramble station and Jack had walked Hazel to her street. She'd offered him a warm drink, hoping he'd come inside but also knowing it might not be a good idea. She didn't know if she could trust herself to hold back with him. Jack had politely declined, said he was exhausted and that he needed to get back. Perhaps he'd been battling the same yearnings as her or maybe he couldn't bear the thought of being close to someone again. There could be many reasons why he'd left her at her door, but Hazel found she didn't mind; she needed time and space to think too.

Before he left, Jack handed her a small object wrapped in brown paper and told her to open it when she got inside. She'd been intrigued and practically ran up the stairs to her flat. Fleas had greeted her with her usual enthusiasm, asked for her dinner then watched as Hazel had opened the gift. Inside she'd found the pretty resin robin she'd been looking at on the stall and something inside her had trembled as if there was an earthquake. The robin was now sitting on her bedside table and it was the first thing she'd seen that morning when she'd woken after a restful night's sleep.

Robins were said to symbolise new beginnings and good fortune and Hazel certainly felt that she'd had a fresh start coming to Little Bramble and that meeting Jack was good fortune. Whatever direction their friendship took, she knew that he had brought something special to her life.

❊

Jack opened Bella's front door and his heart skipped a beat when he found Hazel on the doorstep. She was wearing a different coat to yesterday and a light blue beret along with jeans and ankle boots. She looked younger, somehow, and he thought it might be because of how the colour contrasted with her pale skin and blonde hair, almost adding depth to her luminous eyes.

'Hey,' he said softly, not wanting to bring everyone else rushing to the door, although Aster was already at his side, wagging her tail in wide arcs.

'Hey yourself.' She smiled. 'I brought your jumper back.'

'Oh. Thanks.' He accepted the paper bag she'd been holding.

'It's washed and ironed.'

'That was quick.' He felt his heart sink. Had he been hoping she wouldn't wash it so he could catch her scent within the fibres? 'What are your plans today?'

'I've done my washing and ironing, given Fleas a good brushing – she's moulting like you wouldn't believe – and I wanted some air, so I decided to pop this over to you. What are you up to?'

'Well, this morning we went up into Bella's attic to dig out the Christmas decorations and, after that, we picked up a tree so we're about to decorate it.'

'How lovely,' Hazel said. 'Well . . . I'd better let you get back to it.'

'Would you like to join us?' he asked quickly.

'Oh no. I couldn't impose like that. Bella and Lee have been so kind, letting me join you yesterday and for lunch last week and . . . I'd better not.'

Bella appeared at Jack's side. 'Better not what?' she asked.

'I just asked Hazel to help with the tree but she's worried she'd be imposing.'

'Nonsense!' Bella pushed Jack aside and reached for Hazel's hand, making Jack laugh. 'Come on in, Hazel. I need a hand unravelling the bloody lights anyway as they're all tangled.'

'That's me off the hook then.' Jack was smiling as he closed the door then turned to follow Bella and Hazel through to the lounge.

Just when he thought things couldn't get any better . . .

Hazel sniffed the air. 'It smells amazing in here. Deliciously festive.'

'I have my mulled wine candle burning,' Bella gestured at the coffee table. 'And Lee has made mince pies.'

'Yum.' Hazel licked her lips.

'We'll decorate the tree then have some refreshments and watch a Christmas movie.' Bella smiled at Hazel. 'How does that sound?'

'Wonderful,' Hazel said but she felt like squealing with delight. She'd only come to return Jack's jumper and now she'd been invited in to help with festive activities. Since her parents had died, she'd missed being part of a family, especially at Christmas because it hadn't felt the same with just her and Lennox, especially as he'd been out so often, leaving her alone. Bella was such a kind person – even if Jack hadn't existed, Hazel would still have been incredibly grateful to be her friend. Bella was actually undoing some of the damage Valentina had done when she'd stabbed Hazel in the back. After that had happened, Hazel had thought she'd never trust another woman again, but she just knew that Bella would never do that to a friend, and it was comforting to know that women like her existed.

The TV was tuned in to YouTube and Christmas hits played on the screen, from Mariah Carey to Wham! to Elton John. Hazel found herself accepting a glass of eggnog from Lee and tasting it tentatively as she'd never had it before. It was quite nice, creamy and strong, and she knew she'd have to drink it slowly because it was like an alcoholic milkshake and could easily be drunk too quickly.

'Here are the lights.' Jack held out a tangled mess and Hazel eyed it.

'It's a good job I like a challenge.'

'Good luck.' He winked.

'Every year when we put the decorations away, I say to Lee, "Wrap them around something to stop them getting tangled",' Bella said. 'And every year he doesn't listen.'

'Hey!' Lee looked affronted. 'I do my best.'

'I know, darling, but it always takes us ages to untangle them the next year.'

'It's part of the fun.' Lee grinned and Bella swatted him playfully.

'I'm going to go and finish baking with Penny, so shout when you need me.' Lee left the room.

Hazel sat on one of the sofas and placed her glass on the table then set the fairy lights on her lap. Jack and Bella stood in front of the tree that they'd set near the window overlooking the driveway, discussing whether the branches were even.

'We picked this up this morning from the farm shop just outside the village,' Jack said. 'I don't think I'll ever get the scent of pine off me after the struggle we had trying to tie it to the roof rack.'

'It was quite funny.' Bella laughed.

'It's a beautiful tree,' Hazel said, thinking of how she'd always wanted to get a real tree but Lennox had said they were messy and clichéd and would just leave pine needles all over the floor. Hazel's parents had always had real trees which smelt amazing; they held, for Hazel, the real aroma of Christmas. Her parents had always planted the trees in their large garden afterwards and some had thrived while some hadn't made it, but they bought them from a sustainable tree farm so they had been doing their bit for the environment.

She had made a lot of compromises with Lennox, far more than he made, and now that they were separated she could see that clearly. Sometimes she wanted to go back in time and give herself a good shake and at others she felt sorry for the innocent girl she'd been.

'Does it look even now?' Jack asked, tilting his head.

'It's perfect,' Hazel replied and he gazed at her so intently that her stomach flipped over. She dropped her gaze to the lights on her lap, aware that a flush was crawling up her neck and would soon bloom in her cheeks.

When she next looked up, Jack and Bella were helping Bobby to hang decorations on the tree. It was sweet to watch, like a scene from a movie, and Hazel couldn't look away. But then she noticed what was happening. Bobby would hang a decoration on one side of the tree then accept another from Jack and while she was looking for somewhere to hang things, Bella would sneakily adjust or move the one she'd just hung. This went on for some time and Hazel found herself laughing softly.

Bella looked up and caught her watching them and she winked then she came over and crouched next to Hazel.

'Let's have a look at how you're getting on with the lights, shall we?' Bella said loudly then she leant closer. 'Please don't tell anyone.'

'Tell anyone what?' Hazel asked.

'That I'm a closet control freak.'

'What?' Hazel laughed. 'Are you?'

'I can't stand a messy tree so I let the girls decorate it then I tidy it up a bit.'

'I can understand that. If it's going to sit in your lounge for a few weeks, then it needs to be tidy.'

214

'It does.' Bella winked. 'Otherwise it drives me mad.'

'At least this way Bobby is helping without realising that you're making adjustments.'

'My thoughts exactly. Part of the reason Lee's staying in the kitchen is to avoid this bit. Before the girls came along I used to adjust his decorating too.'

Hazel snorted and Bella joined in. Bobby looked over at them. 'What's so funny, Mummy?'

'Uh, just a joke Hazel told me.'

'About what?'

Bella frowned. 'Ummm . . .'

'Was it a knock-knock joke?' Bobby asked. 'I know lots of those.'

'Oh no,' Bella muttered under her breath, 'now we've woken the beast.'

'Knock, knock.' Bobby put her hands on her hips and awaited a response.

'Who's there?' Hazel asked.

'Avery.'

'Avery who?' Hazel played along.

'Avery merry Christmas to you.' Bobby chuckled. 'That's a good one, isn't it?'

'Very.' Hazel agreed.

'Knock, knock.' Bobby grinned at Hazel.

'Oh God.' Bella sighed, reached for Hazel's glass and knocked back her eggnog.

'Who's there?' Hazel licked her lips.

'Gladys.'

'Gladys who?'

'Gladys Christmas. You too?'

Hazel giggled. 'I'm very glad, Bobby.'

'Knock, knock.'

'OK, Bobby.' Jack put a hand on her shoulder. 'Why don't we get this done and you can tell more jokes later?'

Bobby pouted. 'But I love telling jokes and Hazel really likes it. Don't you, Hazel?'

'I do.' Hazel inclined her head, but she lowered her eyes to the lights and made a show of weaving a thread in and out to try to free it.

'I'll get you another drink.' Bella stood up and took Hazel's glass. 'And I think I'll get myself a large one.'

'Where's this fat little snowman going?' Jack held the decoration out to Bobby. She took it from him and walked around the tree.

'Here?'

'Brilliant.' Jack smiled. 'And this one?'

Hazel released the thread of lights and soon she'd managed to line them up neatly on the sofa so they were ready to wrap around the tree or the mantelpiece. She cleared her throat loudly and Jack turned around.

'Wow! You've done it already. You're a genius.'

'It wasn't exactly rocket science but hey, I'll take that.' Hazel looked at her handiwork. There was definitely a sense of achievement in what she'd done.

'Come and help?' Jack held out a hand and she got up and went to the tree.

When all of the decorations had been hung, Jack sent Bobby to get her parents and Penny.

'Thanks for that.' Jack tidied the smaller boxes that had held the decorations into one large box. 'You doing OK?'

'Yes, good, thanks. You?' His eyes slid away from her and he gazed at the tree.

'I'm better than expected. I was dreading Christmas but it's turning out well so far.'

'Same here.'

'Bobby didn't make you want to tear off your legs and stuff them into your ears to avoid hearing any more jokes?'

'No.' Hazel shook her head. 'She's very cute and I enjoy her sense of humour.'

'That's a relief.'

They locked eyes and Hazel felt that strange fluttering building inside her again. She wasn't sure if it was nerves, excitement, lust or a combination of them all. It was, though, she knew for sure, because of Jack. He just had this effect upon her and it made her feel like grabbing him and snogging his face off but also turning and running away. It was exhilarating to feel like this about a man. Jack had been through his own kind of hell, though, whatever it had been, and the last thing he needed was to be messed around, so she had to be careful with both of their feelings. Anyway, she had no idea if he liked her in the way she seemed to like him. There had, she thought, been signs, but she didn't have much faith in her ability to read people after what had happened in Scotland.

'Ta da!' Bella entered the room carrying a tray that she set down on the coffee table, careful to avoid knocking over the mulled wine candle.

'The mince pies look delicious,' Jack said, breaking eye contact with Hazel.

Penny and Lee appeared along with Bobby, who had icing sugar over her chin and T-shirt.

'Penny made them and I was her assistant.' Lee smiled proudly at his eldest daughter.

'We have clotted cream or brandy butter to go with them and there's lemonade for Bobby and me and more eggnog for the adults.' Penny pointed at the tray. 'Please help yourselves.'

'Let's just get the lights hung first,' Bella said.

Jack helped her to hang them on the tree and when they switched them on, there was a collective gasp of approval. Then they sat down on the sofas and Penny handed them all a festive napkin and offered everyone the plate with the mince pies. Hazel took one, then Jack, who was sitting next to her, passed her a small glass bowl of clotted cream and she spooned a blob onto her mince pie. Bella handed her a full glass of eggnog that she sipped, savouring the warmth of the brandy in it as it reached her belly.

'Well then,' Jack said. 'Thank you very much for this, Penny and Lee. And here's to a very merry Christmas.'

'Cheers!' They all raised their glasses.

Hazel had to fight back a moan as she bit into the mince pie. The pastry was buttery and crumbly and the fruit was plump and juicy, the cream a perfect companion. Along with the eggnog, which seemed stronger this time, she was in heaven.

When she'd finished, she knew she could easily have eaten it all again.

'Another?' Penny asked.

'Oh, I couldn't.' Hazel shook her head. It wouldn't be polite to stuff her face.

Jack nudged her. 'Enjoy yourself.'

'Oh, go on then.' Hazel shrugged. 'I have no willpower.'

After her second mince pie and when she'd finished her eggnog, she felt full and slightly tipsy.

'That was just amazing. Penny, you are a very talented young lady.'

Penny beamed.

'And me?' Bobby asked, keen to be praised too.

'Definitely.' Hazel nodded. 'That tree looks wonderful.'

'Oh, I forgot!' Bobby jumped up and ran from the room. She returned quickly with something in her hand. 'Where are we going to put the mistletoe?'

'We could fix it over the doorway so that every time people walk through they have to kiss,' Lee said.

'Ew, Daddy!' Penny made a retching noise. 'That's just because you're looking for an excuse to kiss Mummy more and it's so gross.'

Lee raised his eyebrows and Bella giggled.

'I wonder if it works.' Bobby pursed her lips then looked at Hazel. Hazel's heart started to thump. 'I think I'll test it.'

Bobby skipped over to stand in front of Hazel and Jack then she reached out and held the mistletoe over Hazel's head. Hazel glanced around the room and everyone was watching.

'Go on, Uncle Jack. It's bad luck if you don't.'

Jack cleared his throat then he turned towards Hazel. 'Is this OK?' he whispered.

Hazel gave a brief nod.

Jack moved closer and gently cupped her face with one hand then he brushed his lips against hers. It was the softest of kisses but Hazel felt the room spinning as he moved away.

'Yay!' Bobby's shout made Hazel jump. 'It works just like magic. Now your turn, Mummy and Daddy.'

As Bobby took the mistletoe to her parents, and Penny muttered about how she was never kissing anyone, *ever*, Hazel raised her eyes to meet Jack's. His cheeks were flushed and he looked disorientated, exactly how she felt.

'I guess now we've had our Christmas kisses it's time for the annual Christmas movie,' Lee said, getting up to grab the remote control. 'We've already narrowed it down to a choice of three, so it's time to cast your votes. Do you want *A Christmas Carol, National Lampoon's Christmas Vacation* or *Home Alone*?'

Hazel held her breath and looked around. She didn't want to pick a movie that everyone else didn't want and she could barely think straight after the kiss.

'*Home Alone!*' Bobby shouted.

'*A Christmas Carol,*' Penny said.

'*National Lampoon's,*' Lee added.

'I don't mind,' Bella said. 'You know me, I love them all.'

'Hazel?' Jack asked.

'Uh . . . I don't mind at all.'

'Nor me.' Jack sat back and folded his arms over his chest. Hazel noticed that he seemed to be breathing quite quickly.

'That's not helpful.' Lee furrowed his brows. 'We have one vote for each movie and three abstainers. Please vote or we could be here all day.'

'It's OK, Daddy, I have more jokes.'

'*National Lampoons!*' Bella snapped. 'And the same for Jack and Hazel.'

Hazel pressed her lips together and kept quiet, aware that Bella was desperate to avoid more knock-knock jokes.

'*National Lampoon's Christmas Vacation* it is then.'

Lee sat on the sofa between his daughters and Bella, and Hazel shifted her position on the sofa next to Jack to see the TV better. It was an enormous TV, though, so she suspected she could have watched the movie from the driveway.

As the music started, Hazel settled into her very comfortable seat, resisting the urge to press her fingers to her lips to touch where Jack had kissed. The light was fading outside, the tree lights were twinkling, in the grate a fire glowed and the candle on the coffee table flickered. Jack was warm and solid next to her and she felt relaxed with him and his family. Their arms occasionally brushed against each other, making her skin tingle, and during the funny parts of the movie, he glanced at her and smiled and her heart squeezed.

When she was close to Jack, she felt like there were possibilities ahead, whatever they were. And she was having fun, enjoying what was happening, and so when their hands both happened to rest on the sofa cushion between them, and their little fingers touched, she didn't pull away – and neither did he.

Chapter 19

'What do you think?' Hazel asked Clare.

'I like them.'

Clare was sitting on the opposite side of the desk to Hazel in her office, a selection of mini bouquets laid out in front of them.

'And because they're dried, I'll be able to keep them afterwards?'

'You will. You can use them as a wall display or on a shelf or just pack them safely away.'

'Thanks for picking them up.' Clare gently touched one of the bouquets, a faraway look in her eyes, and Hazel wondered if she was picturing herself holding the bouquet as she walked along the aisle towards Sam.

'It's no problem. When I saw them at the festive fayre, I thought they'd be perfect. There was a whole stall selling things like this.'

The bouquets were made of dried wildflowers as well as cream and red roses entwined with stalks of lavender, sage and rosemary. Tied with twine, they were pretty and rustic. Hazel had bought three, one for Clare, one for Jenny and a spare in case Clare wanted someone else to have one.

'And what about favours for the tables at the reception?' Hazel asked.

'I've got some ideas and Kyle said he'll help me.'

'And the bistro is catering?'

'Yes. We're going simple with a festive buffet featuring things like turkey, cranberry sauce and stuffing rolls, mini cheese tartlets, nut roast and lots of breads, olives and nibbles.'

'Good idea,' Hazel said, thinking of the three-course sit-down meal she'd had organised for her own wedding reception. Lennox had wanted a cooked meal served with champagne, fine wine and a fancy dessert. All the money they'd spent on it had been wasted as they had cancelled too late to get it back; Hazel hadn't wanted to anyway as the Georgian hotel they'd booked for their wedding was owned by a family who regularly hosted weddings she planned. She knew that they would have lost out had she and Lennox pushed to get their money back and just couldn't do it. Instead, she'd asked if they could donate the food to a local shelter to avoid wasting it all. As for the honeymoon . . .

Two weeks in Italy, honeymooning on the shores of Lake Garda, had been gifted to mutual friends who'd been able to jet off at short notice. There was no way that Hazel could face going alone and she didn't want Lennox and Valentina to enjoy her honeymoon. Italy had been Hazel's dream destination, her choice, and she'd paid for it as a wedding gift to Lennox. She knew their friends had enjoyed the trip because they'd messaged to thank her, but she'd been unable to look at Instagram for ages afterwards because she feared seeing photographs and imagining the time she would have had there. It was amazing, she thought now, how Lennox had taken so much from her, like a tornado that had sucked her life into it then spat out the remains.

'Hazel?' Clare was staring at her as if waiting for an answer.

'Sorry?' Hazel shifted in her seat and took a deep breath.

'You looked lost then. Are you all right?'

'Y-yes, I'm fine, thanks.'

'Are you sure? I'm a good listener.' Clare's tone was soft and encouraging. 'You look like you could do with a chat.'

'Oh, it's nothing, really.'

'You won't know this,' Clare said, 'well, not in detail anyway, but I'm divorced. Before I came back to Little Bramble I was married, but after over twenty years together my husband turned around and told me that he wanted out.'

'Goodness, I'm sorry.'

'I'm not.' Clare laughed. 'Not any more, that is. At the time it was dreadful and I was . . . a bit lost. But now I've found myself again. Coming back here was the best thing I could have done and, funnily enough, Kyle followed me. He was meant to be returning to university but he's settled into life here and is happy. He says he'll go back when he's ready but I'm not convinced. He's madly in love with the vet nurse, Magnus Petterson, and they're even talking about moving in together. I sometimes wonder if I should push him to go back and continue his education but then it's his life and he has to make his own decisions. We all do.'

Hazel nodded, gazing down at her hands which were folded in her lap.

'I digressed then, Hazel, but my point was that relationships break down. I'm not prying, but if that's what happened to you then I understand what it's like. It might have happened differently to my marriage breakdown but it all hurts and leaves scars. I was terrified of falling in love with Sam and yet . . . it's different.'

'You're very much in love.' Hazel met Clare's steady gaze again.

'Yes, we are. But it took us time to get there, to reach a place where we could put faith in each other. If you have been hurt – and I suspect I'm right about that because you haven't denied it – then it doesn't mean that you can't fall in love again. If you meet someone who's different to your ex, don't be scared to give him or her a chance.'

Hazel swallowed then inhaled deeply. There was sense in Clare's words and yet the idea of giving someone her heart again seemed so daunting.

'Also . . . don't be afraid of letting me know the truth because you're worried it might be bad for business.' Clare winked at her. 'Nothing's going to stop me marrying Sam, nothing short of him running away the day before the wedding – and if he does that then I'm going to bloody well hunt him down!'

Clare laughed but then she looked at Hazel and covered her face with her hands and groaned. 'Oh God, was that what happened to you? Have I just put my foot right in it?'

Hazel felt her lips curving into a smile in spite of how she felt because Clare had definitely hit the nail on the head.

'So you're a wedding planner whose groom ran away?'

'Something like that. Not ran away exactly, more decided that my maid of honour was more desirable than me.'

Clare gasped. 'That is awful! I am *so* sorry. But you know what? Screw them both. You don't need people like that in your life. My ex went off to discover himself as if he hadn't a care in the world. We're on friendly terms now but there were times when I could have punched him in the kidney.'

Hazel sniggered. 'In the kidney?'

'Yeah. And I called him a lot of names when I was ranting about what an idiot he was – piss-kidney, tosspot, knobhead and more. But when I calmed down and took some time to think about it, we'd fallen out of love a long time before and neither of us was happy. Splitting up freed us both. I know that you probably don't feel that way right now . . . Of course, I don't know how recently this all happened to you, but you'll get past this and hopefully you'll feel that you had a lucky escape.'

'I already do. It happened back in the summer but I stayed in Scotland because I had things to sort out financially and emotionally, I guess. I am glad I left, though, and I feel like I have the chance to start again here.'

'It's a good place to have a new beginning. You know, it sounds to me as if your ex got off lightly. Some women would have exacted a terrible revenge on him for cheating like that and ruining their wedding.'

Hazel pressed her lips together.

'You didn't, did you?' Clare leant forwards, her interest piqued.

'I couldn't help myself. I was devastated at first and kind of numb with disbelief, but then anger took over and it was such a relief after feeling so sad that I harnessed it and I . . .'

'Oh, go on, tell me. I won't repeat it to a soul.' Clare grinned and leant closer.

'Well,' Hazel said, 'I knew Valentina's Netflix password because we'd watched movies together lots of times, so I signed into her account and changed her preferences.'

'What did you change them to?'

'Movies and boxsets that had a message in the titles like *Indecent Proposal, I'm Thinking of Ending Things, Clueless, Marriage Story, Someone Great* . . . things like that to get her thinking. I don't know if she'll even have noticed but it gave me a small scrap of pleasure to think of her annoyance at having her original list changed.'

'That's brilliant!'

Hazel shrugged. 'It wasn't as dramatic as some things I could have done but it helped a bit.'

'What about your ex?' Clare asked.

'I left some raw chicken under the driver's seat in Lennox's Range Rover. It was a high-spec vehicle and he paid it more attention than he ever paid me, to be honest, so I thought it might hurt him when it started to smell.'

Clare was laughing now and Hazel felt relieved. She'd been worried about admitting to what she'd done as she hadn't told anyone before, but Clare clearly found it funny.

'It would have been easy enough for him to clean it out but the smell would've been pretty rank for a while. I just needed to do something, even though it was petty.'

'I think you did well. They deserved it, anyway.' Clare dabbed at her eyes with a tissue, having laughed so much tears had welled.

'But I don't want you to think I'm unprofessional. Weddings are my business and I believe in true love and happy ever afters.' Hazel sat up straight and goosebumps rose all over her body. What she'd just said – it was true. She did believe in love and being happy. At least Lennox hadn't taken that from her.

'See?' Clare winked. 'You just spent time with the wrong one. Open yourself up to life and the right person will come along. Not that I'm saying you have to be in a relationship or anything like that, but a beautiful young woman like you should have plenty of suitors.'

'Suitors?'

'Why not? It sounds a lot better than notches on your bedpost.'

'I like it. I'm available for suitors to call on me in my parlour.'

They laughed then and Hazel felt so much better. Speaking to someone who'd been through difficult times and come out of them really helped. Clare had been hurt, had lost her old life and yet she was happy now, possibly far happier than she had been before. Sometimes it was good to move on and start over.

'Anyway, about the ice sculptures you added to your list of wants for the wedding . . .' Hazel turned her laptop around. 'What do you think about these?'

✻

Jack had been for a run, had walked Aster (twice), cleaned the apartment, done his washing and ironing and popped to the village shop to pick up some groceries because he wanted to make dinner for Bella and Lee (all with Aster's company). They had a parents' evening with Bobby's teachers that evening and he thought it might help if he made dinner and watched the girls.

He'd let himself into Bella's home and made a start on dinner just after three. He was making lasagne so he could get everything ready then let it rest before popping it into the oven. He'd also decided to make garlic bread as well, so he'd made a dough and kneaded it and it was currently proving. After he'd washed up and tidied everything away, he went through to the lounge and turned the tree lights on, then lit the fire.

His gaze fell on the sofa where he'd sat next to Hazel just two days before. He'd been conscious of her at his side, of how their hands had touched and how neither of them had moved away. They had kissed under the mistletoe and, though it had been awkward in front of his family, he had enjoyed it. His feelings for Hazel were confusing him because he liked her – more than liked her – but he also knew that they'd both experienced difficulties in their pasts and wondered if it was even possible to overcome those things to find a way forwards with someone else. Also, he didn't know if he wanted to be, or even could be, with anyone else. His heart was still so fragile, as if there was a hairline fracture along it that refused to heal. Perhaps he was getting carried away with Hazel because Little Bramble was such a long way from Swansea and from what had happened to him there. Perhaps it was like a holiday romance. And yet he found that difficult to accept, because when Hazel walked into a room, it lit up, and surely that had to be real?

The front door opened and Bella, Penny and Bobby piled inside and Aster raced out to greet them.

'Quick, shut that door!' Bella said, 'It's freezing out there and we don't want Aster running out.'

'Hello, Aster! Something smells good, Mummy,' Bobby said. 'Did you put dinner on already?'

'I've been in work, Bobby, so I suspect we have Uncle Jack to thank for that delicious smell.'

As they entered the kitchen, Jack smiled at them. 'Hello, ladies. Good to see you all. How was your day?'

The girls competed to tell Jack how busy school had been then shrieked with delight when they discovered the donuts he'd bought them on the kitchen table.

'Do you want a cup of tea with them or a cold drink?' he asked, as if he didn't know the answer.

'Tea, please!' they both replied.

He made tea while Bella went to change and the girls ate donuts and drank their tea in front of the TV in the kitchen. When Bella came back downstairs, she was wearing jeans and a sweatshirt with her UGGs.

'That's better.' She accepted a mug of tea. 'I'm happy to dress smartly for work but it's a relief to get a bit more comfortable. Let's go and sit in the lounge, shall we? I could do with putting my feet up before I have to go back out again.'

'What time do you have to go back?' Jack sat on the sofa opposite his sister.

'Five thirty. Lee's going to meet me there.'

'Well, I've made lasagne and I've got the dough for garlic bread proving so you don't need to worry about dinner.'

Bella cradled her mug between her hands. 'It's just wonderful to get home and hear that, Jack. I know I don't work full-time now but even so, having someone else make dinner and light the fire for when I come home is wonderful. I'll miss you when you leave.'

'Don't think about that now. I've got a few weeks left here yet.'

He didn't want to think about it either.

'I know, but I've missed you over the years and now that you're here, I know exactly how much. I swear it's as if I was in denial – and now you're with me I don't want you to leave again. Can't you just fall in love with Hazel and stay in the village?'

Jack blinked then rubbed at the back of his neck.

'Did I just say that out loud?' Bella shook her head. 'That's working with little ones all day. They say what's in their heads without a second thought and sometimes it knocks my filter off. I'm sorry, I didn't mean to make you feel awkward. It's just that . . .'

'I barely know her.' Jack sipped his tea.

'I know and it was wrong of me to say that. I'd say I was joking, but with your circumstances in mind, it would be an inappropriate joke. I just want to see you happy.'

'I appreciate that.'

'How *are* you feeling?' she asked, curling her legs up underneath her.

'About what?'

'About everything?'

'I'm loving being here with you, Lee and the girls. It's good to be with family again, makes me realise that I have been lonely. I'd shut myself away, literally and figuratively, tried to stop myself feeling anything much at all. But being here, it's impossible to stay shut down. I already feel so different, as if I'm coming back to life again.'

'That's so good to hear.'

'I have you to thank.'

She shook her head. 'No, Jack. I think you were at a stage where this needed to happen. At some point, you needed to make some changes and this is the start of that.' She turned and gazed into the fire then asked softly, 'And what about Hazel?'

'What about her?'

'I'm not blind. I've seen you two together and there's definitely a spark. She likes you, I can tell, and I think you like her.'

'I do like her, but as I said, I barely know her.'

'You have to start somewhere.'

'What if this is wrong, though? What if I'm projecting onto her or something?'

'In what way?'

'She's the first woman I've been near since I lost Danni. Since my world fell apart. You don't come back from that easily. What if I'm trying to make something with Hazel, even on a subconscious level, because she's pretty and funny and sweet? Perhaps I don't have actual feelings for her and this will just lead to one of us getting hurt.'

'That's all possible, I'm sure, but it's been a year now and you can't question everything you feel for the rest of your life. I know that with Danni you were young and you fell head over heels and you just knew that she was the one. But things can be different when you're older and when you've been hurt. Hazel has had her own difficult times but that's far more likely when you get together with someone in your thirties and older. Life scars us all in some way, but it doesn't mean you have to sit at home alone, knitting and watching soaps for the rest of your days. You're young, Jack, you have every right to another relationship. Hell, Danni would want that for you. Can't you see that?'

Jack shifted in his seat. He was feeling a bit uncomfortable because of the heavy nature of the conversation but he could see that Bella was making sense. Life did scar people but it could also be wonderful.

'Look,' he said, 'it's early days and Hazel and I are friends. She's very attractive and I do . . . fancy her.' He felt his cheeks warming up. 'But we need to get to know each other a bit better first.'

'I understand that.' Bella finished her tea and set the mug on the table. 'But it's almost Christmas and there's a wedding approaching, so who knows what could happen under the mistletoe?'

He raised his eyebrows. 'Bobby's Christmas wish might come true?'

'I hope so, Jack, and that's why this year we need to reset things so you can have good memories of the festive season that will, hopefully, help you to heal from the sad ones.'

He cleared his throat. 'Sounds like a plan.'

'Good.' She stood up. 'I'd better go and see what the girls are doing. Oh, before I forget . . . there was an official invite posted through the door when I came down this morning.'

'What for?'

'The wedding. Clare and Sam must have been out delivering them late last night or perhaps it was Kyle. Anyway, your name is on it too as Clare promised.'

'Great news.' He frowned. 'What about Aster?'

'She's invited as well. So we can all go together.'

Jack smiled. He would be a guest at the wedding that Hazel was planning. She would be there. It would be festive and romantic and who knew what might happen? He would try, he decided, to go with the flow, as Bella had suggested.

'There's just one problem,' he said as they went through to the kitchen.

'What's that?'

'I have no idea what I'm going to wear.'

'Well, brother dear, as you know, I'm a great help with clothes shopping.'

Bella winked at him and he was sure he felt his credit card shiver in his wallet.

Chapter 20

Friday had rolled around again and it was time for the joint hen and stag party at The King. Sam and Clare had told Hazel that they didn't want separate parties because they wanted their friends and family together and were only actually having the do because their friends had insisted. To Hazel, it sounded like a good excuse for a party. She'd finalised some plans for the wedding during the day, gone for a long walk in the fresh air then gone home to shower and change.

As she dried her hair, she thought about her own hen weekend. She hadn't wanted one but Valentina had planned it regardless and they'd jetted off to a spa hotel in Barcelona. They'd gone with eight others, none of them close friends, but women they knew from their time at school and work, and it had been fine. The days had been spent having beauty treatments and the nights had been raucous alcohol-fuelled affairs that had made Hazel quite uneasy. She'd taken her time with the cocktails that the others had thrown back as if they were juice, and she'd been aware of Valentina watching her like a hawk. Had her best friend been after Lennox then? Had they already been meeting behind her back even though Lennox had sworn it was just a one-time thing? Valentina had tried hard to get Hazel drunk, but she had kept her wits about her without even being aware why.

Hazel's trust had been destroyed by the woman she'd cared about, by the friend whose shoulder she had cried on after she'd lost her mum and her dad. And it hadn't all been one way. Hazel had been there for Valentina too, through pregnancy scares, a dodgy mole removal and the grief she'd suffered when her estranged father had got in touch only to want money from her. Their friendship had longevity and yet it hadn't been strong enough to resist an affair. Valentina could've had any man she wanted but she'd had to go after Hazel's. Was it because she loved a challenge and Lennox was the one man she shouldn't have wanted?

As for Lennox's stag party, it had involved a week in Amsterdam and when he'd returned and she'd asked how it had gone, he'd laughed and tapped the side of his nose then said, 'Babe, you know that what happens in Amsterdam stays in Amsterdam.' A few photographs had shown up on social media, posted by Lennox's friends, but they hadn't looked too bad to Hazel. There had clearly been a lot of beer and shots involved and a fair amount of horseplay, but apart from that she found that she didn't want to know.

Shaking her head, she pushed the thoughts away then turned off the hairdryer. None of it was relevant now, anyway. Life was strange in that way; one day something could be incredibly important and the next, things shifted and something that had seemed like the end of the world no longer mattered. Lennox's behaviour was none of her business now and she wished him well. She'd told him so only that day when he'd sent another text, then another. He wanted to speak to her, was desperate to talk about what had happened. Hazel had tried to say very little in her replies, had told him to take care of himself and hoped he'd leave it at that, but he'd kept texting all afternoon until she'd turned her phone off. She had work to do, a night out ahead and Lennox was dragging her back to a past that she wanted to forget.

She emptied her bag and left her phone on the coffee table. She wasn't going to switch it back on because she didn't want to speak to Lennox. It was hard leaving someone behind but he wasn't her problem now; he had chosen to turn to someone else and Hazel was moving on. So why wasn't her mind free and why did her heart feel so heavy?

She needed to find something to wear. That would help take her mind off things. The frustration of dressing to go out always did these days.

Half an hour later, she'd settled on black jeans with knee-high boots and a sheer purple blouse over a black camisole. She'd straightened her hair and it fell to her shoulders, sleek and glossy, and she'd put on some makeup, a dusting of mineral powder, mascara, blusher and lipstick, and she felt better. She wasn't a big fan of makeup, but she always felt more confident when she put some on, a bit like putting on war paint before heading into battle. Not that she saw this evening as a battle, but she'd been surprised and very pleased when Clare had invited her. It meant that she was being accepted into the community and she'd have the chance to get to know more locals.

She put on her coat, grabbed her bag and set off for The King.

✳

'Are you sure Lee didn't want to come?' Jack asked as he walked with Bella to the pub.

'He really didn't.' Bella flashed him a smile. 'There's some documentary on TV that he wants to watch with Penny and he's very tired this week, so he said he'd be glad to have an early night.'

'I would happily have babysat,' Jack said. 'You two could've come together then.'

'It's fine.' Bella slid her arm through his. 'I'm glad to have an evening out with you anyway. Lee will be snoring his head off when we get back, I bet.'

It was a clear night, the sky velvet black pricked with stars that sparkled like tiny diamonds. Their footsteps echoed in the night air and their breath appeared in white puffs in front of them that quickly dispersed. Frost was already forming on cars, making them sparkle in the glow from the streetlights. Christmas lights flashed in the windows of houses and shops, and woodsmoke permeated the air as fires burned across the village to ward off the cold.

When they reached The King, Jack gazed at its rustic façade, its history evident in its structure. Parts of the pub had apparently been there since the 1600s and Jack found that intriguing because it made him wonder how many people had passed through it on their journeys, how many had lived and died within its walls. Jack really liked that about Little Bramble: it had so much history and was such a pretty place to live. He could see how happy Bella was here and what a good place it was for the girls to grow up. Could it be the place where he settled too?

The windows of the pub glowed with orange light and coloured lights raced around the roof. He could hear music and laughter as the door opened and a man stood there, staring out into the night. He was tall and broad, most of his face covered with a big bushy beard, and he carried a large rucksack over one shoulder. He stared at Jack and Bella for a moment, then stomped off into the night without so much as a hello.

'Who was that?' Jack asked.

'No idea.'

'He didn't look too happy,' Jack said.

'He didn't. Let's hope he finds what he's looking for.'

They entered the pub and Jack let the grumpy man slip from his thoughts as they went through to the function room.

❄

Hazel looked around as she entered The King but she couldn't see anyone she knew so she made for the function room at the rear of the pub. It was packed as she entered and squeezed her way through to the bar.

'Evening.' Bella's cheeks were flushed and her eyes were shining. 'You look gorgeous.'

'Oh, thanks.' Hazel glanced behind Bella to see if Jack was there too. 'So do you.'

'Ha! I doubt it, but thank you.'

'Bella, you're stunning.'

'So my husband tells me but you know how it is. We never see what others do when we look in the mirror. Before I left home, Bobby told me my eyelashes are too long with mascara on and that my lipstick is too pink.'

'What?' Hazel shook her head. 'She probably didn't want you going out.'

'I hope that's what it was because I keep wondering if I do look like I've put too much makeup on.'

'You don't, I promise, and I like your lipstick too. It's a pretty shade.'

'You're very kind. It's one I had at the bottom of my makeup bag. I don't wear much for work and we rarely go out so I thought I'd put some on this evening. Do you want a drink?' Bella asked.

'I'll get them.' Hazel pulled out her purse. 'What do you want?'

'It's OK, I have to get one for Jack anyway.'

'I'll get his as well.'

'Go on then.'

Hazel ordered their drinks then followed Bella to a table where Jack was sitting with Connor.

'Hazel got you a drink,' Bella said as she handed Jack the bottle of beer.

'Thank you!' He smiled.

'Sorry, Connor, I should have asked if you wanted something.' Bella winced but Connor shook his head.

'I'm fine, thanks. Emma's around here somewhere and she's got the money so she should appear soon with our drinks. I think she must have got lost on her way to the bar though . . . probably chatting to someone.' He rolled his eyes but he was smiling.

'You look nice,' Jack said as Hazel sat down next to him.

'Thanks. So do you.'

He looked down at the table and fingered a beer mat. 'How was your day?'

'Good, thanks. Just tying up loose ends for the wedding and I had an email from a couple who are thinking of getting married in the spring. They said they could do with some help so I'm meeting with them next week to discuss.'

'That's brilliant news.'

'I just hope it all works out. It's hard starting a business, especially in a new area, and I'm probably mad for doing it but I just had to get away from Scotland and I need to earn. I wouldn't know what else to do.'

'I wish I could help,' Jack said. 'But I wouldn't have a clue where to start.'

Hazel shook her head. 'It would be brilliant to have a business partner but it's the kind of business that you have to love to be a part of.'

'Love weddings, you mean?'

'Yes.'

'Do you love weddings? I mean, after what happened.'

Hazel swallowed hard, searching for her professional answer. But this was Jack and she didn't feel the need to deceive him. 'I did – and I do. Weddings are such happy and hope-filled occasions. Just because mine went wrong – well, the day before did anyway – doesn't mean that all weddings are doomed.'

'I love how you say that.'

'Doomed?'

'Yes.' He grinned. 'It sounds so much better with your accent.'

'Don't.' She shook her head. 'I'm self-conscious enough about my accent around here.'

'I love it.' Jack looked away. 'Your accent, I mean. I could listen to you all day and not get tired of it.'

'How many of those have you had?' Hazel gestured at his beer.

'Not enough to start waxing lyrical.' He grinned and she gazed at him, wishing things were different and that the reason she'd come here was different, that she hadn't had her heart broken and that Jack hadn't either. If only they were ten years younger and fresh with youth and enthusiasm for life. But they were hardly over the hill in their thirties, were they? And people married at all ages. Clare and Sam were both in their mid-forties and they'd found love. Clare had told her all about it and Hazel knew from the weddings she'd planned that lots of people had a bumpy ride before they found the person they wanted to spend their life with.

'Good evening, everybody!'

The voice came from the loudspeakers on stands either side of a small, raised platform in the corner of the function room. Hazel stood up and she could see Kyle standing there, looking surprisingly like a cowboy.

'Thanks for coming to help us celebrate Mum and Stepdaddy Sam's hen and stag party.'

A cheer spread through the room.

'Less of the stepdaddy!' Sam shouted from the bar, waving a fist playfully.

'Yes, well . . . we shall see.' Kyle grinned. 'To kick things off this evening we've got a very special warm-up planned for

242

you so grab a partner, roll up your sleeves and get ready to cha-cha, swivel, chassé and grapevine.'

Hazel looked at Bella, who appeared to be as confused as she was. Then there was a whooping sound as two 'cowboys' ran into the function room carrying colourful cowboy hats that you might find at a fancy dress store. They started handing them out and when Hazel received hers, she put it on her head and slid the strap under her chin.

'Yes, darlings, tonight we are going to be line dancing!'

Hazel bit the inside of her cheek. She'd never tried line dancing – it had always looked challenging. She wasn't the most coordinated of people and the idea of trying to keep up in a room full of people filled her with anxiety. She looked at Jack and he'd gone pale.

'Are you any good at this?' he asked her.

'Never done it before but always thought it looked hard.'

'I think so too.'

'Shall we try to sneak away?' Hazel muttered.

'We could.' Jack glanced in the direction of the exit.

'Ah, come on, you pair,' Bella grabbed their hands and dragged them towards Kyle. 'This will be great fun!'

Shania Twain's 'Any Man of Mine' burst from the speakers and Kyle led the way.

Jack looked around him. The function room was full of rosy-cheeked people smiling, swaying their hips and moving in time. He'd managed to keep up with Kyle but Hazel had made him laugh as she clearly had no coordination at all and ended up spending a lot of time catching up. But she was laughing at herself and still trying and he admired that about her. And as for Bella . . . His sister appeared to be quite tipsy but she was giving it her all on the dance floor. Line dancing was proving to be a lot of fun with such good company.

When the song ended, Bella grabbed his arm. 'I am pooped!'

'You look it.' Her cowboy hat was perched at the back of her head, she had a sheen of sweat on her brow and her cheeks were glowing. 'It was so much fun though.'

Kyle came over to them.

'How was that?' he asked.

'Brilliant,' Hazel replied. 'I was rubbish but I did enjoy it. Do you hold regular sessions?'

'Not line dancing, no, but I do hold tai chi classes at the village hall and there are others there like yoga. There's always plenty to do in Little Bramble.'

'It sounds like it.'

'You'll be happy here, my new friend.' Kyle wrapped an arm around Hazel's shoulders. 'I am and I had no idea I'd end up moving here.'

Jack watched Hazel's face as she gazed up at Kyle. She did look happy and she was clearly enjoying the evening. There was something else in her eyes and he thought it was hope. She was hopeful that she would be happy in the village and he could understand that. Everyone needed hope and after what she'd been through she really deserved it.

'Well done, Kyle.' Clare and Sam joined them. 'That was a fantastic surprise.'

'Yeah, thanks, Kyle.' Sam smiled.

'No problem.'

'And I love the cowboy hats.' Clare tilted hers back on her head. 'I think we should wear these all the time.'

'At the wedding?' Kyle cocked an eyebrow.

'Ha! Ha! Perhaps not at the wedding.' Clare looked at Sam and he shrugged. 'But I will hold on to mine.'

'Drinks?' Sam asked.

'Definitely.' Kyle, Clare and Sam went to the bar.

'You go and sit down,' Jack said to Bella and Hazel, 'and I'll get the drinks in. Hazel, what do you want?'

'I'd love a lemonade.' Hazel replied. 'I'm quite thirsty now.'

'Coming right up.'

'Thank you.'

Jack got the drinks then took them back to the table. Hazel was staring at her phone and had gone very pale.

'Hazel? You OK?'

She gave a small nod.

'You sure?' Bella asked. 'You look like you've seen a ghost.'

Hazel tucked her phone in her bag and accepted the lemonade from Jack.

'Thank you.' She drank it down like a shot then wiped her mouth with the back of her hand. 'I'd better be going.'

'What?' Bella turned to her. 'But the night is young.'

'I know, b-but something's come up.'

'That's a shame,' Jack said, disappointment surging in his chest. 'I think Kyle has got some other fun things planned.'

Hazel bit her lip and Jack wanted to take her hand and ask her what was going on, but he knew it wasn't his place to pry.

When Hazel stood up, Jack did too.

'Are you going straight home?' he asked.

'Yes.'

'Would you like me to walk you back?'

She met his eyes and smiled sadly. 'No, it's fine. I-I'll be fine.'

'OK.'

Hazel put her coat on and hooked her bag over her shoulder. 'I'll just say goodbye to Clare and Sam and then I'll be off. Enjoy the rest of the evening.'

Jack watched her leave, feeling deflated. It shouldn't matter if she wasn't here – after all, he was there with Bella – but knowing that Hazel was sad about something and wouldn't be there to enjoy the rest of the party worried him.

Ten minutes passed and he felt restless and in need of some fresh air. He told Bella, who was chuckling away with Kyle as he regaled her with stories about what Goliath the Great Dane had been up to, then made his way through to the bar and out of the door. The air hit him like a freezing wave and he zipped his coat up.

He took a few deep breaths, gazing out at the green, then something made him blink hard and peer out into the night. Was that Hazel standing at the edge of the green with a tall man? They appeared to be having a heated conversation and he wondered what it could be about. She'd said she was going home but she hadn't got very far.

He crossed the road, needing to get a bit closer to see if it was definitely her.

'But why did you need to come here?' she asked, her voice fraught with tension.

'I needed to see you, Hazel. I made a huge mistake. I-I can't live without you.' The man's accent was clearly Scottish.

Jack's stomach clenched. Was this him? The man who'd hurt Hazel? Had he come all this way to see her?

'You have to live without me, Lennox. You made your choice.'

Jack squinted through the darkness and as the man turned slightly, he saw that it was the grumpy man with the beard he'd seen earlier that evening.

'Hazel, I love you. Please . . . please give me another chance.'

Hazel gasped and covered her mouth, then Lennox lurched towards her and hugged her. Jack froze, not sure what to do, wondering if he should go to her aid, but when her arms encircled Lennox's neck, he knew he had to leave them to it. He'd thought there had been something between him and Hazel, that their kiss, however brief, had been the start of something, but apparently, he'd been wrong.

❋

Jack turned and trudged back to The King. His heart was heavy and he felt confusion swirling like a fog in his mind. And yet he wasn't naïve enough to try to reason away what he'd just seen. Sometimes you took back the people who hurt you because the thought of life without them was too much to bear. Would he have taken Danni back had she done that to him? He didn't know, and he'd never know, because Danni was gone and so, it seemed, was the chance of anything happening with Hazel.

Chapter 21

Hazel unlocked the front door to her office and stepped inside. Lennox followed right behind her and she pointed at the stairs. 'Go on up and I'll lock the door.'

'OK.' He plodded up the stairs, a large rucksack bouncing against his back.

Hazel locked the door then rested her forehead against it for a moment, trying to calm herself down. She couldn't believe he'd turned up in Little Bramble. What the hell was he thinking? She'd been having such a good night, had thoroughly enjoyed line dancing and chatting with Jack, Bella and others and then she'd checked her phone and found a text message from Lennox. He'd driven all the way from Edinburgh to find her. Not only had he got her number from her website, but also her location and then he'd spent the afternoon and evening walking around trying to find her. He'd told her that he hadn't wanted to ask in the pubs in case word got back to her but as the evening had worn on he'd become frustrated and finally asked at the late-opening village shop and been told that Hazel was probably at the party at The King. That was when he'd messaged her to tell her he was waiting outside.

Hazel had felt as if the sky had fallen in when she'd seen the message. He'd asked if he should come inside the pub, but that would have been awful, her two worlds colliding, and so she'd told him she'd meet him outside. At first, he'd been calm and spoken quietly, but when he'd realised that she wasn't about to melt into his embrace, he'd become increasingly emotional and eventually flung himself at her. He was a giant of a man and seeing him crying had affected Hazel deeply. Lennox was tough; he didn't cry and he didn't lose control, but he'd sobbed on her shoulder on the village green and she'd had to try to comfort him. Even after all he'd done, she couldn't turn him away when he was that upset. She'd loved the man, part of her probably still loved him in some way, and even though he'd hurt her she wasn't horrid enough to tell him to get stuffed.

He'd turned up without anywhere to stay and it was getting late. Hazel's head was fuzzy from the alcohol she'd drunk earlier so she was struggling to think clearly and she'd told him to come back to hers. What else could she do? Let him sleep in the car on a freezing cold December night? Tell him to find a park bench or get back in his car and drive back to Scotland?

She sucked in a deep breath then trudged up the stairs and unlocked the door to her flat. Inside, everything was as she'd left it before she went out that evening, but it felt different now because this was her safe space and it was being invaded by the Ghost of Christmas Past.

'Do you want tea?' she asked as she removed her coat and hung it up then did the same with Lennox's coat.

'Do you have something stronger?' he asked.

'I haven't got whisky if that's what you're after, but I do have white wine in the fridge and some red in the cupboard.'

'Wine would be great, thanks.'

His voice, his accent . . . they were so familiar; unwelcome tears pricked at her eyes as old emotions surfaced. It was an involuntary reaction. Why had he come here to mess up her life when she was just starting to get back on track? Putting distance between them had been therapeutic for her, she'd felt like she could make progress, but now he was here and all the things she'd tried to forget were flooding through her again.

'What shall I do with this?' he asked, holding up his rucksack.

'Just leave it in the hall for now,' she said.

They went through to the kitchen and Hazel grabbed a bottle of red wine and a glass and set them on the table, then she filled a glass with water and drank it down. Fleas appeared to greet her, twirling around Hazel's legs, her body fluffy and comforting.

'Have some wine with me?' Lennox asked as he held out a full glass of red.

'I'd rather not.'

'Go on.' His eyes pleaded with her and so she accepted the glass, not having the energy to argue, then got another from the cupboard for him.

'Let's go and sit in the lounge,' she said, leading the way, Fleas trotting ahead.

Hazel sat on the one sofa, expecting Lennox to take the other one, but he sat on the same one as her. She pressed herself against the arm, wanting space between them, a sense of disbelief permeating everything. Was this really happening or would she wake up at any moment with a sigh of relief?

Lennox took a sip of wine then set his glass on the coffee table.

'Hazel, I'm sorry if I surprised you but I had to see you. These past months have been awful without you.'

She stared at him, pressing her lips together because she didn't want to react. She needed to stay outwardly calm, however annoyed she felt inside.

'I made such a huge mistake and Valentina – well, it was just wrong.'

'Lennox! It's been *months* since I found you with her. In that time, you moved her into our home and—'

'No! She didn't move in.'

'As good as.'

'She stayed there sometimes but she didn't move in. It was all too soon for that. Sleeping with her was a huge mistake and I—'

'Shagged her the night before our wedding and ruined everything.'

He blinked as if stunned.

'What's wrong? I said *shagged*? Sorry, was it *making love*?' Hazel hooked her fingers around the last two words. She'd kept her tone calm but inside rage was bubbling. It was a rage she'd only expressed when she was alone and now she worried it would take over. But she'd never really let it rip with Lennox, never let him know how angry she was at how he'd betrayed her. Leaving chicken in his car to rot was a more passive-aggressive revenge. Perhaps it was time to get it all out and clear the air.

'No! No, it wasn't. I thought I had feelings for her but it was just . . . sex.' He looked up at her from beneath his fair lashes, his thick sandy brows almost swallowing his small eyes completely.

'Well, that's all right then. As long as it was *just* sex.'

'Hazel, please, this isn't like you.' He combed his fingers through his bushy beard and she noticed for the first time that evening how unkempt it was and how he had some white hairs in it now that caught the light. 'You're always so calm and cool . . . so reasonable.'

'I beg your pardon!' She slammed her wine down on the table and some of it sloshed over the side and onto the coffee table. '*Reasonable.* You cheeky bastard, Lennox! You can't do that one to me any more. It's not *unreasonable* of me to be angry that you betrayed me, that you shagged my best friend and business partner and left my life in tatters. And you often accused me of being unreasonable as a way to keep me quiet. I totally see that now!'

He looked at her, his eyes widening, then he covered his face with his big hands and hunched over. Hazel stared at him, wondering what he was doing, then she noticed that his shoulders were shaking. He was crying again.

Her anger evaporated and she reached out tentatively to him, placing a hand on his shoulder and patting it.

'I'm selfish,' he muttered through his hands. 'You're right. I've not been honest with you or myself and I made a huge mistake and I regret it. No one understands me like you did, Hazel.' He peered up at her, his face wet, his eyes red-rimmed.

'I think what you mean is that no one will put up with you like I did.'

He sniffed hard and Hazel handed him a tissue from the box on the table.

'You were so patient and you did put up with a lot from me.'

'I loved you, Lennox.'

That set him off again and she waited while he sobbed, knowing that he needed to get this out of his system too. When he stopped crying, he blew his nose loudly and grabbed another tissue to dry his face then he picked up his wine and sat back, balancing the glass on his knee.

'I screwed up, didn't I?'

'Big time.'

Hazel reached for her wine and drank it down, patting the sofa next to her to encourage Fleas to jump up. The cat did so and she snuggled closer to Hazel, rubbing her head against Hazel's arm. Lennox held out a hand to Fleas but she ignored him. He had always made it clear that he'd never liked Fleas and now she was making it clear that she felt the same way about him.

'Is there no chance for us to get back together?' Lennox asked in a small voice.

Hazel sighed and stroked Fleas. Was there the slightest possibility that she could have Lennox back in her life? Could they, a couple with so much history between them, ever be the way they were again?

'I'm sorry,' she said, shaking her head. No, it could never be the same, nor would she want it to be. What they'd had wasn't perfect, she knew now there had been much that could have been improved, but it was all she'd known and she had accepted Lennox as he was. Had loved him as he was. But a lot had happened since then and she'd been able to spread her wings, to see that there was a life away from what they'd had, to see that she could cope alone. She'd had no choice – but it was so good to know that she could rely on herself and that she was enough. She was stronger than she'd ever realised. If someone else came into her life then she would be able to have a relationship on different terms, not feel forced to compromise to the extent where she was bending over backwards to accommodate the other person. Lennox had got his own way such a lot of the time. He wasn't a bad person but he had been spoilt as a child and then spoilt by Hazel in turn and all because she'd loved him and believed she needed him. After her parents died, he was all she'd had left and so she'd clung to him, but she knew now that she didn't have to live her life like that.

'I came all this way . . .' Lennox finished his wine and put the glass on the table. 'Doesn't that prove to you how much I love you and need you?' He was persistent, she had to give him that.

'It proves to me that you *think* you need me. You and Valentina didn't work out and now you're lonely so you came back to what you know. But you don't need me, Lennox, and you don't love me. If you loved me, you wouldn't have cheated.'

He hung his head. 'I'm sorry, Hazel. You deserved better.'

'Yes,' she said. 'I did.'

Hazel stood up with Fleas in her arms.

'I'll get you some blankets and you can sleep on the sofa. But tomorrow you need to go back to your life and I need to get on with mine.'

'OK,' he replied sadly.

When Hazel had given him some blankets and a pillow, she brushed her teeth and washed her face then closed her bedroom door and got into bed. Fleas was already there, a gorgeously fluffy foot warmer.

Hazel had thought she'd struggle to sleep with Lennox in the next room, with her heart aching as all the awful emotions from the past year had been rehashed, but as soon as she lay down, she felt herself drifting.

She'd been strong, had avoided sinking into the old ways she'd lived for so long, and though she did feel pity for Lennox, she knew that she no longer loved him as she once had. It might have been a shock seeing him this evening but it had turned out to be a positive thing because she finally knew for certain that Lennox was part of her past.

❄

Jack handed Bella a large glass of water.

'Thanksh.' She grinned up at him. 'Hic!'

Jack had plastered on a smile and done his best not to worry about Hazel when he'd gone back inside the pub. The last thing he wanted was to ruin the party for everyone and what would be the point? Hazel had hugged Lennox, despite everything that had happened – granted, Jack only knew the bare bones of the story – and so she must have decided to forgive him. It shouldn't bother Jack. Nothing had really happened between him and Hazel and it looked as if she had feelings for the large Scotsman so she should follow her heart. But Jack couldn't help feeling like he'd lost something that evening and it was as though a dark cloud had settled over him.

'You OK?' Bella leant forwards, squinting at him. Her eyes were glassy and her hair was like a bird's nest. She'd had a great evening and, in spite of his own sadness, Jack had enjoyed seeing her relax and let her hair down. 'You sheemed sho shad after Hazel left.'

Jack shrugged, trying to ignore her slurring. 'I'm fine. I guess I'm just a bit worried about her.'

'But why?' Bella picked up her water and drank some.

'Get that all down you or you'll have a headache in the morning,' he said.

'I will.' She stared at the water for a moment then met his gaze. 'But why're you shad?'

'Worried,' he corrected her.

'That.' She nodded.

'When I went out for some fresh air, I saw Hazel with a man.'

'No!' Bella shook her head. 'Doing what?'

'Hugging him.'

'Who?'

'I think it was her ex.'

'From Shcotland?'

'He certainly was some big Scot,' he said.

'Well, bloody hell!' Bella's eyes were wide and she was staring into space. 'But he . . . he's a cheat.'

'Seems like he's come to find her and she's forgiven him.'

'Do you think?'

'They were hugging. Hazel probably still has feelings for him. I just hope she'll be OK.'

'You don't want her to be hurt again?' Bella tilted her head. 'I don't.'

'She'll be OK.' Bella stood up, nodding. 'And sho will you.'

'I guess so.' Jack got up.

'What's going on down here?' Lee appeared in the doorway in his dressing gown and slippers. 'Is my wife drunk?'

'A little bit.' Bella put her thumb and forefinger together and grinned at her husband.

Lee slid his arm around her waist and kissed her head. 'Best get you to bed with a glass of water and two paracetamol then.'

'Good plan.' Bella giggled.

'I'll get going.' Jack went to the back door. 'Night.'

'Shee you tomorrow,' Bella said. 'And Jack . . .'

'Yes?'

'Don't worry. Everything will sheem better in the morning.'

'I hope so.'

Jack let himself out and closed the door behind him. As he made his way up the steps to the apartment, he hoped Bella was right. Tomorrow would be a new day and whatever news it brought, he would be fine. He just hoped that Hazel would be OK and that she would take her time before she made any decisions about her ex because she'd been so brave moving to Little Bramble and starting over, and he didn't want her to get hurt again. He knew how it felt to have his life turned upside down and he also knew how hard it was to move on. To have someone from your past turn up must be incredibly difficult and he could understand how hard it would be not to try to turn the clock back. Familiarity could be comforting, even if it wasn't always good for you.

He opened the door to the apartment and went inside, shutting the darkness, the cold wind and the thoughts he didn't want in his head outside. All he wanted now was to escape into sleep. He wondered if Hazel was doing the same thing, then he remembered that it wasn't up to him to wonder about her any more.

Chapter 22

Hazel had woken early, fed Fleas, dressed then left her flat. Lennox hadn't stirred and that was fine with her because she hadn't wanted to speak to him again. Instead, she'd left him a note asking him to be gone by the time she got home, which she'd told him would be late morning. She knew that if she hung around until he woke then they'd have to talk. It would be awkward and he might try to change her mind again and she just didn't have anything left to say to him.

She walked through the village, savouring the crisp morning air. She felt different, as if she'd been through a kind of transformation. And in a way she had. She'd had contact with the man who had turned her world on its head and she was fine. More than fine. She now knew for certain that she no longer loved Lennox and it felt great.

When she reached the village hall, she climbed the steps and went inside. The smell of coffee and baked goods met her nostrils and she realised she hadn't eaten breakfast and was quite hungry. She promised herself a good breakfast later, once she'd done what she'd come to do.

In the main room of the hall, she looked around. She'd expected there to be more people here at Saturday morning tai chi, but there were only six others and the room was cold and felt empty.

'Morning!' Kyle waved at her from the stage. Disappointingly, he wasn't wearing his cowboy hat.

'Hi.' She smiled at him.

'Grab a mat from the back and find a spot. We'll start in five minutes. I want to wait to see if anyone else turns up first because we usually have a far better turnout than this.'

Hazel nodded, got a mat then took a place at the back. After Kyle had told her about the tai chi classes he ran, she'd been intrigued and wanted to see if it was as relaxing and energising as people claimed. Looking around, she thought it would have to work miracles to get this lot energised, but then most of them were people who'd been at the hen and stag party and so it was likely that there were some hangovers in the room.

She sat on her mat, crossed her legs and took some slow deep breaths, enjoying the quiet. Footsteps in the hallway made her glance at the doorway and she saw Clare, looking far brighter than everyone else in the room and wearing a long-sleeved pink top and black yoga leggings, a mat rolled up under her arm. She spotted Hazel and came over to her then placed her mat on the floor.

'Morning.' Clare's tone was chirpy. 'How are you feeling?'

'Oh, I'm fine, thanks. You look chirpy.'

'I feel fine. I took it easy last night, although not everyone did, and I think that's why it's so quiet this morning. Even my mum and Iolo haven't made it.'

'It was a good night,' Hazel said.

'Sam and I had a great time.'

'Is he still in bed?'

'No. He has surgery this morning so he was gone by the time I'd had my breakfast.'

'I guess animals still need to see the vet, even if it's the weekend.'

'Exactly. He doesn't work every Saturday as he takes it in turns with his business partner.' Clare looked at the stage where Kyle was drinking from a bottle of water. 'My poor boy! He overdid it a bit last night and he's paying for it now. I moved in with Sam a while back but Kyle still lives at my mum's cottage. He sent me a text this morning asking if I thought anyone would want to attend tai chi today and I told him that he couldn't let his regulars down. Besides which, it's one of his jobs so he needs the money.'

'Poor Kyle.'

'Right then.' Kyle walked to the front of the stage. 'It looks like this is it, so let's make a start, shall we? Hazel . . ?'

'Yes?'

'You haven't done tai chi before, have you?'

She shook her head.

'I'll take it slow for you then. Just follow what I do and don't worry if you don't get it first time. It takes a while to get used to the unfamiliar movements.'

'Don't listen to him,' Clare muttered. 'He's taking it slow for himself and his headache.'

Hazel giggled and Kyle glared at her from the stage.

'Focus please, ladies. We'll do some warm-up stretches first then progress into tai chi.' Hazel was amazed at how flexible Kyle was as he bent at the waist and his forehead touched his legs, then he sank into the splits before placing his head on the floor in front of him.

'Now into tai chi, class.'

Kyle started to move in a calm and controlled way, creating slow, sweeping arcs with his arms, his legs slightly bent, and Hazel did her best to follow him. She was initially self-conscious but soon found herself lost in the flow of movements, focusing on trying to coordinate arms, legs and hips while moving slowly and breathing deeply. It certainly wasn't easy, but Clare whispered to her that she'd get the hang of it if she persevered.

When the class came to an end, Hazel was tired but also relaxed and her head felt clear. This would be a good way to spend Saturday mornings, a positive way to start the weekends, and she decided to make it a regular thing, even though she had a feeling she'd ache tomorrow. As much as she loved her job, she had to have hobbies and interests outside of working hours and this could be one of them. She knew now how important it was to do things for herself.

'Did you leave early last night?' Clare asked as they rolled up their mats.

'A little bit.' Hazel glanced at Clare, hoping she wasn't offended.

'I thought so. I was going to introduce you to someone but I couldn't find you.'

'Sorry.'

'Don't be sorry. As long as you had a good time.'

'It was a lot of fun.'

Hazel took her mat to the back of the hall then returned to Clare.

'Fancy grabbing a coffee?' Clare asked. 'Although I don't have a hangover I could do with some caffeine and a bacon roll wouldn't go amiss either.'

'Sounds good to me.' Hazel nodded. The longer she stayed away from her flat, the better chance there was that Lennox would be gone when she returned home.

Clare spoke to Kyle, who muttered something about going home to bed with two ibuprofen, then they made their way to the café, which was only a short walk from the hall. Winter sun was struggling through the clouds, making the frost that had coated the village sparkle so it looked as though tiny diamonds had been scattered everywhere overnight. Everything looked fresh and clean and Hazel's mood improved further. Last night had been difficult but she felt lighter, as if a weighty burden had been lifted from her shoulders and she could breathe properly again and see the world in a whole new light. She guessed that closure did that for a person.

At the café, she got a table near the window while Clare ordered at the counter then came to join her.

'It smells good in here.' Hazel sniffed the air appreciatively. 'I'm so hungry I feel like I could eat everything.'

'Me too!'

They laughed together.

'You know . . . even though the wedding is so close now, I can't believe I'm getting married.' Clare held out her left hand and gazed at her engagement ring. 'It doesn't feel real. And to know that I'll be wearing that incredible dress is like a dream come true.'

'It's a beautiful dress and I can't wait until Sam sees you in it.' Hazel pictured Sam's eyes widening when Clare walked towards him on their wedding day; he'd probably get emotional and it would be wonderfully romantic.

'Are you OK?' Clare asked, reaching across the table and giving Hazel's hand a squeeze.

'Yes, thanks,' Hazel said, 'Just thinking about how fabulous your wedding is going to be.'

'And all because of you.' Clare grinned.

'It's because you and Sam are such a great couple and you're so in love. Everything else is just window dressing.'

'Don't be soft.' Clare shook her head. 'I'm delighted we met you and that you're planning our wedding. It's saved me a huge amount of stress, Sam too.'

'You and Sam have something special. It's restored my faith in love.'

'Really?' Clare tilted her head.

'Absolutely. Last night – last night I left early because I had a text message. From my ex.'

'Oh.' Clare winced. 'Bad?'

'Not terrible, but he'd come to Little Bramble.'

'What?' Clare's eyebrows shot up her forehead. 'But I thought he lived in Scotland.'

'He does. But he wanted to see me.'

'Oh dear,' Clare sighed. 'Are you all right? Is he still here?' She looked around as if expecting to spot him.

'I left him at my place.'

'He stayed with you?'

Hazel chewed at her lip. 'It was late and he didn't have anywhere to go and I couldn't leave him to sleep in the car.'

'You're too kind. After what he did to you, he deserved to sleep on a pile of dog poo.'

Hazel shrugged.

'OK, maybe not quite that harsh but he certainly doesn't deserve your sympathy.' Clare frowned. 'He did the unforgiveable.'

'That's the funny thing, though. I was worried about how I'd feel if I saw him again, but it was kind of liberating.'

'Aha!' Clare nodded. 'You haven't seen him for a while and now you know you don't have feelings for him any more.'

'Exactly.'

Their coffees and bacon rolls arrived then, so they thanked the waitress then waited until she'd gone to resume talking.

'So he's still at your flat?'

'He was sleeping when I left but I did leave him a note asking him to be gone by the time I get home. I don't want, or need, to see him again. He might be fine or he might want to talk about things again and there's no point. It's over. He had his chance and he blew it.'

'Good for you.' Clare raised her mug and Hazel tapped hers against it.

'Here's to starting over.' Clare grinned. 'Everything will be fine, Hazel. It will just get better from here on.'

'I hope so.'

'It will. Look at me and I've got about fifteen years on you.'

'I am.' Hazel gazed at Clare who was glowing. 'Although I don't think you're fifteen years older than me. I'm thirty-three.'

'OK, thirteen then.'

'You look amazing.'

'You're so kind I definitely want to keep you around.'

Hazel took a bite of her bacon roll. It was delicious; the roll crusty on the outside and soft and fluffy inside, the bacon salty and perfectly matched with the brown sauce.

'While we're here . . .' Hazel took a sip of coffee. 'I wanted to check if you'd decided on bridesmaids. Is it just Jenny?'

'Well, Sam and I have discussed it as he has a sister, Alyssa.'

'I didn't know that.'

'She did live in the village but now lives with her partner, his daughter from a previous relationship and their baby.'

'Do you want her as a bridesmaid?'

'I asked her but she declined. They're coming to the wedding, though. She's a beautiful young woman, a year or so older than you – and her partner reminds me of a WWF wrestler. He's *huge*.'

'Wow.'

'Alyssa had a tough time of it over the years. She was in a motorbike accident over ten years ago and it left her disabled. She uses a wheelchair and I did think she could have had it decorated with flowers if she wanted to be a bridesmaid but she said she'd prefer to sit with her partner, so . . .' Clare shrugged. 'What can you do?'

'What about you? Do you want your mum or Kyle to walk you along the aisle?'

'I've given this some thought and I've decided to walk alone.'

'No problem.'

'I love my mum and Kyle deeply but this is my journey and I feel that it's important that I walk into my new life independently.'

'I love that.'

'Thanks. I don't feel I'm being given away or anything, I'm just joining two families together and uniting with Sam willingly and hopefully, for the rest of our lives.'

Hazel's throat tightened and she waved a hand in front of her face.

'What is it?' Clare leant forwards, her eyes filled with concern.

'I'm just getting emotional again,' Hazel said, her voice wavering.

'Hazel, you really are a sweet thing.'

Hazel tried to smile but her vision blurred so she grabbed a napkin and covered her face. 'Sorry!'

'Don't be sorry. If you can't cry with friends, who can you cry with?'

Hazel allowed herself a few tears then she dried her eyes.

'I don't know what's wrong with me. I've been strong for so long and since I arrived in Little Bramble it's like the floodgates have opened.'

'It's because you're finally home.'

'Do you think so?'

'Definitely. You're settling in and finding your feet and you've been through a great deal. While you were going through it you had to survive, so you probably suppressed your emotions, but now that you feel safe, you're relaxing and letting down your guard.'

'That makes sense.'

'I know. I went through it too.'

'I'm so glad I remembered this place.'

'Me too. You're going to be very happy here, Hazel. Now . . . shall we have another coffee because you don't want to go back too early and have your ex ruin your mood if he's still there, do you?'

'Absolutely not. So yes to coffee. I'll get them this time.'

Hazel went to the counter, sending out a silent thank you to the universe for bringing her to Little Bramble where she did, she realised, feel safe and cared for.

An hour later, she walked home, a spring in her step and a smile on her face. It was a beautiful December day, she had made her new home in a lovely village and she had friends. Her business was already starting to take off and she could rebuild her life here, be happy and make the most of life.

She reached her office and let herself in then plodded up the stairs, praying that Lennox would be gone as she slid her key into the lock.

The flat was silent. She went through every room, relief rushing through her. Lennox had gone, leaving no sign that he'd been there other than a faint hint of his cologne and that would soon disappear like smoke on the breeze. She went into her bedroom and flopped onto the bed, sighing as reality dawned. This was it, then. She'd put things with Lennox to rest and her life was hers again.

Lying there, she frowned. Something wasn't quite right. It was quiet. *Too* quiet.

Where was Fleas?

She sprang up and raced around the flat, checking under the bed, behind the sofa, in all the cupboards. She called the little cat's name, her voice becoming increasingly frantic, her heart pounding.

'Fleeeeeeeeaaaas!' She tried again, checked the entire flat once more, but it wasn't a big place and the cat was clearly gone. 'Oh my God! Where are you?'

Hazel went down to the office and checked around in case, somehow, the cat had got into her workspace but, of course, she wasn't there. So there was only one place she could be. Opening the front door, Hazel peered out at the street. If Fleas had gone out there, it would all be unfamiliar. She might get scared and hide under a car or run into a house or a shop; she could get run over or chased by a dog or hurt in some other awful way. Hazel balled up her hands and pushed them into her eyes, wanting to unsee the horrific images that were racing through her mind. Fleas was her baby, her friend, her companion.

And she was gone.

She closed the door and leant against it. Crying would not get Fleas back. She needed to make a plan and work out where Fleas could be.

Unfortunately, the first thing she had to do was to contact Lennox and find out if he knew anything because when Hazel had left that morning, Fleas had been there, and since Lennox had left, Fleas had gone. *With him?* No. They didn't like each other and she doubted that Lennox would be so spiteful as to take her cat. He knew Hazel loved Fleas and even if Lennox was upset, he wasn't likely to be deliberately mean.

Back in her flat, she scrolled through her contacts and found Lennox's number but it just rang and rang. He was probably driving or so upset with her that he didn't want to speak to her, so she typed out a message instead, hoping he'd see it and reply soon. She sank onto the sofa and something dug into her leg. Shifting position, she pulled it from underneath her and gasped. It was one of the little feather toys she'd bought for Fleas. Fleas loved to chase the feathers and Hazel would tickle her belly with them or run them along the sofa and Fleas would tap at them with her paws.

'Oh, Fleas.' Hazel's heart felt like it would break. 'I can't lose you. Not now.'

Her phone pinged and she grabbed it, finding a reply from Lennox.

Sorry, H, haven't seen the cat. I opened the front door to leave and realised I'd forgotten my toothbrush, so I went back inside and grabbed it. Perhaps Fleas ran out then and I didn't notice. Hope you find her. Sorry for everything. L x

❄

Hazel fired off a reply, resisting the urge to tell him she'd kill him if anything happened to Fleas, then sat back for a moment to calm down. The most likely explanation then was that Fleas, not liking Lennox and wondering why he was there, had run downstairs, through the office then out of the door. Lennox wasn't that observant at the best of times, but if he was distracted by sadness, anger or thoughts of his journey back to Scotland then there was a chance that the cat could have run past him and escaped.

The best thing for Hazel to do would be to walk around the village and hopefully she would spot Fleas herself but if not, she'd leave her number with people and ask them to let her know if they saw her. She found a recent photo of the cat on her phone and sent it to the printer in the office. She'd hand the photo out with her number and call in at the vet's and some of the shops and ask them to put the photo up. She'd even offer a reward if she needed to. She'd do anything to make sure Fleas was OK. Anything at all.

Chapter 23

Jack unscrewed the lid of the bottle of Coke he'd bought at the shop and took a swig. He didn't drink a lot of sugary drinks but after last night's party, he needed a pick-me-up. It was a lovely crisp winter morning and the air felt good on his skin. He'd picked up some pastries to take back for Bella, who was extremely hung-over, and for Lee and the girls. He'd got extra because he knew that Aster would probably want a bit of one too.

He put the bottle in the tote bag he'd found in the garage then strolled back through the village, admiring the Norwegian Spruce on the green and the Christmas lights. The wedding was a week today and he hoped the weather would be as nice as this for the outdoor ceremony. Everyone was looking forward to it and he felt sure it would be a great day for the village.

He looked up and spotted Hazel. She was speaking to a woman outside Turning Heads, the village hair salon, and she looked worried. She handed the woman a piece of paper then turned and looked around. Instinctively, he waved and called her name and when she saw him, she hurried towards him.

'Jack!'

'What is it?' Her eyes were red and she was incredibly pale. 'Did something happen last night with . . .' How could he say Lennox's name without admitting that he'd followed her outside and seen them together?

'What?' She was shaking her head as if her life depended on it. 'Do you mean with Lennox?'

'Who?' He asked the question even though he felt like an idiot for pretending he didn't know what she was talking about.

'My ex, Lennox. He turned up here last night. It's why I left early.'

'Right.' He nodded. 'And you're OK, are you?'

'About Lennox?' She wasn't looking at him, instead her eyes were darting around madly as if she'd lost something. 'Yes. That was all fine.'

What did fine mean? Did she still have feelings for him? Were they getting back together then? Would she pack up and head back to Edinburgh with that cheating scumbag? He certainly didn't deserve her.

'Then what's wrong?' he asked, swallowing his questions about her relationship.

'It's Fleas!' She grabbed his arm. 'I don't know what to do.'

'What do you mean?'

'She's gone missing.'

'When?'

'Today. This morning. Lennox was at my flat and he must have let her out when he opened the door and she's not been out around here yet; I was waiting for the right time and she won't know her way around and she might be unable to find her way home and . . . and . . .'

271

Jack placed his hands on her shoulders. 'Hazel?'

'Yes.'

'Look at me.' He was trying to ignore the fact that she'd said Lennox was at her flat because it meant that he'd stayed the night and Jack didn't want to deal with that right now; he wanted to help her.

She looked at him and he could see the depth of her pain and worry in her eyes. She loved her cat and needed to find her.

'It's going to be OK. We'll find her.'

'We will?' Her turquoise eyes were cloudy, her long hair windswept and she'd clearly been chewing at her lower lip because it looked dry and bruised.

'We will. She can't have gone far. Give me some of those fliers and I'll help take them around the village.' He gently released her shoulders and held out his hand. Hazel gave him all of them, so he counted off a few then gave the rest back to her. 'This is Fleas?' He looked at the photo.

'Yes.'

'She's lovely.'

'Thank you.'

'Right, you go to the rest of the shops on this side of the village and I'll walk the long way around and let people know. I'll hand some of these in at the bistro, the vet's and the café. I bet someone's seen her already.'

'Do you?'

Hazel looked so bereft he wanted to hug her to him, to hold her tight and make all of her worries go away. She deserved to have someone who cared that much about her. He also wanted to ask what Lennox was doing to help find the cat but sensed that this wasn't the right time and so it was better to leave it for now.

'If I hear anything I'll phone you straight away and you make sure to do the same, OK?'

She nodded. 'Thank you so much.'

'No problem.'

He turned and walked away, stopping people as he went to ask about the cat and to show them the photo. Finding Fleas was his priority now, so Bella would have to wait for her breakfast.

Forty minutes later, he'd done the rounds and no one had seen Fleas. With so much woodland nearby, though, it wasn't surprising. The cat could easily have gone roaming through the fields or crept into a woodshed or garage and gone to sleep. She could even have gone inside someone's house without them noticing while they had the door or a window open. He sent Hazel a text telling her he was popping to Bella's to drop off their breakfast and then he'd go out again.

'Bella?' he called as he entered the warm kitchen.

'Over here.' Bella waved him over to the kitchen sofa. 'And not so loud.'

He smiled. 'Headache, huh?'

'Terrible. It's like someone's put a pneumatic drill inside my skull.' She grimaced. 'I haven't felt like this since I was about eighteen.'

'Not worth it, is it?'

'Well, I did have a good night.'

'You did.'

'Didn't you?'

'I did but . . . uh . . . never mind.' If Bella had forgotten their conversation then he didn't want to go through it all again. 'I have your breakfast here.'

He set the bag on the table along with the A4 photographs of the cat.

'What's that?'

'It's Hazel's cat. She's gone missing.'

'Oh no!' Bella stood up but she winced and sat back down again.

'You stay there and I'll make you some coffee.' Jack held up a hand. 'Where's Lee?'

'Looking for some tool in the garage to fix Penny's mountain bike.'

'I didn't realise she had a bike.'

'She hasn't used it for a while but a friend of hers is going out tomorrow and she's decided she wants to join her.'

'At least it's been dry for a while so she won't get covered in mud.'

'Jack, the states that girl has come home in after she's been riding I'm surprised the washing machine hasn't died yet.'

'I didn't think she'd be into something like that. She can be so quiet and reserved.'

'It's girls, Jack. You have no idea what they get up to, believe me. Penny is far tougher than she looks.'

'It sounds like a very positive thing to do.'

'It is. Hey!' She sat forwards. 'If you stay in the village you can get a bike too and go out with her. She'd love that.'

'Sounds good to me.'

'Anyway, you said Hazel's cat's gone missing.'

'She got out this morning and, so far, there's been no sign of her.'

'She's a cat, though. She'll be fine.'

'I hope so. I'll make your coffee then I'm going to go back out and look for her.'

'You're a good man, Jack.'

'You just love me because I bring you breakfast and speak quietly when you have a bad head.'

Bella grinned. 'Hurry up with that coffee, will you?'

Jack took coffee and a pastry out to Lee, who was in the garage with Penny.

'Thanks, Jack. How's my wife?'

'Feeling sorry for herself.'

'So she should be.' Lee winked. 'Self-inflicted headache.'

'Indeed,' Jack said. 'I've got to go. Hazel's cat is missing and I said I'd help look for her.'

'Well, if you don't have any luck I'll help later. I just need to fix this for Penny because she wants to go out tomorrow.'

'Bella said. See you later.'

Jack went out into the garden and was about to head down the drive when he heard a noise. He turned and went around to the back garden, listening carefully.

At the far end of the grass Aster was standing outside the small blue shed, crying and scratching at the door.

'What is it, girl?' he asked.

She whined and scratched again then the door opened a fraction and Bobby emerged.

'Hey, Bobby.'

'Uncle Jack.' Her eyes widened and she shut the door behind her and leant against it.

'What are you doing?' he asked, instantly suspicious.

'Nothing.' Pink spots appeared on her cheeks.

'Nothing?'

'No.'

'Why's Aster trying to get in there?'

Bobby looked down at her trainers. 'Don't know.'

'There's something in there that she wants.'

Bobby shrugged. 'It's a . . . a rat.'

'A rat?'

She nodded.

'Why don't you take her inside then and I'll see if I can catch it?'

'No!' Bobby flung her arms wide and shook her head. 'You can't go in there. It's massive and it has huge teeth and it will bite your leg off.'

'I see. And yet you were OK in there.'

'I hissed at it and scared it but it will bite *you* for sure.'

'Why don't we let Aster in there then? She can scare it off.'

'No!'

'Why not?'

'She'll . . . she'll chase it.'

'But if it's a rat that's a good thing, surely?'

'It's not.'

'Not a rat?'

She shook her head and dropped her gaze to her shoes.

'Can I have a look in there, Bobby?'

'Why? It's not my fault. It just turned up and it was hungry and so I gave it some ham and it likes me so I don't know why I can't keep it.'

'Keep what?'

She sighed and stepped away from the door. Jack opened it and went inside, waiting for a moment while his eyes adjusted to the gloom. There was a small window high on the one wall but it didn't let in much light because of the large trees outside.

Against the far wall was a workbench, what looked like an old chest of drawers and some garden tools. The shed smelt of wood, compost and turps. It was a strange combination but not unpleasant. He looked around, treading carefully in case there was actually a giant rat in there that would savage him as per the ones in the horror books he used to read as a teenager.

'Fleas?' he called softly. 'Are you in here?'

There was a shuffling from under the bench then blue eyes blinked at him and there was a quiet meow.

'Is that you, Fleas?' he asked, crouching down.

The cat crept out from under the bench and came over to him. He held out his hand and she rubbed her head against it then the length of her body, ending with a flick of her tail.

'Hello, girl. Your mummy's worried about you. We'd better get you home.'

He pulled his phone out and tried ringing Hazel but there was no answer, so he sent a text telling her he'd found Fleas and was bringing her home. He gently picked the cat up and was surprised at the lack of resistance she put up in light of the fact that she didn't know him at all. He tucked her inside his coat in case she got cold and opened the shed door.

Bobby was standing there, arms folded, a thunderous look on her face.

'You can't take her. She's mine.'

'Where's Aster?'

'Inside. She wanted to eat the cat, so I had to take her away.'

'Greyhounds don't always get on with cats. They can live together but only after being introduced carefully,' Jack said, remembering something Bella had told him recently. 'And sometimes it just won't work at all.'

'But it's my cat!'

'She's not yours, Bobby,' he explained. 'She belongs to Hazel.'

'What?'

'Her name is Fleas and she's Hazel's cat.'

'Then why was she in our garden?'

'She ran out of Hazel's flat this morning and must have come here to find a safe place to hide.'

'I think she came here because she wants to be mine.'

'Oh, Bobby.' He shook his head. 'I'm sure she likes you but she needs to be with her mum.'

'Can I visit her then?' Bobby asked, hopefully.

'I'm sure Hazel will be happy for you to visit.'

'Now?'

'Probably not now. I'm going to take her back and Hazel will most likely want some time alone with her.'

'Will you ask her when I can visit?'

'I will, I promise.'

'OK then. Bye-bye, Fleas. See you soon.' Bobby reached up and petted the cat's head then she skipped off to the garage.

'Come on then, Fleas. Let's get you home.'

When Jack reached Hazel's office, she was standing outside staring into the distance.

'Hazel?'

She turned and her expression changed instantly when she saw him.

'You found her!' She ran to him and took Fleas from his arms. The cat started to purr immediately.

'I did try to phone you . . .'

'I was asking around the village. I saw that I'd missed your call but then I saw your text and so I was waiting for you to get here.' She snuggled the cat to her chest and kissed her head. 'Thank you so much, Jack. I'm so grateful I don't know what I'd do if I lost Fleas. She's my whole world.'

'What about Lennox?' The question shot out before Jack could stop it.

'What about him?'

'I thought that he was your world again.'

'Oh, Jack, no. It's over between me and Lennox. Seeing him again confirmed that for me.'

He opened his mouth but found that he didn't know what to say.

'Come on.' Hazel reached for his hand. 'Let me make you a drink to say thank you.'

She led him inside and he closed the door behind them, wondering at the enormous sense of relief he felt knowing that Hazel and Lennox were over. It meant that she was free of the man who had caused her so much pain, the man who didn't deserve her. Hazel was a wonderful person and she should only ever be with someone who would love her properly.

Chapter 24

Safely back in her flat with Fleas in her arms, Hazel experienced a mixture of relief and exhaustion. She'd been so worried about Fleas, had wondered if she'd ever see her again, and now she was back and it was all thanks to Jack.

'Take a seat.' She gestured at one of the sofas in the lounge. 'Do you want a drink? Tea? Coffee? Something stronger?'

'After last night, I'll stay off the booze but tea would be great.' He frowned as if something was bothering him. 'Shall I make it, though? You can keep hold of Fleas then.'

'It's fine. I'll get her something to eat then I'll get the kettle on.'

She went through to the kitchen, got Fleas a bowl of food then set about making tea. Her hands trembled as she poured boiling water over teabags so she stopped for a moment and rested her elbows on the worktop, her head in her hands. What a morning it had been! Waking to find Lennox in her home had been weird but she'd told herself it was a good thing that she didn't have feelings for him anymore. Tai chi had been enjoyable, as had been going to the café with Clare. And then coming home to find her baby gone had been dreadful.

'Hazel?'

She stood upright and turned to find Jack right behind her. 'Are you OK?'

'I . . .' To her horror, tears filled her eyes then ran down her cheeks and she shuddered with emotion, hugging herself.

'Hey!' Jack came to her and placed his hands on her shoulders. 'It's all right. Fleas is back safe and she's fine. She was with my niece in the shed, so she didn't get hurt and she didn't even seem that scared when I found her. She came to me readily enough when I said her name.'

Hazel looked up at him. He was tall and broad-shouldered, his eyes warm and earnest and his hands on her shoulders felt reassuring. He smelt good and she could imagine how it would feel to step forwards into his arms and have him hold her.

So she did.

He went stiff for a moment then his hands moved from her shoulders to encircle her, rubbing gently at her back in a way that was comforting but also stirred something inside her. He felt strong and in his arms she felt safe. It had been a long time since she'd been held by a man and felt this cared about, comforted and this . . . aroused.

She tilted her head and gazed up at him. His eyes darkened. Hazel reached up, took his face in her hands and stood on tiptoe so she could kiss him. At first, she touched her lips gently against his, feeling him quiver against her as if he had never been kissed before, and then he was pressing her against him, kissing her harder and she was overwhelmed with an urgent need to be even closer to him.

'Jack!' She gasped as she pulled back to speak to him. 'I—'

Next to them Fleas meowed, breaking the spell, and they both looked down at the cat then started laughing.

Jack gently released Hazel and she straightened her top, smoothed down her hair. Her whole body was tingling and she knew they'd come very close to taking their friendship to a whole new level.

'Wow,' she whispered as she turned back to finish making the tea.

'My thoughts exactly.' Jack squeezed her shoulder, the pad of his thumb rubbing at her nape. 'Perhaps it's a good job Fleas is here or who knows where that might have led.'

Hazel turned and handed him a mug of tea.

'I really like you, Jack . . . and I'm so grateful that you brought Fleas home. You're our hero.'

He smiled and blushed, and again she felt a stirring of something for him – lust and something else, something softer and sweeter. He was absolutely adorable.

'Well, that's today's mission accomplished then.' He peered at her from under his dark lashes. 'And I really like you too.'

❅

Jack sat on Hazel's sofa and sipped his tea. She was at the other end of the sofa, a safe distance between them, with Fleas stretched out on her lap. His cheeks glowed every time he thought about how close they'd come to tearing each other's clothes off in the kitchen. It had been a long time since he'd been kissed like that or felt that much desire and if Fleas hadn't meowed when she had then he didn't think they'd have stopped.

And that was a bit worrying because he did like Hazel. In fact, he liked her too much to confuse things between them.

Hazel's ex had turned up just last night and left this morning. She was probably vulnerable after that and then going through the trauma of losing her cat. Falling into Jack's arms was an understandable reaction. He had wanted her badly, to lose himself in her and to feel the wonderful intimacy of being with another human being, but now that he'd cooled down a bit, he knew that it was complicated.

After what had happened with Danni, Jack knew he was damaged and he also knew that it was more complex than anyone else was aware of. He hadn't told Hazel the full story and he didn't know if he was ready to share it with her yet, if at all. If he was ever to have an intimate relationship with anyone again he needed to know that they were with him for the right reasons, that they wanted him as much as he did them. He wasn't sure that he was strong enough if anything were to go wrong. How genuine were their feelings? Could he trust someone else and most importantly, could he trust himself?

He finished his tea then stood up.

'I'd better get going. Bella will be worried because I dashed off without explaining what had happened.'

Hazel looked up at him and nodded.

'Thank you so much again, Jack. I can't bear to think what would have happened if you hadn't found her.'

'I suspect that Bobby would have had her dressed up like a superhero and that she'd have eaten her bodyweight in ham.'

Hazel yawned. 'Excuse me. I feel really tired.'

'Snuggle down with Fleas and have a nap. It's probably what you both need. You've got a busy week ahead.'

He reached for a throw from the back of the sofa then held it up and Hazel shuffled down, Fleas curled up next to her, and he draped the throw over them.

'Don't worry, I'll lock the door on my way out.'

'Thanks.' Her eyes were already closing. Before he could think about what he was doing, Jack leant over and kissed her forehead, then left her to rest.

But as he pulled the flat door behind him then the front door downstairs, he felt as if Hazel was still with him. Her scent was on his skin and her kisses still burned on his lips. It was as if she had awakened something inside him and, now it was conscious again, it had no intention of going back to sleep.

Chapter 25

Hazel pushed the door to the bistro open and went inside. She was there to confirm the buffet menu for the wedding reception. The bistro was a cosy space, decked out in deep reds, from the curtains to the red-and-white tablecloths and the red votive holders on the tables. It was late afternoon and, being a Tuesday, the bistro didn't start serving meals until seven, so there were no customers. It made her feel like sitting at a table near the window, ordering some wine and watching the world go by.

She admired the Christmas tree in the corner that was draped with tiny gold star lights and the others that were hung along the front of the bar. It was the type of place that she loved to visit, a haven where she could enjoy good food and wine and not have to tidy up afterwards. She made a mental note to book a table there soon.

There was a swing door off to the side of the bar that she guessed led to the kitchen and classical music came from there, something she recognised but couldn't name. The smell of tomato and garlic drifted out, making her mouth water.

'Hello!' she called, not wanting to give anyone a fright, even though Lorna Osborne, the owner, was expecting her.

A head peered around the door to the kitchen.

'Hazel?'

'Yes.'

'Hello!' The woman came out of the kitchen, wiping her hands on a white apron. She had a scarf around her hair and perspiration on her brow. 'Excuse the state of me. I've been frying onions and garlic for a tomato sauce and it's really warm in the kitchen.'

They shook hands then Lorna offered Hazel a drink. When they both had glasses of lemonade, they sat at a table near the bar.

'So, you wanted to confirm numbers and the menu for the buffet?'

'That's right.' Hazel opened her tablet and set it down on the table between them.

'I'm very excited about this,' Lorna said as she read through Hazel's list. 'It's such a wonderful opportunity to cater for a local event and I hope it will be the first occasion of many.'

'It's my first wedding in Little Bramble too so I hope we'll work together again.' Hazel said. 'This could be the start of a beautiful working partnership.'

'Sounds good to me.' Lorna nodded. 'This all looks fine.' She gestured at the tablet. 'I thought that dessert could be a variety of things like mini lemon meringues, raspberry pavlovas, chocolate tortes and almond cakes. What do you think?'

'That's the sort of thing Clare and Sam said they were hoping for and it sounds delicious to me.'

'Excellent. My partner, Serge, is away this afternoon at a food festival in London, getting some inspiration, but he's the chef and he's very talented.' She laughed. 'He cooks such amazing food that it's hard to resist.'

'I can imagine.' Hazel smiled then sipped her drink.

'Is everything ready for the big day?'

'Just about. I need to help Kyle with decorating the village hall on Friday and then we'll be good to go.'

'Who knows? It could be me and Serge tying the knot next, although I'm not sure if we ever will.'

'Not everyone has to get married.'

'That's true and sometimes I think I'd like to marry him and on others I think, if it's not broke why try to fix it?'

Hazel nodded. In some ways she agreed with Lorna but she also wasn't about to discourage someone who could, however far along the road, be a potential customer.

When they'd confirmed times and facilities that could be used at the hall, Hazel packed up and left, but not before Lorna had insisted on giving her what was effectively a takeaway of pasta, chicken, sauces and some side dishes. Lorna said that they had plenty prepared and that she'd like to know what Hazel thought.

Walking back to her flat, Hazel wondered if Jack had been to the bistro and if he'd like to go there with her. She hadn't seen him since Saturday and did wonder if he was avoiding her or if he'd just been busy – she certainly had been. She knew that he had his nieces' school play this evening and had sent him a text saying that she hoped it went well. After the way they'd kissed on Saturday, it could be awkward between them next time they saw each other, but she really hoped not. Seeing him would certainly bring a lot of feelings rushing back and, as Saturday had shown her, she wasn't always able to control herself around him. In fact, some might say she found him irresistible and with a wedding just days away, she shouldn't allow herself to be distracted. She also had a feeling that she didn't know everything there was to know about him, that he might be holding something back. She'd shared everything about her relationship with Lennox and she was glad that Jack knew her whole story now.

Even if she didn't see him before then, she'd see him on the day of the wedding, and if she had time, she'd be able to assess her feelings for him and find out if they were as strong as she suspected they might be.

'Are you looking forward to my school play, Uncle Jack?' Bobby asked as they walked to the school.'

'I am indeed,' Jack said.

'Is it all you can think about?' Bobby tugged at his hand.

'It's all I've thought about for days.'

'Good. That means you're really excited then.'

Bobby let go of him and skipped ahead.

Jack hadn't been entirely honest with Bobby. He was looking forward to seeing her school play but his mind had been swamped with thoughts of Hazel for the past three days, wondering what she was thinking and feeling and if she had regrets about kissing him like that. Jack didn't have regrets but he did think it had been a bit irrational on his part to kiss her. Hazel had been upset and he'd intended comforting her, but being so close to her, smelling her skin and wanting to protect her had all overwhelmed him and when she'd reached for him, he'd been unable to resist.

He hadn't spoken to anyone about what had happened, not even Bella, because it felt private, something that he and Hazel had shared. He also had a disturbing sense of guilt because he hadn't kissed anyone since Danni and, until he'd met Hazel, hadn't wanted to. Did that mean that Hazel was special or that he was healing? Should he be healing yet or should he still be grieving? How long was a person meant to grieve, especially when the circumstances were like his, when all was not what it had seemed to be?

'Whatever's on your mind, try to leave it at the school gates,' Bella said as she slid her arm through his. 'I know you've been troubled since the weekend and I'm not sure why, but don't forget that you can speak to me about anything.'

'I know.' He inclined his head. 'And I am all right. I just have some things I need to work through and they're not quite clear enough in my head to share yet.'

'I'm here when you're ready.'

'Thanks.'

They reached the school and lined up behind the families of the pupils while the pupils themselves went on inside. Jack had dressed warmly because even though the school was just a short walk from Bella's, it was a very cold night and the forecast had been for minus numbers with a warning of icy roads. The sky was clear, the moon almost full and it bathed the schoolyard in a silvery light. All around them people chatted, their breath like smoke in the chilly air, their perfumes and colognes competing for precedence. The lights of the school glowed warmly, promising a cosy interior and a pleasant evening ahead.

When they reached the front of the queue, Jack was assaulted by aromas of chips and paint, of paper and coffee. All schools seemed to smell the same and it tugged at his heartstrings because it brought back memories of his own days at primary school when Bella had been his world. Back then, he'd been innocent, unaware of what lay ahead, unmarked by life or time. Just like Penny and Bobby were, although Penny was in her final year of primary school and would soon head off to the comprehensive where she'd grow up quickly. Primary schools were small ponds where there was a sense of safety and community, where teachers usually had the respect of pupils and where parents were involved. This changed with secondary education as children became more independent, but knowing that they had a home and loving parents was something that Jack and Bella had never taken for granted. Though their parents had moved to Florida, they were still there when Jack or Bella needed them, but they were getting older and Jack tried to spare them worries, just as he knew Bella did. They deserved to have a relaxing and worry-free retirement, to know that their children were happy and successful, getting on with their lives. Jack had tried to get on with his life but he could see that he'd been treading water, waiting for something to happen and now that it had, he was apprehensive about what came next.

'This way.' Bella led him along a hallway that had pinboards on the walls decorated with paintings and poetry, photographs and class lists. They passed one pinboard near what appeared to be the staffroom and Jack stopped suddenly.

'Is that a job advert?'

'Oh yes. It went up today. The school needs another teaching assistant to work with some pupils in Year 5 with a focus on literacy and numeracy.'

Jack looked at Bella and she looked at him.

'You're not interested in applying, are you, Jack?'

He read the advert again, then met Bella's gaze.

'What do you think?'

'Well, if you want to become a teaching assistant, then it's worth a shot and if you think you might still want to go into teaching at some point, it's good experience too. I'm not sure how it would work in terms of a pathway into teaching but you'd certainly have on-the-job training.'

'Would I be suitable, though? I don't have any experience.'

'You have a degree and good literacy and numeracy skills. Plus I think they'd like a male TA because the school is overrun with women. If you're interested, then why not apply?'

'Is it online?'

'Everything is these days. They still post on the boards here as well, though, so that staff know what's going on. Transparency is everything in Little Bramble Primary and I've worked in schools where it's not, so I really appreciate how things work here.'

'I'll take a look at the full job spec when we get home.'

'Please do.' Bella grinned. 'If you got a job here you could stay in the village and it would be just wonderful!'

Jack laughed; Bella's enthusiasm was making him feel excited too.

'There will probably be lots of applicants so I won't get my hopes up, but I will look into it.' And he would, because after spending almost six weeks in the village, the thought of going back to Swansea was less appealing by the day. It wasn't that Swansea wasn't beautiful, because it was, but it didn't have Bella, Lee, Penny or Bobby. It didn't have Aster. And it didn't have Hazel.

There were lots of reasons to stay in Little Bramble and he found that they were starting to outweigh the reasons for going home. But then Swansea no longer felt like home, so perhaps the time had come for him to move – and getting a new job in education would be the perfect way to get the ball rolling.

❄

Jack sat down and placed his coat on a chair to reserve it for Lee, who was coming straight from work. They'd been working extra hours at The Lumber Shed to get things ready for the wedding as well as to get Christmas orders out on time. Penny was already at the school because she was helping out backstage. As a TA, Bella had helped prepare the children during the school day and once she'd shown Jack to the hall and his seat, she'd gone to help get the children ready.

Sitting alone, Jack looked around at the hall. It was, to his mind, a typical school hall with a stage at the front, tall windows on the walls to the right and left of the stage and double doors at the rear. To the left of the stage were doors leading to another room and steps up to the stage, and to the right was a large Christmas tree, groaning with lights and decorations. The smells he'd encountered at the entrance were stronger here, as if the years of school meals, paint and paper had permeated the walls and floors and filled them so they couldn't absorb any more and now they were seeping back into the air.

He turned and spotted Lee at the door so he waved and Lee nodded in response then weaved his way through the chairs to reach him.

'Evening.' Lee was flushed and still wearing his work clothes. The smell of sawdust and varnish came with him and Jack suppressed a smile. 'Everything OK?'

'Great,' Jack said. 'Bobby made me swear that I'm looking forward to this and that I've been thinking about it non-stop for days.'

'As I'm sure you have,' Lee said and winked.

'I most certainly have.'

'Me too. I've thought of nothing else other than how excited I was about sitting in a hall surrounded by the smell of children's feet and old chip fat and frowning at the elderly ladies as they rustle sweet wrappers and call out to their grandchildren.'

Jack laughed. 'School plays, eh?'

'I love it really, although last year at the girls' old school in Woking, the granny who was sitting next to me laughed so hard at one scene that her dentures shot out and landed in my lap.'

'NO!'

Lee gave a dramatic shudder. 'It traumatised me for weeks but Bobby thought it was hysterical when I told her about it and made me tell her the story over and over.'

Jack laughed as the image kept replaying in his mind.

'I'm honoured to be here, Lee. Not having children of my own it's been a long time since I went to a school Christmas play and there's something special about it.'

'I say the same to Bella every year.' Lee nodded. 'It's like a proper start to Christmas. I'll be a bit sad when the girls no longer take part in them.'

'Bella will still be working here, though, and I'm sure she can get you a ticket.'

'I don't think it'll be the same if my daughters aren't involved.' Lee shook his head.

'I guess not,' Jack replied, although if he went for the TA job and got it, he'd be here for future school plays and that thought was quite appealing. There was always something going on in a school, whatever time of the year it was, and he could be a part of that, play an important role in the community and he'd be proud to be involved.

He pulled his phone from his pocket and turned it off, not wanting any interruptions as the play began, then sat back as the lights went down. When the festive music began and a line of very small children shuffled across the stage, a lump rose in his throat and he had to blink hard to clear his vision. This was what really mattered, this was what went on all over the country at this time of year, and whatever he had thought or felt since Danni had died, he knew now that life really did go on.

Chapter 26

The day before the wedding arrived, bringing cloudy skies and a chilly wind that whipped around the village, howled down chimneys and made Hazel's teeth chatter as she walked to the village hall. A few errant snowflakes drifted down and she wondered if there would be more as the day went on. Snow would be lovely for the winter wedding.

She had two large bags with her, each containing decorations, a jar of good-quality instant coffee and chocolate biscuits. It was going to be a busy day and she'd need the caffeine and sugar.

When she reached the hall, she climbed the steps and went inside, smiling as the warmth enveloped her like a hug. Today, instead of the usual scents of the hall, there was a smell of spices and flowers which was fresh and also festive.

She carried her bags into the main room and set them down by the door.

'Good morning!' She smiled at Clare, Kyle and Elaine.

'Hey there.' Clare hurried over to her and hugged her tightly. 'I can't believe it's tomorrow! I'm getting married tomorrow. Oh my goodness, I'm so nervous and excited I feel like I'm going to burst.'

'And she's done this before so it's not as if she's a virgin sacrifice at the wedding altar.' Kyle rolled his eyes, but he was smiling.

'Kyle!' Clare put her hands on her hips and scowled at her son.

'Mother?' He reached for her and hugged her with one arm then kissed the top of her head. 'I'm just trying to reassure you that everything will be wonderful.'

'It looks fabulous in here already.' Hazel looked around at the tables that had been organised into groups. They had dark purple tablecloths and dried wild-flower arrangements at their centres in jam jars that had been decorated with acrylic paints in purple and silver swirls. The chairs were covered with purple seat covers and they had large silver bows tied around them.

'Mum and Iolo did the jars and Mum bought the flowers when I told her about the colours we wanted.'

'They're beautiful. Funnily enough, though, I thought I could smell fresh flowers when I came in.'

'The smell of flowers is coming from the diffuser on the stage.' Clare pointed. 'It's geranium essential oil.'

'I love it.'

'Right, what's next?' Elaine asked, joining them.

'How about coffee?' Hazel offered.

'That is a wonderful idea.' Kyle clapped his hands. 'Then we can finish off here.'

'I had a text from Connor this morning to say that he'll be at the green this afternoon getting things ready there,' Hazel said to Clare.

'Brilliant! It's all so exciting.' Clare placed her hands on her chest, eyes shining.

'You've picked up the dress and everything else?' Hazel asked, just for her own peace of mind.

'Yes, it's at home, ready,' Clare replied.

'You should see Nanna's hat,' Kyle said. 'It's like a hot-air balloon.'

'Kyle, you cheeky sod!' Elaine scowled at him. 'It is not.'

'It's huge.' He circled the air around his head with his hands. 'At least if it snows we'll all be able to shelter under it.'

Hazel bit her lip and turned away as laughter bubbled. 'I'll go and make coffee.'

Jack had agreed to help out at the green with Connor and Lee. Connor's other staff were either at the workshop finishing orders or delivering them, so he was grateful for an extra pair of hands in Jack.

They'd loaded the things Connor had prepared into his van and were on their way to the green now. As they drove slowly past the village hall, Jack looked out of the window and his heart fluttered because there was Hazel, standing on the steps with Kyle. She was flushed and smiling, a mug cupped in her hands, the breeze toying with her hair. And it hit him like a lightning bolt: she was the most beautiful thing he had ever seen.

Connor drove past The Red Squirrel then parked at the side of the green. 'OK, then. Let's get the green wedding-ready.'

They got out of the van and Jack pulled on his hat and gloves. It was chilly and there were snowflakes in the air, the sky looking as though it might be holding a lot more.

He helped Connor and Lee to unload the van and they carried the arch Connor had created from reclaimed driftwood over to the tree, where they stabilised it then set up the matching outdoor table Connor had created in front of it. The registrar would need somewhere to put the documentation and it would be nice for photographs afterwards, Connor had reasoned.

Then they set about fetching the benches that Connor and Lee had made for the guests into rows set at an angle. Everything was made from reclaimed wood of some kind and Connor had said that the arch and table could go in Sam and Clare's garden after the wedding and the benches be given to the village hall to be used for other events.

'That's that done then.' Connor dusted off his hands. 'We just need to get the lights from Sam and then we can add the finishing touches. You want to have some lunch with us, Jack?'

'I'm all right, thanks. Bella's home today so I said I'd go back and eat with her.'

'Tell my lovely wife I'll be home a bit earlier today, will you?' Lee asked. 'Connor said we can finish early as people want to get ready for tomorrow.'

'Of course.' Jack smiled. 'I think I'll pop to the hall first and see how it's going there.'

In other words, see how Hazel is getting on, he thought, hoping that neither Connor nor Lee could read his mind. He jogged from the green to the hall and up the steps.

Inside it smelt strongly of flowers and festive spices that made him think of mulled wine. He went through to the main hall and his mouth dropped open.

'Wow!' he said. 'This looks incredible.'

Hazel waved at him from the stage where she was hanging lights on a silver Christmas tree. There were five of them along the stage in a row, each one twinkling with tiny lights. The room had been converted from a plain old village hall into a winter wonderland decorated in silver and purple.

'Do you think so?' Clare came to his side. 'I hope Sam likes it.'

'I'm sure he will. Is he at work?'

'He's gone to collect his suit and the rings,' she explained. 'As well as the dogs' wedding attire.'

'The dogs are having special outfits too?'

'Coats and collars.'

'Sounds good,' he said.

'And Nanna has the biggest hat!' Kyle grinned at him from a ladder near one of the windows where he was hanging more fairy lights.

'Cut it out, Kyle. You don't have to tell everyone.' Elaine waved a fist at her grandson.

'I'm just preparing them all, Nanna. It could come as quite a shock to some when the wind blows and you drift away like some sort of UFO, never to be seen again.'

Jack laughed as he walked over to the stage and climbed the steps. 'Anything I can help with, Hazel?'

'I think we're almost done, but thank you.'

'You've done a wonderful job.'

'I'm glad you think so. Although,' she said, standing up and pressing her hands into her lower back, 'I can't take the credit for all this. Clare, Kyle and Elaine had done most of it before I even got here.'

'A proper community effort.'

'Exactly.'

'It feels very festive in here.'

'That's what we were aiming for.'

'And very . . . romantic too.'

He held her gaze and her lips parted. He thought of how good she had tasted and found himself stepping closer, then remembering where he was and what their situation was, and stepping back again.

'Romantic is good too,' she said, her voice barely more than a whisper.

'Looks like you two need to get a room,' Kyle said from his position on the ladder.

Jack looked over at him and Kyle held up his hands.

'Just kidding, handsome. Gosh, does no one around here have a sense of humour anymore? What with Nanna and her flying saucer hat and Iolo with his musty old suit and Mum with her . . . her . . .' He furrowed his brows. 'Oh, I don't know, I can't think of something to tease Mum with. But anyhow, I was just saying that Hazel and Jack have that look that people get when they're in love . . . or is it lust?' He shrugged. 'Whatever, I say. Just don't hang around. Get on with it and hurry up and be happy for goodness' sake. Life is short and it's not a rehearsal.'

'Kyle, please.' Clare was shaking her head. 'Remember what we said about filters? Try to think before you speak.'

'Mother . . .' He climbed down the ladder and sniffed. 'There's far too much filtering going on these days. We can't say this and we can't say that and what's the point? We all just need to get on with living and stop worrying so much. If I think two people look like they have electricity between them and one of them is now a very dear friend, then I'm going to say something.'

'But it's not always your place to say something,' Clare said, looking over at Hazel and Jack. 'I'm sorry.'

'It's fine,' Hazel replied, and Jack nodded.

'See?' Kyle cocked an eyebrow. 'Honesty is the best policy.'

'I give up.' Clare held up her hands. 'Right then, are we done?'

'It looks like it.' Elaine smiled as she looked around.

'Do you fancy a coffee?' Hazel asked Jack as she descended the steps from the stage.

'That would be great.'

He followed her to the kitchen, trying not to imagine what it would be like to kiss her again. It was as though something had got hold of him and he couldn't shrug it off, something that was making him a bit crazy and tempting him to do wild things that he knew weren't really appropriate in polite society. It made him feel young and wild and free again. And while he was trying to rein it in, he also wanted to embrace it and do as Kyle had advised. Kyle was right, of course; life was short so you had to grab happiness while you could.

❄

Hazel handed Jack a coffee then they leant against the kitchen island and gazed out of the window that overlooked the garden at the side of the hall.

'Look at the snow!' Hazel said. 'It's starting to thump down now.'

'It'll be cold tomorrow.' Jack followed her gaze.

'Everyone has been warned to wrap up warm and there will be mulled wine and hot chocolate served as well as outdoor heaters, so hopefully it will be OK.'

'I like the idea of an outdoor wedding.'

'Do you?' Hazel asked, wanting to ask him questions about his. With any other friend, she might have asked, but she worried about upsetting Jack or raising things he'd rather not discuss. After all, she'd found it hard talking about what had happened with her and Lennox and it was probably the same for Jack.

'I got married in a small church in Swansea,' he said, looking at the snow and not at her.

'Did you?'

'It was the church Danni's parents got married in and she wanted to marry there too. It was a family tradition and kind of expected, so that's what we did.'

'How was it?'

He frowned as he remembered. 'It went on a bit long, but it was a good day. We were . . . very happy back then.'

He sighed. 'Things were good for a few years. We got along well and she loved her job and I . . . well, I got on with mine. Working in insurance sales was OK. Not my dream job but it paid the bills and there were good commissions. I was happy supporting her dreams anyway.'

He sipped his coffee and Hazel stayed quiet, wanting to give him the space to talk or to let the conversation fade away if that was what he preferred. He was opening up to her and she desperately wanted to know more about him, but she also knew how hard it could be to say some things out loud.

'I might go for a job at the village school,' he said eventually, taking Hazel by surprise.

'Yes?'

'It's a teaching assistant position. I don't have any experience but I do have a degree and Bella said they'd train me on the job.'

'That sounds exciting.'

He nodded. 'It would get me into education and I could either work my way up to be a higher-level TA or study further and go into teaching.'

'It sounds like a good way to find out if it's what you still want to do.'

'I think so. Plus, it would mean that I could stay in Little Bramble.'

Hazel's stomach somersaulted. 'Where would you live?'

'Bella said I can stay in the apartment over the garage for as long as I like, which is very kind of her and Lee, but if I'm lucky enough to get the job then I'll look for a place of my own. I've had an offer on my house so I'll have the equity from the sale to use as a deposit.'

'How wonderful.' Hazel said. 'I'm renting my little flat but I'd like to buy a cottage if things go well here.'

'We're both starting again.' He smiled.

'Kindred spirits.'

'In more ways than one, I think . . .' He put his mug down and stepped closer to her and her heart started to race. 'Hazel, I—'

'Is the coffee ready?' Kyle waltzed into the kitchen and Jack jumped away from Hazel and went to stand by the window.

'It is, sorry.' Hazel indicated the tray of mugs. 'I got distracted.'

'I can see that.' Kyle waggled his eyebrows. 'And I don't blame you, sweetie,' he muttered as he picked up the tray and carried it away.

'The ground has quite a covering now.' Jack peered up at the sky. 'Could be a very white wedding indeed if it keeps going.'

'Jack?' Hazel licked her lips. 'You were about to say something before Kyle came in.'

He shook his head. 'It was nothing. There's no hurry. I'd better be going because Bella's expecting me.'

Disappointment coursed through Hazel. 'Oh . . . OK.'

'Hey . . .' He shook his head. 'It's all good and tomorrow will be wonderful.'

'It will.' She wished he could stay a bit longer but knew he had things to do too.

He swilled out his mug and hers then set them in the dishwasher.

'Have a good afternoon and I'll see you tomorrow.'

'Bye, Jack.'

She watched as he made his way along the hallway, fighting the urge to chase after him and ask him what he was going to say. This was all so confusing, emotional and unexpected. She'd moved to Little Bramble to escape her ex and ended up liking another man – more than she wanted to like him. She hadn't imagined this happening for years, hadn't thought she'd even be able to entertain the thought of being near another man again after having her heart so cruelly broken. But sometimes, it seemed, the heart made its own decisions and though terrified of having feelings for Jack, she couldn't seem to fight them, and the more that time moved on, the more she found she didn't want to fight them anyway.

And if he did get a job in the village school then he'd be around permanently too. That meant there would be more time for them to get to know each other and that, perhaps, they could pick up where they left off the other day.

Chapter 27

The day of the wedding dawned and Hazel was awake early following a restless night, her sleep filled with nightmares about grooms who didn't turn up and brides whose wedding dresses had shrunk in the wash. When she finally gave up on getting any rest, she wrapped herself up in her fluffy dressing gown and trudged to the kitchen for coffee and toast that she carried through to the lounge.

She was about to snuggle up with Fleas on the sofa when she realised that the light was strange, even for December, so she went to the window and opened the blinds.

'Oh . . .' She stared out at the street below. Everything was white. Cars, trees, pavements, the road . . . It had snowed heavily overnight and though it had stopped for now, Hazel wondered if it would snow more later.

She went to the sofa, sat down and pulled the throw over her and Fleas, then reached for her mug. Snow had been something she had envisioned at the wedding, but that was rather a lot of snow. Still, it was fine. Everything was fine. She'd send some texts to people from the village like Connor, Bella, Marcellus the postman and Jimmy Burton who owned The Red Squirrel and they'd sort it all out. And, of course, she could message Jack too.

Just as she was about to eat her toast, her mobile buzzed and she glanced at the screen. It was Clare, and from what she'd said in the text message, she was not feeling as calm as Hazel was trying to be . . .

❄

'Where are you going so early?' Jack asked.

'To help dig.' Bella pulled a hat over her hair and stuffed her feet into snow boots.

'Dig?'

'Yes, idiot, haven't you seen the snow?'

'Of course I have.' He had because he'd come over from the apartment early to check if Bella needed him to do anything this morning and because he'd run out of milk. 'But I thought Hazel wanted snow.'

'Some snow but not *that* much snow. Hazel sent a group text asking for help. Didn't you get it?'

Jack scratched his head. 'I left my phone next to my bed.'

'I'm sure she messaged you too. Actually, she did because I saw your name on the top of the message.'

'I'd better come and help then.'

'I'll do you a coffee in a travel mug and you can have a mince pie.'

'For breakfast?'

'It is almost Christmas so it's allowed.'

'I like that rule.'

'Me too.' Bella grinned at him. 'Now go and wrap up warm.'

'Yes, ma'am.'

※

At the green, Hazel looked around feeling a combination of anticipation and dismay.

'That's a lot of snow, hey, Hazel?' Marcellus David stood with his hands on his hips, a frown on his face. Even his lilting Caribbean accent couldn't thaw the green this morning, but Marcellus' avuncular way made her feel certain that he could help to fix this. 'Don't you worry now, we'll get this sorted for little Clare and make sure she has the best wedding ever.'

'Thank you so much,' Hazel smiled at him and he squeezed her shoulder.

'No problem, Hazel, but we'd better get digging.'

'Of course.' She picked up the spare shovel he'd brought. 'We need to ensure that there's an aisle here for them to walk along and to clear the benches off so people can sit down.'

'Best get those outdoor heaters lit soon and they'll help to melt some of it.' Bella had arrived and if Hazel hadn't been holding a spade full of snow, she'd have thrown herself at her and hugged her.

'Thanks, Bella.'

'No problem.' Bella turned. 'Hurry up, Jack.'

Jack was dragging a cart behind him. 'It's not easy to move this through the snow.'

'Put some muscle into it, little brother.'

'It's easy for you to say that.' Jack grimaced as he pulled the cart onto the pavement then across the snow-covered grass towards the tree.

'We've brought more spades and coffee and mince pies for energy.'

'Brilliant.' Hazel's heart swelled with gratitude for these wonderful people.

'Here, let me do that.' Jack came over to her side with a spade.

'I'm capable of doing it.' Hazel straightened up and met his gaze.

'I'm not suggesting for a moment that you're not.' He adjusted his bobble hat. 'But if I dig this over then you can go and check on the bride. I'm sure she could do with some reassurance this morning.'

It made sense after the message Hazel had received. 'And you're all happy to do this? Are you sure you don't want me helping too?'

Bella, Jack, Connor, Marcellus and Jimmy stood there looking at her, smiles on their faces, spades in their hands. Then, as if summoned by some invisible force, more villagers appeared, carrying garden tools, pushing wheelbarrows and some even had buckets of hot water.

'Hello!' Emma Patrick smiled as she arrived with her father, Greg, who was holding a lead with a greyhound at the end of it. Emma and Greg were wrapped up against the cold, but the greyhound seemed to be wearing more layers than either of them with just her nose and eyes visible. 'I've come to help dig and Dad and Harmony will supervise.'

'Thanks, Emma.' Hazel's face twitched as she tried to control her rising emotions.

'It looks like we've got this covered. Go check on the bride.' Jack winked at her and Hazel's chest filled with warmth. She'd been worried about how she'd deal with the snow and keep the day running smoothly but the community of Little Bramble had come together to help and it was wonderful.

'Thanks so much!' She blew kisses at them all, then hurried to Clare and Sam's cottage, keen to reassure them that the day would be exactly what they had dreamt of.

At Clare and Sam's she didn't even need to knock, the door swung open and Clare stood there, hair in rollers, white dressing gown stained with what looked like foundation around the collar and a face so pale she looked as if she could fit in with the waxworks at Madame Tussauds.

'Come in!' Clare stepped back and Hazel followed her. 'Excuse the state of me but I started to do my makeup then I started crying and it streaked so I washed it off and was about to start again but I—'

'Hey, it's OK, Clare. It's all going to be OK.'

'Better than OK, I keep telling her.' Kyle stood in the kitchen doorway wearing a zebra print kimono with a wide headband holding his hair back from his face and what looked like false eyelashes on one eye. 'I've tried to get her to have a glass of champagne but she keeps refusing.'

'I think that's exactly what you need.' Hazel nodded at Kyle over Clare's shoulder and they all went into the kitchen.

'Where are Sam and the dogs?' Hazel asked.

'Gone for a long walk to calm down, I think. He said he needed to clear his head.'

'That's probably wise.'

'And Mum was winding him up by being so wound up herself. He's going to drop the dogs back later then go and get ready at Connor's so he can see Mum in her finery for the first time when she walks towards him along the aisle.'

'Lovely.' Hazel bobbed her head. 'And what about Elaine?'

'Getting ready at hers then she said she'd be here.' Clare shrugged. 'She's probably trying to persuade Iolo to wear something tidy because he lives in jogging bottoms and shorts. Having been a vicar for so long, until he retired last year, he doesn't believe in wasting money on clothes when he says the ones he has are perfectly good and he can donate more money to charity.'

'Right, sit down while I take my coat off then we can have a look at your makeup. And Kyle,' Hazel tilted her head, 'we might need to take a look at yours too.'

'I'm fine, darling.' Kyle fluttered his one eye. 'I was just trying these on to see if they suited me, but Mum can have them back now.'

'Kyle, I don't want them.' Clare shuddered. 'They're like insect legs and I just know I'll end up with them stuck somewhere other than my eyes.'

'That can happen.' Hazel said, remembering a bride who'd gone through exactly that. She'd been so emotional at her wedding ceremony that the false eyelashes she'd worn had slid down into her cleavage and no one had noticed at the time, but when her wedding photographs had come through it looked as if she had a hairy chest. The photographer had, thankfully, been able to airbrush them out but it could have been a disaster.

'I knew I should have hired someone to do my makeup but I just thought I wouldn't wear much and I didn't want to look like a clown or a Kardashian because while they're all gorgeous, it's just not me to wear that much eye makeup and I wanted to look like myself and . . .' Clare slumped into a chair. 'And it's snowed so much and what if it's too much and . . . Sorry, I think I'm a bit anxious.'

'Well, firstly, the green is being cleared as we speak, and it just so happens that I have some skills of my own in the bridal makeup department.'

'You do?' Clare's eyes filled with hope. 'And you can make me look natural and not like RuPaul? Again, he's fabulous, but I don't want to look overdone or like I belong on a drag show or—'

'Mum! Have a bloody drink and calm the fudge down.' Kyle pressed a flute of champagne into Clare's hand then poured another and held it out for Hazel.

'Oh no, I'd better not. Busy day and all that.'

'I'm not taking no for an answer.' Kyle raised his eyebrows. 'Have a drink with the bride and let's get this day started as we mean to go on.'

Hazel relented and accepted the glass. 'All right then.'

'To a wonderful white wedding.' Kyle clinked glasses with Clare then Hazel. 'Or is it silver wedding?'

'Sorry?' Hazel frowned, thinking he must be referring to the colour scheme for the reception.

'Well, Mum and Sam are getting on a bit, so their heads are silver, therefore it's a silver wedding of sorts.'

Clare shook her head. 'You're a cheeky thing, Kyle! I might have some grey hairs but not that many.'

'No, Mother dear, because the stylist at Turning Heads covers them all up for you.'

Hazel looked at Clare and saw that her shoulders were shaking and concern filled her.

'Clare?'

Clare snorted. 'Sorry! It's just that Kyle always makes me laugh.'

'Distraction at its finest.' Kyle gave a small bow then winked at Hazel with his false eyelashes. He was trying to take Clare's mind off her worries by teasing her and it seemed to be working.

'Now get that champers down your throat then Hazel can make you beautiful.'

Clare did as she was told then placed her empty glass on the table and Hazel got to work.

✱

Jack stood back and rested his hand on his spade. He'd worked up quite a sweat but the green was already looking more presentable. Not that the snow wasn't pretty, because it was fresh and soft and clean, but at least now there was an aisle for the bride and groom to walk along, the benches were clear and dry and the outdoor heaters had been lit to warm the area up. Someone had also brought some faux fur throws and set them on the benches for people to sit on or under and Jimmy had set up his mulled wine and hot chocolate stall behind the Christmas tree so people could get hot drinks.

'Good job, baby brother.' Bella patted his back.

'We have done well, haven't we?'

'Lee would've been here too but I asked him to get the girls up and ready. Penny has started taking longer and longer in the bathroom and we all need to get in there at some point this morning.'

'The mince pies went down well.'

'They did. Penny will have to make some more for us at home.'

'Hello, everyone.' Marcellus stood in front of the driftwood arch with his hands raised. 'Thanks so much for your help this morning. It makes me so proud to be a part of this community. Today is a very special day and now Clare and Sam can have a fabulous wedding and we can all celebrate afterwards at the village hall. Get yourselves off home to get ready and we'll see you back here later.'

Jack packed up the cart again then he walked home with Bella, hoping that the day would be everything the bride and groom had hoped for and more.

Chapter 28

'Not long now!' Bella squeezed Jack's hand. They were sitting on one of the benches on the green with Lee, Penny, Bobby and Aster, all of them wrapped up in warm coats, boots, hats and gloves. The faux fur throws on the benches provided extra insulation and the heaters that had been placed at the end of each row gave off enough warmth to take the bite out of the air.

The village choir were standing to one side of the driftwood arch and the registrar was behind the table, dressed in a sheepskin coat and deerstalker hat, along with what Jack thought might be ski gloves because they made her fingers look like well-stuffed sausages. The choir had run through a medley of carols and now they were singing 'Silent Night'. It made the hairs rise on the back of his neck because it was so beautiful and because it had been Danni's favourite. What would she have made of all this? he wondered. She'd never wanted to move away from the place where she was born and grew up, so Jack certainly wouldn't be considering moving to Little Bramble and he didn't know how he felt about that. There had been many good times with Danni, some wonderful Christmases too, and he had some lovely memories of their time together, but he also had some difficult ones . . .

'Look!' Bella nudged him and he followed her finger.

It was Hazel. Wearing a long silver-blue padded coat with a loose silver beret and silver knitted gloves, she looked like an ice princess. She had a tablet in her hand and a serious expression on her face as she strode to the front. Clearly, she was in business mode and he had to admit that she looked very attractive when she was focused; her strength and resilience impressed him again.

Sam arrived next and walked towards the front of the aisle, pausing along the way to greet people. He was wearing a silver suit with a purple tie under a wool coat. His head was bare but there was a heater near the front so Jack assumed he'd be OK. Sam leant over to kiss a woman in a wheelchair on the cheek who had a young baby in her arms and he guessed she must be Sam's sister. Next to her was a giant of a man, with his arm protectively around her shoulders.

When Sam reached the arch, he spoke to the registrar for a moment and then he turned and Jack saw the anticipation and excitement in his smile as he waited for Clare to arrive.

The choir moved seamlessly from carols into 'This Will Be (An Everlasting Love)' and all heads turned around.

First, came Elaine and Iolo, arms linked, smiles on their faces. Elaine's hat was enormous and made Jack think of a hula hoop with a bucket in the middle. When they were seated, along came Kyle, a huge grin on his face. He was wearing a leopard print suit with a luminous pink tie, matching hat and shoes. At his sides walked two dogs, Goliath the Great Dane and Scout the yellow Labrador. Even the dogs looked proud in their purple coats lined with silver padding and with sparkling collars around their necks, each with a ribbon tied to it.

'The wedding rings are tied to the ribbons,' Bella whispered.

'Nice touch,' Jack replied, rubbing Aster's head as she pulled at her lead, probably wanting to greet the other dogs. 'You can play with them later,' he said softly to her.

When Kyle had gone to stand at the side of the arch, there was a collective gasp. Clare stood at the end of the aisle with Jenny. They hugged then Jenny made her way along the aisle to the front. She looked lovely in a purple gown that fell to her boots and a matching purple cape and seemed to float past as the material of her dress and cape billowed out behind her.

And then came Clare . . .

She looked beautiful, her face illuminated by the fairy lights that twinkled round them in the late afternoon, and also by joy, because she was about to make a commitment to the man she loved. Her champagne silk dress and matching faux fur wrap contrasted with the silky brown curls that fell to her shoulders. Her green eyes were fixed on Sam alone as she walked towards him.

When Clare reached Sam, he took her hands and they gazed at each other as if they were the only people on the green. Around them, lights twinkled on the arch, the large Norwegian spruce and on all of the surrounding trees.

The choir fell silent and a sense of expectant peace settled over the village.

Then the ceremony began.

❄

Hazel sniffed, struggling to hold back tears as Clare and Sam untied the ribbons on their dogs' collars then placed the rings on each other's fingers as they spoke the vows they had written. It was a moment Hazel had witnessed many times before but it never ceased to be special; it was as if the love between Clare and Sam shone out of them and wrapped itself around all who were present.

A tear rolled down her cheek and she wiped at it absently. She'd thought that she'd be married by now, spending her first Christmas with her husband. But seeing Clare and Sam, she was glad, because what she'd had with Lennox had been nothing like this and so she knew, absolutely, that it had been wrong. They'd both had a lucky escape because they'd got out before they were married and, though it had been terribly painful at the time, it had been for the best.

She glanced around and saw Jack a few rows back next to Bella and her family. And then, as if sensing that she was looking at him, Jack met her gaze. Something jolted through her and she gasped. She averted her eyes but not before she'd seen that whatever she'd felt, Jack had felt too.

When the bride and groom kissed, the choir began to sing 'At Last' and everyone clapped and cheered.

❋

While Iolo, apparently a talented photographer, snapped photos of the bride and groom, the guests made their way to the village hall. There was a buzz of excitement in the air and Jack found himself enveloped by it. This day was about two people coming together to share their love with family and friends and it had been wonderful so far.

'Are you going to dance with me later, Uncle Jack?' Bobby asked as they walked to the hall.

'Uhhh . . . I'm not much of a dancer.' He shrugged.

'Of course he will,' Bella said. 'Everyone dances at weddings.'

'I guess that means yes then,' he said, nodding at Bobby.

'Yay!' she said then she grabbed Penny's hand. 'Come on, Penster, let's get there first so we can find our table.'

Penny rolled her eyes at Jack but she hurried on ahead with her sister anyway, clearly keen to know who she was sitting with.

'You OK?' Bella asked.

'Me?' Lee replied.

'No, you dolt! I was asking Jack. Why wouldn't *you* be OK?'

'Because I'm cold and hungry and can't wait to get you on the dance floor, my love.' Lee grinned at her.

'I'll save you a dance.' Bella took her husband's hand. 'But I was asking Jack.'

'I'm fine,' her brother said. 'It was a great ceremony.'

'And you're . . . all right?'

'I'm better than all right. Seeing Clare and Sam so happy and being here with you guys has helped me see that life goes on. I can't change what happened and unless I want to give up and waste whatever time I have left, I need to look forwards.'

'You have an interview now to look forward to, don't you?'

'I do.' He'd received an email to say that he would be interviewed in January for the teaching assistant role. He'd only sent the completed application off the day after the show and the head teacher's PA had emailed him late last night, telling him that they'd like to interview him after Christmas. It made his stomach churn with nerves but he kept telling himself he could do it, he had a good head on his shoulders and he had a lot to offer professionally. Just because he'd been in the wrong job for so many years didn't mean that he couldn't switch careers and follow the path in education that he'd always dreamt of.

'You'll be brilliant at it,' Bella said, 'and we can all be together as we should have been.'

'I hope so,' he replied.

'Come on then, you lot, let's speed up a bit because I'm starving now and I'm a bit worried that Bobby will have got there, found out she's not happy with where she's sitting and is moving place cards around as we speak.' Lee shook his head. 'Goodness only knows what she might do. Clare will probably be on the children's table and Sam will find himself in the kitchen.'

Jack laughed. Lee was exaggerating but he could imagine Bobby doing something to upset the apple cart. She was a sweet girl but she was still young enough to put herself first most of the time, except when it came to him, he thought. She had, after all, asked Santa to make Jack happy instead of getting her any Christmas presents and that was a very selfless act indeed.

Chapter 29

Hazel walked around the hall taking photos on her phone. Iolo was there in the role of official photographer, but she thought it was always nice to have unofficial shots too and had encouraged the guests to take some then share them with the bride and groom after the big day was over. It was amazing what images guests could capture and always nice to see a variety of perspectives. As part of the package she'd offered Sam and Clare, she would gather the best unofficial photographs and put them together as a photo book to go along with the official photo album.

When they'd got back to the hall following the ceremony, guests had been served flutes of champagne or non-alcoholic festive punch. The DJ who'd been hired for the evening had set up on stage and he played requests until Clare and Sam arrived and received a round of applause.

The buffet provided by the bistro had been delicious and there had been plenty to go round. Hazel's tummy was full and she'd allowed herself a glass of champagne to toast the bride and groom as Kyle, Connor and Elaine made speeches. Alyssa had also said a few words but then her baby had started crying so she'd had to finish quickly.

And now there was dancing.

Hazel was circulating with her smartphone, but try as she might, she couldn't stop her eyes seeking out Jack. He looked smart and very handsome – but best of all was the fact that he'd been smiling constantly. Being with his family was clearly very good for him and she was glad to see how happy they made him. She also wasn't surprised because Bella, Lee and their daughters were lovely people and would bring happiness to anyone's life.

'We've a special request this evening from Sam,' the DJ announced over the microphone. 'He's asked us to play a song that many of you will know well and which is the perfect wedding theme. So now the bride and groom will take to the floor for their first dance to 'I've Had The Time of My Life' by Bill Medley and Jennifer Warnes.'

The song began and Sam and Clare made their way onto the dance floor. Sam took Clare in his arms and gazed at her as if she was the only other person on the planet. Hazel's vision blurred and she blinked hard, keen to watch the couple she'd become so fond of as they danced to the uplifting song. When they launched into a professional dance routine that would have got them at least a seven on *Strictly Come Dancing*, everyone cheered. They moved gracefully around the floor, their eyes locked, as they circled each other, twirled and shimmied.

Kyle came to Hazel's side.

'What do you think?' he asked.

'That's incredible. Where did they learn to do that?'

'I might have taught them a thing or two.' He waggled his eyebrows.

'You're amazing, Kyle.'

'I try.' He blew on his fingers then dusted them on his jacket. 'And you're pretty cool too, Hazel. Thanks for planning this fabulous wedding. It must be a fascinating job and I bet there's never a dull moment, is there?'

'There never is,' she replied.

'I'd be interested in finding out more about being a wedding planner.'

'I'd be happy to talk you through it anytime—'

'Excuse me.' A tall man with long blond hair, a hipster beard and piercing blue eyes appeared in front of them. 'Sorry to disturb you . . .' He had a strong accent, his voice rising and falling in a way that Hazel placed as Norwegian. 'But I'd like to have this dance, Kyle, if I may?'

'Hazel, this is my partner, Magnus.' Kyle grinned at her. 'Isn't he wonderful?'

Hazel watched as Magnus led Kyle away and they started dancing, performing the same moves as Clare and Sam. Everyone gathered around, clapping and tapping their feet until the finale where Sam swept Clare off her feet and kissed her passionately. The song changed to Ed Sheeran's 'Perfect' and more couples joined them on the dance floor. Hazel stepped away, her heart aching at the beautiful song and at what it meant for so many people.

She saw Bobby dragging Jack to the floor and she wondered if he could dance as well as he could skate. Bobby held his hands and stepped from one foot to the other and Jack did the same, smiling down at his niece. Hazel snapped some photos, thinking he and Bobby would like them, then she wandered around taking more of other guests, the Christmas trees on the stage and of the whole room. A village hall might not seem like the ideal location for a wedding reception to some people but to Hazel, it was perfect. They had everything they needed here, could convert it to make it suitable for lots of different occasions and it meant that all the people who mattered could be present without soaring costs and transport issues.

'Excuse me.'

Hazel looked up from her phone. Marcellus David was holding out a hand.

'Would you like to dance, Hazel? I don't like to see a beautiful young woman standing at the sidelines when she should be dancing.'

'Oh . . .' Hazel accepted his hand. 'Thank you, Marcellus. Yes, please.'

He led her to the floor as Chaka Khan's 'I'm Every Woman' came on. Marcellus was a good dancer and Hazel followed his lead, smiling as he twirled her around then strutted his stuff, making her laugh. Around them people danced, some showing off moves that were seriously impressive, some doing a basic shuffle, and the atmosphere was incredible. As the song came to an end, Hazel was breathless – Marcellus had a lot of energy. The music slowed and Hazel thanked him for the dance then turned to leave the dance floor, but someone was blocking her way.

She looked up into Jack's eyes and a shiver ran down her spine.

'Dance with me?' he asked.

She felt weightless, feeling that she could drift away with happiness as he took her in his arms, one hand on her waist, the other holding her hand. She rested her head on his chest and moved in time with him. Around them lights twinkled like thousands of stars and time seemed to slow right down as Hazel relaxed into Jack's embrace. For the first time she felt she understood what people meant when they talked about being lost in the moment.

Jack was like an anchor, holding her there, offering her nothing and yet everything, because the only thing that was guaranteed was the here and now.

❄

When the song ended, Jack wanted to keep holding Hazel. It had been a wonderful day and he felt happy and content. He had watched two people who loved each other make a commitment in front of friends and family. He had drunk champagne and eaten delicious food, danced with his nieces and sister and laughed – a lot. Throughout the reception he'd been conscious of Hazel as she'd wandered around, taking photographs, checking people had what they needed and being the epitome of the social butterfly that being a wedding planner required. Hazel was professional yet warm, attentive and sincere, tireless in her efforts.

When he'd seen her dance with Marcellus, he'd known that he had to hold her, dance with her, gaze into her eyes. But now the song was over and he didn't want to let go.

'I could do with some air,' she said.

He nodded his understanding and they weaved their way through the hall, collected their coats and went out into the hallway. Hazel opened the door and stepped outside, then turned to look at Jack. With the green behind her, lit up as it was, she looked like some sort of ethereal creature. Her eyes seemed lighter than usual, her cheeks glowed and her lips were parted as if in question.

Jack glanced behind him at the hall where lights flashed and the beat of the music vibrated through the walls. People were having a good time; they had everything they needed to be happy and he could too. As he'd grabbed his coat, Bella had caught his eye. She'd seen him with Hazel; had smiled her approval.

Hazel held out her hand and Jack took it then they descended the steps and hurried away into the night.

✶

When they reached her office, Hazel fumbled with the key as she tried to get it into the lock. She was trembling from the cold but also with nerves. She wasn't sure if this was a good move but she was also tired of worrying, wanted to lose herself for a while without thinking and hesitating and trying to do the so-called right thing.

She had feelings for Jack and believed that he had feelings for her too. They were both adults and yes, they had pasts, but they also had the here and now and perhaps that could be enough.

Finally, the key slid into the lock and she turned it, almost tumbling inside as the door swung open. Jack followed her up the stairs and into her flat.

Hazel removed her coat and boots then stood there, waiting, wanting Jack to make the first move. He shrugged off his coat, letting it fall to the floor, stepped closer and took her face in his hands, ran the pad of his thumb over her lips, making her moan with need. Then he kissed her and everything else slipped from her mind. There was no more worry, no more fear, no more hesitation . . .

There was Hazel and there was Jack . . . and then they became one.

Chapter 30

Jack woke up with a jolt and blinked. He had slept like a log in Hazel's bed with her lying next to him, one leg draped over his, her arm across his chest.

He lay very still, not wanting to disturb her. Her breathing was deep and regular and in the grey light of dawn that seeped through the curtains he could see her eyelids fluttering. She was so beautiful that his chest hurt. He hadn't been with anyone other than Danni since he was a teenager and it had been strange and yet wonderful, more wonderful than he could have imagined. There was a chemistry between him and Hazel that had carried them through the night on waves of pleasure as they had explored each other's bodies then fallen asleep still wrapped around each other. Each time they had stirred, they'd ended up making love again and now Jack felt sated and yet . . . incredibly vulnerable.

He held the thought for a moment. Why did he feel vulnerable?

His feelings for Hazel were more than just desire; they were deep and intense and that made him vulnerable to being hurt again. What if it was the same for her? What if they ended up hurting each other without meaning to, just as had happened with Danni?

The need to get outside and run flooded through him and he bit down on his lip as he slid out from under Hazel, then located his clothes and dressed quickly. He thought about leaving her a note but worried that she'd wake and then he'd need to face her and he couldn't do talk right now. He had to be alone. He needed time to think.

He glanced into the lounge to check the cat was safe then he left the flat, pulling the door behind him, and jogged down the stairs and out through the front door. As he hurried back to his apartment, he was barely aware of the snow falling on and around him or of the drifts he had to plough through because he was so busy trying not to give in to the pain in his heart.

❆

Hazel woke to find Jack gone. Her first reaction had been shock and intense sadness, then frustration and anger. She'd made a cup of tea then got back into bed, trying to understand why he had left before she woke. She knew some things about Jack's past, knew that something had happened between him and his wife, was aware that any relationship breakdown would affect future intimacy. She didn't want to judge him for being nervous or afraid and yet she was devastated that he'd left without saying anything. She knew how it felt to be vulnerable, she was going through it too, but she had been able to put her pain aside and to find closure. But perhaps it was still too early for Jack to do the same.

Last night had been incredible. They had held each other, been as close as two people could be and Hazel had discovered a passion inside her that she hadn't known existed. Her feelings for Jack weren't fleeting and she wanted to be with him, but she knew that might not be possible because it had to be right for Jack too.

Fleas padded into the bedroom and jumped up on the bed and Hazel finished her tea then snuggled back down. The sheets smelt of Jack and she pressed them to her face, keen to hold on to last night for as long as she could, though her cheeks were wet with tears and she made no effort to wipe them away.

❄

Jack pulled his keys from his pocket as he reached the top of Bella's driveway, then froze because Bella was staring at him from the lounge window.

It was barely six a.m. but she was up and had seen him coming home.

He raised his hand and she gestured at the side of the house, so he went around and she let him in through the kitchen door.

'Coffee?' she asked.

'Please.'

He pulled out a chair at the kitchen table and sat down then hung his head in his hands. What was he going to do?

Bella placed a mug in front of him then joined him.

'You're up early,' he said.

'I'm always awake early but it's not every morning that I see my brother doing the Walk of Shame.'

He looked up and she smiled at him.

'Sorry,' he said.

'Why are you sorry? You're a grown man and what you get up to is your business. They call it the Walk of Shame but you have nothing to be ashamed of.'

'But I'm a guest in your home and—'

'Jack,' Bella sighed, 'I saw you leave with Hazel last night and I was happy for you. She is lovely in every way.'

'I thought you'd be disappointed in me.'

'But why?'

'Because I spent the night with her.'

'The only thing I'm disappointed about is seeing you creeping back here at this time. Why aren't you still with her?'

'I . . .' He swallowed hard. 'I woke up and panicked and had to leave.'

'Did you speak to her before you left?'

He shook his head.

'Oh, Jack, that's not good. Imagine how Hazel will feel when she wakes.'

'Don't. Please don't.' He rubbed at his eyes and tried to fight the tears that stung them. 'I don't want to hurt anyone.'

'Tell me what's wrong.'

He looked up and took some deep breaths as he tried to control his emotions. 'I like her . . .'

'I know you do.'

'A lot. I think I have feelings for her.'

'Well, that's good, Jack, surely?'

'I don't know. What if I'm wrong? What if *this* is wrong?'

'You've been through a terrible time, and I feel for you, I really do, but this is different.'

'There's more to it.'

'Is there?' She reached for his hand. 'Tell me.'

So he did and it was like a spring uncoiling. When he'd finished, he felt like he could sleep for a month.

'Do you know what you need to do now?' Bella asked.

'Have a shower and go to bed?'

She shook her head. 'You need to go back to Hazel's and tell her what you just told me.'

His mouth fell open. 'I can't do that.'

'Why? Because it would mean laying all your cards on the table and being completely honest with a woman you care about?'

'Yes.' He nodded. 'I'd be completely exposed.'

'And?' Bella raised her eyebrows and held his gaze.

He was silent, forcing himself to think, then: 'You're right. If Hazel and I are to have any chance of being together, I need to tell her everything.'

'Well, go on then, because if she's already awake, I bet she feels bloody awful. I know I would.'

He got up and pulled his coat back on then went to the back door. He paused and turned back to Bella.

'Thank you. I don't know what I'd do without you.'

'You don't need to wonder about that because I'm right here.'

He hugged her then left, knowing that she was right and he did owe Hazel far more respect than he'd shown her this morning. She deserved total honesty and so that was what he was going to give her.

By the time Jack got back to Hazel's, he was white from head to toe. The snow was coming down heavily and Little Bramble was like a winter wonderland. Everything seemed muffled, even his breathing as he pressed the intercom button outside the office door.

What if she was furious with him for leaving this morning and refused to listen to him? What would he do then?

He would fight for her, beg her to listen to him because they couldn't leave things like this. They'd both been through too much.

When Hazel answered the intercom, Jack said hello, but she didn't buzz him in. He waited, wondering if she would change her mind, but then the door to the office opened and there she was.

'Hazel – I'm so sorry.'

She gave him a small smile.

'What can I do for you, Jack?'

'I'm so sorry for running off. I panicked – and though it's no excuse, I really feel awful. Can I come in, please? I want to tell you something.'

She pursed her lips for a moment then sighed. 'But shake that snow off first because you look like some kind of yeti.'

He looked down at himself and realised she was right.

Upstairs in her flat, she made them tea then they went through to the lounge and sat down. Jack took the same sofa as her, not wanting to put distance between them, but didn't try to touch her – not yet. He needed her to hear what he had to say first.

'I'm so sorry, Hazel.'

333

'You don't need to keep apologising, Jack. I'm not going to pretend that I wasn't hurt to find you gone this morning but I'm sure you have reasons for leaving like that, though I do think you could have handled it better. I've been through a break-up too, as you know, but I don't want to let it affect the rest of my life.'

'A break-up?' He rubbed at his forehead. 'I know what Lennox did was terrible. But . . . It has been difficult for me but it's not that. Not a break-up. See, my wife, Danni, didn't leave me. She was killed in a car crash.'

'Oh God! Oh, I'm so sorry.'

'I'm sorry that you didn't know, that I wasn't clear about it. I just – I've found talking about it so hard and I-I just assumed you knew. I thought Bella might have told you.'

Hazel nodded. 'Bella told me you'd been through some tough times and that if you moved here, you'd be alone. I assumed she meant your wife had left you. I had no idea about the crash.'

'It was awful. I thought I'd never get past those dreadful first days. But there was more to it than losing her in the crash. It was . . . more complicated.'

'Tell me. I want to understand.'

He sighed. 'I did love Danni. For a long time, she was my world. I did everything I could to make her happy and I made some sacrifices, but I was happy to do that for her, for us. In the last year of our marriage, though, I started to feel that the time might be right for us to start a family. I tried to speak to Danni about it and initially she was quite positive but then, as weeks turned into months and we still hadn't made any concrete decisions, I asked her to sit down and have a serious conversation about it. She was non-committal and I found it hard but I didn't want to put too much pressure on as her job was exhausting, mentally and physically, so she had to feel the time was right too. However, the last time I asked her if we could try, she agreed. She said it could happen quickly or take a year or more, so we had to be patient.'

Hazel watched his face as he spoke. This was hard for him and there was pain in his eyes. It must have been awful to hope that he was going to have a baby soon then to lose his wife in a fatal crash.

'We'd been trying for a while, but not really trying because Danni kept making excuses about being too tired or she'd go out. We'd have needed a miracle to actually conceive. I even started wondering if it was the right decision because a gulf had opened up between us and we weren't as close as we'd been before.' He rubbed at his face, the memories clearly hard to dredge through. 'Then she died.'

Hazel put her mug on the coffee table and shuffled closer to Jack, then took his hands in both of hers. Whether he wanted to be with her or not, she had to be there for him. She cared about him and seeing him in pain hurt her.

'I'm so sorry,' she said softly.

'Me too. It's tragic that she died so young. She was a brilliant nurse and she'd have gone far in her career and helped so many people. But after she died, they gave me her things . . . things she had in her car on the night of the accident. Her mobile phone was in her bag and in my need to feel closer to her when my grief was raw I read her text messages. There was one there to me that she hadn't sent but had composed weeks before. It said that she loved me but not in the way she used to. That she'd fallen out of love with me but felt trapped by my sacrifice – because I'd given up my teaching dreams to support her. She said she felt terrible about it and was trying to get past it but when I started pushing to start a family, it made everything worse. She felt suffocated. I did that to her, Hazel. I loved her but she fell out of love with me. I was vulnerable and needed her and wanted a future with her but the very thing I did to make her happy made her feel trapped.'

'Jack, that's awful!' Hazel hugged him. 'But it certainly wasn't your fault. You did what you thought was good for her and for your marriage. It's natural to want to start a family, especially if you've both expressed a desire to have children.'

He looked up and his eyes were filled with sadness.

'In her bag there was a prescription for contraceptive pills. She'd been taking them without me knowing, so when I thought we were trying to get pregnant . . . we weren't.'

Hazel squeezed his hand. 'Oh, Jack.'

'I feel terrible because I made her unhappy by planning and hoping and I must have misread her all that time. I didn't see how unhappy she was, how trapped she felt, and I'm terrified that could happen again. If she'd been honest with me, I would have tried to change or we could at least have spoken about things. But she didn't tell me and I guess I didn't want to see it. Danni died with secrets in her heart and I feel as though I never really knew her. If I had, then I'd have known that she wanted out, that she needed a different life. I would never have consciously made her feel guilty for falling out of love with me.'

'I know you wouldn't, Jack. You're a good person.'

'But can you understand why I'm scared? What if *we* got together and made commitments but then you wanted out?

Can I trust myself to see the truth? To not stifle you and want things that you don't?'

Hazel wrapped her arms around him and kissed his forehead.

'Jack – Jack, you've carried this pain for over a year and I can understand why you're afraid. But there's one thing that can stop anything like that ever happening again.'

'What?' He looked at her, a flicker of hope in his gaze.

'Honesty.'

She stood up and took his mug from him.

'Come back to bed? I want to hold you and I think you need to be held.'

He nodded.

'Hazel . . .?'

'Yes?'

'If we're being open and honest, you need to know this . . .' He took a deep breath. 'I love you.'

'I love you too, Jack.'

Epilogue

'And this is for you.' Bella handed a beautifully wrapped gift to Hazel.

'Thank you so much.' Hazel smiled and placed it on her lap.

She was sitting next to Jack in Bella's lounge. It was Christmas morning and she could barely contain her joy at being included in this wonderful family's celebrations.

Jack had stayed with her last night so they could be there for Fleas and open her cat stocking with her. Then they'd come to Bella and Lee's early to be with the girls while they opened their gifts.

Hazel and Jack had agreed to be honest with each other about how they were feeling every day, so that if something changed or if one of them was worried or tense, they'd be able to discuss it and hopefully overcome it. They had also agreed to take things slowly but in the six days since the wedding, they'd spent every night together and she didn't want to be without him. He seemed to feel the same and so they were both walking around with big grins on their faces, hiding yawns caused by their night-time activities, and sharing secret smiles throughout the days.

'Aren't you going to open that?' Jack asked.

'I will in a moment. I just wanted to watch everyone else opening their gifts.'

'You're a sweetie.' He wrapped an arm around her shoulders and kissed her cheek and she leant her head on his shoulder.

'We're having a very special brunch today,' Bobby told Hazel from her position on the floor by the tree where she was surrounded by a pile of colourful paper.

'Are we?' Hazel asked.

Bobby nodded. 'Smoked salmon, cream cheese, prawn and salmon mousse, scrambled eggs with chives, bagels and champagne with orange juice.'

'That sounds wonderful,' Hazel said.

'Daddy and Penny made it. We'll have dinner later on this afternoon and if we're still hungry we'll have turkey sandwiches for supper.'

'I'm looking forward to it all,' Hazel said.

'I'm glad you came for Christmas.' Bobby got up and went to Hazel's side.

'I'm very grateful that you all invited me.' Hazel was fighting the emotion that had been welling inside her all week.

'Of course we'd invite you, silly, you're family now.'

'Is that right?' Hazel felt her bottom lip wobble.

'Open your mug.' Bobby pointed at the parcel.

'Bobby!' Bella shook her head.

'Ooops! I meant open your surprise gift.'

'OK.' Hazel pulled at the Sellotape then tore away the wrapping paper to find a small box. She opened the lid and pulled out a mug.

'Read the side.' Bobby sat next to her now with her hand on Hazel's arm.

Hazel read it but her eyes filled with tears and she pressed her lips together hard.

'Don't close your eyes.' Bobby laughed. 'It says . . . *When you join this family, it's for keeps.*'

'Oh!' Hazel blinked hard. 'That's lovely.'

'So whatever happens,' Bella said and smiled, 'we're here for you and always will be.'

Hazel couldn't speak. She was sandwiched between Jack and Bobby now as they both hugged her.

'You have very soft hair, Hazel, and you smell nice.' Bobby kissed her cheek. 'I'm so glad Santa listened to me.'

'Did he?' Jack asked.

'When we went to visit him in his grotto, I asked him for something special for Christmas and he made my wish come true.'

'Are you allowed to tell us what you asked for?' Jack winked at Hazel.

Bobby screwed up her face. 'I think it's OK now because my wish came true. I asked him to make you happy, Uncle Jack, because you'd been so sad since you lost your wife.'

'Thank you, Bobby.' Jack reached for her and pulled her into a hug. 'You don't know how much that means.'

'It's OK.' Bobby patted Jack's head then went back to unwrapping gifts.

'Daddy, we'd better warm up the blinis.' Penny said standing up. In a red velvet dress with a red headband and wearing the small pearl earrings from Hazel and Jack, she looked quite grown-up and Hazel knew that Bella and Lee must be proud of her. Then it hit her that she'd get to see Penny and Bobby grow up and she felt very privileged indeed.

'We better had, my angel.' Lee stood up.

'I'll give you a hand.' Bella picked up a pile of paper and balled it up.

Bobby was playing with a small plastic unicorn and Christmas hits were playing on the TV. The room was cosy with the fire crackling in the grate and the tree lights twinkling. Outside, snow was falling, deepening the covering already on the ground. It had snowed every day this week and was meant to continue for a few more days and it had turned Little Bramble into the perfect winter wonderland.

Hazel's phone pinged and she grimaced, hoping it wasn't Lennox with some message about how sad and lonely he was, but when she pulled it from her cardigan pocket, she saw it was from Kyle.

'Wishing us a Merry Christmas?' Jack asked.

'Yes.' Hazel nodded then read the rest of the message. 'And he said he's come into some money. His father gave it to him for Christmas and he wonders if I'm looking for a business partner.'

'Are you?'

'I think so. At least, I might be soon. I mean, my last business partner let me down but so did my fiancé. If I can put *that* pain behind me and move on, then I'm sure I can consider taking on a business partner.'

'Kyle's great.'

'He is. He has so much energy and enthusiasm and it would be nice to have someone else investing in the business. He mentioned that he'd like to find out more about being a wedding planner and I think he'd be perfect. If the business grows as I hope it will, then I'll need someone else on board anyway.'

'Have a think about it and see how you feel after Christmas.'

'I will. I'll just text him back to say Merry Christmas and ask if we can have a proper chat in the New Year.'

'Good plan.'

Once she'd tucked her phone into her pocket, Jack placed a hand under her chin and tilted it gently.

'I have a feeling that the New Year is going to be a good one.'

'Me too.'

Penny popped her head around the door. 'Brunch is ready! Come and get it!'

'Come on, Unicorn, let's have some salmon and eggs.' Bobby jumped up and danced out of the room with her new toy.

'Come on then.' Jack stood up and took Hazel's hand. 'Let's eat. I've worked up quite an appetite this week.'

'Me too. I have no idea why.' Hazel giggled coyly as they carefully crossed the lounge, trying not to step on any of Bobby's new toys or the gifts that were scattered everywhere from the chaotic opening that morning.

Hazel paused at the door and looked back at the room. It was exactly how she'd imagined a perfect family Christmas would be. Her last thought before she turned away and followed Jack was that her mum and dad would be smiling down on her now and her mum would be repeating the words that Hazel knew made a lot of sense:

You have to come through the darkness before you can appreciate the light.

Hazel had many lights in her life now and she knew she'd always appreciate every single one.

Acknowledgements

My thanks go to:

My husband and children, for your love, support and encouragement. You – and the dogs, of course – are my everything.

My wonderful agent, Amanda Preston, and the LBA team.

The amazing team at Bonnier Books UK – with special thanks to my fabulous editor, Claire Johnson-Creek, for seeing the potential in my stories and making them shine, and to the very lovely Jenna Petts, for all your hard work and enthusiasm. Also, to the lovely Katie Meegan for her hard work getting the book ready for publication.

Thelma for your love, support and wise words over the years. I hope that if I ever reach ninety, I'm as energetic and inspirational as you.

My dear friends – in no particular order – Sarah, Dawn, Deb, Sam, Clare, Yvonne, Emma, Kelly and Caryn for always being there.

My very supportive author and blogger friends. You are all amazing!

All the readers who take the time to read, write reviews and share the book love.

The wonderful charities Greyhound Rescue Wales and Hope Rescue for the incredible work you do every single day.

**Don't miss Cathy Lake's perfect feel-good
Christmas story . . .**

Recently divorced, the family home sold and her son all
grown-up, Clare is at a crossroads. She's dedicated her
whole adult life to her family, and now it's time she
did something for herself.

In the lead-up to Christmas, Clare decides that a bit of time
in the countryside might be just what she needs, so she moves
back to Little Bramble, the village she grew up in. But living
with her mum for the first time in years – and not to mention
Goliath the Great Dane – can be challenging.

When Clare finds herself running the village Christmas show,
it feels like she has purpose in her life again. Bringing together
people from all sides of the community, and all walks of life,
will Clare manage to pull off a festive feat like no other?
And will she find the new start in life – and possibly
love – that she's been looking for?

Available now. Read on for an extract.

Chapter 1

'Look at me, Mum!'

Clare Greene's heart fluttered. She turned, expecting to see her son, but instead her gaze fell on the empty space in the back garden where the swing used to be. The house and garden were full of ghosts and, as she made her way round one final time, she was being assaulted by memories and voices from the past.

Closing her eyes, Clare could picture her son, Kyle, swinging high, remember her anxiety that he'd fall off and hurt himself. But his laughter as he'd soared through the air and the joy on his face as he'd called to her, keen to garner her approval, had made the fear worth it. Her ex-husband, Jason, had taken the swing down years ago, but it had stood there for a decade, from the time Kyle was seven, and he'd had so much fun on it. Kyle was twenty-one now and at university in Bath studying performing arts – a grown man and no longer her little boy.

A cold wind whipped around the garden, tugging at her coat, and she shivered. Time had passed so quickly: she was forty-five and often felt that her life had passed her by, that she had practically sleepwalked through the days. If only it were possible to have some of that time back to savour the good times . . .

Her heart lurched and she pressed a hand to her chest. Looking down, her eyes found her wedding ring. As difficult as it would be, she really needed to take it off. Jason had removed his when the divorce was finalised, sighing at the white mark that remained on his finger. Just like the emotional scars left by the end of their marriage, it would take some time for physical marks like that to go.

She trudged back up the garden to the semi-detached house, went in through the French doors and closed them behind her, lifting the handle slightly until it clicked, then turned the key. There was a knack to locking these doors. They should have had them fixed years ago, but it was one of a list of jobs that had never been done and now it would be someone else's problem. But the new owners would also have so much to enjoy here. Clare had loved her home and was sad to leave it, but she knew it was time, even though her throat tightened as she realised she would never walk on the lush green lawn again, never sit on the patio as she savoured her morning coffee, never listen to the jazz drifting from next door on sunny afternoons. Her fragrant roses would be tended to by someone else, the shed would house the tools and bikes of others, and the birds that flocked to the feeders would become accustomed to different humans.

Slipping out of her garden shoes and into her plimsolls, she made her way through the open-plan kitchen diner with its large fireplace and driftwood mantelpiece, her soft rubber soles seemed strangely noisy on the wooden boards, the sound echoing around the empty house, making it feel as though she had company. The furniture had been moved into storage and the clothes and belongings she couldn't bear to part with, such as Kyle's baby photo albums, from a time when people had actually printed photographs, were packed in her treasured Mini Countryman, the remaining finance on it cleared with some of her half of the house sale. The car had seemed to groan under the extra weight but she felt compelled to take them with her.

She passed the lounge where she had given birth to Kyle three weeks before his due date, taken by surprise as she'd thought the pains were practice contractions. He'd slid out onto the rug, red and furious at his early arrival. Kyle's entry into the world had been dramatic and he hadn't changed a bit; he still enjoyed being the centre of attention. Clare had been just twenty-four then, so young and innocent, convinced that life had plenty to offer and that she was destined for something special, even though she hadn't had a clue what that something would be.

How things changed.

In the hallway, where the October sun streamed through the window above the door, she took slow deep breaths, treasuring the sights, sounds and scents of home, storing them safely in her heart. Who knew when she would have a home of her own again? When her vision blurred, she knew it was time to get moving.

Her mobile buzzed in her pocket, making her jump, and she pulled it out to check the screen, expecting a message from the removal company. When she saw Kyle's name, her heart lifted.

Hey Mum,

Hope you're OK. I know today will be difficult, but you can do it! When one house door closes another one opens and all that. Let me know when you're safely at Nanna's.

Love you millions! X

Clare hugged her mobile to her chest for a moment, thanking the universe for the gift of her precious boy. Whatever happened, she had a wonderful son and she would always be grateful for that. After firing off a quick reply, she slid her phone back in her pocket then opened the door and stepped outside, put the key in an envelope and posted it through the letter box, preparing to start the next chapter of her life.

❄

Clare was ten minutes away from the village where she had grown up, but it would probably take her twenty to get there because she was stuck behind a tractor. Her Mini ambled along through the narrow country lanes and her feet ached from braking and pressing the clutch as she had to stop/start the car. Behind her, a row of cars was building and she knew it wouldn't be long before some of the drivers started beeping at her, pressurising her to overtake. But Clare knew better; these lanes could be deadly and visibility was poor. There was always the risk of crashing into some idiot taking the bends at sixty miles per hour.

The whole journey from Reading to Little Bramble in Surrey only took about forty minutes, but she had to admit that she hadn't made it very often, particularly over recent years. There had always been an excuse, whether it was a dinner with Jason's colleagues from the prestigious law firm in Reading where he had been a partner, or an author event at the library where she had worked for twelve years as a library assistant (a job she had adored until they'd had to make some staff redundant six months ago due to cutbacks), or generally just feeling too tired to make the effort. A lump formed in her throat from the guilt. Her mum was seventy-five, fit and healthy, a busy member of her local community, but she wouldn't be around forever and in some ways she'd taken her for granted. They hadn't ever been that close but, even so, she was aware that she could have made more of an effort to visit.

She turned the radio on and listened to the DJ chatting to a celebrity author called Cora Quincy about her latest self-help book. Cora was all of twenty-five but spoke as if she'd lived a long and difficult life. Admittedly, Clare had read about Cora (a fashion model turned actress turned author who'd married someone from a boyband Clare could never remember the name of) online, and knew that she had endured a challenging childhood, but even so, her tone was slightly patronising. Clare had been married for almost as long as the woman had been alive – surely she had more life experience to draw on, more wisdom in the bank? And yet here she was: homeless, jobless, clueless about what came next.

The traffic came to a standstill as the tractor stopped to make way for an approaching car. Clare pulled up the hand-brake and turned, gazing at the hedgerow to her left, almost bare of leaves now in October's colder days. Dark twigs poked out of the hedge, threatening to scratch any vehicles that got too close, and others stretched up to the sky like gnarled brown fingers. Beyond the hedges were fields where farmers grew corn and vegetables, where livestock roamed and nurtured their young.

As a child, Clare had thought she'd grow up to be a vet or own her own stables. She'd loved the wildlife around the village, had been a keen horse rider who had spent Saturday mornings at the stables then worked on Sundays at the local farm shop just outside Little Bramble, where she got to feed the chickens and ducks in her breaks, care for the motherless lambs in spring and play with the fluffy collie pups. Yes, she'd had a good childhood, even if she hadn't been as close to her mum as she'd have liked. At university, she'd studied English Literature (after deciding at sixteen that taking A-levels in the sciences was not for her), met Jason, and her ambitions had slipped away like smoke on the breeze. She'd been so infatuated with him, so taken by his apparent maturity and intelligence that she'd have followed him to the end of the earth if he'd asked her, so when he proposed, she'd accepted without hesitation.

The tractor started moving again and Clare released the handbrake and set off again at a snail's pace.

'Oh, absolutely!' Cora's decisive tone burst from the car speakers and broke into Clare's thoughts. 'I'd spent far too long worrying about what everyone expected of me, trying to be that perfect creature that pleased the world, and then one day . . . BOOM! I had an epiphany! I was like, alleluia! Eureka! And all that jazz.' She giggled, clearly very pleased with herself.

'And so . . . do you have a message for our listeners?' Darryl Donovan, the long-time Radio 2 DJ asked.

'I do, Darryl, I really do. Whoever you are and whatever you've been through, put yourself first. Decide what *YOU* really want and go for it! I realised, and your listeners can too, that I had to live my life for *me* before I could be with anyone. If you don't love yourself, how can you possibly love anyone else?'

Clare rolled her eyes. It was all very well saying that at twenty-five. It was a message Clare had heard many times in the past, but not one she'd ever managed to take on board. She'd been a daughter, a wife, a mum, a library assistant (although that had been something for her because she'd enjoyed it so much) so her roles had been centred around others and she'd been content with that. The idea of shaking off those responsibilities and doing things solely for herself seemed unimaginable.

Now, for the first time in her life, Clare realised that she felt very much alone.

Clare had always been a daddy's girl and tried to make her father proud whenever she could. When he'd died ten years ago, he'd left a gaping hole which she'd struggled to fill. She didn't have a close relationship with her mum. Elaine Hughes had always been busy with her own life – for many years with her job as a drama teacher, then later on with her work as a chief examiner and as chairwoman of the village amateur dramatics society. With Jason bringing his and Clare's marriage to an end, she was no longer committed to making him happy, but this in itself was another difficult loss to deal with. And then there was Kyle: her darling son, her reason for everything, her joy. But Kyle was grown up and had gone off to university, leaving Clare feeling redundant in that aspect of her life as well, especially after losing her job. Her whole life had changed when she'd least expected it. She'd been prepared for Kyle leaving home, but losing her job and her marriage at the same time was too much.

Would it be possible for Clare to start again and live her life for herself? Could she turn things around and discover what it was that she really wanted?

The left indicator on the tractor started flickering and it pulled into a layby, so Clare put her foot down on the accelerator and drove past it, singing along to the uplifting track from the eighties that the celebrity had chosen as her theme tune.

Perhaps the young woman wasn't so naïve after all.

❄

Sam Wilson unclipped the soft leather lead from his yellow Labrador's collar then watched as she ran ahead, her long tail wagging, nose pressed to the ground. He looked forward to his twice-daily walks with Scout. It was his time out, his time to breathe deeply and enjoy the peace and quiet. He'd have walked anyway, but having Scout for company made the walks around the countryside surrounding Little Bramble even better. The two-year-old Labrador was good company: she enjoyed being outside as much as Sam did and she didn't feel the need to fill their time together with random chatter or demands. As long as she was fed and walked, could snuggle on the sofa and was praised for good behaviour, Scout was happy, and that made Sam happy too.

Moving to the village over three years ago had been a fresh start for him and for his younger sister, Alyssa. After years of living in London, renting flats and saving hard, Sam had wanted to put down roots and settle somewhere quiet, friendly and beautiful. Little Bramble was perfect, and when a colleague in London told him that a former university friend of hers was looking for a partner to invest in her village veterinary practice, Sam had felt a flicker of hope that he hadn't experienced in a long time. He'd travelled to the village to meet Miranda Fitzalan and had liked her blunt, no-nonsense approach, her devotion to the animals in her care – and the very reasonable asking price for a share of the practice. Miranda's former business partner had decided to retire to Spain and she was looking for someone keen to enjoy being a part of village life. Sam's years of saving and investing his money wisely had finally reaped a reward.

Scout came running back to him, a chunky stick in her mouth. She dropped it at his feet and looked up at him, wagging her tail, her mouth open in what looked like a wide smile.

'You want to play, do you?' He reached out and rubbed her soft head and she barked in reply. 'OK then, girl. Ready?'

He picked up the stick then swung his arm back and threw it as far ahead as he could, laughing as Scout scampered after it, knowing that this process would be repeated many times before they reached home again. Repetition and routine were the things that kept his life moving forwards and he didn't think to want for more.

Return to the village of Little Bramble in . . .

Emma Patrick's life is spiralling out of control. On the cusp of her 50th birthday, she suddenly realises that she's been so focused on work that she's lost any real connection to people.

When Emma's ageing father needs her help, she decides to go back home to the countryside to spend some time with him. But returning to Little Bramble after years away is filled with complications and people she'd rather avoid.

To her surprise, as Emma settles in she finds herself loving village life. When the opportunity to get involved in the running of the summer fête comes her way, soon she's embracing jam making, cake baking and bunting. And with romance brewing, Emma begins to doubt the glamorous life in London that she worked so hard to build . . .

A feel-good, uplifting summer read. Available now.